# THE AGATHA PRINCIPLE
## and Other Mystery Stories

## Elizabeth Elwood

To Viv + Ron,
Best Wishes,
Elizabeth Elwood.

iUniverse, Inc.
Bloomington

The Agatha Principle and Other Mystery Stories

This is a work of fiction. All of the characters, names, incidents, organizations, and dialogue in this novel are either the products of the author's imagination or are used fictitiously.

iUniverse books may be ordered through booksellers or by contacting:

iUniverse
1663 Liberty Drive
Bloomington, IN 47403
www.iuniverse.com
1-800-Authors (1-800-288-4677)

Because of the dynamic nature of the Internet, any Web addresses or links contained in this book may have changed since publication and may no longer be valid. The views expressed in this work are solely those of the author and do not necessarily reflect the views of the publisher, and the publisher hereby disclaims any responsibility for them.

Any people depicted in stock imagery provided by Thinkstock are models, and such images are being used for illustrative purposes only.

Certain stock imagery © Thinkstock.

ISBN: 978-1-4759-0443-7 (sc)
ISBN: 978-1-4759-0445-1 (hc)
ISBN: 978-1-4759-0444-4 (e)

Library of Congress Control Number: 2012904801

Printed in the United States of America

iUniverse rev. date: 4/16/2012

*For The Vagabond Players*

# Contents

# The Agatha Principle
# Cast of Characters

*January, 2010. An amateur production of Agatha Christie's* The Mousetrap *is in rehearsal. The show is a fundraiser for the Children's Society and will be performed for one evening only at the Old Chandler Theatre-Restaurant. The cast is made up from members of the Law Society.*

## The Players

Jordan Hope, professional actor hired by the lawyers to direct the play
Andrew McCardle, Crown prosecutor playing the role of Major Metcalf
Günter Sachs, corporate lawyer playing Giles Ralston
Henri Gerard, corporate lawyer and wealthy entrepreneur playing Mr. Paravicini
Sylvia Barnwell, civil lawyer playing Miss Casewell
Norton Barnwell, Sylvia's husband, a defence lawyer who plays Christopher Wren
Terry Gleason, a young lawyer articling with Sylvia's
firm who plays Sergeant Trotter
Jeannie Dunbar, also articling with Sylvia's firm, playing Mollie Ralston
Judge Mary Worthington, highly regarded member
of the judiciary who plays Mrs. Boyle

## The Staff of the Old Chandler

Walt Wozchinski, owner/operator
Claudia Capelli, senior manager
Pauline Waverly, bookkeeper
Bill Jones, doorman
Guglielmo Bergonzi, bartender
Kurt Liddle, technician for Gaslight Players, the OC's resident theatre company
Winifred Barton, wardrobe mistress for the Gaslight Players

## The Guests

Detective Constable Bob Miller, VPD
Philippa Beary, Sylvia Barnwell's younger sister
Chloe Harker, retired teacher who lives with Winifred Barton
Amy and Frank Steele, wealthy sponsors of the Gaslight Players
Thomas and Geoffrey Barnwell, Sylvia and Norton's sons
Mai Ling, the Barnwell's nanny

# THE AGATHA PRINCIPLE

# I

The corpse lay in Blood Alley, huddled like a sleeping vagrant amid the dumpsters that lined the high brick walls at the back of the Water Street shops. However, at seven o'clock on a cold January evening, it was unlikely to be noticed by the solitary walker who was entering the far end of the old throughway, which once had been home to the butchers that gave the alley its name and now contained the odd trendy restaurant amid the parking-garage entrances and rear shop doors.

The walker passed through Blood Alley Square, serenely unaware of its grim history of public executions, his thoughts on other pressing and immediate matters. The previous day's snowfall had been cleared to form a pathway, and his footsteps echoed eerily on the patchwork pavement of grey granite stones, red bricks and concrete slabs. The area was deserted, and he accelerated his pace, suddenly aware that his decision to dodge the icy sidewalks and walk the rough stones of the alley had not been wise when the shops were shut and dark had closed in. Some light filtered down from the apartment windows that overlooked the square, augmenting the soft white beam of the single streetlamp and the shimmering reflection from the snow, but the palely golden shafts seemed to heighten the menace in the shadows, and when he saw an opening on his left and realized it was a back entrance to Gaoler's Mews, he turned and headed towards the arcade. The shops were closed, but their overnight lights created a welcoming glow.

The path in the snow was narrower here, and he kept his eyes down and watched his step carefully. As he neared the entrance to the mews, the light spilling from the corner coffee-shop window illuminated a set of footprints in the snow. Someone had come from the other end of the alley and had cut diagonally across to the mews rather than follow the cleared path. Curiously, he noted the unusual shape of the prints and the way they curved from the dumpster at the right of the passage; then the thought swept from his mind as the distant sound of the Gastown steam clock reminded him that his rehearsal would be starting soon. He hurried through the arcade and emerged onto Water Street without noticing the reappearance of the strange footprints in the pile of snow by the curb or the square heel mark that was now plainly delineated in the shallower snow at the edge of the mound. The snow had started again, and he pulled up his collar, wrapping his scarf snugly around his neck to hold it in place. Only another two blocks and he would reach his destination.

And back in Blood Alley, the soft flakes drifted down, blanketing the footsteps by the dumpster, concealing the bloodstains in the snow, and making a cold, white shroud for the body that lay slumped in the shadows of the wall.

\*           \*           \*

The walker who had emerged from the alley was Jordan Hope, a skilled thespian with considerable experience and high expectations, and once safely under the lights of Water Street, he reverted to his earlier preoccupation. His current professional engagement was threatening to tax his patience to the limit and he wondered if the remuneration was worth the aggravation. If there was anything worse than having to direct a bunch of amateurs, he thought testily, it was having to direct a bunch of professional amateurs. Lawyers, he suspected, were going to prove the worst of the lot, particularly since their fundraiser for the Children's Society happened to be an Agatha Christie murder mystery. During the preliminary reading of *The Mousetrap*, his cast members had made it plain that they had far greater knowledge of crime and police procedure than he did, not to mention far higher incomes. Every supercilious lift of an eyebrow had reminded him that, unlike their humble director who was earning a paltry fee that probably constituted his sole income for the month of January, his performers were donating their time. His actors had insisted that they needed no vocal direction since they were accustomed to public speaking, and when he had attempted to discuss character interpretation with the judge who was playing Mrs. Boyle, she informed him that she needed no assistance since she had dealt with every possible perversity of human nature over the course of her career. The last straw had come when the handsome and humourless litigator who was playing Giles drew him aside to explain with Teutonic solemnity that he was not to take offence if his actors argued over points of staging since they were creatures of far superior intelligence than the normal riffraff one would find in the theatre. Jordan still steamed at the memory. No wonder, he thought venomously, that Shakespeare had said, "Kill all the lawyers." Yes, he decided, as he headed into the Old Chandler for the first blocking rehearsal, it was definitely time he took charge.

Fifteen minutes later, his cast was assembled in the vast rehearsal hall that dominated the backstage area of the theatre-restaurant. Jordan contemplated the circle of faces. His actors stared back at him, their countenances forming a collective challenge to his authority. Squashing his negative feelings about the group, for there was a job to be done, and Jordan was nothing if not professional, he coolly assessed his performers. They would do, he decided. The individuals suited their parts well.

Andrew McCardle, media darling and anti-drug crusader, was ideal for Major Metcalf, for he was suave and assured, and like the character he portrayed, he stood on the side of the angels—as did Judge Mary Worthington, who was well known as a woman with a strong social conscience. But the judge was playing against type. Her role was the unpleasant Mrs. Boyle who expressed no regret for having placed three helpless children into a catastrophic foster-care situation. Jordan admired the serene, grey-haired woman; however, he did not find her approachable. High-principled people who were renowned for their probity were often revered, but rarely liked.

At the junior end of the spectrum, the two youngest performers sat together. They looked vaguely conspiratorial, possibly due to the fact that they were both fresh out of university and articling with the same firm. Terry Gleason, who played the faux-policeman, Trotter, was clearly besotted with Jeannie Dunbar. Dunbar was darkly beautiful and lacked the fresh innocence that was needed to play Mollie, although Jordan had to admit that she acted well and disguised her sophistication on the stage. However, when not in character, she seemed worldly-wise for one so young. Her belladonna eyes reminded Jordan of some of the young women of his pot-smoking youth and there was an edge to her that he found distasteful. A woman with no scruples, he decided, though that might stand her in good stead in her chosen profession. A promiscuous little minx, too, thought Jordan, recollecting the come-hither looks she had cast his way when they were first introduced.

Jordan's eyes slid around the circle and lit on the only married couple in the play. Sylvia and Norton Barnwell were a study in opposites. Sylvia's blonde elegance went with an extremely business-like air, which made her a credible Miss Casewell. Her husband, with his receding hairline and wire-rimmed glasses, looked totally wrong for the flamboyant Christopher Wren—a wig would definitely be in order—but his vaguely ineffectual manner was not inappropriate, if only it could be channelled to work onstage. The man was certainly bubbling over with enthusiasm, which was more than could be said for the other members of the cast who sat there as if they had been hauled in by a press gang.

The remaining two roles were adequately cast. Mollie's husband, Giles, was being played by the Teutonic prig who had so annoyed Jordan earlier. Günter Sachs was stiff and humourless, but then, so was Giles, and Günter was certainly good-looking, which was always advantageous in a male lead. Jordan glanced at the gnome-like man seated next to Günter. Side by side, they looked like Beauty and the Beast. Still, Henri Gerard, who played Mr. Paravicini, might be deficient in looks, but he was reputed to be as fabulously rich as the fairytale beast. It was Gerard who had arranged for the production to take place at the Old Chandler. The wealthy corporate lawyer had provided financial backing for the theatre-restaurant, and it could well be his money that was paying for the current production. That might, Jordan mused, be the reason for the grim set to his jaw that marred the man's usual affable countenance.

Jordan decided a pep talk was in order. He called his team to attention.

"The object of this venture may be money for charity," he began firmly, "but we owe it to the audience to give them full value for the exorbitant ticket price. We also have an obligation to the Gaslight Theatre Company to ensure that the product on their stage does not damage their reputation with their regular clientele."

"Not likely," snorted Terry Gleason. "Antiquated Dame Aggie is hardly the sort of fare to bring Gaslight audiences in."

"I sense attitude," said Jordan. "The cry of the theatre snob: 'Dame Agatha sucks but she brings in the bucks.' Don't underrate her. For one thing, this show is extremely topical because it deals with an issue that's constantly in the news—foster care. Every month or so, a story about a social worker's mistake hits the headlines. The play may have been written in the fifties, but the subject matter is still relevant. Revenge is as powerful a motive today as it has ever been."

Jeanne Dunbar spoke up before Jordan had time to draw breath.

"You sound as if we have to play it straight," she protested. "Surely we can have some fun with it. I mean, it's so archaic!"

Jordan's tone hardened.

"I do mean you to play it straight," he stated. "It may not be the world's greatest drama, but it's a mystery, not a farce, and don't any of you forget it. In other words, no camp acting from smart-asses who rate the piece as a lumbering dinosaur. Neither do I want to see a raft of modern interpretations that are alien to the intent of the piece."

Jordan shuddered, recollecting a particularly dire production of *The Mousetrap* where the director had dredged up cheap laughs by portraying two of the characters as flagrantly overt homosexuals. "Remember the era in which the play was written," he cautioned his cast. "Agatha Christie would have been well aware of the gay/lesbian issue, though it wasn't talked about as much then, but she would be appalled to see Christopher Wren played as a screaming fairy, especially since Mollie's husband is supposed to be jealous of him. And Casewell's gender-bender personality is more for creating mystery than to make a statement about gay pride."

"Thank heaven for that," muttered Sylvia under her breath.

"So I want strong, disciplined performances. Good pace, clear delivery and no gimmicks. This play is a classic mystery. It's a perfect example of what I call *The Agatha Principle*, and I expect you to listen to what I say, follow my direction and do it right."

Norton raised a tentative hand. His blue eyes blinked behind his spectacles.

"Yes," said Jordan. "You have a question?"

"I was just wondering," said Norton curiously, "what you mean by *The Agatha Principle*."

"Oh, sorry," said Jordan. "I'd assumed that was obvious. *The least likely person is the killer, and no one is really who they seem.*"

*         *         *

Detective Constable Robert Miller strode down the sidewalk, dodging the icy mounds, which were all that remained of the record Christmas snowfall. The white drifts, which had blanketed the city for weeks, had finally diminished into hard-packed piles, leaving the streets of Vancouver vaguely resembling a moonscape. Yet as Miller glanced up through the spindly branches of the trees that lined the sidewalk, he realized that the lull in the weather had only been a temporary respite, for the lowering sky threatened another fall of snow. Winter, it seemed, was never to end.

It was only three in the afternoon, but the round glass balls hanging from the iron lamp standards were already alight. Distantly hearing the famous Gastown steam clock piping the hour, Miller put on a burst of speed. Having invited Philippa Beary to meet him for coffee, he didn't want to annoy her by being late. He had the distinct impression that the young singer was a highly disciplined individual who took casual dates as seriously as rehearsal calls.

However, as he approached the wide intersection where the statue of Gassy Jack on his barrel of whiskey looked sadly bereft without its usual ring of admiring tourists, Philippa was nowhere in sight. Miller breathed a sigh of relief, which manifested like a wraith in the frigid air. He slowed his pace. Then, just as he reached the corner, a petite redhead bobbed into view from the other side of the historic figure. Miller's face broke into a smile. Even in jeans and a turtleneck, which just showed under her navy winter jacket, Philippa exuded style and elegance. It was probably her stage training, thought Miller, as he watched her cross the square. Her posture would rival that of a soldier on parade. To his delight, when she reached him, Philippa's smile mirrored his own.

"This is nice," she said. "Are you working in Gastown today, or did you make a special detour to meet me?"

Miller was tempted to lie, but couldn't quite manage it.

"I did have business here," he admitted. He took her elbow and steered her around the tall maple that towered over the statue. "Where do you want to go for coffee?"

"Mirella's is good. It's on the next block. We can cut through the arcade and dodge the snow." She pointed to a passageway between the shops on the far side of the street.

"Lead the way." Miller fell into step beside Philippa and found that she was leading him back the way he had come. Exactly the way he had come, it transpired, when the arcade forked to the left and came out on the street where the Old Chandler Theatre Restaurant was located. At this end, the arcade was framed by a jewellery store and a Royal Bank. Philippa could not resist a quick glance at the jeweller's sparkling display, but Miller's eyes were automatically drawn to the red brick building on the other side of the road. Then, noticing that Philippa was ready to move on, he followed her onto the street.

They walked past the bank and strolled along until they reached a tiny deli that nestled between a toyshop and a used bookstore. The lower half of the coffee-shop window was covered with red and white checked curtains, but Miller could still make out a glass counter crammed with tempting delectables. He followed Philippa inside and was greeted by the pungent aroma of freshly ground coffee. Behind the chatter of the patrons, the lyric tones of Pavarotti singing Neapolitan songs emanated softly from a speaker at the corner of the room. Miller joined Philippa at the counter, and once they had ordered, they settled themselves at a table by the window.

Miller's eyes slid back towards the glass pane. From where he sat, he had a clear view of the Old Chandler. Beside the entrance was a large poster announcing an upcoming dinner-theatre event but he could not make out the title of the play. Philippa followed his glance.

"*The Mousetrap*," she said. "That's the next production."

"You have good eyesight."

"Not really. I just happen to know that the Agatha Christie is coming up. My sister and brother-in-law are in it."

"You mean they act as well as do puppet shows and sing country and western?"

"You're thinking of Juliette and Steven. I'm talking about the other ones—Sylvia and Norton. You know, Bonnie and Clyde. You must remember them."

Miller looked suitably embarrassed. His first meeting with the members of the Beary family had been on the occasion of Philippa's arrest en route to a Halloween party. The young detective had not been thrilled to discover that his suspect was the daughter of a city councillor and the sister of an RCMP detective inspector, and he recalled Philippa's oldest sister, Sylvia, and her husband, Norton, very well. They were members of a prestigious downtown law firm, and they had arrived at the police station, still dressed as thirties gangsters, to act in Philippa's defence.

"Yes, I remember them. Sylvia and Norton are the lawyers." Miller saw no point in prevaricating. "Why are they involved in a play?"

"The Law Society mounts a fundraiser each year on behalf of the Children's Society and the minute Norton heard about the project, he was raring to get involved. He tried his hand at acting last year and was the surprise hit of the show in spite of the fact that he has no natural ability, so he's very gung-ho about the project. Sylvia wasn't going to participate, but one of the women dropped out so she stepped in to fill the gap. She's not overly enthused, but she believes in supporting charitable causes and she's so efficient that she's bound to do well."

"Why the Old Chandler? Isn't that an expensive venue for a charity project?"

"One of the partners in Sylvia's firm wangled the use of the facility free of charge—as long as they were prepared to use it during January when the resident professional troupe has its down time."

"How did he manage that?"

"He's a part-owner of the OC. A sort of sleeping partner."

Miller looked surprised.

"I read an article about the Old Chandler," he said. "It was about the owner-operator who started it. His name's Walt Wozchinski. It didn't say anything about a partner. Do you know his name?"

"Henri Gerard."

"French Canadian?"

"From St. Boniface, I think, but he must have been here for quite a while. He's a corporate lawyer, but he's very into the arts and he put up the majority of the funds when the warehouse was bought and converted. He sounds like a real character. According to Sylvia, he looks like a bald, middle-aged troll. He wears elevator shoes, but he still can't look her in the eye, and she's only five foot four. However, like many rich, ugly men, he loves to date beautiful women—and spoil them too. Sylvia says he buys bottles of Chanel the way you and I buy cups of coffee. She likes him a lot, but she says he's making a fool of himself over one of Wozchinski's senior employees."

"Did your sister mention a name?"

"No, but I could ask her." Philippa speculatively studied her companion. His interest seemed more than casual. "I guess you get to know quite a few lawyers in your job," she said.

"A few," Miller admitted. "Not so much know them as know of them—the prominent ones, anyway—the prosecutors who nail all their cases and the tough defence lawyers who get off the people we haul into court."

"Sylvia has one of those in her show." Philippa grinned. "The first type," she added, "the kind you like. Andrew McCardle. Do you know him?"

Miller smiled.

"Not personally, but he's the hero of the drug squad. He has a phenomenal record of convictions. He's also famous for his philanthropic work on behalf of kids who are trying to get off drugs. Who else is involved?"

"I only know of two others. One is Günter Sachs. He's another corporate lawyer. He's playing Giles—that's the good-looking hero in the play. I've never met him but I've heard about him." Philippa's eyes twinkled. "He was supposed to be my blind date last Halloween but, as you know, I never made it to the party."

Miller ignored the dig.

"Who's the other one?"

"She's a judge. Mary Worthington."

Miller nodded. "Interesting lady. She tried the Jackson case."

Miller felt no need to elaborate. The Jackson case had filled the headlines for a solid month in 2008 when a pair of ill-fated aboriginal children had died in foster care. The tragedy had caused a major shake-up in many a government department.

"It's very ironical casting," said Philippa. "The judge is playing a character who gets murdered because of the heartless way she dealt with a foster-care case, yet Sylvia says Mary Worthington would move Heaven and Earth to right a wrong if she felt an injustice had been done."

"Yes, she does have that reputation."

Miller looked out the window again. Philippa watched her companion shrewdly. He seemed fixated on the red brick building. She peered through the window and tried to see what had captured his attention. The Old Chandler stood five storeys high, its late-nineteenth-century façade lined with rows of tall, square-paned windows with grey granite sills. The highest row was crowned with sunray transom windows, and above the decorative arches, an elaborate stone cornice stretched the length of the building. Philippa had never been inside the theatre-restaurant, but she had read about the conversion of the ship-supplier's warehouse and she knew that the décor resembled a Tudor banqueting hall that would have far better graced a sixteenth-century mansion. She vaguely recalled that a deal with a California entrepreneur who mounted medieval spectacles had somehow collapsed, and she assumed that when the theatre evolved in its place, there had been neither the funds nor the inclination to redecorate the interior. She could understand why. The building stretched all the way from the corner to the lane that bisected the block. It was a big space to redo once, let alone twice.

She turned back to Miller. His eyes were still riveted on the restaurant. Philippa's curiosity was piqued.

"Why are you so interested in the Old Chandler?" she demanded.

Miller hesitated.

"Oh, come on," cajoled Philippa. "There must be something going on there. If you don't tell me, I can find out from Richard."

Miller scowled.

"Just because your brother's an RCMP detective inspector, it doesn't mean he's going to blab everything you want to know about police business."

"No, but he fills me in if he thinks there's some way I can help him. If I know what's going on, I can tip you off if I pick up any pertinent information from Sylvia."

Miller unbent a little.

"All right, but I don't want you getting involved. I'm here this morning because there was a stabbing in Blood Alley two weeks ago. The young man who died was the Old Chandler's bartender. The body was hidden by the snow for several days, and then it took us a while to find out who he was because his coat and wallet were stolen and no one had reported him missing. He was due for a couple of weeks leave and was supposed to be heading off for a skiing holiday at Whistler."

"On his own?"

"So I was told."

"Did you find out who killed him?"

"It appeared to be a random mugging as he was walking home. He lived in one of those apartments that front onto the square."

"Why did they steal his coat?"

"Evidently it was a pretty expensive leather one."

"So some little thug demanded his coat and wallet, and, when he handed them over, killed him anyway."

"No. There must have been a struggle. He was killed with his own knife.

The girl who lived in the apartment across the hall from him identified it. She told me he always carried a flick-knife in his pocket."

"How did she know that?"

"She had a fling with him when he first moved in. It lasted a couple of months so she got to know him pretty well. Sounds like he was quite the ladies' man. A real Latin lover. His name was Guglielmo Bergonzi."

"Lover's tiff? Is she a suspect?"

"No. She was out of town. Besides, she's a free-wheeling type—not a crime-of-passion personality."

"So you think it was a simple case of a mugging that went wrong?"

"Probably. But I'm not entirely satisfied because the old boy who acts as doorman at the Old Chandler told me he's worried that there's something going on that's not on the up-and-up. He hinted at organized crime and intimated that the drug squad might want to keep an eye on the place."

"What did the other staff members have to say?"

"I haven't talked with any of them yet. The doorman was the only person there. He's a nice old fellow. Bill Jones—every bit as down to earth as his name—and given what he told me, I'm thinking it might not be wise to go in gangbusters and put Walt Wozchinski on guard, which is what will happen if I focus my murder investigation on his staff. A more subtle approach might be called for."

"Sylvia will go bananas if she finds out her charitable project is operating out of a den of iniquity," said Philippa.

"Yes, well, don't tell her," said Miller, "but by all means ask her for backstage gossip, and if you hear anything of interest, let me know. Anyway, the place isn't a den of iniquity. The Old Chandler has a respectable clientele and there are no drug dealers or prostitutes hanging around the premises. It's the last place you'd suspect, but that makes it ideal for concealing illegal funds."

"Isn't a back-lane stabbing unusual for drug gangs? I thought they went around shooting each other in public places and terrorizing innocent bystanders. And don't you have a special task force to deal with that?"

Miller's brow darkened.

"Yes. It's a nightmare. We have a huge number of illegal arms in Vancouver, thanks to some crooked dealers who reactivated guns that were imported for the film industry. But you're talking about gangs. The doorman suspects that the Old Chandler may be run by the people at the top of the chain— the ones who supply the gangs—and it's a sickening fact that there are some highly respectable citizens who have achieved their wealth and status through collusion with crime rings."

"Richard gets steamed on the subject too," said Philippa, "especially if it's cops who turn out to be crooked."

"Or judges or lawyers or politicians. The corruption can go pretty high up. I hope for your sister's sake that the doorman's anxieties are unfounded. The last thing any law firm needs is a bad apple amid their numbers."

"Are you sure I shouldn't warn Sylvia?"

"No. I don't want you to tell anyone. If the doorman is right about what's going on, then it's possible that the bartender had figured it out too. He might have been killed because he knew too much. I'd just as soon you stayed right away from the place, though I suppose you're going to see the show."

"Well, yes, I am. Why don't you come with me?" suggested Philippa. "It's a one-night event. They're charging the earth because there's dinner during the interval and dancing afterwards, and everyone knows they're paying through the nose because of the charity. It's going to be quite the swanky occasion."

"So how much 'earth' are these tickets worth?" Miller asked warily.

"Five hundred dollars."

"Each!"

"Yes, but we don't have to pay. Sylvia asked me to come and look after her children … well, only two of them. Chelsea's too young for the show, but Mai Ling—that's their nanny—is bringing the boys and I said I'd meet her there and make sure they behave. Sylvia gave me two tickets in case I wanted to bring a date. You'll be a great help keeping the boys in line. I'll simply tell them that you're a cop."

Miller looked sceptical.

"That won't work if they're the sons of two lawyers. They've probably been taught that cops rank lower than tadpoles in the big pool of justice. My status won't carry any weight at all. Aren't your parents going to be there to keep an eye on them?"

"No. Mum and Dad have a Council event that night."

"What about your puppeteer sister and her singing spouse?"

"They won't come down from the Sunshine Coast for one night, especially mid-week. Stephen doesn't just sing with his band; he's a full-time teacher."

"So you're the only back-up for the nanny. Well, at the prices they're charging, you and the nanny might be the only people there. Who's going to pay five hundred dollars to eat dinner and sit through a play?"

"Probably nobody," said Philippa. "The lawyers will be selling the tickets to their corporate clients, and the tickets will be given to employees or favoured customers, or even handed back to the law firm to distribute. It'll only take ten percent of the ticket price to cover the actual cost of the event, so if a corporation coughs up four thousand dollars for a table of eight, all but four hundred of those dollars will be tax deductible. Believe me, the place will be packed. I read that the Old Chandler can seat up to two hundred and fifty, so by my calculations, the children's charity should clock up more than a hundred thousand dollars."

Miller shook his head in disbelief.

"I obviously don't move in the right circles," he said.

"So here's your opportunity."

Miller still looked dubious.

"If it's a swank affair, does that mean you'll be wearing the gorgeous gown that you wore for the Greystone Christmas gala?"

"Not that swanky," said Philippa. "Suits and cocktail dresses, maybe. No one wants to sit through *The Mousetrap* in formal gear."

"Good," said Miller, "because I don't own a tux."

"So you'll come?"

"Yes." Miller leaned back in his chair. "And," he added with a smile, "not just because it'll give me an opportunity to nose around."

"Perfect," said Philippa. "I'll watch the action onstage and you can watch the action offstage. Hopefully we'll both manage to detect the villains."

"You don't know the play?"

"No. It's been running for years in London, but it's one Agatha Christie I've never seen. I've made Sylvia and Norton promise not to tell me the ending. I'm looking forward to it."

The waitress appeared at Miller's elbow and deposited two cappuccinos and two portions of hazelnut caramel cheesecake on the table. Philippa picked up her cup and sipped the creamy concoction. Then she gave a contented sigh and let her eyes sweep the cheerful interior of the café. After surveying the room, she turned to the window and gazed outside at the glimmering lights, which were becoming more and more dazzling against the darkening afternoon. The lighted canopy over the Old Chandler gleamed gold against the shadowy red brick.

She looked back at Miller and gave him a sparkling smile.

"Isn't this lovely?" she said.

Miller had only been watching his companion, but he nodded heartfelt agreement.

"Very," he said.

*     *     *

Bill Jones was worried. A year ago, when he'd returned to Vancouver to live with his daughter, he'd hoped that life would settle into a pattern of tranquility, even if he could not expect happiness. The loss of his wife of fifty years to cancer had saddened him deeply, but he dearly loved his daughter and grandchildren, and genuinely liked his son-in-law, so he had been glad to accept their offer to live in the basement suite of their East Vancouver home. After years of working for a gardening company in Ontario, he had had his fill of physical labour, but when his daughter had mentioned that the position of doorman at the Old Chandler was vacant, he decided to apply. However hospitable his daughter and her family were, he could not live in their pockets twenty-four hours a day, and part-time employment would give him an interest as well as an opportunity to supplement his pension. But the job, which had at first been a lively foray into the world of entertainment, had recently become a source of anxiety, for something was terribly wrong at the Old Chandler. The theatre-restaurant was thriving in the face of an economic downturn that was sinking far more prestigious and long-standing establishments, but the numbers going through the front door did not tally with the rosy picture that the management presented. Bill wondered if the young police detective he'd talked to had taken his concerns seriously. He dared not take any other action for if, as he suspected, drugs were involved, it would be dangerous to ask too many questions. Bill particularly did not want to imperil the nice young woman who did the books, for it was her talk of the robust figures that had first raised his suspicions, and he was quite sure that she was an innocent party to whatever was going on. No, for now he had to stay quiet, keep his eyes open and hope that the police were following through on the information he had passed on.

His meditations were interrupted as a tall, wiry woman bobbed under the canopy. Winifred Barton was the wardrobe mistress for the Gaslight Players, so Bill was used to seeing her on the premises. She was a brisk, but amiable woman, and they shared the occasional cup of coffee together so he knew a little about her. She was only a few years younger than him, a good-humoured spinster who lived with a lady friend from her university years.

"Evening, Bill." Winifred greeted him with a friendly smile. "Quiet tonight, I guess."

"Very. Just a few in the lounge. The restaurant is closed for the charity-group rehearsal. They only have one more run-through before their dress rehearsal. Why are you here this evening?"

"I've been commandeered. Henri asked me to outfit the members of the bar, and I couldn't very well refuse. It's for the Children's Society."

"So I gather. Well, let's hope the lawyers can act."

"Lawyers are the ultimate actors," Winifred pointed out. "Their whole livelihood depends on the art of deception."

"You're cynical this evening," said Bill. "What gives?"

Winifred's smile became rueful.

"It's this show. It reminds me of a case Chloe dealt with many years ago." Chloe was the retired gym teacher who shared a home with Winifred. "Foster care gone wrong—just like in the play."

"What happened?" asked Bill.

"Chloe had an aboriginal student who was into drugs and alcohol. The home environment was terrible so the girl had been raised by her grandparents, but she was continually running away and getting in with the wrong crowd. Then she became pregnant, and ironically, the knowledge she was carrying a child was the one thing that got through to her. She cleaned up her act—Chloe and one of the other counsellors did a lot to help her—and she stayed clean throughout the pregnancy. She finished school and, with Chloe's help, lined up a job. She was seventeen when she had the baby, but her grandparents didn't want her to keep the child and they began a suit to claim custody. Ultimately, the courts ruled that, because of the family history, none of the relatives should be entrusted with the child's upbringing, so even though the girl desperately wanted to raise her own daughter, the baby was taken into care. Two years later, the foster father beat the little girl to death. All the social workers who had been involved were far more interested in justifying their own actions than showing any remorse for what had happened. Later the girl committed suicide. It was a tragic case—and all because some rotten creep introduced her to drugs when she was barely into her teens."

Bill shook his head sadly. "Why can't these kids appreciate that they don't need artificial stimulants to feel happy?"

Winifred shivered and pulled her coat more tightly around her chest.

"Chloe saw some terrible things during the course of her career. That's why I'm glad I went into the rag trade and not teaching. Pandering to actors' vanity—that's my lot. No earth-shattering problems at the Old Chandler, thank goodness."

Bill bit his tongue and refrained from comment. Winifred went on, oblivious to his apprehensions.

"Now, I'd better get in there and see what this cast looks like," she said. "I have no idea who's involved, but unless they're as fat as their oversized fees, I should be able to accommodate them. Gaslight has a good selection of costumes for that period. Wish me luck."

She turned towards the door. Bill opened it for her and held it while she went through. But as he closed it behind her, he said a silent prayer: *Whatever transgressions the police unearth during the course of their investigations, let the decent types like Winifred remain safe and untouched by the rotten core within the Old Chandler.*

# II

On the evening of the performance, the raw winter weather still gripped Vancouver. It was a forbidding night to be venturing out. Philippa had layered scarf, bulky sweater and winter coat over her flimsy cocktail dress, and she could still feel the chill coming off the passenger window in Bob Miller's SUV.

"It's going to snow again," said Miller. "If a blizzard starts this evening, your sister may find half her audience has gone home before Act Two."

"You have four-wheel drive," said Philippa philosophically. "We can stay to the end."

Miller switched lanes and overtook an ancient Plymouth that was crawling along the curb lane. Then he cut back in and accelerated through the yellow light as it changed to red.

Philippa blinked.

"I'd get a ticket if I did that," she pointed out.

"Probably." Miller changed the subject. "So has your sister told you anything more about the goings-on at the Old Chandler?"

"Not really. I only talked with her briefly since I last saw you. She did identify the object of Henri Gerard's lust, though. It's Wozchinski's senior manager—some Italian hotpot that has all the men's tongues hanging out. Sylvia says she brings Lucrezia Borgia to mind."

"Poor Henri Gerard."

"I'll say."

"Any other bits of gossip?"

"Her only other comment was that the doorman was a sweetie—and he must be for Sylvia to say that. The only quality she usually notices is efficiency, or the lack of. Norton called too, but that was just to ask for advice on acting—and I ran into Jordan Hope in the CBC building last week, but those are the only contacts I've had."

"Who's Jordan Hope?"

"The director."

"Another lawyer?"

"Goodness, no. He's an actor ... a very good one. Born in England and trained at RADA, but he's lived here since the early nineties. A top-notch local professional, that's Jordan."

"You mean you can make a living from acting in this town?"

"Marginally. Jordan has done a lot of plays with the Arts Club and the Playhouse—both acting and directing—plus he does film and TV. He did a regular character part on 'Da Vinci's Inquest'—all seven seasons—and he was in the latest *Twilight* epic."

"So what's he doing directing the legal beagles?"

"Earning money. He'll be charging his Equity rate. Everyone takes on extra work directing amateur shows or adjudicating festivals. Why do you think I have my arts-council job? The lawyers are lucky to get Jordan. He's arty, witty and delightful to work with. He directed me in a musical at TUTS once. He taught me a lot."

"Did he have anything interesting to pass on?"

Philippa giggled.

"He said directing a bunch of lawyers was as enjoyable as sitting on a hard church pew when you're suffering from haemorrhoids."

Miller turned onto the ramp that led to the Georgia Viaduct and accelerated to merge with the traffic.

"So which one is the biggest pain in the backside?"

"Günter Sachs, by the sound of it."

"Your blind date that wasn't?"

"Yes."

Miller's lips twitched. He made an effort to keep a straight face.

"Good," he said.

Philippa's eyes narrowed.

"If you make any jokes about arresting me to save me from a bad date, I won't speak to you for the rest of the evening."

"Point taken," said Miller. "Who else did this director talk about?"

"He said my sister was the easiest one to work with because she has crisp enunciation, good posture, and is smart enough to perceive that, in this case, the audience is the judge, and that's who she has to impress."

"What about your non-talented brother-in-law?"

"Funnily enough, Jordan really likes Norton. He says Norton plays Christopher Wren like a wooden soldier, which, of course, he would, because the only other part he ever had is the guardsman in *Reluctant Debutante*, but because the character is supposed to be quirky, it actually works … especially when he's parroting the nursery rhymes."

"Nursery rhymes? In a murder mystery?"

"Agatha Christie is big on nursery rhymes. They show up a lot in her work, though in *Mousetrap*, I think it's just the one about three blind mice."

"You're taking me to a show about inebriated rodents?"

"Very funny! Actually, I believe it has something to do with three children who had problem childhoods … or perhaps a child that died. The motive is definitely revenge. Beyond that I can't tell you anything. But Jordan did say one thing that was interesting."

"Oh, and what was that?"

"He's not impressed with the young woman playing Mollie. She's forever sloping off elsewhere when it's not her scene, so he always has to send someone to track her down when he needs her. Jordan figures she's on drugs."

"Does he, indeed? I wonder where she's getting her supply."

"I guess it could be from someone at the Old Chandler."

"Well, there's definitely something going on there. We've checked the bartender's bank records. Big cash deposits three months in a row, and another slightly smaller one made at an ATM on the evening that he died. He couldn't possibly have got it all on tips. I think Bill Jones was right. There's a drug ring operating out of the place."

"But why would they kill the bartender if he was part of the operation?"

"The girl across the hall said he was pretty full of himself. Maybe he became a liability. The other possibility is that he found out what was going on and was blackmailing the ringleaders." Miller turned the corner and swung into the left lane. "Speaking of my investigation," he added, "you'd better forget about using the threat of my status as a policeman on your nephews. Nothing clams people up faster than being in the presence of a cop. If I'm going to be able to mingle as a guest and ask innocuous questions, I'd better be there as your current boyfriend." He smiled. "If that's OK with you, of course."

Philippa refrained from comment. Instead she said, "We won't need threats to control the boys. They're all right, just high-spirited. Sylvia runs her home like boot camp, so they have a tendency to take advantage when free from their mother's reins, but they know how to behave in public."

"So what are the names of the two gremlins we have to supervise?"

"Thomas and Geoffrey. Tom is nine and Geoff is seven."

Philippa stopped speaking as she saw the high wall of the Old Chandler looming ahead. Miller steered the SUV around the corner and pulled up behind the row of cars in front of the entrance.

"I'll let you off here," he said. "I'll park and meet you in the lobby."

Philippa gave Miller his ticket, retrieved the bouquet she'd brought for Sylvia from the back seat and clambered out of the vehicle. Then she joined the throng of well-dressed people who were congregating on the sidewalk and inching towards the entrance. A broad-shouldered man in a gold-braided uniform stood holding the door for the guests. Philippa smiled at him as she went in and received a kindly greeting in return. Sylvia was right, she decided. Old Bill Jones was a sweetie.

The foyer was already filling up, even though it was only just five o'clock, but the high ceiling gave an illusion of spaciousness in spite of the milling crowd. Eyeing the glittering outfits that were appearing as ladies divested their winter coats, Philippa was glad she had dressed up. Her lemon chiffon mini-dress was just right for the occasion.

She noticed Jordan Hope standing next to a tall, distinguished-looking gentleman with long, silver hair combed back from a high forehead, which, combined with a large beak of a nose, gave him the profile of a benevolent eagle. Both men were formally dressed. They were holding court amid a circle of blue-haired, bejewelled dowagers, and although Jordan appeared to be doing most of the talking, the other man was in no way diminished by the lively presence of the director.

Philippa worked her way through and managed to get Jordan's attention. She asked if she could get her flowers delivered backstage, but before Jordan could reply, his tuxedoed companion snapped his fingers and a wafer-thin brunette in black crepe materialized to relieve Philippa of the bouquet. As the woman slipped away, Jordan put his arm around Philippa's shoulders.

"Darling, meet the owner of this illustrious establishment," he said. "This is Walt Wozchinski. Walt, meet Philippa. She's the possessor of an enchanting soprano voice, not to mention an influential family."

Philippa extended her hand, but, instead of shaking it, Wozchinski suavely raised it to his lips.

"Jordan has failed to tell me your surname," he said smoothly, "or would that be because he does not want to reveal your influential family?"

Philippa felt embarrassed.

"Jordan is exaggerating," she said. "My father is a city councillor, that's all."

"And her bro—" Jordan stopped speaking at a glare from Philippa. He raised his eyebrows, but being an expert at picking up cues, he fell silent.

Walt Wozchinski seemed not to notice. The benign blue eyes had become vigilant. The eagle had lapsed back to its natural state and become a predatory bird.

"Is your father on Vancouver City Council?" he asked.

"No. Burnside."

To Philippa's surprise, the raptorial gaze intensified.

"Excellent! We are contemplating opening a second venue and I have been viewing some properties in Burnside. Will your father be here this evening?"

"No. He would like to have come but he had a prior engagement." Philippa flashed her best stage smile and took command of the conversation. "This is my first time here," she gushed, "but I've read about the Old Chandler. I think what you're doing is wonderful, and I know my father would be impressed. I'd love to know how everything works. How do you manage to run the restaurant when you have a company putting on a regular play season?"

The eagle smiled disarmingly.

"Would you like me to give you a tour?" he offered. "We have time. Come. Let me check your coat and get you a glass of wine. Then I'll show you around."

Leaving Jordan to entertain the dowagers, and feeling slightly guilty knowing that Bob Miller would think she'd abandoned him, Philippa glided away in the wake of the proprietor. This was an offer she could not refuse.

*       *       *

Bob Miller finally found parking on Cordova Street. He was glad that he'd dropped Philippa off because the night air was so frigid it hurt to breathe in. He pulled his coat tightly around his body as he walked back. The stores were still open and the streets were brightly lit. The white glow from the lamp posts was augmented by glittering lights entwined in the branches of the sidewalk trees, and the shop windows were filled with colourful signs advertising January sales. Miller hurried along the Lonsdale Block and turned the corner onto Carrall Street. The statue of Gassy Jack loomed ahead, sharply silhouetted by the light from the street lamp behind it. As Miller drew nearer, one side of the dark shape became outlined in gold as the light from the OK Boot Corral spilled onto the rear of the statue.

Suddenly the silhouette split into two. A dark figure glided forward from the statue. It was as if Gassy Jack had come to life. Miller could make out a long, flapping overcoat and the drooping brim of a hat. As the figure moved into the light, he saw that it was a derelict old man, most likely a street person in search of handouts.

Miller pulled out some change, but then he paused. He was standing at the entrance to Blood Alley. If this was the man's haunt, chances were he'd have known the bartender of the Old Chandler by sight. He might even have seen something on the night the bartender died. Miller put away his change and pulled out a ten-dollar bill. The man was moving away from him now. He was hurrying towards a well-dressed couple who had paused at the intersection. Miller called out and waved. The man glanced back; then, seeing Miller striding towards him, he took off at a run and vanished into the crowds that were coming along Water Street.

"Shit," muttered Miller under his breath. "Walk like a cop, talk like a cop. They can see us coming every time." He stuffed the ten-dollar bill back in his pocket and crossed the road. As he set off alongside the Europe Hotel, he resolved to send the uniformed branch out to chat with the homeless people in the area. Even on a snowy evening, some of them must have been about. One of them might have noticed the bartender as he made his final deadly walk from the Old Chandler.

19

Miller hurried along the sidewalk and joined the line of patrons streaming through the door of the theatre-restaurant. Keeping his face averted as he passed the doorman, he entered the lobby and looked for Philippa.

To his surprise, she was nowhere to be found. Where had she got to? What was she up to now?

\*         \*         \*

Philippa was enjoying her tour. Walt Wozchinski was a superb guide. He was knowledgeable and articulate, and he took a great deal of pride in the work that had transformed the warehouse into a dinner-theatre. The reconstruction had been a massive task, and extremely expensive, judging by the high-quality workmanship and fittings. Wozchinski explained that the front section of the building had been the original chandler's shop, which had run the full width of the building. With its thirty-six foot ceiling, which encompassed three of the five storeys, the shop had been the ideal space to accommodate the lobby, bar and washrooms. However, the restaurant behind exploited the full height of the building.

Rather than enter the restaurant on the main floor, Wozchinski escorted Philippa up the stairs to a landing where a burnished suit of armour held pride of place. They continued to a second level and emerged onto a wide gallery that ran around all four walls, although ornately carved planters blocked access at one end, turning the balcony into a large horseshoe. Dinner tables, resplendent with white linen cloths and gleaming cutlery, were set along the far end of the gallery and halfway down each side.

Philippa moved to the edge of the gallery and found herself looking down on a sea of white-clothed tables, artfully arranged to maximize the audience's visibility of the stage. The hall's brick walls were broken up with wooden beams and decorated with spears, swords and colourful shields that completed the illusion of a medieval banqueting hall. The stage itself was constructed like a Shakespearean theatre, so a portion of the set was hidden beneath the gallery. However, the apron was in view. It held a well-worn chesterfield, a suitably dated end table, a tea trolley and a Parker Knoll wing chair.

As her eyes travelled upwards, she saw that the high walls culminated in a vaulted ceiling created by a series of massive oak beams. A second gallery, narrower and higher than the one she stood on, encircled the room, but it appeared to be only a walkway. Her professional eye noted a row of ellipsoid lights hung below the upper gallery, some of which were beamed onto the blocked-off section of the lower gallery.

"How do people get to that top gallery?" Philippa asked.

"They don't—we don't want our patrons wandering around up there. That's where our offices are located, along with the staff kitchen and lounge. There's a staff elevator that's locked with a security code on the main floor. It's right next to the public elevator that goes to the lower gallery. There's also a stairway at the back of the rehearsal hall, though that's mainly for the performers."

"Why do the actors need to go up there?"

"Sometimes they play a scene from the top gallery—though the audience can't see them unless they move right down to the railing. It's a good setting for a castle battlement or the crow's nest of a ship."

Or an eagle's nest, thought Philippa, noting her host's long, talon-like fingers as he waved his arm skywards. But a very charming raptor, she conceded, as Wozchinski continued the tour, entertaining her with anecdotes and answering her questions. He guided her round the gallery to another flight of stairs that took them down to the main floor. At the bottom of the stairs, he opened a door marked private and ushered her through.

Philippa was even more impressed once she had viewed the backstage area. The dressing rooms were spacious, the tools in the scene shop were top-of-the-line, and the costume room was equipped with bales of fabric, three expensive sewing machines, and four room-length racks filled with clothing from every imaginable era. The rehearsal hall, which formed the central core for the other workspaces, was huge. Philippa's appreciation was obvious, and the more she enthused, the more intense became the gleam in her host's eyes.

"Come," said Wozchinski, leading Philippa across the rehearsal hall, "I will take you to the upper gallery now. It's quite a climb," he warned her, "but there's a landing halfway with a door to the middle gallery, so we can go back that way if you decide not to go all the way up."

Wozchinski was right about the climb. Philippa was determined to make it to the top, but she hoped she wouldn't look too horribly wilted once she returned to join her escort. Ignoring her aching legs and admiring the stamina of her host, she puffed up the final flight. When she emerged from the stairwell, she felt a sudden rush of dizziness, for the staff lounge was tiered with three levels descending to the gallery, and the top level, which was furnished with two leather sofas and a large square coffee table, was higher than the balustrade at the edge of the walkway. Wozchinski, used to the sense of open space, walked down the carpeted tiers and stood at the railing. He was a tall man, and, silhouetted against the void, he appeared poised to take flight.

Philippa regained her equilibrium and walked down more slowly to join him. She looked down cautiously. Below, the restaurant was a mass of swirling bodies and colourful dresses. She tried to pick out her escort amid the crowd but she couldn't see him anywhere. She hoped he wasn't waiting, fuming in the lobby. She raised her eyes again and peered towards a long strip of glass at the far end of the gallery.

"That's the booth," said Wozchinski, following her glance. "It has state-of-the-art equipment. I can show you later. I hope you will give your father a glowing report. It would be helpful to have a councillor on our side in the event that I have to apply for a rezoning."

"I can guarantee he'll be impressed," said Philippa sincerely. Though not, she thought privately, with the other rumours that are circulating about the place. "But," she added deliberately, "he will want to know how you can make a go of a second venue in the current economic climate. Restaurants and theatres are going under all the time. I'm amazed you're doing so well."

If Philippa had expected a reaction, she was disappointed. Walt Wozchinski did not miss a beat.

"Not at all," he said smoothly. "We have good management and a first-class product. Now, we're almost done," he added. "Come this way." He led her to the left side of the gallery where a series of doors lined the wall. These, he explained, were the staff kitchen and the offices. As they approached the last door, it opened and a striking woman stepped out onto the gallery. She had Sophia Loren lips, a creamy complexion, and an artfully styled tangle of tawny hair that emphasized her dramatic cheekbones. Her voluptuous figure was encased in a short burgundy sheath that emphasized every titillating curve and displayed her long, shapely legs to perfect advantage. On her feet were matching suede Fluevog shoes with huge buckles that would have looked ridiculous on a smaller person, but were ideally proportioned for the arresting creature that wore them. Philippa mentally priced the shoes at the best part of four hundred dollars. She suspected that the subtle rose fragrance hovering in the air was equally expensive, but the dazzling diamond on the third finger of the woman's left hand was probably worth forty times as much.

"Claudia Capelli, my manager," said Wozchinski. He introduced Philippa and the woman's lips parted into a smile. However, her glittering hazel eyes were mocking. She complimented Philippa on her dress with an air that implied she was fully aware that her own footwear cost more than Philippa's entire outfit. Then, with a briskness that could not be faulted but still managed to imply that Philippa had no business being there, she led the way to the elevator at the end of the gallery. She stood back to allow Wozchinski and Philippa inside, then stepped in after them and pressed the button. The tour was clearly over.

*     *     *

When Philippa returned to the main floor, she found Bob Miller waiting in the lobby. Rather than lead her into the restaurant, he took her arm and guided her into the cocktail lounge, which was deserted except for a solitary staff member who was wiping off tables at the far end of the room.

"Sorry for abandoning you like that," Philippa apologized, "but it was too good an opportunity to pass up."

"I bet it was." Miller drew Philippa into a corner that was screened by the projecting bar counter. Keeping his voice low, he asked, "So what did you learn?"

"I'll fill you in later. Hadn't we better find Mai Ling and the boys?"

"I found them ages ago," said Miller. "I saw a tiny Asian lady arguing with what looked like two dwarf-sized waiters, so I went over and introduced myself. I must say your sister is a bit of a sadist. If I'd been forced to wear a red waistcoat and a bow tie at your nephews' age, I'd have committed matricide."

"They probably look very cute."

"Cute isn't the word I'd use," said Miller. "More like *a-cute*." He leaned in closer and dropped his voice. "The first thing they did was ask if I was the cop who arrested you."

"How did they manage that?" Philippa whispered. "Sylvia didn't know I was bringing you."

"The younger one said his dad told them you can always tell a cop by the haircut, and the older one said it was obvious because I was eyeing all the guests as if I was trying to figure out who might be a terrorist."

"Little wretches," said Philippa. "So much for you being able to mingle and ask questions."

Miller looked smug.

"Not a problem. I told them I was here undercover and swore them to silence. They were most excited. They won't breathe a word to anyone. I said there'd been a recent spate of jewel robberies and that I had a tip that the thief was one of the people at the next table—which means we won't have to worry about them wandering off because they'll be too busy spying on the group beside us."

"That could backfire in a variety of embarrassing ways."

"Never mind the boys. What did you learn from Wozchinski?" Noticing that the waiter had reached their end of the room, Miller inched closer. By now, he had Philippa backed into the corner and she was finding it increasingly hard to concentrate. Miller was far too good-looking for that much proximity.

Miller seemed oblivious to her discomfort. "I just about flipped when I saw you wandering along the top balcony," he said softly, "especially after your pal, Jordan, told me who had spirited you away. I had visions of you asking one question too many and getting yourself tossed off the gallery."

Philippa steeled herself to ignore her fluttering insides. "Wozchinski was very charming in a rather predatory way," she said evenly. "He reminded me of an eagle, especially when we were up in his eyrie. He let me ask him some pretty detailed questions—I couldn't have got away with it except that he's toying with the idea of starting a second venue in Burnside and he was trying to impress me so I'd rave about the place to my father."

"So what did you learn?"

"He has two managers—one who handles the food services, and a senior one who oversees the cashiers, along with the box-office and front-of-house staff when they have ticketed events. The senior manager brings the cash drawers upstairs to count the take and package up the bank deposits. She's here tonight. Wozchinski introduced us. Her name's Claudia Capelli and the only way I can describe her is to say she's a tropical-zone hottie with eyes like ice. Pricey too. Her clothes look like they come from Holt Renfrew and she walks in a cloud of Chanel."

"Your sister's Lucrezia Borgia?"

"Must be. I can see how Walt Wozchinski could use her to lure in Gerard and get himself a wealthy partner with an impeccable reputation."

"So Henri Gerard might not be a criminal; he could just be a horny, deluded idiot with more money than sense."

Seeing the man with the cloth getting closer and glancing their way, Philippa sidled out of her corner and turned to face Miller. Even speaking softly, she knew her voice projected. It was safer to have her back turned. "It's possible," she murmured. "It sounds as if Gerard has very little to do with the actual running of the place. He just contributed a lot of dollars to get the venture started."

Miller glowered at the waiter—surely the man had to realize he was interrupting a tête-à-tête—then he put his arm around Philippa's shoulders and steered her to the other end of the room. Philippa gently extracted herself and slid onto a barstool. She could focus much better with space around her. She thought back and tried to remember what else she had learned on the tour. Miller prompted her.

"Did you meet any other staff members?" he asked.

"No, but Wozchinski told me how many it takes to run the place. In addition to the two managers, there's a bookkeeper, a publicist, two hostesses, three bartenders, two security guards who double as bouncers, an assortment of waiters, the doorman—that'll be the old boy who tipped you off—plus an accountant to do all the year-end stuff. The janitorial work is contracted out to a cleaning agency, which also provides extra staff for special events."

"What about the Gaslight Players? You haven't said anything about the theatre company."

"I was coming to that," said Philippa. "This is the amazing part. I assumed that the players would operate separately as a non-profit society and give a percentage of their take to the Old Chandler, but the troupe is entirely funded and run by the OC administration."

Miller looked astounded.

"You're kidding!"

"I'm not. The Old Chandler retains four permanent staff for the theatre: a production manager, a set builder, a wardrobe mistress and a lighting technician. Then the actors, crew and directors are hired for each production. Honestly, I can't imagine how they can make it pay. It's a very expensive operation."

"That's what the doorman said, and according to him, the bodies coming through the door don't warrant the rosy figures on the books." Miller grinned. "You've done well. This is proving to be an enlightening evening. It'll be interesting to see what else turns up. Come on," he added, "the nosy-parker with the dishcloth is coming back." He took Philippa's hand and helped her down. "We'd better get moving before everyone starts wondering where we are. Let's go join the others. I can't wait to see if your nephews have identified the jewel thief yet."

*      *      *

The restaurant was packed. Some guests were already seated with plates of appetizers collected from the buffet; many were getting a head start on the bottles of wine that had been placed at the centre of the tables. Others table-hopped and name-dropped, more interested in networking than in satisfying their appetites. However, at one table on the far side of the room, two women sat with two young boys, and the bottle of wine remained unopened. Neither woman looked as if she belonged in the glittering throng. One was a diminutive Asian who could have been anything from thirty to fifty. She was dressed plainly in a white blouse and black skirt, and her attention was entirely devoted to the boys who sat on either side of her. The other was middle-aged, a grey-haired woman in a well-worn pantsuit the same shade as her hair. She looked tired and strangely disconnected from the bustling scene around her.

Chloe Harker had attended many productions at the Old Chandler. Her friend, Winifred, regularly received comps and Chloe enjoyed coming to the plays. But tonight, she found herself strangely preoccupied with the past. As she opened her program and stared at the first name on the cast list, the print on the page blurred and her mind filled with memories. Andrew McCardle had been in Grade Ten during Chloe's fifth year of teaching. He had been a spoiled brat when he first came to the school—a typical West Vancouver boy—very bright, but also given far too much money instead of being encouraged to work for it. It was the following year that had given him the shock that had changed his personality. The disastrous student party where a girl had died from a drug overdose had sobered him up for good. The tragedy had a strong effect on a lot of the students, but Andrew had taken it to heart.

25

That had been the trigger that prompted his first anti-drug campaign—and the initiative had done a lot of good. Other students looked up to Andrew and they had followed his example. If only he had not been so intense, thought Chloe, but he had become fanatic as only the very young can be. It had caused his thinking to be skewed when he first came to the bar. He only saw things in black and white. That was why he made the one bad decision that marked him for life. Chloe remembered the case well, for she had still been teaching at the time. The girl had been another of her students—Deanna John, the teenage aboriginal girl who was so eager to keep her baby. But because she had a history of drug use, Andrew took steps to ensure that she didn't succeed. Chloe would never forget how devastated Deanna had been over the ruling. Neither would she forget the subsequent heartbreak—the death of the child and Deanna's suicide. It had been the saddest event in Chloe's entire teaching career. Andrew had been attempting to do what he thought was right, but the end result was shattering. He's been trying to atone ever since, Chloe thought sadly. I wonder if he's succeeded.

*       *       *

Philippa and Miller paused in the doorway of the restaurant. The room was a riot of colour and sparkling light as rhinestones and sequins caught and reflected the beams from overhead. The scent of expensive fragrances mingled with tantalizing aromas from the buffet, which was laden with a mouth-watering display of finger-food to keep hunger at bay until dinner was served. The noise in the room had risen beyond the comfort level, and shrill bursts of laughter and the clink of glasses punctuated the constant hubbub of private conversations and boisterous greetings.

Miller placed his hand on Philippa's waist and steered her through the crush. Guests were still milling about and waiters were delivering wine to the tables where people had already emptied bottles, so weaving a path to the far side of the room was a challenge. When they reached their appointed table, Philippa saw her nephews seated on either side of Mai Ling. They were working their way through a plate of appetizers and staring intently at the next table, which was comprised of six respectable-looking senior citizens—two of whom Philippa recognized as venerated members of the opera guild—and a modishly dressed couple of indeterminate age. Philippa could not pin down which designer had created the shimmering lilac gown that the woman wore, but she was ready to swear that the glittering evening bag was Versace. The man's suit looked tailor-made. He was broad-shouldered in spite of a lean face, rendered even thinner by his slicked-back red hair, but the fabric of his jacket looked expensive and the fit was exquisite. Corporate clients who had bought the entire table, Philippa surmised.

She turned to her own table, which still had four empty places. Jordan was nowhere in sight—probably backstage giving a last-minute pep talk—but a pleasant-faced, middle-aged woman sat opposite Mai Ling. Miller politely drew out a chair for Philippa and she sat down, greeted Mai Ling and the boys, and then introduced herself to the other woman.

"We've already met," said Miller as Philippa turned to introduce him. "We had lots of time to chat while you were getting your tour. Chloe is a friend of the woman who's doing costumes for the show."

"That's right," said Chloe. "Winifred is backstage, but she'll be out to watch the performance."

"Is Winifred another of the lawyers?" Philippa asked.

"No. She's the resident wardrobe mistress for Gaslight Players. She's on the staff here."

Philippa's interest level increased.

"Do you work here too?"

"Heavens, no. I'm a retired teacher. I'm very much looking forward to tonight's production because one of my former students is in it."

"Oh. Which one?"

"Andrew McCardle. Brilliant young man … well, young by my standards. He'll be well into his forties by now. He's one of the ones you don't forget."

"I've heard about him from my sister," said Philippa. "He sounds like a real go-getter. Was he a mover and shaker in high school too?"

"That's a long story," Chloe said wryly. Philippa listened intently as Chloe recounted the history of Andrew McCardle and the struggles that had molded his character. "Andrew's had a hard time," Chloe concluded, "but he's turned his bad experiences to good use."

Philippa was about to comment, but Chloe glanced up and said, "Here comes Winifred with Jordan. It must be getting close to show time."

Philippa turned to see a tall, broad-shouldered woman crossing towards them. She had steely grey hair, worn in an old-fashioned French pleat, and her horn-rimmed spectacles were equally dated, but her long-sleeved navy cocktail dress was beautifully cut and revealed an athletic figure that would have been the envy of a woman half her age. Jordan was bouncing along in her wake, and when he reached the table, he gallantly held a chair for Winifred, then opened the bottle of wine at the centre of the table.

"So what was with the Scarlett O'Hara routine?" he asked Philippa as he poured her a generous serving that threatened to spill over the brim of her glass.

"What Scarlett O'Hara routine?"

Jordan swept around the table deftly filling the remaining glasses.

"You know. La, Sir, Ah do declare, Ah'd just love to see over yo great big plantation. Li'l me is so bowled over by the things yo clever men can do!"

Miller choked into his wine glass. Philippa looked indignant.

"I didn't sound like that."

"Just about," said Jordan. "So was the tour satisfactory?"

"Yes. Very interesting. I know more about the place now than you do."

"No, you don't," said Jordan. "I direct plays for Gaslight. I know the place like the back of my hand." He hailed a waiter and pointed at the empty wine bottle. "I know how Winifred runs her costume room, I oversee the set builder, I spend hours setting lighting cues with the techie, and I've enjoyed many an evening discussing box-office returns with our sexy, scrumptious manager."

"Speaking of your sexy, scrumptious manager," said Philippa, "I was nearly blinded by the rock on her finger. Who's she engaged to? Don't tell me she's landed Henri Gerard?"

Jordan plopped down the bottle and slid into the chair beside Winifred.

"She has," he said. "He popped the question last night—and made a point of announcing it to all and sundry when he arrived this evening. He's so flushed with delight that he probably won't need any stage makeup." Jordan twisted round and glared towards the waiter. "What the hell is the matter with that poncey idiot?" he added waspishly. "That's the second time I've tried to get another bottle of wine. Do you think the waiters have been told this is a comp table?"

Philippa swivelled round and peered across the room. The server that Jordan had beckoned was holding a bottle of wine, but he had averted his gaze and was talking with another waiter. However, the second waiter took the bottle and brought it to the table. In a trice, Jordan was mollified. He proceeded to top up the glasses, but Philippa kept her eyes on the first waiter. He was now staring at their table. He was a thin young man with hair so short it was shaved at the back with only some streaked blonde spikes on top, and he wore a gold loop in his right ear. His dark eyes were ringed with long lashes that Philippa could have sworn were daubed with mascara, and, with a jolt, she saw that they were trained on Bob Miller. Feeling uneasy, she leaned towards Thomas and spoke quietly to him.

"Tom, did you tell anyone about Bob being with VPD?" she asked.

Thomas vigorously shook his head.

"No," he said indignantly.

Jordan's head spun round.

"What have the boys been up to?" he asked.

Philippa was saved from replying by a shrill cry from the next table. The lilac fashion plate was trilling Jordan's name and waving her Versace handbag in an attempt to get his attention.

Jordan blew her a kiss.

"Hello, darling," he crooned. "Fabulous to see you. You look marvellous as usual." Turning back, he muttered sotto voce to Philippa, "By the end of the evening her cheeks will be as purple as her gown. Very lush-ious lady, that one."

"She's a stunning dresser," said Philippa.

"Of course she is. Hubby, Frankie, makes a fortune importing hardwood flooring, and he never seems to mind how much of it little Amy fritters away on designer clothes. Still, she fritters quite a bit in our direction, so who am I to complain?"

"They donate to the Gaslight Players?"

"Regularly. They're loaded. Holiday home and yacht in the Bahamas, chalet at Whistler, New York townhouse, and a condo in Maui. You name it; they've got it. Now," he added, reaching over with both arms and ruffling the boys' hair, "are we set to do some sleuthing?"

Philippa blinked, startled.

"The play," said Jordan. "Or does everyone already know the ending?"

"I do," said Chloe. "Winifred and I saw it in London in the seventies."

"We don't," said Philippa. "What about you two?" she added to Thomas and Geoffrey. "Did your mum and dad tell you who did it?"

"No. They said we had to guess, and if we get it right, we get a trip to McDonald's and a movie."

"What do we get?" asked Miller.

"We can have our own contest," proposed Philippa. "If I win, I'll take you to dinner and a movie, and if you win, you have to treat me—not McDonald's though."

Miller grinned.

"I'm game," he said. "Sounds like I win either way."

"And if neither of you get it and we do," said Geoffrey, "then you guys can take us to McDonald's and a movie too. OK?"

"Deal," said Miller.

"So," Jordan intoned dramatically, as the lighting in the room began to dim, "turn your chairs forward, everyone, because the play is about to begin."

Henri Gerard had some time to wait before his entrance as Mr. Paravicini. He sat in his dressing room, his thoughts straying from the task at hand. Why did he feel so restless when the future looked so good? His investments were thriving, his practice was booming and, best of all, Claudia Capelli had finally accepted his proposal. His friends had said all along that she would, but he had not been so confident, and the joy he had felt initially was turning to apprehension. What if Claudia found out what he'd done to eliminate his rival? Henri's face darkened as he thought about Guglielmo Bergonzi. Guglielmo had been so breathtakingly handsome. All the women had flocked to him and Henri was well aware that Claudia had been no different. He flushed as he recalled all the things he'd discovered about the predatory womanizer, and he shuddered at the memory of their final confrontation. The whole business filled him with disgust. Thinking about it made his stomach churn. Still, he had no regrets. It was good that the man was dead, Henri thought bitterly. For all his good looks, Guglielmo had been a waste of space. Greedy, sensual and lacking in all principles.

Henri took a handkerchief and wiped his brow. The lights on the makeup mirrors were hot, and the sweat was already starting to run down his face. The intercom broke into his thoughts and reminded him that he was due to come on stage. He tossed the handkerchief onto the counter and stood up. It was time to take his part in the murder play.

\*       \*       \*

Act One ended to a round of applause. Philippa suspected it was more for the prospect of dinner than for the play as the main course was to be served during the intermission. The waiters quickly distributed the entrées, and the guests speculated about the plot while they devoured their braised salmon. Those who knew the play discussed the merits of the production and dropped hints about the outcome, while those that were viewing it for the first time exchanged theories as to who would turn out to be the killer. The wine continued to flow so abundantly that Philippa decided very few people would care about the solution by the time the curtain fell. However, her nephews were keen to have their contest, so once she finished her entrée, she wrote her guess on the back of her place card and added it to the pile begun by Miller and the boys.

The intermission seemed to go on for an unnecessarily long time and Philippa started to feel restless. The washroom lineups had diminished, the plates had been cleared, and even the waiters were looking towards the stage and tapping their watches. She was dying for a cup of coffee, but the side tables were still laden with hors d'œuvres, so she suspected that she would have to make do with water until after the final curtain. As she reached for the jug to refill her glass, she noticed a woman approaching their table. It was the slender brunette who had taken Sylvia's flowers backstage before the show. The woman headed straight for Chloe Harker and gave her a hug. Chloe seemed pleased to see the newcomer; however, after an exuberant but brief exchange that the whole table could hear, the woman moved on. Chloe apologized to Philippa for not introducing her.

"Pauline Waverly is another of my ex-pupils, but she's on duty so she didn't have time to chat."

"What does she do here?" Philippa was curious. The woman's svelte black dress and smart French-braided hair seemed far too elegant for a junior employee. "Is she a hostess?"

"No," said Chloe. "She's the Old Chandler's bookkeeper."

"Didn't I hear her say something to you about Andrew McCardle?" Philippa asked.

Chloe nodded.

"Yes. She's thrilled to meet up with Andrew again. She had quite the crush on him in high school."

"Were the two of them in the same grade?"

Chloe shook her head. "No. Andrew was in her sister's grade. Pauline was three years younger. Andrew dated her sister for a while and Pauline absolutely worshipped him"—her face clouded momentarily—"but as I told you earlier, everything went wrong. Every student in the school was shaken by the tragedy at that party, Andrew most of all. He became obsessed with his anti-drug campaign and they all drifted apart."

"Pauline is an excellent bookkeeper," Winifred chimed in. "Very reliable. Sweet girl too. The nicest member of the permanent staff, other than our doorman who's an absolute love." Winifred smiled fondly. "Old Bill at the Old Chandler. He's a major draw for our clientele. I bet he'll be holding doors and jollying people along when he's a hundred and ten."

Not from the way I heard him talk, thought Miller. However, out loud he said, "Your owner-operator strikes me as pretty smooth too. He was laying it on thick with the rich bitches out in the lobby."

Winifred's voice acquired an edge.

"Yes," she said. "Walt can turn on the charm when it's needed."

"As can we all, dear," said Jordan. "And it's a good job Walt can do it or we'd all be a few dollars poorer. Darling Guglielmo had a great manner with the ladies as well. Poor beggar."

"Hardly poor—well, not in life, anyway," Winifred said wryly. "He was pretty well heeled for someone who worked behind a bar."

"With those looks, no wonder." Jordan arched his brows knowingly. "Big tips from rich ladies who wanted more than a swizzle stick with their cocktails."

"Who's Guglielmo?" asked Miller with studied innocence.

"The cougar-magnet who got himself killed in Blood Alley." Jordan shuddered. "Would you believe I used to cut through that alley en route to this place? Never again," he vowed.

"Surely you didn't go through there at night?" cried Winifred.

"Well, no, but the muggers work all hours, don't they? And I did actually go through one night when the sidewalks were particularly icy. I figured the rough stonework in the alley would make for easier walking. It was the night of our first blocking rehearsal. Horribly creepy. As soon as I reached the mews, I cut back out to the street."

"For heaven's sake, Jordan," said Winifred. "That was the night Guglielmo was killed. Don't you pay attention to the news?"

"No," said Jordan. "Why?"

"The police put out all sorts of bulletins asking if anyone had seen anything suspicious."

"I didn't see anyone. Not a soul."

"Then you were lucky," retorted Winifred, "because Guglielmo left here just before six-thirty, and you arrived soon after seven, so you could have run into the same mugger who killed him. I read that the body was lying against a dumpster right by Gaoler's Mews."

Jordan gulped.

"Oh, good grief!" he said. "I must have gone right by it."

Miller had been listening with avid attention. Philippa could sense how hard he had found it not to interject, but now he cut in with a question.

"There was snow on the ground," he said. "Did you see any car tracks?"

Jordan raised his eyebrows.

"Car tracks? That would be a very up-market mugger."

Philippa grinned at Miller's discomfited expression. Jordan, however, did not appear to notice. He rattled on without missing a beat.

"I did see footprints, though. In fact—" Jordan paused and his eyes lit up. "They came from the direction of the dumpsters," he cried, "and cut over to the entrance of the mews. That could have been the killer!"

"What did the prints look like?" Philippa asked, keen to help Miller in his quest for information.

Jordan thought for a moment.

"Rectangular," he said decisively, "with a big heel. Bit of an unusual shape

… definitely not Wellies or Uggs … more like a cowboy boot with the toe cut off. Man must have had a wide foot."

"Did you see where they went at the other end of the mews?"

"No. Didn't notice. Besides, there's more than one exit to the mews. He could have gone out a different way. Do you think I ought to pop into the police station and tell them about it?"

"Yes, you should," said Miller. "You might recognize the shape if you looked through some computer mockups."

"How exciting," said Jordan. "I will, but not for a few days. I have a gruelling schedule next week and I'll barely have time to breathe, let alone visit the cop shop."

"You should make time," Miller said bluntly; then seeing Jordan's surprised reaction, he moderated his tone. "Shame about the bartender," he said sympathetically. "Sounds like he was a pretty popular guy."

Philippa heard a muffled sound, a sigh, or perhaps a sob, from the next table. She glanced round. To her surprise, Amy Steele was looking their way, though her eyes did not seem to be focussed on anyone. Jordan was right, thought Philippa. The Old Chandler's benefactress was into her cups, and maudlin with it. The impeccable makeup looked blotchy, and, as Philippa watched, a tear gradually made its way down the woman's cheek.

"Shhh, everyone. Cut the conversation." Winifred spoke sharply, drawing Philippa's attention back to her own table. "Act Two is about to begin."

The lights had finally started to fade.

Jordan leaned in, determined to have the last word. His clearly projected stage whisper reverberated eerily in the darkness.

"Guglielmo wasn't popular with everyone," he said. "He would have been corked up permanently in one of his wine bottles if some of the husbands and boyfriends had got their way."

*     *     *

Judge Mary Worthington was already dead. Knowing that she had a long wait until the end of the show, she had brought a book to read, but after staring blankly at the same page for several minutes, she tossed it aside. She should have realized how impossible it would be to concentrate, especially here at the Old Chandler, where her anxiety over her old friend was in the forefront of her mind. The last few weeks had been unbearable. She had no idea what she should do; yet doing nothing was like a slow death to her soul.

Of course, Henri had always had an eye for beautiful women, and despite his plain appearance, the combination of his wealth and Gallic charm had ensured that his interest was usually reciprocated. He'd enjoyed his bachelor existence—well liked, if not loved, by his conquests—so why had he become so ridiculously besotted with Claudia Capelli. There would be no affection there. The woman would bleed Henri dry and discard him. Judge Worthington had seen enough during her years on the bench to recognize the type—a lethal partnership of charm combined with total lack of empathy. Henri would be destroyed if the marriage went ahead ... or perhaps ... The judge's head started to throb as the thought that had been simmering below the surface for the last few weeks surged to the fore. Perhaps Henri was already past redemption. For the hundredth time, Judge Mary Worthington mentally relived the evening of the first blocking rehearsal, reviewing the details with the same precision she applied to the cases that came before her court.

It had been a Monday, so the theatre-restaurant was closed. Henri had offered her a ride, but warned that he had to go in early as he had arranged a meeting with Walt Wozchinski prior to the rehearsal. He had suggested that they pick up coffees and sandwiches en route and work together on their lines once his meeting was over. Mary had been happy to accept the offer, for she knew the Old Chandler was full of quiet spaces where she could sit and study her script while she waited for the meeting to run its course.

They had arrived at five-thirty and were let in by the young security guard who was on duty that evening. When they entered the lobby, they saw Claudia Capelli coming from the lounge. The manager was casually dressed in sweater and jeans. She was there for the meeting, or so she said, and the moment Henri set eyes on her, Mary became invisible. As the judge stood there, ignored and embarrassed, she became aware of sounds coming from the lounge—the clinking of bottles and glassware. She glanced through the open doorway and saw Guglielmo Bergonzi organizing stock at the bar. Sensing a reaction behind her, she turned to see Henri, eyes narrowed, staring towards the lounge and glancing speculatively towards Capelli. However, a smile from Capelli had erased the frown from his face. The manager tossed her tawny mane of hair, took Henri's arm, and murmuring seductively, led him to the elevator. Mary was left in the lobby, her mortification made worse by the sympathetic glance of the security guard. The guard had been kind. He had chatted to her. He had told her that the bartender was going away on holiday and had come in to ensure that things were in order for his replacement. Mary had barely listened, wanting to get away and hide her distress.

She had gone up to the middle gallery, where, gradually, she had calmed down and forced herself to concentrate on her script. After a while, she remembered glancing at her watch and seeing that it was ten past six. Soon after that, she heard a door opening and voices overhead. The meeting had drawn to a close. Henri's voice carried clearly to where she sat. His tone had been light, but beneath the jocularity, there had been intensity as he'd suggested that Capelli meet him for a drink after the rehearsal. Capelli had laughingly declined—something about going to her sister's for dinner—but said she'd see him the following day.

Mary tried hard to recollect what had followed. There was the sound of movement on the upper gallery; then she had heard the clang of the elevator. A few minutes later, the voices became audible again, now coming from the main floor, but it was hard to distinguish any words other than Capelli's ringing *Ciao, Cara* as she prepared to leave. Mary had heard the main door opening and closing. After that, there had only been the low murmur of men's voices. Deciding this would be a good time to reclaim Henri, she had stood and walked to the stairs—but as she reached the landing, she heard a woman speaking. She paused and looked down toward the lobby, fearing that the manager had returned, but it was only Winifred Barton, the Old Chandler's costume mistress. She was talking with Walt Wozchinski and the security guard. Henri was nowhere in sight. After a brief exchange, Wozchinski went out the front door. Winifred Barton and the security guard disappeared through the doors that led into the restaurant.

Mary started down the final flight of steps, but then she heard voices in the lounge: Henri talking with Guglielmo Bergonzi. The smarmy baritone of the bartender was unmistakable. He spoke softly, so she could not make out his words, but she could tell that his tone was provocative. And Henri had been provoked. Mary had never heard him sound so angry. For a moment, he sounded incoherent with rage. Mary had hesitated, unsure whether to go down and intervene, but after his initial outburst, Henri had become calm again. She could not hear what was being said, yet the tone of the conversation had changed. It was matter-of-fact, businesslike. Suddenly she heard footsteps, and, realizing that the men were coming out to the foyer, she drew back. Guglielmo came first, but Henri was right behind him. Neither noticed Mary standing on the stairs. Guglielmo crossed the lobby, banged the front door open and strode out into the night. Henri followed, and by the time Mary had come down the stairs and crossed to the doorway, both men had disappeared into the inky darkness.

As she stood in the doorway, she heard movement behind her. Winifred Barton had returned. She asked if the bartender had left, and Mary confirmed that he had. She didn't mention Henri. Winifred had looked at her watch and commented on the time. It had been twenty-five past six. Then she had muttered something about a dinner date and hurried off down the street. Mary had gone back inside. She remained in the lobby for a while, waiting for Henri to return, but when the other cast members began to arrive, she gave up and went through to the rehearsal hall. Henri did not reappear until just before seven o'clock. He said nothing about where he had been and Mary did not ask him. But she knew that sometime within that half-hour, the bartender had died.

The judge pressed her hands to her head in an attempt to stop the pulsing in her temples. She knew that many a case had been lost because a lawyer had been foolish enough to pose a question that he did not know the answer to in advance. But how could she possibly ask Henri the question that persistently intruded into her own troubled thoughts? The answer might be more than she could bear.

$$*\qquad*\qquad*$$

*The Mousetrap* ended punctually at nine o'clock. Jordan had trained his cast well.

"That was a crappy solution," said Miller dourly, as the lights came up. "Who's going to guess that the cop did it?"

"It is a bit of a cheat," agreed Philippa. "I knew the killer had to be one of the foster children, but I certainly didn't suspect Sergeant Trotter." She turned to her nephews who were waving their place cards and gloating over their potato chips. "How come you two little imps figured it out?"

"It was easy," said Thomas. "He had to be in disguise because he didn't have the right haircut for a cop."

"Good point," said Philippa. She turned to Jordan. "In that case, we can blame you."

"Not at all," said Jordan. "He's a fake cop. You could construe that to be an important visual clue. You boys are very observant," he added to Thomas and Geoffrey.

"So does that mean we get to stay around until the end of the party?" asked Thomas.

"I don't think so," said Philippa. "McDonald's and a movie. That was the deal."

"McDonald's and a movie times two," pointed out Thomas. "You and Mr. Miller have to take us out as well."

"That's right," said Miller. He turned to Philippa. "Well, now that we've flunked sleuthing, how about another drink? That was a long second act. All those interrogations gave me a thirst."

"Later," said Philippa. She noticed that the band was starting to set up. The waiters were ushering people out to the lounge, and she realized that the main floor was going to be cleared for dancing. "There's going to be a hiatus while the tables are moved," she said, "which means the lounge will be unbearably crowded for the next half-hour. Why don't we go congratulate Sylvia and Norton? Then, by the time we come back, the dessert bar should be ready."

Jordan slid his chair back and stood up.

"Good idea. Come on, everyone. Follow me."

Mai Ling beckoned to the boys. "Come, we go tell your parents how much you like the play, and then I take you home."

By the time their party got backstage, a lot of people had already arrived and were congregating in the rehearsal hall. Norton spotted Philippa and emerged from a cluster of friends, his bony face beaming with delight under a light-coloured wig that vaguely resembled a haystack that had been run over by a threshing machine. His smile grew even broader when she told him he'd done well. Philippa spied Sylvia amid the crush, so leaving Norton basking in the attention of his colleagues, she waved to her sister and forged her way over.

Miller had been standing aside and he failed to notice when Philippa moved away. His attention had been caught by a couple who had entered from the dressing-room corridor. The young actress who had played Mollie had changed out of costume and now wore skin-tight leggings, high-heeled boots, and a gold lamé tunic with a cowl neck that plunged almost to her navel. Her companion seemed transfixed by the alluring neckline. He was a beefy young man, incongruously dressed in an outfit that belonged more in a Wild West gambling house than at a Vancouver fundraising party. Miller recognized the unruly mop of blonde hair right away. It was the actor who had portrayed Sergeant Trotter. However, Trotter had very little time to enjoy his co-star's cleavage, for another woman joined the couple, grabbed the actor's arm and marched him away. Jeannie Dunbar tossed a dagger-laden glare at the woman's back, and then flounced off into the crowd.

Miller turned away and realized that he had lost his own date. He glanced around, and then picked her out on the far side of the room. She was with her sister. As he watched, Sylvia thrust a darkly handsome man towards Philippa. It was the performer who had acted the part of the young husband in the play. Self-importance personified, thought Miller, sourly recalling how the man had radiated lascivious enjoyment every time he'd kissed the spaced-out creature playing his wife. To Miller's annoyance, the man was now ogling Philippa with a similar degree of lust.

"Don't worry," a voice hissed in Miller's ear. Jordan was passing behind him. "She won't be able to stand him. I couldn't."

Miller didn't share Jordan's confidence. He threaded his way through the crowd and positioned himself at Philippa's side. Günter Sachs did not notice, for he was making an elaborate show of kissing Philippa's hand.

"I am so very glad to meet you at last, Miss Beary," he said. "We should have met before if it hadn't been for the clod of a policeman who caused you so much grief on Halloween. You should have sued him. You still could, in fact, and I would be most happy to handle the case if you decide to pursue it."

Philippa's eyes danced merrily and she tossed a wicked smile in Miller's direction.

"What a good idea! Perhaps I shall," she said.

Günter took her at her word.

"We could discuss the options over dinner one night," he suggested.

Philippa murmured a non-committal reply. Then she politely extracted herself and moved away with Miller. The rehearsal hall was rapidly clearing, so they joined the line of people filtering through the warren of backstage corridors and soon were back in the main restaurant. The waiters were still clearing the last of the tables, but the buffet along the rear wall was now filled with dessert platters, so they each took a plate and helped themselves to an assortment of éclairs and petits fours. Then they poured cups of coffee and strolled up to the first gallery. There were only a few couples present, all seated at the tables nearest to the elevator, so they walked round to the far side so that they could enjoy their desserts and talk in private.

As they sat down, Philippa's cellphone rang. It was Sylvia.

"Are the boys with you?" Her sister's voice sounded suspicious.

"No. Why?"

"I thought as much. Mai Ling took them back to the restaurant, and then she managed to lose them. I called Tom's cell and the little wretch said they were with you."

"They're probably just exploring. That's what little boys do."

"Maybe, but I expressly forbade them to go off the main floor, and if they're telling me whoppers, you can bet they're up in the gallery."

"Well, we're on the lower gallery and they're not here," said Philippa, "and I can't see them up top either. Do you want me to come and help round them up?"

"No, it's all right," said Sylvia. "Just watch out for them in case they come up there. I'll call them again and tell them to report back immediately."

Sylvia rang off and Philippa put her phone back in her purse. Miller was grinning.

"Supermom having trouble keeping them under control?"

"Yes. Maybe we should go and help."

"Nonsense," said Miller. "Those two can look after themselves. They'll be stalking the people who were sitting next to us. Relax and enjoy your dessert."

Philippa started on her éclair, but as she ate, she kept a watch on the galleries to see if her nephews showed up. As her eyes swept the area, she noticed Judge Mary Worthington standing at the gallery railing above the stage. She was carrying a dessert plate and a cup of coffee, and she stood for a moment and contemplated the scene below. Then she moved back and disappeared from view.

Philippa saw a flicker of movement directly above the spot where the judge had been standing. A man was peering over the upper gallery. It was the blonde waiter. She wondered what he was doing there. His manner was decidedly stealthy. A second or two lapsed. Then he started as if he had heard something and bobbed out of sight.

Philippa turned to scan the other end of the room. There was still no sign of the boys, but a woman had appeared on the top gallery. Even at a distance, the svelte brunette with the French-braided hairstyle was easily recognizable. It was Pauline Waverly. Presumably, she had come out of the staff elevator. She was carrying a tray, and as she neared the staff kitchen, the door opened and Bill Jones emerged, followed by a thin young man with long black hair tied back in a ponytail. Probably the techie, Philippa decided, noticing how the man was dressed casually in a black T-shirt.

Pauline Waverly handed the tray to Bill Jones. Philippa smiled as she watched the exchange. The elderly doorman deserved a quiet hour to enjoy his dessert and coffee, but before he could take his tray into the kitchen, another figure walked down from the stage end of the gallery. It was the young woman who had played Mollie. She headed straight for the man in the black T-shirt, gesticulating with far greater verve than she had demonstrated during the play. Philippa chuckled inwardly. No wonder Jordan had found Jeanne Dunbar so irritating. One of his frequent complaints about amateurs was the fact that many of them reserved their best performances for the post-show party.

Philippa finished her éclair and stood up. Stepping forward, she peeked over the railing and saw that the band was in place on the stage. Miller came to join her at the rail, and they watched for a couple of minutes as the musicians chatted and tuned their instruments. The conductor looked at his watch; then decisively, he picked up his baton and gestured to his combo to get ready. As he raised his arms, the overhead lights dimmed. The restaurant took on an eerily iridescent aquamarine hue, which gradually transmuted into rose, and then continued through a spectrum of colours as the band rolled into the wedding song from *Blue Hawaii*.

Philippa became self-consciously aware of Miller's shoulder brushing against hers in the dark. The sentimental tune thrummed gently below them. "Guaranteed to appeal to the generation that dominates the audience," she said lightly.

Miller hummed a couple of bars. "This is nice," he said. "I'm glad you asked me, and not just because of my investigation. Would you like to dance?" he added, taking her by surprise.

Philippa's eyes widened. Then she smiled and nodded.

Miller stepped back from the railing and held out his hand. Philippa moved forward and floated into his waiting arms. To her surprise, Miller expertly swept her away from the tables and guided her into the open space near the end of the gallery.

"Very good," said Philippa admiringly. "We certainly won't be able to refer to you as a flatfoot."

"Hey, I'll have you know I spent a whole month once taking ballroom dancing lessons."

"No!"

"Yes. I was undercover. We were investigating a dance studio. Now why don't you stop talking and enjoy the moment. Can't you tell I'm trying to romance you?"

Philippa fell silent, grateful that the dim lighting masked the flush that she knew had bloomed on her cheeks. The changing colours of the room were subtle and focussed on the dance floor below, but the galleries were bathed in shadows and it felt as if she and Miller were suspended in space, enclosed in a world of their own. The upper gallery had dissolved into darkness and they could see no more than a few feet along the centre tier. Even the other couples on the gallery might not have existed. But after a moment, over the pulsing harmonies of the band below, she became aware of an irritatingly disruptive noise overhead. Miller had heard it too.

"Someone talking on a cellphone," he said irritably. "Wish he'd keep his voice down. How can I murmur seductively in your ear with that in the background?"

"He isn't talking that loud," whispered Philippa. "It's the acoustics of the building carrying the sound down to us. He must be in the upper lounge."

Miller cocked his ear towards the upper gallery. "He has a very didactic tone," he observed. "Must be one of the lawyers who was in the show."

"Oh, well, our dance is over anyway," said Philippa, pulling back with a sigh.

The band rolled out the final bars of the song and a ripple of applause came from below. Then, in the pause that followed, Philippa sensed rather than heard a change in the rhythm of the noise from overhead, and her singer's ear detected the timbre of a second voice.

A moment later, there was a flurry of movement up above. Philippa had trouble later pinning down the sequence of events because it all happened so fast. But as the drummer rattled out the introduction to the next song, a strangled cry came from overhead. The conductor froze and looked up, and the combo ceased playing. There was a shrill shriek, which must have come from someone on the ground floor, and almost immediately, it was followed by a dull thud. And then bedlam broke out below.

Philippa and Miller raced to the railing and looked down. All they could see was a sea of bodies surging forward, circling something at the side of the stage. The coloured gels overhead continued to turn in sequence, transforming the writhing mass of humanity from blue to violet to green, and rendering the scene surreal and indecipherable. Then, abruptly, the coloured floods vanished. The main lights came up and the walls of the Old Chandler reappeared. Someone called loudly to ask if there was a doctor in the house.

By the time Philippa drew back from the rail, Miller was already racing towards the stairs. Pleasure was over for the night. Philippa didn't know exactly what had happened on the main floor, but she knew one thing for sure. Her date was back on duty.

*      *      *

Walt Wozchinski had called for a doctor, but the gesture was futile since Andrew McCardle had been killed instantly when he plummeted to the ground from the upper gallery. Wozchinski was surprised, but not shaken, when Miller revealed that he was a homicide detective with VPD and, wisely, the owner-operator did not demur when the young constable took charge. However, he insisted that McCardle's death must have been an accident. Nevertheless, Miller was sceptical. He knew there had been a second person on the upper gallery, and when no one came forward to admit being present when McCardle toppled over, Miller became convinced that the lawyer had been pushed.

Within the hour, the Major Crime Section was on the scene and the IDENT team had been called in. Miller's partner, DC Ho, arrived shortly after eleven o'clock, and the rest of the night passed in a blur. The predicted snow had started again, and Miller did not envy the two uniformed constables who were given the job of taking names and contact information from the assembled guests, all of whom were anxious to leave because of the weather. By the time Miller and DC Ho had narrowed down the list of people who had access to the upper gallery in the appropriate time frame, it was one o'clock in the morning and they had a large number of highly indignant patrons on their hands. Miller was relieved to be able to dismiss them and concentrate on the few individuals who were in a position to give him relevant information. Philippa was willing to stay, but he asked Bill Jones to call a cab for her. He needed to get a detailed account of everything she had seen and heard over the course of the evening, but he would be able to talk to her later, and it would be far easier for him to concentrate on the case if he did not have to worry about her nosing around and possibly putting herself in danger. So with a promise to contact her the following day, he handed her over to the doorman and returned inside to gather preliminary statements from his limited pool of suspects. Ruefully Miller

Elizabeth Elwood

reflected that he felt as if he had stepped back into the play again, except that in this case, a lot more than a trip to McDonald's depended upon the outcome.

# IV

Philippa was working on grant applications at the Burnside Arts Council when Miller finally came by for her interview. Cheerfully, she abandoned her computer, poured him a cup of coffee and settled down to pool their information. The snow floated down in large feathery clumps outside the wood-framed window of her office. Miller was reminded again of the play, but at least, unlike Sergeant Trotter, he had not been obliged to travel on skis to get his interview. However, if the overcast sky was any indicator, that could come yet. He turned away from the bleak exterior and made notes while Philippa outlined the events of the evening from her own perspective.

When she had finished, he said, "Any thoughts or theories you want to add?"

Philippa hesitated for a moment. Then she voiced the idea that had been troubling her, even though she knew it was far-fetched.

"This is fanciful," she admitted, "but the whole theme of *The Mousetrap* was revenge, and McCardle was connected with that horrible case of the child who was killed by his foster father. Is it possible that life is imitating art?"

"Possible, yes," acknowledged Miller, "but the murder is more likely to be drug-related. If Bill Jones is correct and the Old Chandler has connections to organized crime, then Andrew McCardle will have been killed because he saw something he shouldn't have seen on that upper gallery. He had to be stopped from blowing the operation wide open."

"Yes, you're probably right. What was he doing up there, anyway?"

"He went to the top gallery to find a quiet spot to phone his wife. She's in L.A. with their children. She says her husband called her at half past ten. They talked for a couple of minutes, and that must have been what we heard when we were dancing."

"McCardle talking to his wife?"

"Yes."

"But there was a second voice, wasn't there?" said Philippa. "Just at the end … right before he fell. You heard it too. Someone else joined him there."

"There's no doubt about that," agreed Miller. "McCardle's wife heard her husband say, 'Hang on, I'll be right with you.' Then he told her he had to go and rang off. She has no idea who was there with him."

"Couldn't she tell whether it was a man or a woman?"

42

Miller shook his head.

"No. But the good news is we've reduced our suspects to seven people."

Philippa's jaw dropped.

"You've got to be kidding! How can you possibly do that? There were over three hundred people present."

"The Old Chandler is big on security. There were surveillance cameras on the exterior doors, including the one at the top of the fire escape that connects with the staff kitchen. Not that we needed that camera as Bill Jones was in the kitchen. He'd have seen anyone who came through."

"All that means," protested Philippa, "is that the killer was already inside the building. You still have a ballroom full of potential murderers."

"Let me finish," said Miller. "There were cameras on the backstage corridors as well, and the monitors revealed who went through to the restaurant before the dancing started. Unless the person who spoke to McCardle was already on the top gallery, it had to be someone who either remained backstage or was on the stage end of the lower gallery."

"We could see the lower gallery from where we sat," Philippa reminded him. "The only person there was Judge Worthington."

"Exactly, which puts her on my list."

"What did she have to say for herself?"

"She says she took her dessert and coffee to the gallery because she had a headache and she needed to sit somewhere quiet. About eight feet back from the planters that block off the stage portion of the gallery, there are enclosures with benches that act like wings if the actors have a scene up there. This is where the judge sat. She didn't notice anyone else in the area, but given the dim lighting and the fact that the wall of the enclosure limited her vision, she wouldn't have seen people unless they stood right in front of her. However, she says at one point she heard someone moving and she's quite definite that the door of the stairwell opened and shut while she sat there."

"Then someone must have been on the stairs. Perhaps it was the murderer searching for McCardle ... peeking through the door to see if he was there."

"Possibly, but whoever it was didn't have to be the killer. There are other routes to the top gallery."

"Only the staff elevator, but no one could use that unless they had the access code."

"Right," said Miller, "and I know who used the elevators during the key period. There was a group on the other side of the gallery from us. They were sitting at the table closest to the public elevator, and they were quite definite that, although several people came up that way, no one went down. Once up, people were using the stairs to go back to the main floor. This tallies with what my witness on the main floor said. She's an elderly lady who was feeling overheated and went to sit in the armchair by the washrooms. She couldn't see round the corner to observe which elevator people were using, but she was able to describe the people that went by. She mentioned half a dozen or so, only three of whom could have known the code to the staff elevator. Claudia Capelli went by with the cash drawers, Bill Jones followed soon afterwards, and Pauline Waverly went by a little later with the tray of dessert and coffee that we saw her give him when he came out from the staff kitchen."

"Did this lady see any of them come back down?"

"No. When the band started playing, she went to the washroom. Pauline Waverly must have come down soon afterwards, because I saw her talking with Wozchinski when he was calling for an ambulance. Claudia Capelli did not appear until later. She says she had to go back into her office as there was a lot of cash lying about and she had to lock it in the safe. Bill Jones was pretty shaken up—the old guy is pushing eighty, after all—but when he heard the commotion, he came down and helped keep order. He was pretty exhausted as the night wore on. We questioned him early and sent him home as soon as we could. The only other persons on the top gallery were Jeannie Dunbar and Kurt Liddle, the technician. Liddle had been there all evening. Dunbar went up the backstage stairway soon after the show ended."

Philippa furrowed her brow.

"What was she doing up there?"

"Hanging out with the techie. They struck up a friendship over the course of rehearsals. Dunbar apparently has more than one relationship on the go. Your sister had quite a lot to say about her. Dunbar's only twenty-four and she's articling with your sister's firm. She's thick as thieves with Terry Gleason—the one who played Sergeant Trotter. He's articling there too—and the word around the office is that they're having an affair."

"So why did she head up to see the techie? Why didn't she spend the rest of the evening with Gleason?"

"He's married," said Miller, "and his wife was there. Anyway, the techie has another attraction. Your sister figures Dunbar went up to the booth so she could smoke a joint—or get something even more potent. She says the girl is not only promiscuous, but also has a drug dependency. Needless to say, Dunbar will not be invited to join your sister's firm. Anyway, it's just as well for us that Dunbar went up to the top gallery because, other than the killer, she must have been the last person to see McCardle alive."

"Really? She spoke with him?"

"Yes. McCardle was in the lounge when she came out from the stairwell. According to Dunbar, he was punching in numbers on his cellphone, but when he saw her, he closed the phone, called her over and invited her to sit down. Then, to her amazement, he gave her a lecture on the evils of drugs. She says she was touched by the depth of his concern for her—that, of course, was sarcasm—but she was mad as hell that he was treating her like a schoolgirl who needed counselling. Since she couldn't afford to offend him, she heard him out, then went to the staff kitchen where she'd arranged to meet the techie. Liddle confirms this, as does Bill Jones and Pauline Waverly—and you and I know they're telling the truth because we saw all four of them talking outside the staff kitchen just before the lights dimmed for the dancing. Too bad the lights didn't stay on a bit longer. We might have seen where they went from there."

"Where do they say they went?"

"Waverly slipped into the washroom before coming down in the elevator. She insists that she was already on the main floor when McCardle fell, but I haven't come across anyone who can substantiate her story."

"What about the others?"

"Bill Jones went back into the staff kitchen after Waverly left, and the other two headed for the booth."

"So Dunbar and Liddle were together when McCardle fell?"

"No. Liddle was in the booth, but Jeannie Dunbar went to the washroom."

"Then surely she must have seen Pauline Waverly? Even if Waverly had come out of the washroom, Dunbar would have seen her at the elevator. It's right next to the ladies' loo."

"Evidently not. She says she didn't see a soul. It's possible that both ladies are telling the truth. Waverly could have been in and out before Dunbar got there."

"Or one of them could be lying. Still," mused Philippa, "Kurt Liddle had to be in the booth when the lights went down. He was controlling them. And he must have been there when McCardle fell because he brought them up after the uproar started. I'm surprised he reacted so quickly. It's not always easy to hear what's happening outside when you're in a booth."

"He wasn't that quick," said Miller. "The floods changed colour several times before the main lights came up. There was a delay of at least two minutes. Liddle says he didn't hear McCardle yell, and only realized something was wrong when the band stopped playing. After he raised the lights, he came out to see what had happened. By that time, Bill Jones, Claudia Capelli and Jeannie Dunbar were all on the gallery. Theoretically, any one of them had the opportunity to commit the crime. Pauline Waverly did too. It was so dark up top during the dancing that none of them could see more than a few feet away, and the booth is high enough up that someone could sneak round in front of it without the techie seeing them. However, it's also possible that none of them are guilty. I do have one more suspect."

"The waiter!" cried Philippa. "The weird-looking one with the blonde fuzz and the earring. I saw him up top. And he was acting strangely all night, not to mention staring at you as if he knew you were a policeman. You didn't notice, but he was deliberately avoiding you."

Miller's face became inscrutable.

"Yes, I'm aware of that, but I think it may have been for other reasons."

"I don't know why you're discounting him," Philippa persisted. "There's no legitimate reason why a waiter would be on the top gallery, and I tell you, he nearly had a fit when he saw you. There was something very peculiar about him."

Miller sighed.

"Look," he said, "you've got to stop going on about the waiter. I shouldn't be telling you this, but you have to know because, if you say anything about him to someone else, you might put him in danger. He's a policeman. He's there because of the information we received from the doorman."

Philippa went bug-eyed.

"He's undercover?"

"Yes. That's why he didn't want to come to our table. He recognized me, and he was afraid that he might inadvertently give the game away. Besides," Miller grinned, "he was embarrassed. The persona he's adopted isn't exactly traditional cop."

"So he was up top because he was snooping about. What was he looking for?"

"He's been watching Claudia Capelli. If there's a money-laundering operation going on, Capelli and Wozchinski have to be involved because they're the ones who take the cash drawers up to the office. They do the tallies, make the bank deposits and give the figures to the bookkeeper. If the bar and box-office figures are being inflated, those two have to be complicit. But we still don't know who is bringing the drug money in. That's what Constable Cliffe has been trying to discover. He reckons it's being delivered by a patron during the restaurant's operating hours. He was watching to see if anyone went up to the office, but unfortunately, McCardle came up and saw him there, so he had to duck away and wait for another opportunity."

"OK, cancel the waiter, but then who *is* your other suspect?"

"Henri Gerard."

"Surely not," Philippa protested. "I thought he seemed like a really likeable little guy."

Miller raised his eyebrows.

"That's a bit of a wild assumption considering you only saw him do a part on stage."

"No, I met him. I talked with him briefly before I went home. He was in the lobby while I was waiting for my cab. The poor man was dreadfully distressed. I can't see him as a killer."

"He had the opportunity," Miller pointed out. "He was still backstage when McCardle fell."

"Did anyone actually see him there or are you just making the assumption because he didn't show up on the security camera in the passage?"

"Actually, your sister saw him. Remember how she was combing the area hunting for your nephews. They hadn't answered when she tried to call them the second time and she'd gone to see if they'd snuck backstage again."

"Where had the boys got to?"

"I have no idea, but they weren't backstage. The security cameras picked them up leaving the area with Mai Ling about fifteen minutes before the music started. And when McCardle fell, the boys were back with their nanny and getting their coats on. But in the course of her search for them, your sister saw Gerard in the rehearsal hall. He could have been the person that Judge Worthington heard on the stairs. What's more," said Miller, "Gerard might have had a motive for killing the bartender too."

Philippa looked horrified. "Really? What would that be?"

"Claudia Capelli. According to Pauline Waverly, Guglielmo had been working his charm on Capelli ever since he started at the Old Chandler. A fat little frog like Gerard would have a hard time competing with a hunky Italian half his age."

"I don't believe it," said Philippa stubbornly. "Besides, I can't see Claudia Capelli giving Guglielmo the time of day—not when she had a multi-millionaire primed to pop the question."

Miller leaned back and gave Philippa a lazy smile.

"The bartender was supposed to be pretty hot," he reminded her, "and all women can be tempted given the right circumstances."

Philippa flushed. "*Some* women might be," she retorted.

"Pauline Waverly thinks Capelli *was* tempted. She thinks the two of them were having an affair. Gerard could have been mad with jealousy. It fits. He was in Gastown the night the bartender died. And look at his footwear. Those elevator shoes he wears could well have made the marks your pal, Jordan, described."

"So could Terry Gleason's cowboy boots," argued Philippa. "And come to that, Claudia Capelli's shoes could be a fit. Didn't you notice those clunky Fluevog shoes she wore? They were gorgeous—jazzy burgundy suede platforms—wide and rectangular with big heels."

Miller looked sceptical.

"Capelli would hardly be wandering around snowy streets in suede dress shoes."

"Fluevog makes lots of boots too."

"Why would she kill him if they were having an affair?"

"All right, I know it's not likely, but Henri Gerard seems a real stretch too. Unfortunately for you, clunky is in fashion. Even your present-day muggers are probably wearing boots with heels like fence posts—and you said yourself that the bartender's death could have been a robbery that went wrong. There's no guarantee the two murders are connected."

Miller sighed.

"True, but my gut instinct tells me that they are. I just hope I'm not heading off on a wild-goose chase by trying to link the crimes."

Philippa flashed him an encouraging smile and refilled his coffee mug.

"Oh, well, have some more coffee," she said. "A jog for the brain. Cheer up. Once your crime-scene crew has finished, the restaurant will reopen, and then your mole is bound to find you a lead. Something is bound to break soon."

Philippa did not realize how quickly her words would come true. Two days later, an observant woman police constable noticed that a derelict individual, well known to the local force due to his frequent overnight sojourns in the cells, had inexplicably acquired an Yves St. Laurent leather coat. Upon questioning, the Badger—which was the name the constables who periodically fed and lodged him had christened him—swore that he had nothing to do with the murder. The coat, he insisted, had been found in a dumpster down by the CPR tracks. More questioning dredged up the information that, prior to the Badger's diligent efforts to clean it, the garment had been blood-stained—on the outside, not on the lining—and a wallet, with money and credit cards intact, had been in an inside zip-up pocket. Why the bartender had taken off his coat on such a cold night was a mystery, but since it would be an exercise in futility to kill someone for an expensive garment and then discard it, along with a well-stuffed wallet, the murderer was definitely not a mugger. Miller did not know whether the man's death had resulted from his connections with organized crime or from his relationship with the glamorous manager of the Old Chandler, but one thing was for sure: It was time to put the heat on Walt Wozchinski and Henri Gerard.

*     *     *

The two men were brought down to the station the following morning. While DC Ho questioned Walt Wozchinski, Miller conducted the interview with Henri Gerard. The corporate lawyer had his solicitor in tow, a sharply dressed woman of indeterminate age who pinned both Miller and the young constable who was taking notes with a stare that could have frozen hot coals. Gerard vehemently denied having anything to do with the murder. However, after a lengthy consultation with his solicitor, whose glacial gaze began to encompass her client as well as his inquisitors, he broke down and said he was ready to make a statement. Pleading with Miller to be discreet and not reveal to his fiancée what he was about to recount, Gerard admitted that he had taken steps to get the handsome bartender out of Claudia Capelli's life. Gerard's story was pathetic, but it rang true. He had hired a private detective to watch Guglielmo, and his worst suspicions had proved correct. Claudia Capelli had been a frequent visitor to the bartender's apartment. However, she was not the only one. Another woman had appeared even more often than Claudia, and there had been several other instances where the bartender had brought women home for one-night-stands.

Knowing that he could not tell Claudia what he knew without destroying his own relationship with her, Gerard had to devise another plan. Finally, he decided to confront Guglielmo with the evidence of his affairs. The opportunity arose on the night of the first blocking rehearsal. Claudia had left, so there was no danger of her overhearing. Guglielmo was alone in the bar and Gerard grasped his chance. However, the encounter did not go as he had planned. When he produced the detective's report, the bartender had laughed in his face. Guglielmo had boasted that Claudia meant nothing to him. She was a diversion—a test of his powers of seduction—and he had no problem breaking off with her ... for a price. Gerard was enraged and disgusted, but he forced himself to get a grip on his temper and discuss terms. This was his opportunity to get rid of his rival, and he agreed to pay up.

However, he had no intention of writing a cheque, so he took the bartender to the bank across the road and withdrew the necessary cash from the ATM. Once the transaction was complete, he had left. He was agitated and he needed to walk off his anger. He had headed up Water Street, and, by the time his black mood dissipated enough for him to notice his surroundings, he had reached the Delta Hotel. He had a drink in the bar to steady his nerves, after which he had come back to the Old Chandler for the rehearsal.

Gerard ended his story and looked across the table at Miller. The lawyer's eyes were sad, rather than defiant. Miller believed he had been telling the truth, but he thought the man had been foolish.

"Do you really think that would have been the end of it?" he asked sceptically. "Don't you think there would have been further demands for money?"

Gerard laughed bitterly.

"Oh, no. That's the irony of it. Guglielmo had no need of my money. He'd been getting a regular allowance from his other woman. What's more, she was planning to divorce her husband and marry him. She was waiting for him up at Whistler."

Miller was stunned.

"That was his ski holiday?"

"Yes. Two weeks of luxury living at her chalet, after which they were heading for the Caribbean. He was set for life. He'd already planned to walk out of Claudia's life permanently."

"But if he was not coming back, why did you pay him?"

"He only told me after I'd given him the money and he'd deposited it in his own account."

Miller's eyes grew speculative.

"That must have made you angry," he said. "What did you do then?"

"I was outraged ... speechless. I walked away."

"You didn't say anything at all? You didn't tell him what you thought of him?"

"No. What was the point?"

"What was he doing as you left?"

"Tucking his deposit slip in his wallet. If you don't believe me, ask the security guard who was on duty that night. He'd come out to have a cigarette. He was standing in the lane on the other side of the road. He must have seen us. I noticed him as we went into the bank, and he was still hovering when we came out. Check with him. He'll tell you that I left on my own."

"Don't worry, I will," said Miller. "Do you know who the bartender's other woman was?"

Gerard nodded.

"Yes. I recognized her from the photos in the PI's report. It was Amy Steele. She's one of our sponsors."

Miller's eyes bulged. "How did Guglielmo figure he was set for life if he ran off with her? Doesn't her money come from her husband's company?"

Gerard seemed to relax as the focus of Miller's questions moved to a third party. He steepled his fingers and assumed a professional air. "Actually, no," he said. "I suppose I have to tell you this, given that you're conducting a murder investigation, but Amy is one of my clients, and, in fact, she has a great deal of money of her own. She's from a very wealthy family. Frank's company was formed on funds from her private income, but having helped him get started, she's made it clear that she's not pouring any more cash into it. Her husband can't touch her money. It would have come as a shock if he'd found out that Amy was planning to leave him."

Miller's face was grim.

"Maybe he already knew," he said.

The door opened and a uniformed constable popped her head through.

"There's a young woman asking to see you," she told Miller.

Miller had learnt what he needed to know for the time being. He wrapped up the interview and left the constable to oversee the signing of Gerard's statement. He came out of the interview room, curious to see who had come into the station and wondering if his visitor had some connection with the case. When he reached the front desk, he was surprised to see Philippa chatting with the duty sergeant.

"This is an unexpected pleasure," he said. "What brings you here?"

Philippa moved away from the desk and lowered her voice.

"I had to come downtown for an audition. I did call, but you were busy, so I figured I'd just drop by."

"How did it go?"

"What? Oh, the audition. It was fine. Look, the reason I'm here is that my nephews have been on at me. They're demanding the McDonald's dinner that we promised them, and they want it to be tonight, the reason being that they need to talk to you and they don't want their mother to know. I think we'd better go along. Knowing my nephews, they'll clam up if you try to push them into making a formal statement. Can you spare some time to hear what they have to say? It could be important. There's a McDonald's near where they live in Deep Cove, but if you're really busy, I can pick them up and bring them downtown."

Miller nodded.

"That would help," he said. "I have some critical stuff to deal with, but I can get away around five. There's a McDonald's on the next block. I'll meet you there. Sounds like we're going to find out where the little devils got to when they disappeared for fifteen minutes." He frowned thoughtfully. "I wonder," he murmured. "Look, can you hold on a minute. I need to make a call and the number's in my file."

Without waiting to hear Philippa's answer, he turned and headed back down the hall. Mildly miffed that she had not been invited to accompany him, and flushing because Miller had made it plain that the McDonald's dinner was strictly business without any social component, Philippa sat down in the waiting area. For want of something better to do, she pulled out her phone and sent texts to her nephews confirming that she would pick them up at quarter past four. Miller was a good five minutes before he returned, but the grin on his face indicated that his call had produced something gratifying.

"What was all that about?" Philippa asked.

"I just phoned Mrs. Bede," he said. "You know—the lady who was sitting outside the main floor washrooms—the one who gave me a list of people who could have used the elevators. Well, it turns out she neglected to mention two young boys because she assumed they wouldn't be relevant to my investigation."

Philippa's eyebrows shot up and her fit of pique evaporated.

"Thomas and Geoffrey went up in the elevator?"

Miller shook his head.

"No," he said. "But they came down. And considering that they were supposed to be out in the main part of the restaurant, I can't wait to find out how they managed that. This should be the most interesting McDonald's meal I've ever experienced."

*      *      *

After Philippa left, Miller's afternoon proved frustrating. He was anxious to interview Frank Steele and find out where he was the night the bartender died. Less urgent, but still on the list of things-to-cover, was contacting the people who could confirm Henri Gerard's story.

However, a call to Frank Steele's home proved fruitless. Frank and Amy, their next-door neighbour informed him, were spending the week at their house in the Bahamas. They would not return until the following Monday. Next, Miller headed for the Old Chandler, but there, too, he struck out. Tracking down the security guard who had been on duty the critical night turned out to be a time-consuming task. The man was not one of the in-house employees, so the receptionist was only able to provide a phone number for the security company that supplied temporary workers. After trying several locals and getting nothing but a recorded message, Miller finally got through to an employee who gave him the man's name and a cellphone number. However, every attempt to reach the guard was met with voicemail. After several tries, Miller left a message and headed out onto the street. If he hurried, he would just have time to walk up to the Delta Hotel and check Henri Gerard's alibi. The lawyer's appearance was distinctive. Somebody should remember whether or not he had been in the hotel bar. But to Miller's annoyance, even this venture failed to produce results. The hotel bartender had been on duty every night for the first week in January. He did recall Gerard coming in early one evening, but couldn't say with certainty which evening it had been.

By this time it was past four o'clock. Miller was tempted to buy himself a drink to fortify himself for the encounter with Philippa's nephews, but thought better of it. He needed a clear head to deal with the junior Barnwells, both of whom seemed to have the same laser-sharp brains as their aunt and mother. So he made one more attempt to contact the security guard, after which he gave up, returned to his car and set off for McDonald's.

Philippa and the boys had not arrived when he got there, so he called her cellphone and took the boys' orders. He had seen enough of his sister's children to know that kids were rarely cooperative when they were hungry. By the time Philippa and her nephews walked into the restaurant, Miller was seated at a corner table surrounded by Big Macs, fries, soda pop, Chicken McNuggets and two coffees. Thomas and Geoffrey clambered into their seats, issued a polite 'thank you' and dived into their dinners.

Thomas demolished his burger quickly and started on his fries. Geoffrey ate more slowly, his eyes warily moving between his plate and DC Miller, as his brother explained why they had needed to talk privately. Philippa sipped her coffee and listened in amazement to the tale her nephew unfolded.

"You see," said Thomas between mouthfuls, "after you told us about the jewel robber, we kept a lookout on the next table. Six of the people were so old they were probably born the same time as the dinosaurs, so we figured the thief had to be the redheaded man with the expensive-looking wife. Anyway, we asked that costume lady if she knew who he was and she said his name was Frank Steele and he and his wife were often at the Old Chandler. She said he made his money importing hardwood flooring, which made us think he was more likely to be into smuggling if he was a crook. Mind you," he added, "after the play, we had second thoughts because we thought you might have invented the story about the thief because *you* were up to something."

Philippa choked on her coffee. Thomas was unapologetic.

"Well, in the *show* the cop was the villain."

"Trotter was a fake policeman," Philippa pointed out.

"Yes, I know," said Thomas. "That's what made us wonder about crooked cops. But anyway, after we came out from backstage, we saw Mr. Steele heading towards the washrooms. He went into the corner where the elevators are …" Thomas paused and looked defensively at his aunt. "And this is where you're not to get mad at us or rat on us to Mom and Dad."

Philippa rolled her eyes, but nodded agreement.

"Well, we ditched Mai Ling and took off as fast as we could so that we could beat him to the gallery before he came out. We ran up the stairs, but when we got to the gallery, the elevator was still going up. He was in the one for the staff. The lights had gone out, except for all the coloured stuff on the dance floor, and we figured no one would see what we were up to, so we shot back the other way, climbed over the planter and ran to the backstage stairwell so we could go up top and see what he was doing."

Geoffrey chimed in.

"It was really spooky in the dark. When we came out of the stairwell, Mr. McCardle was up there. He didn't see us, because we crept round the other side of the gallery, but we could hear him."

"Did you see anyone with him?" Miller cut in eagerly.

"No. He was yapping on his cellphone," said Thomas. "We weren't really interested in what he was doing. We wanted to see what Mr. Steele was up to."

"And did you?"

"Yes," said Thomas. "We ran to the other end of the gallery and snuck along the section below the booth. Mr. Steele was already out of the elevator. He'd stopped by the room at the end. The door was open and the light was on so we could see him really well. He was talking to the lady who'd been downstairs earlier bossing the waiters around." Thomas grinned. "The real sexy-looking one."

"With weird shoes," Geoffrey added.

"Claudia Capelli," interjected Phillipa. "She's the manager."

"Did Mr. Steele hand anything to her?" Miller asked.

"We don't know, because just at that moment, my cellphone rang."

"That will have been Sylvia after she talked to me," said Philippa.

"Yeah," grumbled Thomas. "I didn't want Mom to know we were there so I shut it off quick. Steele kind of glanced around, but I guess when he didn't hear anything, he figured it was OK. Anyway, he went inside the office and we thought we'd better not stick around, so we hoofed it to the elevator and went back down that way. Then we ran over to the coat check and pretended we'd been there the whole time waiting for Mai Ling."

"The importer must have the code," said Miller. "He's obviously part of the operation. I bet he brings his flooring in from China."

Philippa gave Miller a cautionary glance, reminding him of the boys' presence. He changed tack and grinned at the boys.

"Well, you're a smart pair of operators. You've earned those burgers. I'll make a bargain with you. You don't breathe a word of any of this to anyone else, and I won't tell your mother what you were up to."

Thomas gave Miller a calculating stare.

"He's not really a jewel thief, is he?" he said. "These days, everything's to do with drugs. He and that manager lady must be in it together. Mr. McCardle must have figured out what they were up to and that's why he was killed. Which one of them do you think pushed him over the top?"

"You ask too many questions," said Miller.

"So why don't you answer them?" said Thomas.

"Because it's my job to investigate, not explain," said Miller firmly. "Now, before we order anything else for you two little bottomless pits, you can answer one more question. Did you see anyone else on the top gallery?"

"We heard voices, but we couldn't see. It was too dark. Why don't you ask the other cop? He must have been up there somewhere. We saw him sneak up the backstage staircase when we were talking to Mom and Dad after the show."

Miller started to look apoplectic.

"What other cop?"

"The one that was dressed as a waiter," said Geoffrey. "He was watching that manager lady all evening."

"So maybe he was new and needed direction."

"Uh-uh," said Geoffrey. "He was a cop. You can always tell—"

"By the haircut," groaned Miller.

"That's right," said Thomas. "So now do we get dessert?"

# V

Miller had no trouble acquiring the necessary warrants for a search of Frank Steele's warehouse. Steele was not only a suspected drug dealer; he had also become the prime suspect in the murder investigation. However, Capelli and Wozchinski were also implicated in the money-laundering process, and Miller wanted to avoid alerting any one individual while apprehending the others. Finally, he and DC Ho decided that a three-tier operation was needed. After consultation with their senior officers, a plan was set in place. DC Ho would bring Frank Steele in for questioning; then, once Steele was in the station, Miller would go to the Old Chandler to talk with Capelli and Wozchinski. At the same time, the drug squad would raid Frank Steele's warehouse.

The operation was scheduled for the Monday that the Steeles returned from the Bahamas. All week, while he waited, Miller brooded about the murder of Guglielmo Bergonzi. Henri Gerard's testimony had offered a likely solution, for Steele had a strong motive, but Miller was still troubled over the bloodstained coat. That one piece of evidence niggled at his mind. It did not fit the scenario.

Finally, Monday arrived. Frank Steele was apprehended at the airport, and the drug squad moved in on his warehouse. Miller headed for the Old Chandler, having ascertained that Capelli and Wozchinski were already in the building. He had high hopes that the day's work would serve to wrap up the entire investigation. However, as he pulled in to park at the end of the block, his cellphone rang. It was his partner.

"Thought I'd better step out for a moment and pass this on," said DC Ho. "We may get Steele for the drug charges, but we won't get him for murder—not for the bartender, anyway. He was in Taiwan and it sounds as if there are multiple witnesses to prove it. Looks like he's in the clear."

"Not if he hired someone to do it," grunted Miller.

"That's true, but if he didn't, we're back to square one. Keep that in mind when you're talking with Wozchinski." Ho rang off. Muttering under his breath, Miller put his phone away. Then he locked his car and set off down the street.

It was an unsettling day, the pale sky casting an unforgiving glare that accentuated the age of the heritage buildings while obliterating their charm. The stark scene suited Miller's mood. Too many dead ends, and now the possibility of a contract killing, always near impossible to prove—and yet, the more he thought about it, the more he was convinced that Frank Steele was behind the bartender's death. With Steele's criminal connections, it would have been easy for him to hire a hit man, and easy for the assassin to make the murder look like the theft of an expensive leather coat that went fatally wrong. Guglielmo must have tried to slip the knife from his pocket as he handed over the coat ... an attempt that obviously failed because it gave his attacker a lethal weapon of opportunity. Still, thought Miller, a hit man wouldn't have been loitering in Blood Alley on the chance that the bartender would come straight home. He would have been tipped off about his quarry's work schedule. He would have been outside the Old Chandler, watching for his intended victim to leave the building.

As Miller approached the Old Chandler, he glanced towards the shops on the other side of the road. He had not noticed before, but the arcade was directly opposite the lane that ran down the side of the theatre-restaurant. Another mews, another alley. An ideal spot for someone to watch and wait. Gastown was full of nooks and crannies, shadowy corners where someone with evil intent could lurk. From the arcade, a hit man could have seen anyone who left by the main door or the stage door. He would have been sheltered from the snow and sheltered from view—except from someone who was standing in the lane and looking towards the street.

Miller walked the few steps up the lane and stood by the stage door. From there, he had a clear view of the bank and the arcade. The security guard, outside enjoying his cigarette, would have seen Henri Gerard and the bartender in front of the bank. The light from the streetlamp would have beamed down where they were standing. The guard would also have seen anyone who was skulking in the arcade for there was a lantern mounted on the wall by the entrance—unlit now, but at night, it would have cast a glow all around the alcove.

Miller decided to try the security guard again. He whipped out his phone and punched in the number. Still only voicemail. He shoved the phone back in his pocket and walked the last few steps to the theatre-restaurant.

The red brick building appeared drab in the morning winter light, the grey-granite sills mottled and stained, and the opaque windows darkly reflecting the street scene and the watery sky. Two hard winters had taken their toll. The ornate panelling on the heavy front door looked weather-beaten and the brass handle was discoloured with verdigris. It was long before opening time but Miller tried the door anyway. It was locked. The staff probably used the entrance on the alley, he decided, but he banged on the door in case someone was in the lobby. Stepping back to wait for a response, he read the heritage plaque beside the door. The warehouse had been constructed in 1898, designed to house a ship chandlery and hardware business that could supply gold prospectors heading for the Klondike. A ball had been held in the warehouse when the building first opened. Miller wondered ruefully if any fatalities had marred *that* celebration. For all the advances in subsequent years, he doubted if Vancouver was any safer than when the building had first been erected.

There was still no sound from inside. He was about to give up and go round to the side entrance when, suddenly, the door opened and he found himself face to face with a security guard. It was a young man, and he was talking on his cellphone. Miller felt a surge of excitement. With any luck, the individual he had been seeking had fallen right into his lap. He showed his ID, and when the guard admitted him, asked if he had been on duty the night of the first blocking rehearsal for *The Mousetrap*.

The guard ended his call and snapped his phone shut.

"That was me," he said.

"Good. I'm here to see Walt Wozchinski and Claudia Capelli, but I need to ask you some questions too."

"No problem. Mr. Wozchinski stepped out for a few minutes but he'll be back any time. The manager is up in her office. Just let me call up and tell her you're here."

"No need for that. You can take me up and we'll talk on the way."

The man hesitated, but something in Miller's expression stopped him from arguing. He shrugged and told Miller to follow him.

The guard set off down the hall and Miller fell into step beside him. Faintly, he could hear the distant sound of a vacuum, but otherwise, the place was eerily silent. When they reached the staff elevator, the guard punched in the security code. The door slid open and they stepped inside. As they ascended, Miller asked, "How well did you know Guglielmo Bergonzi?"

"Didn't really know him. I knew who he was. Couldn't help it, considering his reputation with the female customers."

"On the night he died, what time did you come on duty?"

"Five o'clock. I was on the evening shift. The restaurant was closed, but the lawyers had a rehearsal so someone had to let them in and out."

"Did you see Bergonzi when you arrived?"

"Yes. He was in the bar. He'd come in to organize the stock for the guy who was going to fill in while he was on holiday."

"Was anyone with him?"

"Just the manager, Ms. Capelli."

"What was she doing there?"

"No idea. They were both yattering in Italian. I think she was helping him check the stock, but she came out as soon as Mr. Gerard arrived with the lady judge."

"Then what?"

"She took off with Gerard. They had a meeting with Wozchinski up in the office. I chatted with the judge for a bit, and then she went up to the lower gallery to study her script."

"Go on."

"The meeting ended and they all came back down."

"All?"

"Wozchinski, Capelli, Gerard and Winifred Barton. She's the wardrobe mistress."

"Then?"

"They all left, except for Winifred. She wanted to get something from her costume room."

"Who left first?"

"Capelli. Then Wozchinski. Mr. Gerard went in to talk with Guglielmo and I went backstage with Winifred. She went to the costume room and I went out for a smoke."

"Out where?"

"The stage door. It opens onto the lane."

"What time would that have been?"

"Around six-thirty. I needed to be back on the door by quarter to in case any of the lawyers arrived early."

The elevator door opened and Miller stepped out onto the gallery. He was surprised to find how dark it was on the upper walkway. The posts that formed the base for the arched roof jutted out at intervals, creating shadowy alcoves and concealing doorways, while the curved beams of the vaulted ceiling were so close overhead that they cut even more of the light from the wall sconces. The security guard started to move ahead, but Miller called him back. He wanted to finish his questions before they reached Claudia Capelli's office.

"Guglielmo Bergonzi left the building while you were outside," he said. "Did you see him when you were standing in the lane?"

"Yeah, he was outside the bank talking with Mr. Gerard."

"How long were they there?"

"Not long. Maybe a couple of minutes."

"Did they leave together?"

"Couldn't tell you. My phone rang so I didn't pay attention. Once my call was finished, they'd gone."

Miller felt a surge of irritation. Another closed avenue. However, he kept his voice even as he continued.

"What about other people on the street? Did you see any strangers hanging about … anyone you hadn't seen before?"

The guard looked blank. "Strangers? No. It was like the Arctic out there. The stores were closed. The street was pretty well empty."

Vaguely, Miller was conscious of a door opening further along the gallery, but he still had one more question to ask, even though he realized it was a long shot, given the security guard's addiction to his cellphone.

"Could you hear what Henri Gerard and the bartender were talking about?" he asked tersely.

"Not really. I could hear their voices, but I couldn't make out what they were saying."

The guard hesitated, and thinking he had finished, Miller was about to move on. But then the man spoke again. "Why don't you ask Ms. Capelli," he said. "She was standing in the arcade. She'd have been able to hear what they were saying."

Miller stared incredulously. For a moment, he had trouble taking in the import of what the guard had told him. Finally, he managed to speak. He forced himself to keep his voice calm.

"I thought she'd left a good ten minutes before the others came out."

"Well, yes, she did. I remember at the time thinking she was waiting for a cab and wondering why she hadn't stayed inside, because she wasn't wearing a coat and she must have been freezing. Later, I found out she was engaged to Mr. Gerard, so I figured she'd been waiting for him."

"Are you absolutely certain it was her?"

"Oh, yeah. The lantern over the entrance was lighting up her multi-coloured sweater—and that tawny mop of hair. It was definitely her."

Miller felt the adrenalin pumping through his body. She wasn't waiting for Gerard, you naïve idiot, he thought. She must have been waiting to go home with Guglielmo. He rapped out another question.

"Was she still there after the others had gone?"

"No."

"You're quite sure?"

The intensity in Miller's tone woke the guard out of his complacency. His expression changed from mild inquisitiveness to horror. "Christ!" he said. "Don't tell me she was waiting for Guglielmo!"

Miller did not reply. He was recalling how the arcade provided an undercover route between the Old Chandler and Blood Alley. On a cold winter evening, the bartender would have gone that way. Miller could not be sure whether Guglielmo had secretly arranged to meet Capelli, or whether she had decided to surprise him and spend the night with him before he left for his holiday, but either way, she would have waited for him in the arcade. When he came out of the Old Chandler with Gerard, she would have ducked back and stayed out of sight, so even if Guglielmo knew she was meeting him, he would have assumed she had gone on ahead.

Miller tried to picture the scene. Once the two men reached the bank, curiosity would have made Capelli creep forward to find out why they were together. Her rage at hearing the bartender's plans must have been all-consuming. Miller could well believe that Hell would have no fury like a scorned Claudia Capelli. She must have gone further down the arcade to wait, and when Guglielmo reached her, he would have had no idea of the burning hostility beneath her smile.

And there's the solution to the bloodstains on the coat, Miller thought triumphantly. Capelli was cold, so Guglielmo took his coat off and gave it to her. In fact, knowing the knife was in the pocket, Capelli most likely asked for the coat. Then, when they reached Blood Alley, she took her revenge on the man who had played her for a fool.

Miller came out of his reverie and looked up. Over the guard's shoulder, he saw a shadowy figure standing further along the gallery. Claudia Capelli had come out of her office. Miller knew right away that she had overheard. She was statue-still, but poised with the intensity of a tiger ready to spring. The Lucrezia Borgia eyes met Miller's, and the ferocity of her stare momentarily rooted him to the spot. It was the image he had visualized as he had mentally played out her final confrontation with the bartender in Blood Alley—and in the few seconds that he hesitated, Capelli turned, raced to the next door and disappeared into the staff kitchen. Galvanized into action, Miller shoved his way past the security guard and ran to the door. It was locked from inside.

"Get this door open," he barked to the guard.

The security guard produced a batch of keys, but while he was trying to find the right one, there was a crash from the other side of the door.

"What the hell was that?" asked Miller.

"It's the door to the fire escape. She must have gone out that way."

"Can she get back in?"

"No. She'll have to go down now. It'll take her a while. You can beat her if you hurry. You'll be there before she reaches street level."

"You're sure she has no way to get back in further down?"

"No. All the fire-escape doors open from the inside."

Miller raced back to the elevator. The guard loped after him. They entered the elevator, and Miller called for backup as they descended. The moment the door slid open, he darted out and raced down the hallway. The security guard followed close on his heels, and they burst through the front door and out onto the pavement. As Miller ran along the sidewalk, he could hear the sound of an approaching siren. The fire escape was almost at the corner. Two women, bundled in winter coats and wool toques, stood chatting at the base of the steps. Both were holding Starbucks cups and they looked startled as Miller barged between them and peered up the black metal staircase.

There was no sign of Capelli.

Stunned, Miller turned on the women and asked if anyone had come down while they were standing there. They shook their heads. Miller whirled round and snapped at the security guard, "I thought you said she had no way of getting back in."

"She doesn't. She must have bluffed us." The guard shrugged apologetically. "I guess she just opened and closed the door, then waited for us to go."

Miller's eyes narrowed.

"She'll have waited until she heard the elevator and then come out, which means she'll be coming down the backstage stairs. You stay here," he instructed the guard, "in case she comes out the front. The squad car can go up the lane and cover the stage door. I'm going back in."

Miller sprinted inside, calling the squad car as he ran through the restaurant and directing his reinforcements to head for the alley. He shot through the connecting door to the backstage area and raced across the rehearsal hall. There was no sign of Capelli, and the stairwell was silent as he started up, but as he reached the third flight, he heard the sound of footsteps overhead. He slowed down and tried to move quietly, but the bare wooden treads creaked with age, and, after a moment, he heard the footsteps overhead falter; then they began again, but now they were retreating. He started to sprint, and the footsteps ahead speeded up too, but by the time he had climbed the fifth flight, he could tell he was gaining on his quarry. He rounded the corner and looked up. Capelli was nearly at the top of the stairs. As he started up the final flight, she darted up the last few steps and disappeared through the door into the lounge.

Miller raced up after her and shot through the open doorway. Then he froze, bewildered. The lounge was empty. He glanced around. Then he scanned the two sides of the gallery. Capelli was nowhere in sight.

He stepped down to the lower tier, carefully scrutinizing the gallery walkway. Capelli could not have reached the offices in such a short time, but she might have ducked below the railing. Miller stood very still, watching for any sign of movement. As he waited, he was suddenly conscious that he was standing where Andrew McCardle had stood before he fell to his death. The railing was low, dangerously so for a tall person like McCardle. It would have caught him at the top of his legs, and, with the force of the push, it was no wonder he went over.

As the thought flashed through his mind, Miller became aware of the subtle fragrance of roses. He sensed movement behind him, and in the split second that followed, he realized he had fallen for another old trick. Capelli had been hiding behind the door. He lunged sideways just in time. The momentum from the shove that would have hurled him over the top carried Claudia Capelli forward, and as he watched, helpless, she pitched over the railing and disappeared into the void.

The blood-chilling scream that followed was mercifully short, but for weeks afterwards, Miller was haunted by the terrified cry and the sound of the impact as Capelli hit the ground.

As he pulled himself to his feet and steeled himself to look down, his phone rang. It was DC Phil Ho. Still feeling dazed, Miller only half took in what he was hearing as his partner reported the results of the raid.

DC Ho was crowing.

"Wait till you hear what they found in the warehouse bust," he said jubilantly. "It's the biggest stash of heroin I've seen in my entire career. This is huge. I've got a search warrant coming for the Old Chandler offices, also for the private homes and offices of the owners and head staff members. The fraud squad will want to go through everything with a fine toothcomb, so we're going to have to shut the place down. We're keeping Frank Steele in, but you'd better keep an eye on Wozchinski and Capelli. I'm arranging the arrest warrants now, and I'll be over there shortly."

Miller looked down towards the rag-doll figure on the ground below. A small circle of people hovered anxiously around the body. They appeared to be members of the cleaning staff. The security guard had come back inside and was talking rapidly into his phone. In the distance, Miller could hear an approaching siren.

"Save yourself a job," he said shortly. "You'll only need one warrant now."

# VI

Bill Jones had been correct in his belief that the Old Chandler had been used to launder drug money, and two weeks later, Miller was able to inform Philippa that her 'eagle' had landed, or more appropriately crash-landed, for Walt Wozchinski and Frank Steele were under arrest. The arrest of the pair was a coup for Miller and the officers of the task force on drugs. The breaking of the ring resulted in the seizure of a huge haul of illegal drugs and halted one of the major sources that had been bringing such substances into the country.

However, the solution to the murder of Andrew McCardle was not so simple. Miller had thought his investigation over with the death of Claudia

Capelli, but his assumption had been premature. DNA evidence confirmed that Capelli had killed the bartender, but she could not have been responsible for McCardle's death. The police search of the Old Chandler's office had disclosed another security camera, this one well hidden, and the same tape that provided incriminating evidence of the money-laundering operation also provided Capelli and Steele with cast-iron alibis for the murder. Both had remained in the office from the time Philippa's nephews saw Steele enter until after McCardle fell. Neither one could have pushed the lawyer to his death.

The restaurant had been closed since the arrests, and would continue to be shut until the fraud squad finished its investigation. The Old Chandler's future was sadly uncertain now it was apparent that the only thing that had kept the enterprise profitable was the huge infusion of drug money that had come in on a regular basis. Henri Gerard was under investigation too, although to date, nothing had been found to prove he knew about the illicit operation. If Gerard had been involved, he had concealed it well, so the fraud squad had their work cut out for them in their search to link him to the drug ring. Still, even if Henri Gerard did not lose his freedom, thought Miller, he would probably lose his shirt. Privately, Miller felt sorry for the wealthy lawyer. Gerard was devastated by the death of his fiancée, but his horror when presented with proof of her crimes was so genuine that Miller was inclined to believe he had merely been an innocent dupe, lured in by his infatuation for Capelli.

Miller had been too busy with the investigation to see Philippa since their dinner date with the boys, but the following Monday, he had arranged some on-site interviews at the Old Chandler, so he called Philippa to see if they could meet for lunch after he was through. Philippa suggested that they meet again at Mirella's, and she went downtown early so that she could do some shopping beforehand. She got off the Skytrain at the Granville Station and spent a productive hour at Pacific Centre acquiring gifts for the members of the Beary clan who had imminent birthdays.

By eleven-thirty, she had finished her shopping, and although her lunch date was not until noon, she decided to go to Mirella's early and get in out of the cold. She pulled her coat collar high around her neck as she walked down to Gastown. It was another overcast morning, and she quailed as she peered up at the leaden clouds. The weather forecasters were predicting more snow, and, she reflected, they were probably right. She shivered and picked up her pace.

However, as she hurried down Water Street, she could not resist stopping to gaze in the windows of the Fluevog shoe store. A pair of turquoise suede platforms caught her eye, and the huge gold buckles reminded her of Claudia Capelli. Right beside the shoes was a pair of black boots. They had large, square heels, and toes shaped like a duck-billed platypus. The name on the label was

*Wicked.* Frighteningly apt, thought Philippa, remembering the manager's cold eyes and the horrific tale that Bob Miller had recounted.

Conscious that she had become chilled standing outside the store, Philippa continued on her way, walking more rapidly and rubbing her arms to restore circulation. She hurried by the square, wishing that she could be as impervious to the weather as Gassy Jack, who stood stolidly on his barrel, indifferent to the solitary pigeon perched on his head. Impatiently hopping up and down to keep warm, Philippa waited for the traffic to clear; then she crossed the wide intersection between the maple-lined square and the flatiron structure of the Europe Hotel. She hurried alongside the hotel, and soon she reached Mirella's.

When she entered the brightly lit café, she saw two people that she recognized. Jeannie Dunbar and Kurt Liddle were seated at a table by the back wall.

Philippa ordered coffee, and while she waited for her drink, she strolled over to their table. She introduced herself, and deliberately ignoring the other girl's indifferent air, she raised the subject of the closure of the Old Chandler.

"It's such a shame," she prattled. "We had a fantastic evening there … well, of course, until Mr. McCardle fell. Poor man. I just hope his spirit is deriving some comfort from the fact that the police have broken a major drug ring. He did so much to help people who were hooked on drugs."

Jeannie Dunbar's tone became petulant.

"Maybe if he hadn't stayed on the gallery to give me a lecture, he wouldn't have been there when the killer came up. I'm sorry about what happened to him, but the man was a bore. An utter fanatic. It all stemmed from guilt, you know."

Philippa blinked. Then she recalled the sad tale that Chloe Harker had related.

"You mean that awful case with the foster child?"

Jeannie looked scornful.

"No. He was hung up on a girl who died when he was in high school."

"That was common knowledge," said Philippa. "It's the incident that started him on his anti-drug crusade."

"Yes, but what Andrew told me isn't common knowledge. He was so determined to get through to me, he told me something he'd never told anyone else."

Through the window, Philippa caught a glimpse of Miller coming across the street. With him was old Bill Jones. They were talking earnestly, and Philippa wondered what new information the doorman was imparting to her friend. With her ear partly attuned to what the girl at the table was saying, Philippa watched as the two men approached the café.

Jeannie Dunbar was unaware that her audience had been distracted. She continued, her voice dripping with indignation and venom. "It was Andrew," she said bitterly, "who gave the girl the Ecstasy tablet that killed her."

Philippa's eyes widened. Dunbar had her full attention now.

"Are you absolutely sure?" she gasped.

"Of course I am," snapped Jeannie. "He explained the whole thing. He'd been going with this girl for a while and he thought it would loosen her up so she'd finally let him screw her."

Out of the corner of her eye, Philippa saw that Miller had entered the café. Bill Jones came in behind him. Miller saw Philippa right away and started towards her. She shook her head, and he stopped, immediately picking up her signal that he hold back.

Jeannie had not noticed him. She went on with her tale.

"What Andrew didn't know," she spat, her hard-edged stage voice projecting like a knife through the hum of voices in the café, "was that his girlfriend had some asthmatic condition. The next thing he knew, she was in convulsions. He was such a bloody hypocrite. All those years, people have been feeling sorry for him because he was so traumatized by that incident in high school, but he was the one who was responsible for the girl's death."

Philippa drew in her breath, barely believing what she was hearing.

"Yes, it's something, isn't it?" Jeannie looked pleased to see Philippa's stunned reaction. "So much for Andrew's saintly image. He—"

Philippa cut in. There was a question she had to ask.

"Did you tell anyone else this story?"

"Yeah. I was really steamed, so I told Kurt."

"Did anyone hear you?"

"The old boy was there, and that woman who does the books. They were listening."

"Pauline Waverly?"

"Yeah, that's the one. She seemed pretty shocked. She didn't say anything though."

Miller edged closer. Philippa's eyes locked briefly with his, and then she turned back and asked Jeannie Dunbar another question.

"Did McCardle, by any chance, tell you the name of the girl who died?"

"Why is that important?"

"Believe me, it's important. It was Waverly, wasn't it?"

Jeannie shrugged.

"How should I know? He didn't tell me that. Why? Are you implying there was some connection between Andrew and that accountant?"

"There *was* a connection between them," said Philippa. "They were at school together. He was three years ahead of her, but he dated her sister."

Philippa spun round to face Miller. "Chloe Harker told me about it," she cried. "Don't you see? The girl who died must have been Pauline Waverly's sister. Go back to the records of the tragedy. I bet you'll find that the girl's surname was Waverly."

But before Miller could respond, another voice broke the silence. It was the doorman of the Old Chandler.

"No," he said. "It wasn't Waverly. You can leave Pauline out of this. The girl who died was Pauline's sister's best friend. Her name was Janie Jones."

\* \* \*

The following week, Philippa went downtown to meet Jordan Hope. The director had been horrified to hear of Bill Jones' arrest and he had offered Philippa lunch in return for a full accounting of the case.

"It's really aggravating," he complained. "From all I've heard, Walt and Frankie deserved to be clapped in jail, and Capelli, gorgeous as she was, was pure poison. Thank the Lord she took a dive over the gallery," he added with a notable lack of piety. "Can you imagine the havoc she would have wreaked in a women's prison? Instant oblivion was a much better ending."

"Jordan, really! Don't be so heartless."

"I'm not at all heartless, but Claudia was. I'm glad the taxpayers were saved the expense of a trial. But never mind La Capelli, why Bill Jones? He was by far the nicest one of the bunch. Whatever made him kill Andrew McCardle?"

"He didn't actually push McCardle over," said Philippa. "They weren't even standing by the balcony rail. They were on the upper step. McCardle staggered back when Bill shoved him. Then he lost his footing, and the momentum as he lurched down the steps carried him right over the railing. Bill didn't mean to kill him. Hopefully, he'll only be facing a manslaughter charge."

"Yes, but what triggered the incident? Come on, Philippa—the only reason I offered to buy you lunch was to get the inside story. Earn those expensive scallops on your plate and tell me something I don't already know. How did Bill Jones know McCardle? I thought he'd spent most of his life in Toronto."

"Only the last thirty years. He was originally from Vancouver. Bill Jones and his wife had two daughters who went to the same school as Andrew McCardle. Bill's daughters were good friends with the Waverly girls because both sets of sisters were three years apart. The older girls, Janie Jones and Jennifer Waverly, were both crazy about Andrew McCardle. He was interested in Jennifer for a while, but then things cooled off—Pauline says her sister was only fourteen and was hesitant about putting out, and Andrew, being a randy fifteen-year-old who was desperate to get laid, transferred his attentions to Janie. However, she proved equally reserved, so although she let Andrew single her out at parties and school events, she was very good at making sure they stayed with the crowd. Then one of his friends told him how easy it was to loosen a girl up with Ecstasy."

"So he gave Bill's daughter the E pill?"

"Yes, and she died. But no one ever knew who had given Janie the Ecstasy, except the friend who had encouraged McCardle to try it on her."

"And being teenagers, they closed ranks and kept quiet." Jordan nodded. "Yes, I can just see it."

"Exactly. Bill and his wife were devastated. Old Bill had a complete breakdown. He quit his job, and the family moved away. They couldn't bear to stay in Vancouver, and they ended up in Ontario, where Bill gradually pulled himself together. He spent the rest of his working years employed at a garden centre. When his younger daughter grew up, she married a Vancouver man, so she moved back here, and she became reacquainted with some of her former friends, including Pauline Waverly, who had just started working for the Old Chandler. After Bill's wife died, he returned to B.C. to live with his daughter, and when the doorman's job became vacant at the Old Chandler, Pauline suggested he might like to take it. And that's how he came into contact with Andrew McCardle again."

"But how did he find out, after all this time, that McCardle was responsible for his daughter's death?"

"Through Jeannie Dunbar. You know how passionate McCardle was on the subject of drugs. He'd go out of his way to try to help people with addictions, and Jeannie Dunbar was someone he could see heading for a major crash. He wanted to save her, but she had a real attitude and he couldn't get through to her."

Jordan sniffed.

"I'm not surprised. I couldn't get anything through her pot-addled brain either. Why did he open up to her of all people?"

"She asked him why he cared, and he told her," Philippa said simply. "Maybe he'd been wanting to tell someone all his life. It must have been a terrible burden to carry."

"So all those years of anti-drug crusading were merely atonement. What a sad tale. I take it that Jeannie, instead of being moved to reformation by these confidences, took it upon herself to spread the story to anyone and everyone who crossed her path."

"Well, not quite that bad, but unfortunately, Bill was standing beside Kurt Liddle when Jeannie threw her little tantrum. What she said hit Bill like a tidal wave. I felt terrible when he started unloading on Bob Miller at the café. He was so distraught, but he was determined to give the police all the details."

"Well, that's typical of Bill," said Jordan. "He wouldn't let anyone else take the rap for something he'd done. I'm surprised he didn't own up right away."

"I think he was in shock. He has no recollection of walking round to where McCardle stood. He just remembers seeing him talking on his cellphone. He says McCardle saw him waiting, ended his call, and said, 'Just chatting with my family.'"

"Unfortunate choice of words," said Jordan.

"Yes. I gather Bill muttered, 'What about my family?' He says McCardle looked blank and said, 'Sorry?'"

"And?"

"Bill literally saw blood in front of his eyes. He cried, 'You should be sorry! She was my daughter!' And he shoved McCardle hard in the chest."

"And McCardle staggered back and toppled over."

"Bill doesn't remember anything after that. He just blanked out. He heard the shouting below, so he went down and carried on, on autopilot, I suppose. The police could see how shaken he was, and given his age, they were very easy on him and sent him home early. When he eventually came out of his fog and thought about what he'd done, he saw how bad it looked that he hadn't told the truth right away. He's been longing to get it off his chest, and when he heard me getting close to the truth, he found his opportunity. Poor old fellow. I feel so sorry for him."

"Me too," said Jordan. "He was such a great doorman. A real presence. Hard to believe he spent his working years in a garden shop. I'd have pinned him as something much more authoritarian—a sergeant major, or something like that. He had the bearing of a real old soldier."

Philippa helped herself to a piece of bread and wiped up the sauce on her plate.

"You're not far wrong," she said. "Before Janie died, Bill was with VPD. That was the career he gave up. He was a policeman."

Jordan's jaw dropped. Then he started to laugh.

"What's so funny?" demanded Philippa.

"I can't help it," snorted Jordan. "It's so utterly perfect."

"What are you talking about?"

"*The least likely person is the killer and no one is really who they seem.* Let's face it; we really ought to have figured it out."

"Why? Bill may have been the least likely person, but there was no question about who he was."

"But we were doing *The Mousetrap*," crowed Jordan. "Don't you see? The murderer was a policeman! Besides, the solution was glaring at us through his nickname."

"Huh? I don't get it."

"No, you're too young and you're too far detached from your British heritage. But your Dad would understand. He would know the old English term that used to refer to the law."

Jordan paused dramatically and reached for his wine glass. With an aggravatingly languid air, he sniffed the bouquet and took a leisurely sip.

"Oh, for heaven's sake," snapped Philippa. "You're not on the stage now. Just tell me. What is the blessed term?"

Jordan grinned and raised his glass in a toast.

"The Old Bill," he said gleefully. "Here's to him."

# THE MAN IN THE CAGE

Robin Forrest loved Kippie. The diminutive chocolate Labrador belonged to—no, that was the wrong word—was living with Constable Mark Clancy, the young policeman from the Port Moody Police Department who had been dating her sister for the last six months. Mark, who appeared quite besotted with the beautiful blonde enchantress who was the oldest sibling of the Forrest clan, was good-naturedly tolerant of Robin. He was also very happy for the ten-year-old girl to walk the little female Lab while he and Tracy were otherwise occupied, but as he saw how attached the young girl was becoming to the animal, he felt the need to caution her. He told her that Kippie had been a candidate to become a sniffer dog in Port Moody, but now that all the police forces were switching to cross-trained German shepherds, the Labs were only going to be used at Canada Customs. Therefore, if Kippie made the grade, he would have to give her up. Robin couldn't understand how anyone could have a dog that they knew they would lose at some point in the future, and she hoped desperately that Kippie would fail the tests, for then, she had been told, the dog would be put up for adoption. However, Mark discouraged her firmly, pointing out that Kippie was probably going to be accepted in spite of her small size and the fact that she'd had surgery for a torn tendon in her knee, because, even with the preliminary training he'd provided, Kippie had proved to have an exceptionally good nose. Still, ever the optimist, Robin began an intense campaign with her mother, hoping to persuade her to adopt Kippie if the dog did not make the grade.

The Forrest home was located in the section of Burnside that stretched along Burrard Inlet and looked across to the mountains of the North Shore. It was a dank February day. Heavy clouds hovered on the peaks, and the mountainsides melded into the dull slate grey of the ocean. The afternoon was gloomy and overcast, but the rain had stopped by the time Robin walked home from school. Monday was Tracy's day off, so Robin hurried along the sidewalk, hoping against hope that her sister's boyfriend would be there. As she turned the corner to her own street, her heart lifted. Mark's car was parked in front of her house.

She opened the garden gate and saw Mr. Bates coming round the side of the house. Off for his afternoon walk, thought Robin, hoping that she didn't meet him when she went to the park with Kippie. Mr. Bates was the tenant in the basement suite and he disliked dogs. Robin didn't like him at all, but her mother said they had to be charitable because life had dealt Mr. Bates a series of terrible blows. Robin sympathized, but she still didn't like him, especially as he'd been making a play for her mother ever since he'd discovered his landlady was a widow. Robin had been quaking at the thought of him becoming a regular member of the family, but fortunately her mother had made it quite clear that she wasn't interested in him *that* way.

Mr. Bates came down the path and Robin stepped aside to let him pass. He barely acknowledged her as he walked by and disappeared through the gate. Robin scowled, remembering the insincere way he fussed over her when her mother was around. Putting the tenant out of her mind, Robin hopped up the front steps and went through the front door. Kippie raced to greet her. Robin knew the dog was not supposed to jump up, but Mark and Tracy were nowhere in sight so she tossed her backpack into the corner and let the dog leap about and cover her with kisses. Then she grabbed Kippie's leash, hooked it on her collar and set off for the park.

Cliffside Park was only four blocks away. It stretched along Burrard Inlet, a hundred-acre tract of partly cultivated land that accommodated tennis courts, a swimming pool, a playground and a rose garden, and partly bushy trails that zigzagged down to the water. The torrential downpour of the morning had ceased. Now there was only a light mist permeating the air, but it cast a grey pall over the area, making the park dull and unwelcoming in the late-afternoon light. Above the playground towered three huge maples, black against the watery sky, their skeletal branches laden with abandoned birds' nests that blended onto the dark wood like sinister growths feeding off the trees.

The off-leash trails were on the far side of the park so Robin kept Kippie on her lead. It was unlikely that many people would be out on such a dreary day, but she knew that Mr. Bates' daily walk always included a stroll through the park, and once before, when he had seen Kippie running free in the playground, he had threatened to call the SPCA. Robin bridled indignantly at the memory, but she could not risk a complaint or a run-in with a pound officer since Mark was not really supposed to let her take the little Lab out unsupervised. Focussed on the dog at her side, she proceeded through the playground and crossed the rose garden, scarcely noticing the pruned stumps of the bushes protruding from the sodden earth, but her attention was drawn to the tennis courts by the thump, thump, thump of tennis balls.

As she entered the path that ran between the courts and the pool buildings, Kippie lunged towards the high mesh fence, and Robin had to pull her back and make her heel. A solitary man was on the tennis court. He was a burly individual who seemed indifferent to the weather, for he was dressed in dark blue chinos, a black sweatshirt and a red ball cap. Watched by a solemn row of seagulls perched on the fence, he was practising his serve, repeatedly hitting balls across the net, and then moving to the other end of the court once his supply of balls had been used up. In the misting rain, the painted concrete had turned a shimmering green, gradually darkening to black on the far side of the enclosure where another cluster of the bizarrely decorated maples loomed above the high fence. In the dwindling light, the chain-link fence transformed the playing area into a gigantic, menacing cage. Robin was glad that she was on the outside of the grey wire.

As she reached the end of the court, a clang startled her and made her jump. Kippie leapt at the fence and barked furiously. A ball had bounced and hit the green garbage container by the wire fence. Robin pulled the dog back, but although Kippie stopped barking, she strained forward, sniffing eagerly at the corner of the enclosure. Robin glanced down. A sports bag was lying inside the fence. This was what had caught the dog's attention. As she tried to pull the Lab away, she heard an angry voice. The man had come to retrieve the ball.

"Get that dog away from my bag! Take off, kid."

Robin started to apologize, but something in the man's eyes froze the words on her lips. She dragged Kippie after her and hurried away. When she reached the gate at the trail entrance, she glanced back, apprehensive in case the man had followed them, but he had resumed his practice on the tennis courts. The balls were repeating their steady, one-way trajectory over the net.

Once well into the trails, Robin slipped the leash from Kippie's collar and the dog bounded eagerly ahead with the slightly uneven gait that had resulted from her corrective surgery. The bushes were still sodden from the morning rain, and drips from the overhead branches fell on her head as she walked, but Robin did not care. Kippie raced back and forth, sniffing here and there, and Robin felt her spirits soar. Her love for the little creature was so immense that she could not conceive of them ever being parted. Kippie was such a small Lab, surely the runt of the litter. How could she ever make it as a police dog?

As if Robin's thoughts had somehow conjured up an image so vividly that it had materialized before her eyes, a line of figures appeared at the far end of the trail. At the head of the group, leashed and held by a giant of a man wearing a distinctive peaked cap, was a large, fierce-looking German shepherd. The uniforms and the yellow raingear were unmistakable. Six RCMP officers were coming up the path.

Kippie's head rose as she saw the dog. She was too far ahead for Robin to grab her, and it was obvious that she wanted to run and meet this new acquaintance. Robin gulped. Praying that Kippie would obey, she hollered a command for her to come. To her relief, Kippie turned and ran back to her. Robin clipped on the leash and stepped to the side of the trail to let the squadron by. The officers passed in silence, but the woman constable at the end turned back and smiled at Robin.

"Nothing to worry about," she said. "This is just a training exercise. Carry on with your walk."

Robin waited until the policemen had disappeared from view, but stopping had made her conscious of how wet and chilled she had become. She noticed that the trails had darkened, so, keeping the dog on the leash, she turned up the path that would lead her back to the parking lot. When she emerged from the trees, she glanced towards the tennis courts. There was no sound of racquet hitting balls. The man had gone.

Relieved, she led Kippie back through the parking lot. A silver Chrysler 300, glistening brightly in the rain, had arrived during her absence, though there was no sign of the driver. Robin grinned as she noticed the licence plate— KIP 100. "See, Kippie," she laughed. "You're one hundred percent. The best dog in the world."

As she entered the path by the tennis courts, the dog pulled eagerly ahead. When they reached the edge of the fence, Kippie sniffed eagerly at the wire, but the sports bag that had caught her attention earlier was no longer there. Robin dragged her away, but before she could continue along the path, a dark object caught the corner of her eye. She glanced up, and then she gasped. The tennis court was not empty after all. A bundle of clothes lay beside the net at the centre of the court. Robin's stomach lurched and her knees felt suddenly wobbly. She recognized the red cap lying beside the bundle of clothes. The man was still there.

Remembering the training corps of RCMP officers, Robin dragged Kippie after her and started running back towards the woods.

＊　　　　　＊　　　　　＊

Two days later, the file concerning the body on the tennis court came to the attention of Detective Inspector Richard Beary. As the RCMP, like every police force in the Lower Mainland, was stretched to the limit with preparations for the 2010 Winter Olympics, Richard hoped fervently that the death would not turn out to be a suspicious one. Richard was drinking his morning coffee and reading a security update on his computer screen when Detective Sergeant Bill Martin entered his office to give him a preliminary report.

"The dead man's name was Gordon Havering," said Martin. "His sister identified him. He was an ex-military man who had been dishonorably discharged because of his addiction to cocaine, so it's possible he simply had a heart attack. We'll know for certain when we get the autopsy results. He lived a couple of blocks from the park and he used to go there regularly to practise his serve, but no one ever saw him playing a game with a partner."

"Who discovered the body?" asked Richard, still with one eye on his computer screen.

"A child who was walking her dog. Fortunately, there was a training corps in the park at the same time—Jean Howe was part of the group, and she'd spoken to the child earlier—so the little girl ran to fetch her right away."

Richard nodded. Constable Howe was a resourceful and reliable member of the uniformed branch.

"Jean says the little girl who discovered the body referred to him as 'The man in the cage'—and given his solitary nature, the epithet is quite appropriate."

Richard was still only half-listening. Sergeant Martin cleared his throat loudly. Then he continued with ponderous deliberation. "Now," he said firmly, "there's one very puzzling factor about this caged corpse."

Richard put down his coffee mug and became more attentive.

"What would that be?" he asked briskly.

"The child who found the body had passed by the tennis courts when she first arrived at the park. She told Jean that there was a sports bag inside the enclosure, and that her dog had been extremely interested in the bag. Evidently, Havering became very angry and told her to keep the dog away from it."

"So? It probably had his lunch in it."

"Possibly, but the bag had disappeared when she came back. Jean couldn't find it anywhere, and it would be easy enough to recognize. The girl said it was unusual. It was black, with an orange picture of a cannon imprinted on the side. Pretty distinctive."

Richard raised his eyebrows.

"How old is this child?"

"Only ten. She's young, but Jean said she seemed pretty sharp. Her name is Robin Forrest. Anyway, this is the interesting bit. The kid said her dog was formerly a police dog. It was being trained for drug-detection until it had to be withdrawn from the program due to a knee problem."

"One of ours?"

"No, she said it came from the U.S. But she was very insistent that the dog had its nose practically through the wire. That's how eager it was."

"So this could be a pick-up gone wrong. You think the bag contained drugs."

"It seems likely. This girl also saw a car in the parking lot, but by the time she'd run back through the trail, alerted the training squad and come back a third time, the car had gone. However, she was able to give Jean the licence number. This has been traced to a known dealer named Pete Blagg."

"This child sounds a real gem. You'd better make sure you have all this in writing. Has she been formally interviewed yet?"

"No. She took off after talking with the officers in the park. Jean said she seemed anxious to get home. Jean went round to her house later that evening, but no one was home. However, it was far from a wasted trip, because the downstairs tenant came out to see what she wanted, and it turned out he'd been in the park too." Martin grinned. "The tenant was a very useful witness," he said smugly. "He must have walked through the park while the girl was on the trail because he saw the car pull in. It was just as he was leaving the park."

"So he also saw the driver?"

"Yes. The description he gave definitely fits Blagg."

"Was he able to tell Jean what time the car arrived?"

"About four-thirty. He didn't have a watch, but he left his house just after three-thirty, and then walked up to the bank before heading round to the park. He told Jean that his route takes him about fifty minutes. He saw Havering practising his serve on the tennis court, but once he had passed the pool building, the courts were no longer in view. Neither was the parking lot, so he couldn't say whether or not the driver got out and went to the courts."

"Did he notice the mysterious sports bag?"

"No. He was a good hundred yards away and up on a rise, so even if it had been there, he wouldn't have seen it."

"Is this man reliable? What do we know about him?"

"Jean checked into his background. He's OK. He has a tragic history, but drugs are definitely not in the picture. Alcohol was a problem once, but he learned his lesson the hard way."

"How so?"

"Back in 2004, he got falling-down drunk at a pool party. Several couples were present, and the whole event was pretty wild. Later in the evening, after most of the people had left, there was an accident that left one of the men a paraplegic. The homeowner accused Bates of causing the accident, and although the charges turned out to be bogus, he lost everything during the two-year period he was required to defend himself. His wife left him, he had to sell all his assets to pay the lawyers, and then, a year later, he lost his job, again through no fault of his own. He used to be an accountant and a top-notch baseball player; now he's a shell of a man living on welfare." Sergeant Martin shook his head sadly. "It's actually amazing the man *isn't* on drugs, but there's nothing to connect him with the dead man. His evidence checks out plainly enough. The walk he described—which was a daily routine for him—was accurate in terms of time. His description of the car and driver was right on. If Havering's death turns out to be suspicious, I'm willing to bet Blagg will be our man."

"Fine," said Richard. "I hope you're right. With the Olympic circus about to start, the last thing we need is to be bogged down with a complicated murder case. Let's bring him in for questioning. If for no other reason, I'm curious about what was in that bag."

*     *     *

Richard indeed did have more urgent matters on his plate. Security for the Winter Olympics was a billion-dollar enterprise, and the pressure was on to make sure the dollars produced results. Public feeling on the subject was divided, and as the recession continued and government cutbacks hit a variety of community groups, the numbers who were infuriated by the massive spending for the Games tended to outweigh those who were excited that Vancouver was about to be showcased on the world stage.

Robin's mother, who was president of a theatre society that had seen its grant disappear, was in the first category. However, when her daughter proposed that they walk down the hill to watch the Olympic torch pass by, she thawed a little and agreed to go. Once she had seen the smiling white figure jog past, holding the torch high for all to see, her interest increased somewhat. Then tragedy struck. Prior to the opening ceremony, a young competitor died on the slopes of Whistler. After that, motherly concern for all the athletes compelled Mrs. Forrest to pay more attention to the challenges they faced.

Before long, Mrs. Forrest found herself besieged by Olympic ambassadors. Everywhere she turned, she was reminded of what was happening downtown. Her doctor, who was volunteering in the first-aid station, had a fascinating store of tales about the various VIPs, some of whom were so doddery that they deserved a medal for making it around the tea tent. Her hairdresser proudly boasted of a son who was engaged as a dancer for a VIP reception and, due to security, would only learn his destination on the day of the event. And at home, Tracy constantly regaled her mother with descriptions of the pub in the Irish pavilion and the bands playing in front of the big screen in Yaletown. By the end of the first week, as Canada began to take in gold and the national anthem more frequently blared from the television set, Mrs. Forrest became a convert to Olympic fever.

One day, when Robin came home late from basketball practice, she found her mother chatting with Mrs. Silver, their next-door neighbour, who had just returned from a day in town. To Robin's surprise, Mr. Bates, who was usually withdrawn and uncommunicative, came out from his suite and joined in the conversation. He seemed genuinely interested in what Mrs. Silver had to say.

77

"You must go see the cauldron in Coal Harbour and the huge Canadian flag on the side of The Bay," trilled Mrs. Silver. "It's easy to get around if you use transit. We took the Skytrain downtown, and from there we rode the Seabus to the North Shore—that's where the Russian tall ship is moored—and after we returned, we took the Canada line to the Olympic Village and the streetcar to Granville Island. Then we came back to Yaletown on a tiny little Aquabus that looked just like a bathtub toy."

Robin's mother was dubious.

"How crowded is the Skytrain?"

"Very," Mrs. Silver acknowledged. "Every train that comes in is packed like a tin of sardines. We couldn't get on at Stadium. We had to take a train back to the waterfront in order to catch one to get home. But you really should make the effort and take Robin down for a day. Go on a Monday and get there early. Then the line-ups won't be as bad."

"Can we?" said Robin. "I want to go on the zip-line."

"And so you should," said Mrs. Silver.

"What on earth is the zip-line?" asked Robin's mother.

Mrs. Silver explained.

"People climb up a tower and hook onto a cable; then they let fly and ride across to the other side of Robson Square."

Robin's mother shuddered.

"That sounds appalling."

"No," laughed Mrs. Silver. "It's perfectly safe. The young people love it."

Mr. Bates cleared his throat. Robin looked round. Startled, she saw that the tenant's expressionless eyes were focussed on her.

"I'll take you if your mother doesn't want to go," he offered.

Robin gulped. The last thing she wanted was a day out with Mr. Bates. She turned back and glowered at her mother.

To Robin's relief, Mrs. Forrest picked up the hint. "That's quite all right," she said firmly to Mr. Bates. "I'll take Robin down for the day." Then, seeing his lips tighten and sensing his disappointment, she added, "Why don't we all go together?"

*   *   *

The investigation into the death of the man in the cage came to an abrupt halt when the coroner sent the autopsy report. Havering had died of natural causes, if one accepted that a heart weakened through excessive drug use could be called natural. However, there was also forensic evidence indicating that Blagg had been in contact with the dead man, even to the extent of having his hands inside the man's pockets. When presented with the facts, Blagg eventually admitted going onto the tennis court. His story was glib. He had come to the park for a walk, had seen the man lying there, and had gone to see if he needed help. Having concluded that the man was dead, Blagg had left the court, not wanting a run-in with the police given his own less-than-perfect record. He had ducked behind the pool-house when he'd seen the little girl approaching with the dog, and waited until she had gone before going to his car and driving away. He flatly denied taking the sports bag and insisted, with great indignation, that no such item had been anywhere in sight.

"And my Aunt Harriet is the Queen of England," muttered Sergeant Martin, after they had released him. "Walk in the park, my eye. Blagg was obviously Havering's supplier, and the tennis court was their regular drop-off point. The money for the drugs will have been in the sports bag, and Blagg will have just helped himself, once he saw the man was dead."

"You're probably right," said Richard. "But why would he take the sports bag? Why not just dig out the money? And why," he added thoughtfully, "would he have searched the body if the money was in the bag?"

"I don't know," said Martin. "It's a mystery."

"That it is," said Richard. "And it's a mystery we have to shelve because we have more critical things to deal with."

"Roll on the Winter Olympics," grunted Sergeant Martin. "At least we're not freezing our nuts off up at Whistler."

*      *      *

Robin felt guilty for having lied about Kippie, but she didn't want Mark to get into trouble for letting her walk the dog. As long as the police were tipped off to the fact that drugs might be involved, that was really all that mattered. Her conscience also troubled her that she had not told Mark about the incident, but she was scared that he would stop her outings with Kippie if he knew what had happened. So she had kept quiet, and not even her mother knew about her adventure in the park. She'd had one anxious moment when Mr. Bates had stopped her in the garden to tell her about the police officer who had come round to ask questions. The tenant was curious to know what Robin had seen in the park, and although she admitted to alerting the police about the body on the tennis court, her innate distrust of Mr. Bates made her hold back the detail of the missing sports bag. To her relief, when she pleaded with him not to tell anyone of her experience, he agreed that it would be their secret. As the days passed and no more police officers appeared to ask questions, Robin's feelings of unease abated, and by the time the day arrived for her trip downtown, she had thrust the incident to the back of her mind. All she could think of was the exciting excursion ahead.

The journey into Vancouver was a foreshadowing of what was waiting in the downtown core. The Skytrain was packed, and Robin was squeezed onto the single seat at the very back of the last coach on the train. She was quite happy to be sitting there, rather than with her mother and Mr. Bates who sat on the seats adjacent to her alcove, for the outlook from the end of the train was fascinating. She watched the moving picture outside the window, a mesmerizing panorama of tracks disappearing around curves and into dips, then rising back into sight, occasionally splitting into two and then returning to a single line. Periodically, a train would rocket into her line of vision, startling her as it shot into view on her right, after which it would snake off into the distance, gradually diminishing until it vanished around another bend.

Finally, the robotic voice over the PA announced that they had arrived at Stadium Station. Robin struggled to her feet. Trying to stay close to the others, she wriggled past the standing passengers and pressed her way through the doors. As she tucked in behind her mother and scurried along the platform, she was glad she hadn't brought a purse or backpack. Mr. Bates had been right about that. He'd emphasized that they should put everything in their jacket pockets so that they didn't have to deal with the hassle of being checked by security guards. But she still wished she was having her day out without him tagging along, and she knew that her mother, for all her sympathetic manner towards Mr. Bates, would have preferred that too. Their tenant's impassively polite manner did not make for easy companionship.

"Come on, darling. Don't get left behind."

Robin's mother fell back and took her daughter's hand. Swept along in the flow of bodies, they reached the end of the platform and were funnelled into single file as they started down the stairs at the east end of the station. Robin glanced ahead as she followed her mother down to the street. Mr. Bates was already on the sidewalk. His pudgy face had become a misty red blur in the reflection from his Canada cap, but as she reached ground level, Robin could see that his eyes still retained their usual blank expression.

*Honestly*, thought Robin, *why did he even bother to come?*

\*             \*             \*

On the day that Robin and her mother ventured downtown, Pete Blagg came once again to the attention of the RCMP. Although a small-time villain, Blagg was active in several Lower Mainland municipalities, and when Richmond RCMP officer, DC George, who happened to be a friend of Constable Mark Clancy, was investigating Blagg's connection to an underground cache of marijuana, he came across Robin Forrest's name in the file. Knowing that

Robin was the sister of Mark's girlfriend, he called his buddy to find out what was going on.

"What's this?" he demanded. "Have you seen this report?"

"What report?"

"About Kippie and your girlfriend's kid sister?"

"What!"

"Keep cool. I'm sending it over to you right now. You've got to check it out."

"This is news to me," said Mark, moments later, as he brought the page up on his computer screen and started to read. "She never said anything about this. Silly kid."

"Kippie's a reject from the NYPD drug squad? Is she on something?"

"No, of course not," snapped Mark. "She'll have invented that story thinking that I'd get into trouble if she told them I'd been letting her walk the dog. Oh, Jesus!" Mark froze and stared at the screen in horror.

"What?"

"That sports bag. I've seen it."

"The black one with the cannon?"

"Yes. That same day. I was at the house. That's why Robin had Kippie. I was upstairs with Tracy, and we heard the clang of the garden gate so I looked out to see if it was Robin. But it was the Forrest's tenant. He was coming back from his walk and he was carrying a bag just like that." Mark's eyes flashed to the corner of the screen and noted the name on the file. "I'm ringing off," he snapped. "I have to get hold of Inspector Beary."

A few moments later, after impressing the constable at the other end with the urgency of the situation, Mark was put through. Quickly, he relayed the information about the bag.

"You've got to get out to the Forrests' house," he told Richard. "God, if only she'd said something."

"Calm down," said Richard. "If their tenant is into drugs, we'll deal with it. It isn't a red alert."

"The girl misled you, sir." Mark struggled to keep the note of hysteria out of his voice. "I told Robin that Kippie was a candidate for the drug squad so as not to upset her, but the dog's actually intended for a different program. It's not drugs. It's explosives!"

*       *       *

Mrs. Forrest had heard that the Ontario Pavilion had a big-screen film presentation that began with a sweeping view of Wolfe Island, so she suggested they begin their tour there. With the help of directions from ubiquitous policemen and friendly volunteers in blue, they wound their way through the labyrinth of fences, all the while listening to a steady stream of announcements from the stadium loudspeakers telling ticket-holders where to go for the upcoming hockey game. However, when they reached the pavilion, the line-up was so long that they decided to keep going. They turned back, cut up past the casino and the Yaletown stage, and strolled along the water until they reached Beatty Street. Scalpers stood on every corner, but they declined the offer of event tickets and forged on until they reached Starbucks. They stopped for drinks, and then ambled over to the Queen Elizabeth Theatre plaza where a demonstration of First Nations dancing was in progress. To Robin's delight, the friendly chief invited the spectators to join him, and she giggled as she saw her mother drawn out onto the square. Mr. Bates seemed indifferent to the antics on the plaza, though he did not appear to mind waiting while Robin and her mother enjoyed the festivities. When the dancing stopped, they walked up Georgia Street and then crossed over to Robson Square. Mrs. Forrest was captivated by the murals and the art gallery flower wall, but Robin was impatient to get to the zip-line. She urged her mother on, and they worked their way through the milling crowds until they found the end of the queue.

"So do I get to go on it?" Robin demanded, squinting up at the high towers on either side of the square.

Her mother demurred.

"It doesn't look safe to me. Besides, there's a long wait. Do you really want to stand around all that time?"

To Robin's surprise, Mr. Bates intervened.

"There's no hurry," he said calmly. "We can have another coffee while Robin waits in line." He gestured to a table at the side of the open-air café. "We can keep an eye on her if we sit there."

"Great," said Robin. "And after I'm done, we can go on the streetcar."

"But what about the cauldron?" said Robin's mother. "I thought that was the main purpose of the trip today."

"No rush," said Mr. Bates. "That's the last thing we're going to see."

*       *       *

"Why wasn't Havering's army record checked?" snapped Richard. "If we'd known he'd worked with explosives, it would have set off some alarm bells."

"The autopsy indicated he died naturally," pointed out Sergeant Martin. "It wasn't a murder case and it didn't warrant any further investigation." He turned off the freeway and started up the hill that climbed to the northeast end of Burnside. "We're lucky the Forrest girl has a cop for a boyfriend," he mused.

"Bates is used to seeing Mark Clancy around the place, so he won't go into a panic when he shows up. Clancy will be able to suss out the situation for us."

"He ought to be there by now," said Richard. "The Port Moody station must be less than ten minutes from the Forrest home. I just hope he has the sense to keep calm."

"Easier said than done," growled Martin. "We don't even know what kind of device Havering created."

The radio cut in. Jean Howe's voice came over the air.

"EDTS has been notified, sir, and they have a technician ready to come in as soon as you give the word."

"Is Mark Clancy at the Forrest house yet?"

"Yes. And the older daughter is there. Her mother and sister have gone downtown sightseeing, but Tracy is home. She's waiting with Clancy. Clancy said to tell you that they're sure the tenant is out, because whenever he's home, the TV is blaring, and Tracy hasn't heard any noise down there all morning. She has a key and she's ready to let you into the basement suite."

"Good. With any luck, whatever nasty little gadget Bates has acquired will be there, and we'll be able to cordon off the area and get the disposal team in before he has a chance to use it. Has the girl any idea where he's gone?"

"No. She couldn't say."

"OK. Once I've confirmed the place is empty, I'll let you know and you can give the disposal team the go-ahead. I'll need the uniformed branch out too. We'll have to evacuate the street while they're working."

He pulled up in front of the Forrest home. Tracy was standing by the gate, and she opened it as they approached. Richard beckoned to Sergeant Martin, and they followed Tracy round the side of the house. Mark Clancy was waiting impatiently at the entrance to the basement suite. Tracy went down the short flight of cement steps and unlocked the door; then she stood aside for the others to go by. Telling Tracy to remain outside, the three policemen entered the suite.

Sergeant Martin was first through the door. He froze the moment he stepped inside.

"Look!" he hissed, pointing to the far side of the room.

A thread of light filtering through a crack in the curtains illuminated an orange cannon that seemed to hover in the darkness, apparently floating on air. Then, as their eyes adjusted to the dim light, the sports bag became visible against the dark wall. As they moved closer, they saw that the bag was open. It was empty, except for a towel and a plastic tube of tennis balls.

Richard glanced around the room. Nothing appeared out of the ordinary.

As his eyes swept the area, he spotted an envelope propped against the toaster on the kitchen counter. Picking it up, he tore it open and began to read the letter inside. His face paled.

"What is it, sir?" Mark Clancy's face was pinched with anxiety.

"It's a suicide letter," said Richard tersely. "We're dealing with someone who's completely alienated from society, and he's intending to take as many people with him as he can."

"Christ!" said Martin. "Are you telling me we're too late?"

The door flew open and Tracy burst into the room. A grey-haired woman followed her.

When Tracy spoke, she confirmed Richard's worst fears.

"Mrs. Silver says our tenant went downtown with my mom and sister," said Tracy. Her face was pale, and she looked beseechingly at Richard. "Will they be all right?" she asked. "What has Mr. Bates done?"

Richard gave Mark Clancy a stern glance to keep him from blurting out the crisis that they were facing. Keeping his voice calm and trying not to reveal the chill that he felt, he patted Tracy on the shoulder.

"Don't worry," he said. "You go back upstairs. We'll take care of everything from here on. Your mother and sister will be just fine. But you can give me their cell numbers so I can contact them. I don't want you calling them, OK. And," Richard whipped a card out of his pocket, "I want you to email photos of Robin and your mother to the address on this card. Got that?" Tracy's hand trembled as she took the card, but she nodded. Then she gave Richard the phone numbers and left. With a mistrustful frown, Mrs. Silver followed her out.

As soon as they had left, Richard's manner changed.

"Get Jean to alert security and let them know there are pictures coming," he told Martin. "There'll be a photograph of Bates in the files because of his court case." He pulled out his cellphone and began to punch in numbers. "We have to pinpoint their exact location. You stay here, Mark," he added. "I want you to talk to Mrs. Forrest when I get through. Keep it casual. Just find out where they are."

"Clever bugger," grunted Sergeant Martin. "A man on his own would be a magnet for the security guards, but if he's with a woman and a child, he's practically invisible. No one is going to believe a man with his wife and child is going to blow himself up."

He headed out to the car. Mark looked questioningly at Richard.

"They're not answering," muttered Richard. "Where the hell are they?"

*       *       *

Robin was standing on the platform at the start of the zip-line when she heard her phone ring. High up above the crowd, the tone was crystal clear, but she was already in the harness and ready to leap into the void, so there was no way she was going to take the call. With a delicious quiver of excitement, she launched herself into space and felt the rush of exhilaration as she hurtled across the square. Within seconds, she had reached the platform on the other side and the ride was over. Unmindful of the hum of voices below, punctuated with blaring announcements from the loudspeakers, she peered down towards the café table where she knew her mother had been sitting. After a moment, she saw a hand waving, and she beamed and waved back. By the time she had descended to ground level, she had completely forgotten the phone call.

"So, was it as thrilling as you thought?" laughed Mrs. Forrest.

Robin beamed. "Even better. Can we go on the streetcar now?"

Mrs. Forrest shook her head.

"Mr. Bates and I were talking about that while you were in line," she said. "If we go up to Granville Island now, we'll have to backtrack to see the cauldron, so we should really have our streetcar ride just before we're ready to leave town. We're almost at the waterfront now, so we should go to the cauldron next. And then we can get something to eat."

"OK," said Robin equably. "Can we go to the Cactus Club? Mrs. Silver said they have big screens all over the restaurant. We can watch the events while we eat. There's sure to be something exciting on."

"Yes, there probably will be," said Mr. Bates.

For a brief moment, Robin could have sworn she saw a flicker of animation in the man's eyes, but when she looked again, the enigmatic glint that had flared with the fleeting intensity of a lightning flash had been shrouded by the tenant's habitual empty stare.

*      *      *

"Still no answer?" Mark Clancy's fists were clenched so hard that his knuckles had turned white.

Richard shook his head.

"I'll keep trying," he said. "They may have their phones on, but the noise level could be drowning out the ring tone."

Mark frowned. "Are you sure I shouldn't warn them about what's going on, sir?"

"No. If they panic, they could tip Bates off, and that might be all it takes for him to trigger the bomb."

"But even if our guys spot him, how are they going to grab him without taking a chance that he'll set it off? He probably only has to pull a string or press a button. How can you prevent him?"

"I'll think of something," said Richard. "The main thing is to locate where they are."

"Why don't you call Robin's cell if you can't get hold of her mother?"

"I've already tried it," said Richard. "Neither one is answering."

"Here," said Mark, whipping out his own cellphone. "Why don't I text her? Kids don't bother with voicemail, but they check their text messages all the time." He started to punch letters in. "She's used to getting messages from me," he said. "She'll think it's something to do with Kippie, so if she sees it, she'll answer right away."

The door opened and Sergeant Martin came back into the room.

"The descriptions have gone out," he said. "I'd say within fifteen minutes, every security person and member of the force will have the info and be on the lookout. The trick is going to be getting him before he detonates his explosives. I wish to God we knew what he has."

"Whatever it is, he'll need to use his hands," said Richard. "Our people are going to have to pick their moment."

"Yeah, well, he's not going to accommodate us by doing jumping jacks," growled Martin.

Richard barely heard, for an idea had started to come to him. He turned to Mark.

"What sort of kid is this Robin?" he asked. "Is she a sensible girl, or one of those spinny, spaced-out ones?"

"The first type," said Mark. "She's a bright kid. She's great with Kippie. She's very calm, and she takes instruction well."

"Jean said she was a good witness," added Sergeant Martin, "other than telling her a whopper over the dog's history."

The ring of Mark's phone startled them. He opened it. Then he looked up at Richard and said, "It's her. She's sent a text message, and … Oh, Jeez. You don't want to hear this. They're heading for the cauldron."

"Give me your phone," said Richard. "I want to answer that message."

*     *     *

Down at the waterfront, the crowds were getting thicker. The cafés reaped the benefit as people flagged and needed somewhere to sit and recoup their energy. Others soldiered on, determined to see the sights, in spite of sore feet and aching backs.

Shirley Babbit was in the latter category, but she was not enjoying herself. Her husband had insisted on bringing the children downtown, but after several hours of struggling through crowds and trying to keep track of the smaller family members, Shirley's patience was wearing thin—especially as it was quite plain that the children were missing the point of the entire exercise. Their youngest daughter was too little for such a lengthy day out, her older sister did nothing but whine every time they passed a vendor hawking tawdry souvenirs, and her five-year-old brother was only interested in stuffing his face with as much junk food as he could persuade his father to buy. That is, when his father was not sidetracked by another flat screen parading the latest event or medal ceremony. Shirley was getting very little help in ensuring that the children did not get lost, and she resolved that, as soon as they had climbed to the top of the viewing platform and taken their picture of the cauldron, they would head for home.

Enviously, Shirley watched the family standing ahead of them in the line-up. The woman appeared cheerful and unruffled, and her husband was so calmly impassive that he looked as if nothing could stir him into a display of temperament. Their daughter was a model of patience as she waited in line, staying at her father's side. The girl actually seemed a little tired, Shirley thought, eyeing her more closely, but in spite of the fact that she was rather wan, not a complaint or grumble passed her lips.

Shirley turned around as her three-year-old wriggled and pulled away from her. Two men stood in the line behind them. They were casually dressed, but they didn't look to Shirley as if they were having fun. However, the taller man fielded the little girl and nudged her back to her mother. Shirley thanked him, but his eyes were already gliding past her towards the front of the queue.

The line inched forward. They were almost at the steps now. Shirley's husband drew out a roll of mints and gave them to their son, who was grumbling yet again about being hungry. Then he picked up their three-year-old and hoisted her onto his shoulders.

"How long is it going to take?" demanded their older daughter.

"Only another ten minutes," said Shirley. "Not long."

"Boring," came the reply. "This has to be the most totally lame thing we've done all day. What's so special about a stupid flame?"

The girl opened her Blackberry and began to text her friends.

Shirley pushed her gently forward as the line shifted another foot. As it moved again, the family in front of them reached the steps.

All of a sudden, for no apparent reason, though Shirley thought the milling crowds might possibly have jostled her, the girl in front of them tripped forward. To Shirley's surprise, instead of getting up, the child rolled onto her rear end and began to cry.

"I've hurt my ankle," she sobbed.

Then she raised both hands to her father and said, "Mr. Bates, please help me up."

Shirley had just registered the fact that the man could not be the girl's father after all, when dramatically and unceremoniously, she was shoved out of the way by the men who had been behind her.

One grabbed the man's outstretched arms and the other slapped a pair of handcuffs on him.

And then they led him away.

Instantly, an army of policemen and security guards surrounded the steps, though where they had come from, Shirley had no idea. The little girl hopped to her feet, and one of the policemen patted her on the back and said something to her quietly. Then she took her mother's hand, and they slipped out of line and followed the policeman to a waiting squad car that had materialized at the side of the road.

"Now that was cool," said Shirley's older daughter, holding up her Blackberry and showing her mother the picture she had taken of the arrest.

"I wonder if we'll ever know what that was all about," mused Shirley.

"I doubt it," said her husband. "It'll just be the RCMP over-reacting about some minor little thing. Come on. People are moving forward again."

He put his hand on his wife's back and gently propelled her towards the steps. As the line slowly inched upward, Shirley continued to ponder the significance of the scene that had played out in front of them, but once she stepped onto the viewing platform, the strange incident was forgotten. Following her children to the railing, she felt a thrill of patriotic pride. There was something quite magical about standing level with the Olympic flame.

And on the road below, unnoticed by the people on the viewing platform, the police car pulled out and turned towards Georgia Street. Robin twisted round and looked out through the rear window. For a long time afterwards, the picture framed in that window was imprinted on her mind—the cauldron rising majestically above the crowd, its yellow flame flickering steadily against the smooth blue sky.

*      *      *

Mrs. Forrest shuddered whenever she remembered that day. She was glad that she had not known what was going on for she was sure she would not have been able to disguise her panic. When she heard the story from the beginning and was told about Robin's man in the cage, she could not help concluding that the real man in the cage had been her tenant who had never been able to get beyond the injustices he had suffered throughout his tragedy-ridden life. She shivered to think that under that placid exterior, he had been as dangerous as a pent-up lion.

But in the immediate aftermath of the incident, there was too much relief and exhilaration to brood. Olympic fever grew as the Games drew to a close.

From sea to shining sea, Canadians were euphoric, for their athletes, who had never before won gold on their own territory, had taken fourteen gold medals, more than any team had ever won at the Winter Olympics. The final victory in the hockey game was the icing on the cake.

Tracy and Mark ventured downtown for the closing evening, although they had to link arms and put their heads down to burrow their way through the wall-to-wall bodies in order to move along the street. However, Robin and her mother stayed home to watch the closing ceremonies on TV. They laughed at the opening, with the fizzled fireworks and the clown pushing the fourth arm of the cauldron into place, and they revelled in the hilarious rendition of "The Maple Leaf Forever" with its Mountie Rockettes, jigging voyageurs, virtuoso fiddlers and inflatable beavers. But the most wonderful moment of all came two weeks later when Mark came to visit. As usual, he had Kippie in tow. Instead of whisking Mark away to herself, Tracy brought him into the dining room where Robin was doing her homework.

Tracy had a big smile on her face.

"Mark is here to see you, not me," she told her sister.

Robin looked up, surprised.

"I thought you'd like to know," said Mark, "that the Force has decided that you deserve a medal every bit as much as the Olympic athletes. It isn't gold, but I think you're going to like it."

Robin's eyes grew wide as saucers.

"Don't tease her," said Tracy. "Tell her."

Mark grinned.

"Well, it seems that, even though the surgery was successful, Kippie's knee problem, however slight, is enough to disqualify her from going into the training program, so—"

Mark paused, a tantalizing gleam in his eye.

"So?" shrieked Robin, instinctively knowing what he was about to tell her.

"So she's going to be given to you," he finished. "That is, if you want her," he added. "We're calling it the Kipple Award."

But Robin did not hear, for she was already on the floor, clutching the chocolate Lab to her chest.

Mark put his arm around Tracy's shoulder and guided her out of the room. As he glanced back before closing the door, he knew the right decision had been made.

Kippie did not even watch him go.

# THE WINDOW IN ROOM 21

The road that connects the Sunshine Coast Highway with the tiny community on the Pool Bay side of Pender Harbour is a glorious drive on a bright summer day. It meanders between forests and farms, then follows the perimeter of the lake for a breathtaking mile before rising steeply to the turnoff to Rumrunners' Point. After the fork, it drops rapidly towards a picturesque lagoon that divides two bays at the foot of the peninsula that is known by the locals as Millionaire Mile. However, on a cold winter night when travellers are rare, the road takes on a sinister aura, and the very features that make it beautiful in sunlight become threatening when enveloped in darkness.

One evening early in March, Anne Broadbent travelled the lake road. She was driving a Porsche, but the high-performance sedan was wasted on the journey for she was moving very slowly. There were no streetlamps on the winding road, and the only relief from the inky blackness came from the beam of the car's headlights, which illuminated the gleaming asphalt and provided fleeting glimpses of the thickly forested bank on the right. To the left of the vehicle was a blanket of darkness, a black void where the icy waters of the lake lurked, treacherously awaiting any driver who allowed a momentary lapse of attention to lure him to certain disaster.

Anne braked as she approached the horseshoe bend that preceded the rise. Five more minutes and she would be home. She carefully negotiated the curve, sensing rather than seeing the vast expanse of water beside her; then she accelerated up the hill as the road straightened out. The car came over the top of the rise and began the descent to the bay. Halfway down the hill, there was a fork where a road branched off and ran down to the pub on Pool Bay. Anne glanced to the left as she passed the junction. She caught a glimpse of the lights of the pub and the night became friendly again. One more turn, and the headlights would hit the ivy-draped cedar that stood like a sentry at the edge of her property. As she drove around the corner, the halogen lamps of the marina on Loon Bay sent a welcoming glow up into the night sky. Anne steered the Porsche into her driveway and pulled up in front of the Hampton House Inn.

She got out of the car and looked with satisfaction at her new residence. She had always wanted to run a country hotel, and the lottery win that had allowed her to buy Hampton House had made her dream come true. Anne had fallen in love with the heritage building the moment she set eyes on it. Its history, for her, was part of its charm. The mansion had been a private home during the early part of the twentieth century; then later, it had been used as a TB hospital for the Indians. The small chapel that remained at one end of the building was a legacy from the hospital days. Later, in the seventies, after a small country hospital had been built on Leeds Road, the house had become a bed and breakfast hotel, but sadly, the last owners had neglected the property. Hampton House Inn had stood idle for several years and a lot of repairs were needed to restore it to the point where it could reopen, but even in the small amount of light thrown from the porch, the building radiated old-world charm. Anne was pleased with her purchase. Life had taught her to invest her trust in things, rather than people, and the inn was providing the focus that she needed to keep moving forward. However, the weather was far too cold to stand and admire her acquisition, and anxious to get out of the bitter night air, she hurried inside.

Krypton was waiting to greet her. Given the vastness of the building and the fact that she was living alone, she was glad to have a large, protective dog on the premises. The black malamute was actually very gentle, but his appearance was daunting and his presence made her feel secure.

The hall was warm and blazing with light. The utility bills were high for the inn, but Anne did not believe in shortchanging herself on home comforts. She took off her coat and eyed her surroundings with pleasure. Above dark oak wainscoting, the walls were covered with flocked green and gold striped wallpaper, intermittently dotted with turn-of-the-century sepia photographs of hardy men, who, judging by their dress and the machinery in the background, were pioneers of the coastal logging industry.

Anne hung up her coat and started up the stairs, buoyed by the blast of heat that billowed after her from the main floor. However, as she approached the landing, she felt a chill in the air. The cold increased as she reached the top of the stairs. She moved towards the first room of the second floor. The icy draft was coming from under the door.

Krypton whimpered and he flattened his ears against his head.

Feeling apprehensive, Anne opened the door. The room was dark and freezing cold. She immediately saw the reason why. The window had been opened wide and the linen curtains undulated gently in the wintry breeze that drifted in from the sea.

How strange, she thought. I'm sure I closed all the windows before I went out. She crossed the room quickly. Without looking outside, she shut and latched the window. Then she returned to the welcome heat of the hall. But it was several hours before she grew warm again.

*       *       *

Edwina Beary was in a social mood. She had talked non-stop ever since the ferry had embarked from its mooring at Horseshoe Bay. Bertram Beary wished his wife would go back to the mystery novel she had been reading during their wait at the terminal, but sadly Ruth Rendell had been abandoned for the real-life characters that were in the forefront of Edwina's mind.

Gloomily, Beary watched the grey sea churning by. He should have stayed below on the car deck where MacPuff, the Siberian husky, was languishing in solitary confinement. The company would have been more congenial and the scene could not have been any less dismal. The day was so dark that he could see the reflection of the brightly lit lounge superimposed on the ocean outside the glass. A thin blonde with lanky hair and patchy skin sat in the seat behind them, and the image in the window gave Beary a clear view of her as she talked into her cellphone. Her voice added an irritating obbligato to that of his wife's, and in spite of the proximity of Edwina's incessant chatter, he could tell that the blonde was nervous and anxious, for her forehead was furrowed with tension and the fingers on the hand that did not hold the phone were drumming restlessly against the arm of her seat. Beary watched, fascinated, as the silver and turquoise bracelet on the thin wrist vibrated with the force of the little blows.

Suddenly, the blonde glanced at the window, and her eyes became wary as she caught the reflection of Beary's unashamed stare. The obbligato ceased, and she got up hastily and vanished from view. Resigned, Beary turned back to listen to Edwina, who was still delivering a monologue on the subject of her old school friend.

Edwina's tone was triumphant.

"It's such a perfect outcome," she chirped, "and who could have guessed it would turn out this way? A year ago, Anne was practically suicidal. Colin's defection utterly demoralized her. Thirty-five years of marriage, and then to turn around and leave her for a silly little bimbo who worked as a sales girl in his shop. I mean, it's not as if Anne isn't attractive. She may be sixty years old, but she's absolutely gorgeous. She makes me think of Joan Collins in 'Dynasty'."

Beary felt obliged to interject.

"She's an attractive enough woman," he admitted, "and very comely in a fresh sort of way, but the Joan Collins look didn't materialize until after the divorce. It seems to me that the new image is a byproduct of her lottery win."

"Well, yes." Edwina conceded the point. "She did go out and buy herself a fabulous designer wardrobe, and it's all high-end Laura Mercier make-up as opposed to a dab of cheap lipstick for special occasions. I believe she's had a few acupuncture sessions to get rid of the worst wrinkles too—but then, that's part of her husband's come-uppance, isn't it? I mean, not only did she scoop the pool six months after he divorced her, which means he can't touch a penny of the money, but in spite of her age, she's also become far more attractive than the whey-faced little piece of fluff he abandoned her for." Edwina caught sight of her reflection in the window and checked that her own neatly styled blonde hair was suitably in place. "I'm so happy for Anne," she added, unnecessarily smoothing an eyebrow into line. "Colin must be feeling agonies of regret."

"I always liked Colin Broadbent," said Beary mutinously, "and he has the best fly and tackle shop in the Lower Mainland. I agree that his behaviour has been highly regrettable, but I have no intention of boycotting his business just because he and Anne have split up. And she's certainly getting her own back. She really dug the knife in when she bought her new car. Colin drove at the Westwood Race Track in his youth. His big ambition was to own his own Porsche."

"Serves him right," said Edwina shortly. "He should have treated his wife better."

"As I recall, he always treated her very well. Until his bout of middle-aged lunacy, they were a very happy couple. But then, who knows what goes on under the surface?"

Edwina sniffed. "Under *his* surface, maybe—certainly not under hers. Anne's sweet personality goes right through to the core. She offered us one of her guest rooms, you know, but, of course, I had to refuse. Juliette would be offended if we didn't stay with her."

"I should think so too," muttered Beary. "I like staying with our daughter. Very sensible of her and Stephen to buy a house that sits between the fish and chip shop and the pub."

"That's irrelevant," said Edwina. "The Hampton House Inn is right across the road from the fish and chip shop, and you could walk the three extra steps to the pub. Actually," Edwina digressed, "Juliette tells me that the Pool Bay Pub has new owners. They've fancied it up and renamed it. It's now called Barringer's Break. It's about time, too, when you consider the clientele they get from the Royal Van Yacht Club."

Beary grunted his disapproval.

"Don't worry," said Edwina. "The pub hasn't closed, but they've added a dining room that's big enough for large parties."

"Won't that be competition for your friend?"

"Not really. It might even bring her business." Edwina prattled on happily. "I'm really looking forward to seeing inside Anne's hotel," she said. "The last owners went bankrupt five years ago and it's been sitting idle ever since, but Anne has the money to restore it to its former glory. She's going to remodel the house as glamorously as she's made-over herself."

"Isn't Anne's new image rather wasted now that she's living up the coast and pursuing her dream of running a country hotel?" said Beary. "She can hardly swan around in her Gucky outfits while catering to the tourist trade."

"Gucci," Edwina corrected him. "And it's not a waste. There's lots of social life in Pender Harbour. Several movie stars and multi-millionaires have estates there. Anne's already gathered some very interesting acquaintances." Edwina looked smug. "She's made friends with an influential couple who own waterfront acreage on the point—Grant and Sandra Curtis. You must have heard of the Jamieson family."

"Of course I have. They own half of Vancouver … the half the Chinese haven't bought up."

Edwina flinched. "You shouldn't say things like that," she hissed. "One of these days, your mouth will cost you your seat on Council. There are a lot of Chinese in Burnside."

"True, and they would not be in the least offended," Beary said airily. "I'm acknowledging their industry and prosperity. Property is always a good investment. Old man Jamieson knew that too, though, of course, he originally made his fortune in pulp and paper. It was later that he branched out into real estate and food processing and God knows what else. He was one of the early pioneer barons of British Columbia."

"Exactly, and he left everything to his daughters with the condition that they take care of their mother—who, by the way, is still alive. Anne tells me Olivia Jamieson is one week away from her hundredth birthday."

"Ah," said Beary, seeing the light. "Anne's new friend is one of the Jamieson heiresses. What did you say her name was?"

"Sandra Curtis."

"Right. Now, didn't the other sister die? I'm sure I saw an obit in the paper a while back."

"Two years ago. Cancer. It was very sad. Sandra has sole control of the company now."

"Does she indeed? Well, Anne is certainly running with the elite, isn't she?"

"Better than that," said Edwina smugly. "Sandra Curtis introduced Anne to her brother-in-law. His name's Brandon Manning, and I gather he's very suave and debonair—he runs the fish-processing plant at Daniel Point, so he's very much a part of the family business. He owns a waterfront home and drives a Jaguar," she added gleefully. "Anyway, after two years as a widower, he's ready to make new attachments. Evidently, he's been very attentive to Anne."

"Has he indeed?" said Beary. "Well, she certainly won't have to worry that her new beau is after her money."

"I know," said Edwina. "It's so perfect. It's every woman's dream."

"What? To win the lottery and then top it off by marrying a billionaire?"

"No, of course not." Edwina looked scathingly at her spouse. "To grind a cheating ex-husband's face in the dirt," she retorted.

*       *       *

Anne looked in the fridge and saw her supply of milk was getting low. She ought to pick up some other items too, she thought, as she would be entertaining the Bearys while they were in the area. There was nothing she needed that could not be purchased from the convenience store at the marina. Most people avoided buying groceries there due to the high prices that the Browns were compelled to charge for the extra cost of bringing goods across the harbour, but money was not an issue for Anne and she knew the store could not stay in business without local support. Besides, she took pleasure in making such small shopping trips on foot. She was lonely since the divorce, and the everyday contact with workmen and storekeepers was far less threatening than the glamorous new friendships she had formed, for she was a shy person at heart and she never knew whether people liked her for herself or for her new-found wealth.

Telling Krypton to stay, Anne put on her coat and went out the door. Hampton House was built on a sloping bank above the channel that connected Loon Bay with the lagoon. Therefore, many of the guest rooms overlooked both lagoon and ocean. However, the entrance to the inn was on the landside where a wide parking area stretched the length of the building. Anne waved to the workman who was unloading roofing material from his van and walked round the garden path to the view side of the inn, noting as she did so the empty parking lot in front of the fish and chip shop on the other side of the road. Colonel Codfish would not open until the end of April when the tourist season began.

Once she reached the corner of her property, Anne paused to enjoy the pleasing outlook that always reminded her of a child's storybook map. It was a sweeping panorama that took in Pool Bay, Loon Bay, and the lagoon in between. The main road veered left past the fish and chip shop and encircled the lagoon, and at the far end of the pool, the entrance to the pub path was just visible where it cut between a lichen-covered outcropping and the parking lot of the Royal Vancouver Yacht Club outstation. Once past the RVYC, the road split into two. One branch rose up the hill to Millionaire Mile; the other continued round the lagoon, ending at the Loon Bay Marina and the grey, vaguely Tudor-looking building that housed the general store. A narrow footbridge spanned the channel, enabling boaters and inn patrons to go back and forth without needing to walk right around the lagoon. No cars were parked by the store, and the marina was empty, except for a handful of local boats that were moored there all year round. Winter was bleak in the harbour, but Anne found the desolation of the surroundings soothing. She craved peace and tranquility after the shocks and turbulence of the previous two years.

The day was clear, but very cold, and as Anne looked out to sea, she could see dark clouds hovering above the islands at the mouth of the harbour. She shivered. The sky looked ominous and forbidding. She had been looking forward to coming out for some fresh air, but now she felt the urge to complete her errand quickly and return to the warmth and security of the inn.

She hurried down the uneven stone steps. Below her property was a lane that ran parallel to the channel and dead-ended at the government docks. In the summer, the slope bordering the lane would be a mass of blackberry bushes, pink wild roses and purple periwinkle, but now it was simply a tangled mesh of bare branches with earth and ivy-covered rocks peeking through the brown fronds. Anne walked along the lane and crossed the footbridge. The day seemed almost preternaturally still, and the flag on the pole by the store hung limp and immobile. There was no perceptible change in the atmosphere, but as she walked up the ramp to the store entrance, she noticed a flicker of movement in the posters that lined the notice board on the wall. Then the birdhouse that hung from the front of the blue awning rotated to the right and hovered on a slight angle as if propelled by a steady stream of air.

As Anne opened the shop door, Billy Brown emerged. He grunted a brusque greeting and pointed at the birdhouse. "Weather's going to change," he said. Having delivered this prediction, he plodded down the steps and turned towards the docks. Anne did not doubt his word. The crusty old marina owner was an expert on matters nautical and meteorological. He was also well versed in local gossip. Anne had a sudden thought. She let the door swing shut again and called to Billy.

"Billy, you've lived here a long time, haven't you?"

Billy had already reached the top of the ramp, but he paused and turned back.

"Forty years or so. What do you want to know?"

"Where can I get information about the people who lived at the inn? I know the basic background, but none of the local history books tell much about things that actually happened there."

Billy's weathered face cracked into a grin.

"You want the stuff that the real-estate people didn't tell you, don't you?"

Anne nodded.

"Well," he said, "that won't be in the guidebooks. But there is a book—it was written in the seventies—and I think we have a copy tucked away in the back of the store. You ask my wife. She'll dig it out for you."

Anne was puzzled.

"How can you possibly know that the information I want isn't in the guidebooks? I haven't even told you what I'm researching."

Billy's grin grew even wider.

"You want to know about the window, don't you? That's the story you're after. The window in room twenty-one."

Anne's eyes widened.

"Yes." She waited expectantly, but Billy was aggravatingly silent. "Well, if you know," she continued, attempting to conceal her exasperation, "why make me read a book? Can't you tell me?"

"Just get the book. It can explain far better than I can."

Billy waved a farewell and started down the gangway.

Anne called after him, "Well, at least tell me the title!"

Without looking back, Billy bellowed an answer.

"*Ghosts of the Sunshine Coast*," he shouted. He plodded down the ramp and disappeared around the storage shed on the end of the floats.

Anne felt an inner chill that matched the temperature of the air outdoors. Feeling anxious and apprehensive, she went into the store and gathered the grocery items on her list. Then, directed by Billy's wife, she entered the back room, which was lined with shelves crammed with boxes and ancient items of inventory. Anne flinched. Judging by the layers of dust, all the contents had long been hidden from the light of day. She found the book that she wanted in a pile in the corner. The cover was brown with age, but once she wiped off the grime, an eerie illustration of an old house emerged. With a start, she recognized the building. It was Hampton House.

Uneasily, she returned to the cash desk at the front of the store. As she paid for her purchases, she watched the progression of black clouds in the otherwise motionless seascape on the far side of the window. When she left the store, the air was eerily still, and it seemed even colder than when she had first come out. She set her shopping bag on the stone planter at the side of the store and went into the post office to pick up her mail. Nothing personal, she saw sadly—only an array of bills and a communication from her lawyer. She gathered up her bags and started back across the bridge. The water in the channel was motionless and the lagoon was a glassy reflection of the winter sky. The tide was getting ready to turn.

As she neared the middle of the bridge, a strong breeze sprang up, blowing hard off the ocean. She glanced out to sea and saw that the black scudding clouds were now almost overhead. All of a sudden, it started to rain, heavy drops pounding onto the treated-hemlock planks, instantly transforming the bridge into a black, slippery obstacle course. Anne put up her umbrella, but before she could progress any further, the wind veered to the northwest. A gust swept her against the railings, and the drops of rain turned to freezing hail that blew sideways and whipped into her face. She put down her umbrella again, for it was threatening to blow inside out, and forged her way to the far side of the bridge. Distantly, over the howling of the wind, she could hear the wail of a siren. As she stepped onto the road, the hailstones miraculously softened and expanded into huge fluffy snowflakes. The air became white around her as the swirling blizzard hit. Fighting her way against the white squall, she looked up towards the sanctuary of the inn.

The window in room twenty-one was open again.

*     *     *

"The weatherman didn't forecast this." Beary turned the windshield wipers onto high and peered through the swirling flakes that raced in a continuous stream towards the car window.

"We should never have stopped for coffee in Sechelt," said Edwina. "Do be careful," she added. "We don't want to end up in the lake."

Beary put the Jeep into four-wheel drive and negotiated the next corner. The road straightened out for a merciful stretch, but as they approached the next curve, a dark figure materialized out of the white haze.

"What's that?" Edwina squinted, trying to make out the shape on the road.

"Looks like a cop directing traffic. There must have been an accident."

Beary slowed and came to a standstill. As he drew up, the blue-jacketed figure came round to the side of the car. Beary rolled down the window.

"What's happened?" he asked.

"A car's gone off the road. There are emergency crews around the corner."

"Is it serious?"

The policeman nodded. "It's a bad one. A woman lost control at the hairpin bend and went into the lake. The car is still there. They had to send divers down to get her out."

"Is it that slippery at the bend?"

"No, you'll be OK. The accident wasn't caused by the weather. The squall didn't hit until after we got here and there were skid marks on the road. She must have been speeding."

"Can we get round?"

"Yes. You can get through but be careful. The ambulance is blocking the left side of the road, and there's a squad car and a fire truck behind it. Just go slow. I'll walk you round."

The constable walked ahead and beckoned them on. Beary followed slowly. As he rounded the corner, he saw the ambulance. The rear doors stood open and paramedics and firemen were congregated behind the vehicle. The police car and fire-truck were parked further up by the hairpin, and a handful of people stood nearby in the small grove of fir trees that overlooked the lake. They were pointing down into the water.

As Beary drove past, he glanced toward the ambulance. The crew was sliding a stretcher into the back of the vehicle. He caught a glimpse of lank blonde hair trailing across the pillow and a silver and turquoise bracelet on the thin wrist that lay ominously still at the woman's side.

*      *      *

Anne hurried upstairs and slammed the window shut. Then she went down to the kitchen, made herself a cup of coffee and sat down with the book of ghost stories.

She skipped the first three stories and began to read when she reached the section that dealt with Hampton House. It was a sad story that dated back more than half a century.

*In the summer of 1964, a dance band called The Wanderers was performing at the Whittaker's Hotel in Sechelt. The group had been brought in from Vancouver, and one of the vocalists, a particularly good-looking performer named Shane Paladin, was especially popular with the young women. One of the girls caught his eye. She was an extremely pretty teenager named Marnie Rhodes and she worked as a maid at the hospital in Loon Bay. Paladin used to drive up to meet her after work and they were frequently seen drinking together at the Pool Bay Pub, or on her days off, lying about at the swimming hole on the lake. Towards the end of the summer, the inevitable happened and Marnie became pregnant. Paladin had no intention of settling down, and one night they were seen quarrelling at the pub. They were both drinking heavily and the argument escalated until Marnie burst into tears and ran outside. Paladin followed and they could be heard yelling at each other in the parking lot. The proprietor of the pub went out to intervene, but as he came out the door, he saw them getting into Paladin's car. The car sped off down the hill. Paladin was driving, and whether it was due to speed, or because the two were fighting, he lost control at the hairpin bend. The car went off the road and plunged down the bank into the lake. It didn't sink right away because it landed on a rocky ledge, but it was tilting and slowly going over. Paladin managed to escape, but the girl was drowned.*

Anne felt a chill as she read the next line.

*When the divers went down to bring the girl up, they found her hand wedged inside the handle of the window on the passenger door. She must have been trying to open the window.*

Before she could read any further, there was a knock at the door. Anne put down the book and went into the hall. Artie Briggs, her contractor was standing on the step.

"The plumbers are here," he told her. "We'll need to turn the water off for half an hour."

Anne thanked him for letting her know. Briggs hovered on the doorstep.

"Did you hear what happened down at the lake?" he asked. Without waiting for a response, he continued. "There's been an accident—at the hairpin bend. It was Judy Parsons. You've probably met her—I see her at the pub all the time. She's a shipper-receiver with Jamieson Processing and she was on her way to their annual employee brunch. They were hosting it at Barringer's in the new restaurant. I guess she was in a hurry to get to the party. Anyway, she lost control and went off the road into the lake."

Anne paled. She remembered the siren she had heard earlier.

"Is she all right? Did she manage to escape?"

"No, they had to send divers down. She must have been in the water at least twenty minutes."

"Why couldn't anyone get to her faster?"

"There was no one there." The contractor's eyes bulged with excitement. Gossip was a coastal industry and he was equally proficient in spreading information as he was in laying roof tiles. "It was pretty bizarre. No one would have known she was in the lake, but she was talking to her boss on her cellphone at the time. He heard her scream and then the line went dead, so he knew she must have had an accident. She'd just told him that she was coming along the last stretch before the hill, so he knew where to direct the emergency crew."

Anne cut in and stopped the flow.

"Her boss? Do you mean Brandon Manning?"

"Yes. He was at the staff party, and he called to see why she wasn't there yet. I gather she was one of the organizers, so he was a bit ticked that she hadn't arrived. Evidently she was coming up from town, but she missed the ferry so she was running late. I guess she was speeding. Manning is going to feel pretty bad for having told her to get the lead out."

"Yes, he will," said Anne soberly. "That's horrible."

"Yup, it's pretty sad all right," conceded Briggs. He leaned in closer and riveted Anne with a hypnotic stare. "You know what else they say," he continued. "Her car was an old Ford and it didn't have any of these electronic gizmos that you get today. Everything in the car was manual. And when the divers reached her, they had a hard time pulling her free because her hand was locked around the handle of the car window. Creepy, isn't it? Imagine the poor girl trying to get out."

Briggs shook his head gravely and turned to leave.

"Don't forget to fill your sink and kettle if you want water," he called over his shoulder as he plodded across to the plumber's van at the far end of the parking lot.

Anne closed the door and returned to the kitchen. She turned on the tap, but as she held the kettle under the stream of water, she found her hand was shaking.

*      *      *

Beary stood in Juliette's kitchen and looked out the window. The snow had stopped and the morning sky was clear and a glorious blue. The brown gable and the attic window of the Hampton House Inn peeked out above the huge Colonel Codfish sign on the back of the adjacent building. The giant cod was obtrusively visible in spite of a fig tree that covered half the wall, and all Stephen's efforts to build trellises and screens had been unsuccessful in blocking it out.

Edwina emerged from the guest room, cellphone in hand, and vetoed Juliette's offer to put the kettle on.

"We've been invited to Anne's for coffee," she announced. She slipped her phone into her pocket and put on her coat. "You too, dear," she added to Juliette, "if you'd like to come."

"Another time," said Juliette. "I have a couple of calls to make."

Edwina shook her head at Beary, who was preparing to clip a leash onto MacPuff's collar. "No, he can't come," she said firmly. "He'll have to stay here with Purdy and Quasar." These were Juliette's dogs. Ignoring Beary's mutinous scowl, Edwina opened the front door and beckoned imperiously. Beary apologized to MacPuff, tucked his scarf snugly around his neck and followed his wife out the door.

Five minutes later, they were settled around the fireplace in the parlour that adjoined Anne's kitchen. It was a cozy space, with a small wood-framed window overlooking the flagstone patio between the main building and the ivy-draped wall of the old hospital chapel. Beary surveyed the room, noting with approval the bulging bookcases and wildlife watercolours that lined the walls. The armchairs were worn, but comfortable, and the blazing fire in the hearth bathed the room in a warm yellow light. Anne's coffee was excellent, and the array of cakes and cookies she set by Beary's wing chair was mouth-watering. Krypton lay in front of the fire. He was a huge dog, and as he stretched out on the carpet, chewing and squeaking a green velour frog that was clearly a favourite toy, he filled most of the space between the chairs. Beary turned to observe his hostess. Edwina was right about the Joan Collins look, he decided. Anne was dressed casually, but the clothes were stylish and expensive, and her make-up had the delicately understated glow that he associated with fashion magazines. She was remarkably attractive, but in spite of her newly acquired affluence, he did not think she looked happy. When he had met her before, she had always struck him as a deeply contented woman. Now there was a new vitality, but it came at the cost of her former serenity. It was too bad, he thought. In spite of Edwina's opinions to the contrary, he had always liked Colin Broadbent. He and Anne had seemed right together.

Krypton interrupted Beary's deliberations by dropping the frog into his lap. Assuming correctly that this was an offer intended as a trade in exchange for a cookie, Beary obliged by delving in his pocket and fishing out one of MacPuff's dog biscuits. The dog devoured it in three bites and fixed Beary with a concentrated stare. Beary communed companionably with his new friend while Anne and Edwina talked. Their conversation appeared to be a series of female confidences, so, realizing he had been relegated to the same category as the dog and assumed deaf, he shut his eyes and leaned back to enjoy the fire and to eavesdrop on the snatches of gossip that drifted his way.

Anne's voice was low, but her tone was intense. She obviously felt the need to unburden herself.

"The divorce was my fault," she murmured. "I was so angry. I told him to leave. I hated him so much for betraying me. I couldn't bear to have him near me. But I miss what we used to have. I miss the companionship. We used to laugh so much, and we did so much together. We had so many interests in common."

Edwina raised her eyebrows.

"You sound as if you're sorry you let him go. Don't forget he's the one who caused the break-up by getting involved with that creature from his shop."

Anne sighed.

"The truth is he was having a bit of trouble … you know, in the bedroom department. He was feeling inadequate, and I was busy with my job and simply not taking his problems seriously. He was ripe for the picking when that female set her cap at him."

Edwina sniffed.

"Yes, well, he didn't have to fall off the tree. You're the injured party. Stop feeling sorry for him and start enjoying yourself. What about this new beau who's been squiring you about?"

"Brandon? Oh, yes. I have to admit he's tremendously attractive, but it's not the same."

"Most women would give their eye teeth to be in your situation," Edwina pointed out. She glanced across at Beary to make sure he was asleep. "Very few women," she continued in a low voice, "get the chance to trade in their husbands for someone new and exciting, let alone be able to do it in luxury."

Anne sighed.

"I know. But how can the thrill of being courted by someone new replace the deep bonds of a thirty-year-old relationship? My social life has a lot of surface glamour these days, but there's no substance to the relationships."

"That will come with time. You're still hurt. You're resisting getting involved."

"Yes, I know. Emotionally, I'm a hollow woman. The only driving force in my life right now is the work on the inn." Anne faltered, and a shadow crossed her face. "The trouble is, even that is not proving to be as enjoyable a project as I'd hoped. I'm starting to get uneasy being here by myself."

"But you don't have to live here all alone," said Edwina. "You'll be hiring staff once you're ready to open. Why don't you engage a personal secretary or manager right now? You can afford it, and you'll have someone to work with and help you plan the project."

Anne looked pensive.

"I think I will do that," she said. "When I first came, I enjoyed the solitude. Things were so tumultuous after the break-up. I was living on an emotional rollercoaster for months, and all I wanted was peace … just the freedom to quietly come and go as I pleased. But now …" She hesitated and bit her lip.

"What's wrong? Has something happened?"

"It's the window." Anne's voice dropped to a whisper. "It's uncanny, and quite honestly, I'm finding it very unnerving."

Beary opened his eyes and sat up.

"What window would that be?" he asked curiously.

"The window in room twenty-one. It won't stay shut. I close it and I secure the latch, and the next time I look, it's open again."

"That's bizarre," said Edwina. "Is someone playing tricks on you?"

"I wish it were as simple as that," said Anne. She pointed to the book that lay facedown on the coffee table. "I read that book last night. It was written a quarter of a century ago. It's a series of ghost stories about the Sunshine Coast … local legends, that sort of thing."

"Don't tell me the inn is haunted?" said Beary with relish.

"According to that book, it is," said Anne.

"Really?" Edwina picked up the book and studied the cover. "Goodness! This is your hotel, isn't it?"

"Yes." Anne related the story of Marnie Rhodes while her guests listened, fascinated. The light from the flames in the fireplace danced on the walls, and the flickering movement created an eerie sensation of other presences in the room. Beary's interest was piqued by the tale.

"Intriguing," he said as Anne finished. "I get the significance of the closed window, but how does that relate to the inn?"

"Hampton House was a TB hospital at the time. The girl worked here as a maid. The autopsy was performed here … in what is now room twenty-one. And it was after that that the rumours of a ghost began. The staff noticed that, no matter how often they closed the window in room twenty-one, it was always open the next time they checked. Later, a psychic was called in. She insisted that there was light in the room where the autopsy had been performed." Anne's lip trembled. "It's such a horrible thought … to think that her spirit is constantly trying to escape … that she's trying to get out the window. And what makes it worse, yesterday it happened all over again. Another accident at the same corner … another woman trapped in her car in that cold black water."

Edwina cut in briskly.

"Well, you can't possibly connect yesterday's incident with your book of ghost stories. There will have been bad accidents on that corner for the simple reason that it's a dangerous bend and people drive too fast. And as for the window, there's probably some logical explanation—a tremor, or a lack of stability in the building that works the latch loose. You're not to work yourself into a state over this. Would you like me to stay here tonight? I'll even sleep in the room if it'll help put your mind at rest."

Beary regarded his wife fondly. Edwina's drill-sergeant management skills and total lack of imagination were two of her most irritating qualities, but he had to admit that she never quailed at a challenge and she always tackled what she perceived to be her duty without flinching.

"Oh, Edwina, you don't have to do that," said Anne. "I'll be all right. I love this old house. But it's very disconcerting."

"What you need is more company," said Edwina firmly. "You may have needed peace and solitude after the divorce, but now you need to start socializing again."

"I am socializing. The local residents have been very hospitable. Besides, I see people all day long because there are so many workmen coming in and out. And speaking of socializing, Grant and Sandra Curtis are throwing a party on the weekend to celebrate Sandra's mother's hundredth birthday. It's a glitzy formal affair and they said to invite you to come. Your daughter too. They have a magnificent home on the other side of the harbour. You'll love it."

Edwina demurred.

"We can hardly invite Juliette without Stephen," she said.

"Your son-in-law will already be there," said Anne. "They've hired his band for the occasion."

Beary blinked.

"Country and western music for a formal party?"

"He'll be out in the pavilion. Won't it be a lovely surprise for him to see his wife there as a guest?"

"Indeed, it will," said Edwina. She turned to Beary. "Don't you dare tip him off ahead of time."

Beary turned to their hostess. "I take it then that we're coming."

"Of course you are," said Anne. "Four fit comfortably in the Porsche, so I'll be able to drive you. I'll pick you up at seven."

Edwina frowned.

"I don't have anything suitable to wear for a formal event. We usually do nothing but walk the dogs, go boating and read books when we're on the coast."

Anne beamed at her friend.

"I'll lend you something. It'll be fun ... just like when we were at school. We're about the same size. We'll go through my wardrobe and you can pick whatever you like."

Edwina's eyes sparkled, but the glimmer of joy faded as swiftly as it had appeared.

"What about Bertram?" she said. "His tux is in town."

"Good," said Beary. "I'll stay home with MacPuff."

Edwina firmly squashed that suggestion.

"No, you won't. You can borrow one from Stephen's musician pals. A couple of the guitarists have beer bellies that match your girth."

Beary opened his mouth to argue, but Edwina did not notice. She had already turned back to Anne and was discussing what she might wear for the occasion. Beary was astonished at the ease with which the topic of conversation switched from ghosts to designer clothes. Recognizing a lost cause when he saw one, he tuned out, gave Krypton another dog biscuit and leaned back to enjoy the fire and reflect on what he had learned about relationships past and present.

The rest of the visit passed peacefully. Beary sat by the fire and read about the ghosts of the Sunshine Coast, and when the ladies disappeared to the top floor to explore Anne's walk-in closet, he made a discreet phone call to Broadbent Fly and Tackle Shop. There were two sides to every story, he thought, and he was rather keen to hear the other version. By the time Edwina returned, looking singularly pleased with herself and with a dress bag draped over her arm, it was nearly four o'clock. They bid farewell to Anne and headed back across the road. The temperature had dropped again and the snow crunched underfoot as they walked.

As they started up Juliette's driveway, Beary turned and glanced up to the top floor of the inn. The low winter sun was beaming against the face of the building, causing shimmering rectangles where the rays hit the glass panes of the windows.

But the square at room twenty-one was black and hollow. The window was open again.

$$* \qquad * \qquad *$$

The next day, Juliette was scheduled to volunteer at her children's school, so she left with Jennifer and Laura first thing in the morning. Beary and Edwina leashed all the dogs and set off along the rocky path that provided a scenic shortcut to the pub. The snow had hardened but was not packed down to ice, so walking was not yet treacherous. Beary forged ahead with MacPuff and Quasar, the powerful German shepherd that Juliette had adopted the previous year. Edwina followed with Purdy, the more manageable chocolate Lab.

The path hugged the shoreline for a hundred yards and then entered a tunnel formed from the frost-covered branches of bowed vine maples. At the far end of the tree tunnel was a small garden that, in summer, was dominated by two huge *gunneras manicata* towering above the tiny creek that snaked back and forth between the flowerbeds. Now only mounds of snow marked the truncated piles of the giant rhubarb plants. Beary and Edwina crossed the wooden bridges that forded the creek. Then they climbed the flight of steps to the deck of Barringer's Break and walked out into the parking lot.

They continued past the pub and entered the network of trails that led to a marine park in the east and the lake to the north. In the forest, the snow cover was thinner and walking became easier, although, in places, they had to duck where the weight of the snow had bent branches across the path. Beary and Edwina unclipped the leashes and ambled in leisurely fashion while the dogs raced back and forth, dislodging snow from the bushes and sniffing at ferns and tree stumps. Beary was amused to see how Purdy was careful never to go in front of the other two animals. MacPuff, on the other hand, stayed well ahead, all the while eying Quasar warily, unsure as to which alpha male was going to be the leader. Pack order was very important to MacPuff. Fortunately, Quasar was good-natured, so the walk continued without incident.

The day was clear and bright, and the fresh air was exhilarating. Even after circling the circumference of the marine park, Beary did not feel tired. Therefore, he did not object when Edwina proposed that they take the longer loop back and follow the trail that headed inland to the lake. Twenty minutes later, the forest thinned out to reveal the swimming hole, which was situated a few yards from the main road.

Beary picked up a stick and the dogs ran around him, barking excitedly, but instead of hurling it into the water, he threw it along the shore. The cold snap had been so intense that there had been ice on the lake in December, and the water was still far too cold, even for MacPuff. Beary was intent upon the dogs, so he did not notice the flurry of activity on the road. Edwina was the first to see what was going on.

"Look," she said. "There's a police car at the accident site."

Beary glanced up. "So there is," he said. "Let's go see what they're doing."

He called the dogs and leashed them. As he bent to clip the lead on MacPuff's collar, he glimpsed a patch of red caught on a clump of snow-crusted ferns.

"What's that?" asked Edwina.

"Felt, I think." Beary detached the piece of cloth. "It's shaped like a flower."

Edwina took it from him and peered at it.

"It's a napkin ring," she declared. She peeled the felt band away from the flower and demonstrated how it would work by looping it round her fingers. "The centre is Velcro," she added, "so it probably had some other item—a theme token, or a candy—attached on top. It's the sort of thing you'd see at a banquet. Goodness knows what it's doing in the woods."

Beary was losing interest. "Bit fancy for a picnic," he said and moved on.

Edwina tucked it in her pocket.

"Finders, keepers," she said. "I'll take it home for Laura. She can use it for a doll hat. She still plays with Barbies."

She followed Beary out to the road, which was now clear as the snow had melted off the asphalt and only remained as a crisp white border along the soft shoulder. A solitary policeman stood at the hairpin bend, jotting notes in his book. He glanced up when Beary and the dogs approached.

"That one doesn't look too friendly," he commented, eying MacPuff.

"No," Beary acknowledged. "He has a tendency to chew anything that smacks of officialdom. We've managed a truce with Canada Post, but I wouldn't want to test him on the constabulary. My son is an RCMP detective, but fortunately he's a plain-clothes officer, so it's safe to invite him to dinner. My niece, Adrian, however, is another matter. She's posted up here, actually. You must know her. Constable Wright."

The policeman's face relaxed into a grin.

"Yes, I know Adrian," he said, "and she's told me lots about her uncle. You must be Councillor Beary."

Beary tried not to look smug. He always mentioned his RCMP connections when talking with police officers. Such tactics generally resulted in a satisfactory loosening of tongues.

"Bad business yesterday," he said, nodding toward the lakeshore. "We came through shortly after she went into the lake. Horrible way to go."

"Actually," said the policeman, "she hasn't gone yet … though it's not likely that she'll recover."

"She's not dead?"

"No. She's in a coma. They were able to get her heart and lungs going again. It's remarkable, considering the time she was in the lake. I gather it's a result of the water being so cold, but it'll be a miracle if she pulls through. Silly woman. She was speeding and talking on her cellphone. Mind you, it was because of the phone call that we knew she'd gone into the lake. She was talking to her boss and he heard her scream as she lost control, so he was able to report it immediately."

"How did he know where to send the emergency crew?"

"He was at a company brunch at the restaurant up the hill, and the woman was on her way to join him. She was coming up from town and she'd missed the ferry, so she was running late—which explains why she was speeding—and just before she lost control, she told him she was almost at the foot of the hill, so he knew right away that she must have crashed at the hairpin bend. If he hadn't reported it, she'd still be down there and everyone would be wondering why she was missing. It's strange though," he continued, pointing towards the road, where the skid marks were still black against the asphalt. "You'd think she'd have lost control going round the corner, and that she'd have braked further into the hairpin. But these marks indicate that she jammed on the brakes before she went into the bend."

"Well, if she was going too fast and realized she couldn't take the corner at that speed, wouldn't it be logical for her to brake?" said Edwina.

"Not like that," said Beary, comprehending the policeman's point. "It's as if she panicked just as she reached the corner. She didn't even start to go round the corner. She just shot straight off the end and into the lake."

The policeman gestured towards the soft shoulder.

"She'd have slowed a bit as the car went across the gravel. It looks as if she skidded down the bank. The car would have been only partially submerged because there's a granite ledge that juts out about four feet below the waterline. If she'd acted fast enough, she could have escaped through the window, but the ledge is only about three feet wide, so the car would have slid down into the deeper water fairly quickly."

"Maybe she was unconscious after the crash," said Edwina.

"No, she must have tried to escape because her hand was clenched around the handle that controlled the window."

Edwina and Beary exchanged significant glances, but the policeman did not notice. He shut his notebook and headed for his patrol car. Beary and Edwina waved goodbye to him and set off for home. They had been out a long time and they did not fancy another uneven trek through the forest trails so they decided to walk back along the road. Within five minutes they had crested the hill and were heading down towards the harbour.

They passed the ivy-covered cedar at the foot of Anne's driveway and followed the curve of the road down to the lagoon, but before they started up Juliette's driveway, Beary could not resist the compulsion to glance back towards the Hampton House Inn. As he expected, the window was open and the green curtains were billowing in the breeze.

*       *       *

Saturday was the night of the party. Anne picked up the Bearys at six-thirty and chattered happily as she chauffeured them round to the Madeira Park side of the harbour. A lot of cars were already lined along the street when they arrived at the Francis Peninsula estate. Beary hoisted the trousers on his borrowed tuxedo and followed Anne into the spectacular residence that had been built during the late sixties on the Jamiesons' ocean-view property. Beary had often seen the house from the water when cruising past in the *Optimist*, and from that angle it had reminded him of an upside-down wedding cake layered in tiers down the cliffside, but he had not appreciated how large the building was. The front hall opened onto a vast concourse with twenty-foot ceilings. The room blazed with light from chandeliers within and from tiki torches and floodlights outside, which cast a spectral glow on the precipitous drop to the ocean and also lit the grounds on either side of the building. Round tables covered with royal blue tablecloths and tempting assortments of hot and cold canapés were spaced about the room. The area was already overflowing with guests, and white-jacketed waiters carrying trays of champagne glasses wove their way amid the crowd.

As Beary helped Anne, Edwina and Juliette with their coats, a familiar voice rang out behind him and he turned to see Bob Brady, the Member of Parliament for the Sunshine Coast.

"Beary, you old reprobate! What are you doing here?"

Beary introduced his female entourage and explained the connection between Edwina and her friend. Brady eyed Anne appreciatively.

"I read about your win," he said, "but I didn't realize the jackpot had gone to such a charming lady." He grinned at Beary. "You're doing singularly well tonight, old man. Quite the bevy of beauties."

He zeroed in on Edwina, who was resplendent in the jade green satin creation that she had borrowed from Anne's closet. "Now, I know your old man from way back," he said solemnly, "so I'm well aware that you, being his wife, deserve a medal. Let me find you a glass of champagne." He winked at Juliette. Then he tucked his arm around Edwina's waist and whisked her away. Beary gaped after them. Juliette gurgled with laughter.

"You have to admit she looks nice, Dad," she said.

"Nonsense," growled Beary. "There'll be some item he wants to get through that will need the support of local councils. He'll be working on Edwina with the mistaken belief that she has influence over me."

"She does have influence over you," Juliette pointed out. "Mother organizes all our lives."

"Mere governance," said Beary. "She doesn't control my thinking."

"Whatever," said Juliette. "Where's the band?" she asked Anne. "I want to go and surprise Stephen."

"They'll be in the gazebo." Anne pointed towards the garden. A glassed-in octagon glowed with light at the far end of the lawn, and the flickering silhouettes on the windows indicated that dancing was already in progress. A distant, but pounding beat could just be heard, subtly penetrating the shrill hubbub from the crowd in the room. Juliette draped her stole around her shoulders, swept her long brown hair clear of the fabric and floated off towards the door. Beary looked after her affectionately.

"That was her high-school graduation dress," he said. "She can still fit into it. It's probably the only formal gown she's ever owned."

"She's lovely," said Anne. "Come on, let's go mingle and I'll introduce you to our hosts."

She ushered Beary forward, but before they could navigate their way into the crowd, a handsome, grey-haired man approached and took Anne aside. Beary noticed his proprietary manner. If this was Brandon Manning, Edwina was right when she insisted that her friend had a serious admirer.

The newcomer appeared oblivious to the fact that Anne had someone with her.

"There you are," he said, enfolding her hands in his own. "I've been watching for you. I hope you're not annoyed that I didn't call earlier, but we've been having a difficult time. To be honest, if this party wasn't for Olivia's one-hundredth birthday, we'd have cancelled. You heard about what happened at the lake."

"I did. Brandon, I'm so sorry," said Anne, confirming Beary's speculation about the identity of the newcomer. "I gather it was one of your employees," she added sympathetically.

Brandon nodded. "Yes. It was Judy Parsons. She's my shipper-receiver. She'd had to make an overnight trip downtown—a problem with one of our outlets—so she was on her way back. It was pretty horrible. I was talking to her when she went out of control. I heard her scream."

"That must have been traumatic," interjected Beary. "Did you hear anything that would indicate why she lost control?"

Brandon seemed mildly affronted at the interruption, but once Anne introduced Beary as her guest, he became a model of courtesy and answered the question.

"No," he said. "There wasn't any warning."

"Why was she on the phone?" Beary's tone was disapproving. "It's not only dangerous, it's illegal now."

"I know," said Brandon. "Judy was bad that way. She must have called me three times that morning. She phoned soon after seven-thirty to let me know she'd missed the ferry, and she called again once she was on the nine-thirty crossing. I was annoyed," he said ruefully. "She was in charge of the company brunch, and even though she'd organized everything ahead of time, she was supposed to be there to oversee. It created a bit of confusion because the caterers kept asking me about details that weren't my department at all. Anyway, we managed to get everything underway and the brunch went very well in spite of her absence, and when we were all milling around socializing, she called again to let me know she was on the lake road and would be there in a few minutes. By that time, I'd calmed down and was able to reassure her that everything was going all right, but she kept on asking about stuff that we'd already dealt with. After a couple of minutes, she announced that she should go as she was coming along the last stretch before the hill. She was about to ring off, and then I heard her gasp, and almost immediately afterwards, there was a bloodcurdling scream; then everything went silent. I realized right away that she must have had an accident, so I called 911. I knew it had to be the hairpin. And sure enough, she'd gone right off the road."

"Was she a good driver?" asked Beary.

Brandon shook his head.

"No. She tended to speed at the best of times, and if she was running late, she drove like a maniac. She was a nice enough girl, but she had some problems."

"Her only problem now is whether or not she'll survive," said Beary. "Have you heard anything more from the hospital?"

Brandon's face clouded. "No. There's been no change. It doesn't look good. I wanted to go round to see her, but they're not allowing any visitors other than family—and that's a joke, because her mother lives in Alberta and her only other relative is her brute of a husband. He's a surly individual. He came to the brunch, but he was so put out that Judy wasn't there, he went through to the pub and got drunk. We didn't know where he'd vanished to at the time, so we couldn't even tell him that his wife had been in an accident. It was only after they'd pulled her out of the lake that we found him. As far as I'm concerned, he was the root of all Judy's problems. You know, it's a strange thing, and maybe it's bad taste to say this, but if she hadn't screamed like that, I'd almost have wondered if she hadn't gone into the lake on purpose."

"Suicide? Why would you think that?"

"She'd got herself into a real fix, and I suspect her husband was the one who engineered it."

"What sort of fix?"

Brandon dropped his voice and leaned forward.

"I've been getting reports of under-the-table shipments going to some of the less scrupulous restaurants downtown and there's a very strong likelihood that she was fiddling the books … exaggerating the wastage so that quantities of fish could be sold privately."

"That's an odd sort of embezzlement," said Beary. "Is it lucrative enough to justify the risk of being caught?"

Brandon nodded.

"Absolutely. A cube van loaded with fish, especially if there's a quantity of high-end produce like crab or prawns, is worth more than ten thousand dollars. That much could be skimmed off once or twice a month."

Beary whistled.

"Close to a quarter of a million dollars a year … tax free too. That's big bucks."

"Exactly. I trusted Judy completely, but when I heard a rumour that we had a racket like that going on at the plant, I couldn't ignore it … and the reality is, it couldn't have been going on without her knowledge. She had to be involved."

"How did you find out?"

"From my sister-in-law. She has a godson who is a chef at the Four Seasons Hotel, and he always keeps his ear open for that sort of thing. There's nothing restaurateurs hate more than knowing they're paying the full shot for products when someone else is able to undercut their prices by buying stolen goods. But I should stop talking shop," said Brandon. "You're here to enjoy yourself, not listen to our problems." He gestured towards the blue-covered tables. "You must go and sample the appies. I think you'll find they're exceptional. Curtis Catering at its best." Having pointed Beary in the right direction, Brandon turned to Anne and slipped an arm around her shoulders. "Let me get you something too," he added softly.

Beary could see that his host wanted to have Anne to himself, so obligingly, he left and ambled over to a nearby table where a fashionably emaciated redhead was helping herself to canapés. The woman was piling her plate high, but she could afford to, Beary thought enviously, for she was built like a Watusi and her slender sheath of metallic silver displayed no bulges. Ornamental tangles of rhinestones and onyx dangled from her ears, and they swung like medieval maces every time she bent over the dishes. Beary moved to the other side of the table to examine the fare. He was contemplating which delicacy to start with when he heard a voice at his side.

"Those are good." A solemn child in pink taffeta pointed towards the hot tray of garlic prawns at the centre of the table. "They're Great-Granny's favourite."

"Are they?" said Beary. "Then I will definitely have to try them." He picked up a plate and loaded it liberally. Sensing he was under scrutiny, he looked down at the small girl. Her chin barely reached the top of the table. She handed him her own plate, and assuming that she wanted a refill, Beary obliged by serving her a generous portion of prawns. "And would Great-Granny be the lady who is celebrating her hundredth birthday?" he asked.

"Yes. This is her party."

"So who would Granny be?"

The minute Beary asked the question, he regretted it, instantly recalling that one of the Jamieson daughters had died of cancer two years previously, but the child seemed unconcerned and pointed towards a striking woman in black velvet on the far side of the room. Beary regarded the woman curiously. Sandra Curtis was a commanding presence. A chip off the old-man-Jamieson block, Beary decided. The Watusi confirmed the identification.

"That's Sandra Curtis," she said. "She's the head of Jamieson Enterprises. And the tall brunette standing beside her is her daughter, Sue Brady, who's married to the son of our local MP. Sue is an astute businesswoman too. She runs another of the family companies—Curtis Catering—it's a big firm. She's also Suzie's mother," she added, gesturing towards the blonde curls bobbing at the edge of the tabletop.

"Did the other Jamieson heiress have children too?" Beary asked.

"No," Suzie interjected smugly. "I'm the only granddaughter. One day I'm going to be as rich as Paris Hilton."

"Better behaved, I hope," said Beary, "though if you're descended from old man Jamieson and Bobby Brady, we can't hope for too much."

"It's too bad your auntie didn't have children," said the Watusi, moving around the table and good-naturedly ruffling Suzie's curls. "A few cousins would knock the spoiled-brat edges off you." She turned back to Beary. "The reality is that Sandra has always been the hard-working, family-oriented one. Shirley and Brandon were just interested in living a jet-set existence off other people's efforts. Of course, Shirley's gone now, so Brandon is a solitary leech."

Beary raised his eyebrows.

"I thought Brandon Manning earned his keep. Doesn't he run Jamieson Processing?"

"He does, but that's a minor subsidiary." The Watusi's tone was dismissing. "Sandra wouldn't give him anything more important than that. He's all charm and no competence. He didn't even pick up on the fact that one of his chief employees was skimming off thousands of dollars from the company. Beautiful but dumb, that's Brandon."

"My mom says Uncle Brandon only got a job with Great-Grandpa's company because Auntie Shirley wanted to marry him," Suzie volunteered. "She says he wouldn't notice a bullfrog in the lobster pot unless it leaped up and bit him."

Beary started to feel sorry for Anne's new suitor. No wonder he was courting Edwina's gentle friend. The Watusi helped herself to a second plateful and wandered off, pendulums swinging, into the crowd. Beary finished his last prawn and hunted for a napkin to wipe his fingers. He had been too busy eyeing the food to notice earlier, but now he saw the napkins were encased in rings which were attached to white silk flowers with gold centres.

"You can take that bit off," said Suzie, pointing at the gold protruding from the white silk petals. "It's a chocolate."

"So it is," said Beary. He detached the sweet from its base. Underneath was a circle of Velcro.

"Do you want the chocolate?" asked Suzie, eying it greedily.

"Why? Do you want it?"

"Yes, please, and could I have more prawns as well?"

"You certainly may," said Beary. He scooped another helping onto the child's plate. "Would you like the napkin ring as well," he added. "It would make a pretty hat for your Barbie dolls."

Suzie stared at him scornfully.

"I stopped playing with dolls when I was five," she said. "And my Barbies had their own hats. They didn't wear napkin rings."

"I stand corrected," said Beary, and helped himself to another plate of prawns. There were worse ways to spend an evening than sampling gourmet fare with a pint-sized glutton who had the scoop on the local jet-set gossip. He was beginning to be glad he came.

*        *        *

The following day was Sunday. Once the dogs had been walked, Juliette took the girls to their dance class. Stephen, however, planned to catch up on his marking, so Beary and Edwina left him in peace and headed to the pub for lunch.

They settled at a corner table by the window where they could both enjoy the panoramic view of Mount Daniel overlooking the bay. The pub was not busy. The only other occupants were two elderly couples seated at a table on the far side of the room and a grizzled, weather-beaten ancient who lounged on a stool at the bar. Even from across the room, Beary could see his piercing blue eyes framed in a network of spider-like creases that gave the impression he was perpetually squinting at the horizon. One of the local fishermen, Beary decided. He turned back to study the menu, but before he had read through all the entrées, a waitress materialized at their table.

"He will have mineral water and a Caesar salad," said Edwina, overriding Beary's directive to bring fish and chips and beer. "You drank enough last night to float the Jamiesons' yacht," she told her husband, "and I saw you and that child empty an entire platter of prawns between you. You can't indulge in heart-attack cuisine indefinitely. Something's going to give."

"Not you, obviously," muttered Beary. However, although he never would have admitted it to his wife, he was suffering some effects from the previous evening, so he did not protest. As the waitress headed for the kitchen with their order, a familiar figure came into the pub. It was Beary's niece, Constable Adrian Wright. She came across to greet them, but her expression was sober.

"Lovely to see you both, but I can't stop," she said.

"I gathered that from the uniform," said Beary. "What's up?"

"Juliette says you came along the lake road shortly after Judy Parson's accident. I was wondering if you saw any other vehicles."

Beary was surprised at the question.

"There were quite a few cars on the highway, but we didn't see anyone else on the lake road."

"Nothing passed you going the other way?"

"No. The road was deserted. Why?"

"Because we've had a report that another car may have been trying to overtake Judy Parson's vehicle. If the person driving that car didn't go back the other way, it could be someone who lives down in the bay."

"What makes you think there was another car?" Edwina asked.

"A lady who was walking her dog that morning called in to the station. Apparently, she heard a man cry out a warning. She didn't see him because she was on the trails, but she says the words were quite distinct. He said, 'Christ! Watch out behind you! Hit the brakes!'"

"Kind of contradictory," observed Beary.

"Yes, but if a car were coming up too fast on Parson's tail, and she tried to pull over and ended up sliding towards the lake, the warning would make sense."

"Are you implying that someone ran her off the road?"

"Not necessarily. We've raised Parson's car now, and there was no sign of damage to the rear end. There's damage all along one side, but that's from the rocks in the lake. But even if the other car didn't hit her, its presence might explain the reason she lost control. The accident could have been caused by dangerous driving."

"Hard to prove."

"I know. We need to trace the person who called out to warn Parsons. He would be able to describe the other car."

"He hasn't come forward?"

"No, so keep your ears open." Adrian patted her uncle on the shoulder. "I know how good you two are at picking up on local gossip. Here, I'll let you eat," she added, as the waitress appeared with two large Caesar salads.

Adrian waved goodbye and strode off. Beary picked up his fork and ruefully inspected his plate of greens.

"You know," he said as he speared a forkful of lettuce, "I've been wondering about that accident back in the sixties. It's strange that there's been another almost identical incident."

"Pure coincidence," said Edwina. "There can't possibly be a connection."

"All the same, it'd be very interesting to hear Shane Paladin's version of the accident. I wonder what happened to him."

"Well, that's easy. He was an entertainer. Call your daughter. Philippa will be able to help. She's doing a radio show with Julian Buchanan right now."

"Buchanan? The bandleader? God, he's been around for centuries. I didn't know he was still alive."

"He certainly is," said Edwina. "Philippa says he has more energy than she does. Buchanan will know everyone who was on the circuit in the sixties."

"Yes, he will. Good thinking," said Beary. "I forgive you the Caesar salad." He pulled out his cellphone. "I'll call her right now."

"She won't be home. She had an opera-in-the-schools engagement today."

"Doesn't matter," said Beary. "I'll leave her a message."

He did so in the loud, precisely enunciated tones he used in the council chamber.

"You didn't have to boom," Edwina reproved him. "The entire restaurant will have heard."

"All five people," Beary retorted. "You are singularly crotchety today," he added. "Sore feet from hopping around the gazebo with Bob Brady?"

"Not at all. I enjoyed myself. It's not as if you were in any state to dance. Besides, I learned some interesting gossip. Did you know Bob's son is married to Sandra Curtis's daughter? And they have a little girl, so Bob actually shares a granddaughter with Sandra Curtis. The child was there somewhere last night, I gather."

"The prawn depository," said Beary. "The one in pink. She was full of gossip too."

Edwina looked interested.

"Really? What did she have to say?"

"Mainly that your friend's beau is categorized as utterly useless by most of the family. Beautiful but dumb is the general consensus."

Edwina's displeasure showed on her face.

"That's very unkind," she said. "I thought he was charming. And I didn't get that impression from Bob Brady. He seems to think Brandon is all right. He told me Brandon was genuinely fond of his wife and was devastated when she developed cancer. He nursed her at home, with the help of a palliative team, and was very upset when she died. Bob likes Brandon. The one he doesn't care for is Sandra's husband. According to Bob, there are no flies on Grant Curtis and he doesn't trust him an inch. He said Sandra's husband is a good-looking womanizer who's cagey enough not to get caught, and his exact words about Grant's business ethics were, 'He's a cutthroat megalomaniac who'd cheat his own mother out of her life savings if he needed cash for a deal.' Mind you, from what he said about Sandra Curtis, it sounds as if she's a pretty tough lady herself. He said she doesn't give anyone any quarter."

"They didn't get to be multi-millionaires without stepping on a few toes," said Beary. "It isn't just wealth that accounts for the disparity between the rich and ordinary mortals."

He turned back to his plate and speared the last two croutons. Then he signalled to the waitress to bring the bill. As he did so, the old fisherman uncoiled himself from his barstool and sauntered across to their table. Beary estimated that the man was well over eighty, although he looked fit and vital. The man ignored Edwina and directed his piercing blue stare at Beary.

"You wanted to know about Shane Paladin," he said.

It was a statement, not a question.

"Yes, I did," said Beary. "Did you know him?"

"Not personally. He wasn't a local … just here for the summer. He was a singer working at the hotel in Sechelt. Good-looking fellow … all the girls were crazy about him. He was the lad who crashed his car into the lake and killed young Marnie who worked at the hospital."

"Was he charged after the accident?"

"No. There was an inquest, but he wasn't blamed. He swore that Marnie went nuts and was punching him and screaming at him as they drove down the hill, and that's why he lost control. Since there were witnesses who had seen her giving him hell in the parking lot, the police believed his story."

"How did he manage to escape?"

"There's a ledge about four feet below water level and the car was lodged there. The driver's side was uppermost, and Paladin managed to open the door and get out. Marnie was trying to escape, but because of the angle, the door slammed shut, and the impact was just enough to send the car rolling off the ledge into deep water."

"Feasible," said Beary. "I can see why they'd have to let him off."

The man scowled. "Maybe, but people round here still felt he was responsible. Everyone thought he could have done more to save her, and given that he'd got her pregnant, it was damned convenient for him that she didn't get out. There was even speculation that he slammed the door himself and sent the car over the edge. Feeling ran pretty high. He left the coast and never came back."

"How old was Paladin?" Beary asked.

"Hard to say. He had a lot of face hair, which made him look older, but I think he was just a teenager. Most of the band members were."

"What did he look like?"

"Tall and dark. He looked a bit like that actor in 'Have Gun, Will Travel'—the one with the moustache and sideburns."

"Richard Boone?" offered Edwina.

"Yeah, that's right. Remember that show? It was pretty popular back then. Mind you, I never saw much of Paladin. He and Marnie hung about on their own."

"What happened to him? Did you ever hear of him again?"

The man harrumphed noisily and his face broke into a gloating grin.

"Sure did. He died. Not that long afterwards too … must have been around Christmas."

"What was it? Another accident?"

"Could have been. There was an obit in the newspaper. Just said he died. No details. It didn't even list any survivors. Wouldn't be surprised if he killed himself out of remorse. Whatever the cause, nobody up here was sorry."

"Well," said Edwina, when the man had moved on, "I feel like Alice in Wonderland. Mysteriouser and mysteriouser. Maybe Paladin is the ghost that opens the window."

"Who knows?" said Beary. "Odd, though."

"That he died so soon afterwards. Yes, that is strange. Still, like the man said, it could have been suicide."

Beary nodded. "I shouldn't wonder," he said. "But what I'd like to know is, if he had no survivors, who put that obituary in the paper?"

Beary paid the bill and followed Edwina out of the pub. They walked back on the road, and as they reached the inn, Anne's Porsche came down the driveway. The car stopped at the side of the road and Anne rolled down the window. "Brandon just called with the latest news about Judy Parsons," she said. "She hasn't regained consciousness, but her eyes have opened a couple of times and there are signs that she's going to come out of the coma. As of tomorrow, the hospital is allowing visitors. They're hoping that if people come in and talk with her, something may register and help to bring her round. Anyway, Brandon and I are going in the afternoon. Visiting hours start at two o'clock, so we should easily be back by five. You're heading home the next day, aren't you, so why don't you meet us at Barringer's for dinner? Juliette and Stephen too … my treat. Shall we say six o'clock?"

Without further ado, Anne pulled back onto the road and drove away.

Beary looked after her thoughtfully.

"Your friend is learning the ways of the rich, isn't she?" he commented. "She didn't wait to find out if it was convenient for us, did she?"

"Don't be silly," said Edwina. "It's a lovely idea."

But secretly she acknowledged that Beary was right. Anne's new look wasn't just on the surface. There was no question that money had brought her empowerment. She wondered if it was going to bring her happiness.

*         *         *

Monday was dark and overcast. Sandra Curtis gripped the steering wheel rigidly as she drove along the lake road. She was not looking forward to the hospital trip, but she had to visit Judy Parsons, if only to see what chance there was of her coming out of the coma. It would have been better if the girl had died, she thought bitterly. Better for everyone, including Judy Parsons. Sandra glanced across at her husband. He had insisted on coming with her, but he sat silent and morose in the passenger seat.

"Do you think she'll come round?" she asked him, breaking the silence.

"It's possible." Grant stared straight ahead.

"She was under the water for twenty minutes, for heaven's sake."

"Miracles happen."

"Yes, that's true." Sandra's voice was hard. "And if she does come round, she'll be able to say who she was working with."

"Yes, she will." Grant leaned forward and flicked on the car radio. "And I bet you can't wait to skewer the poor bastard where it hurts," he said venomously. Still refusing to look at his wife, he leaned back and stared out the window.

The car started down the straight stretch towards the hairpin bend and they fell into an acrimonious silence. Sandra slowed to a crawl to take the corner, deliberately keeping her eyes on the road and avoiding looking towards the water. Then she accelerated up the hill and turned right onto the road to Rumrunners' Point. Within five minutes, they reached the long, single-storied building that housed the country hospital.

Sandra turned into the hospital parking lot and pulled up near the entrance. She turned to her husband. "Come on, we might as well get this over with," she snapped. "Then we'll head round to the processing plant. I want to talk to the other staff members in the shipping office."

"What are you going to do about Brandon?" Grant's antagonistic tone matched her own. "Surely you won't leave him in charge of the plant now?"

Sandra gave a cynical smile.

"No. This mess gives me an excuse to bounce him out once and for all. It's not as if we have to feel sorry for him. He has Anne Broadbent nicely lined up for wife-number-two. Marrying wealthy women seems to be his only talent. Still," she added snidely, "he was a faithful husband. Loyalty is a valuable trait. Never forget that."

Grant did not respond. He opened the passenger door and got out. Without waiting for his wife, he strode towards the hospital entrance. With a heart like stone, Sandra followed him.

*      *      *

After they had finished a mid-afternoon cup of coffee, Beary and Edwina walked MacPuff around the lagoon and stopped at the store to pick up a newspaper. The temperature had risen, but dark clouds hovered over the bay, turning the ocean a dreary battleship grey, and a southeasterly wind was starting to blow. A storm was coming in.

Beary stayed outside with MacPuff while Edwina went into the shop. As he waited, a small girl hopped up the steps. She wore a yellow ball cap, sequined jeans and a Hannah Montana Hoody. In spite of the outfit, Beary recognized the solemn face and the blonde curls, which protruded from the back of the ball cap in a ponytail that bounced and danced in the gusting breeze. It was Suzie.

"Where's your pretty pink dress?" asked Beary.

"It wasn't pretty, it was sucky," said Suzie. "I had to wear it because it was a present from my great-grandma. Can I pat him?" she added, looking suspiciously at MacPuff, who stiffened his ears and returned her wary look.

"No," said Beary. "He doesn't like strangers. What are you doing out on your own?"

"I'm not on my own. My dad is fuelling up our boat. We're going back to town today."

Beary glanced down towards the floats. A forty-foot yacht was tied up alongside—presumably one of the smaller launches in the Jamieson fleet—and Billy Brown was busy with the fuel lines.

"Will you buy me a chocolate bar?" Suzie changed tack without a beat.

"I thought you were Paris Hilton the second," said Beary. "You have far more money than I do."

"I don't like spending my money," said Suzie. "It's much nicer if people buy me things."

"I'm beginning to understand why the rich are rich," said Beary. "I'll tell you what," he continued, "I'll buy you a chocolate bar if you tell me what your family has been saying about Judy Parsons and what you've heard about her accident."

Suzie pinned Beary with a direct stare.

"Why do you want to know?"

"Do you want that chocolate bar or not? You'd better make up your mind quickly, because Billy Brown has just about finished down there."

Suzie whirled round to look at the docks. Then she turned back and started to rattle off a string of vaguely connected pieces of information.

"They're all sorry for her," she said, "but they said it was her own fault because she drove like a maniac. And they're mad at her too because they think she's been stealing from the company, and they want her to get better so she can tell them who got her to do it because they figure she was too dumb to think it up by herself." Suzie snatched a quick breath and carried on. "My mom thinks it was a man, because she says Judy didn't have a happy marriage and was searching for a way out … and she said Judy sometimes had a smug look as if she was 'getting it'—whatever that means. What does it mean?" she added, looking Beary straight in the eye.

"Ask your mother," said Beary.

"I did. She said it meant Judy had a boyfriend, but that's dumb," Suzie interjected, offering her own perspective on the situation. "Judy wasn't at all pretty, and she always acted scared and worried, so I can't see how she'd get a boyfriend."

Beary steered her back to the subject at hand.

"So no one has any idea who was helping Judy cheat the company?"

"No, and everyone is cross with Uncle Brandon because he didn't figure out what she was up to, but that's nothing new because nobody ever really liked him except Auntie Shirley. Now can I have my chocolate bar?"

Suzie bent over to tighten the Velcro on her runner. Beary noticed that the bobbing ponytail was decorated with a white silk flower. At its centre was a Disney Cinderella sticker.

"I see you aren't averse to wearing napkin rings, even if your dolls wouldn't be seen dead in them," said Beary.

"That's different," said Suzie. "My mom designs these for her company dinners, and sometimes she makes me ponytail rings from the ones I like."

"And very pretty they are too," said Beary. "Your mother runs Curtis Catering, doesn't she? Did she, by any chance, cater the company brunch at the pub last week?"

"Yes, of course she did. Uncle Brandon wouldn't hire anyone else."

"And did she design pretty napkin rings for the brunch too?"

"Yes," said Suzie. "They weren't as nice as mine though. They were just plain red fuzzy stuff."

"Were they, indeed?" Beary gave an approving nod. "That is most interesting. Suzie, I think you've earned your chocolate bar."

Edwina emerged from the store. To her surprise, Beary handed her MacPuff and disappeared inside with Suzie. Five minutes later, Suzie reappeared with three chocolate bars and a roll of mints. Without looking back, she ran across the grass and down the ramp to the docks, then hopped aboard her father's yacht and vanished below.

"That child has you wrapped around her little finger," Edwina said severely, as they walked back around the lagoon. "You shouldn't encourage her. She's spoiled enough as it is."

"She's interesting," said Beary. "Six years old and she already knows how to make everyone work for her. Just imagine what she's going to be like in thirty years. Old man Jamieson all over again in a Hannah Montana Hoody. Who is Hannah Montana anyway?"

"Ask your granddaughters," said Edwina.

"Later. Right now I have to think."

"What about?"

"Napkin rings." Beary explained how he had discovered the source of the one they had found in the woods. "I wish I could work out the significance," he said, "but whatever it means, there's no question that someone who attended the brunch walked down the trail to the hairpin bend. The Velcro on the ring must have stuck to the person's sleeve or jacket and come loose when brushed against the bushes. If that was the person who called out to warn Judy Parsons about the other car, why didn't he stay to help or report the accident? There's something strange going on."

"But surely you're not suggesting the crash was anything but an accident?"

"I'm beginning to wonder. Perhaps that warning yell was just a cover-up. Maybe the watcher at the side of the road did something to startle her ... threw something, or darted out. He could have engineered the crash and stayed to make sure Judy Parsons didn't survive. Let's face it; her death would have been pretty convenient for whoever got her involved in the scam at the processing plant."

Edwina pursed her lips.

"Brandon suspected her loutish husband, didn't he?"

"Yes, but he was only speculating. He didn't know."

"Still, Judy Parson's husband could have been the person at the roadside. Remember, he disappeared from the brunch and nobody could find him until after she'd been fished out of the lake."

"True, but those sorts of social events are so busy that nobody notices if someone slips out for a smoke or to make a phone call. Anyone at that brunch could have left for fifteen minutes. I think I'll give Adrian a call. The police should be keeping a watch at the hospital because, if I'm right, there could be another attempt on Parson's life. It's possible that someone is out there sweating blood knowing that she might come round and divulge his or her identity."

"But the police can't keep watch indefinitely."

"No, but if the police guard is an undercover cop who looks like a staff member, with any luck, he'll catch the killer in the act of trying again. Come on," he added. "Hurry. Here comes the rain."

There was a crack of thunder and the skies opened up. The deluge was sudden and overwhelming. Edwina put up her umbrella and held it so that Beary could huddle under it, and turning it against the wind, they hurried back. MacPuff pulled ahead with his tail down and his ears flat.

As they reached the bottom of the drive, a deafening roll of thunder stopped them in their tracks. Beary glanced up to see a jagged bolt of lightning streak across the sky behind the inn.

"Oh, my goodness," whispered Edwina. "Look!"

Through the downpour, they could see that the window in room twenty-one yawned open and the curtains were flapping frantically in the whistling wind.

\*       \*       \*

Brandon parked the Jaguar close to the hospital entrance and put up his umbrella before getting out of the car. Then he came round and opened the passenger door for Anne. The rain was already gathering in pools on the asphalt and a miniature river was starting to form at the side of the path. Brandon took Anne's arm and held the umbrella over her as they walked across the parking lot. "Can you manage those?" he asked, nodding towards the bouquet of cut flowers she was carrying. "We'll make this a quick visit," he continued, "and then head over to the restaurant. I'm looking forward to dining with your friends," he added. "They seemed very pleasant."

Anne smiled to herself. Fond as she was of Edwina and Beary, *pleasant* was scarcely the adjective that came to mind. Edwina was a powerhouse of energy, but she was not a relaxing person to be with, and Beary was as rugged an individualist as Anne had ever met, other than her errant husband who had been as outspoken and aggravating as he was entertaining. She and Edwina had often joked that their mates must use the same scriptwriter. *Pleasant* was the sort of adjective she would apply to Brandon himself. She glanced sideways at his handsome profile, thinking how most of her friends would envy her. Perhaps she should count her blessings and let things take the course that he so clearly intended. Many people had told her what a good husband he had been to Shirley. She could do far worse than spend her old age with him.

As they reached the front steps, a streak of lightning flashed across the sky. The clap of thunder that followed was deafening. The storm was right overhead. They hurried inside. Anne shivered as the sinister rumbling seemed to roll in after them, echoing around the lobby and taking an eternity to diminish and die. She followed Brandon to the administration desk, and the receptionist directed them down the hall. Judy Parsons was in a single room at the very end. The atmosphere was bright and cheerful, for the curtains had been drawn to close out the darkened sky and the raging storm outside. There were two floral arrangements on the window ledge, one large and manifestly expensive and one more modest. A row of cards had been arranged beside these. Judy lay motionless at the centre of the room, and a nurse, clipboard in hand, stood beside the bed, talking with Grant and Sandra Curtis. Grant looked up as Anne and Brandon entered.

"She's coming round," he said shortly.

The nurse elaborated.

"She opened her eyes and spoke a couple of words this morning—mostly gibberish, nothing intelligible. Then she drifted off again. She may not do more than wake briefly for the next couple of days, and she won't be able to talk coherently at first, but she'll pull through."

"So she won't be able to tell us anything about what was going on at the plant?" Sandra asked brusquely.

"Not immediately. You'll have to be patient. There may be no point in staying any longer today."

Sandra eyed the still form on the bed.

"No. We'll stay for a while. We might as well wait out the storm."

The nurse hung the clipboard on the bottom of the bed and left the room. Grant turned to the window and opened the curtains. He glowered at the rain. The parking lot outside was awash with rivulets created by the torrential downpour.

"It doesn't look like it's going to let up soon," he complained.

"Then you'll just have to kill time until it does," snapped Sandra.

"Why don't you two go for coffee," Brandon suggested smoothly. "Take a break. We'll stay with her for a bit."

"Good idea," said Grant. "There's no point in hanging around to visit with you two." He took his wife by the arm and steered her towards the door.

"What's the matter with them?" Anne asked after they were out of earshot.

"They're feeling stressed," said Brandon. "Don't let them get to you. Now why don't you ask that nurse to find you a vase for those flowers?"

*       *       *

Beary hung up the phone and came into the living room. He picked his way over Jennifer and Laura, who were sprawled on the carpet watching a video, and sat in the armchair by the window. The curtains were drawn, insulating the household against the fury of the day, but he could still hear the rain pounding against the deck outside. However, the rolls of thunder were becoming more intermittent. The storm was gradually moving away. Edwina was sitting on the sofa, dutifully watching the movie to demonstrate rapport with her grandchildren, but she looked across at Beary and raised her eyebrows.

"Well?" she asked. "What did Adrian say? Is she concerned?"

Beary's face was grave.

"Yes," he said. "She's going to head round to the hospital now to talk with the staff, and another constable will be sent round to stay on guard in the room. It's odd, though," he added. "The police found a witness who has debunked the theory of a car forcing Judy Parsons off the road. One of Anne's workmen was taking his coffee break in his van, and so that he didn't seem to be slacking on the job, he drove up the road and parked at the junction where the road branches off to Rumrunners' Point. He was there from ten past eleven until quarter to twelve. He actually heard the sirens of the emergency vehicles, and that's when he moved on. He insists that no cars came up the hill while he was parked there."

"So why did the bystander call out?" said Edwina.

"Which bystander?" asked Juliette, coming into the room with the tea tray. "Here, this will warm you up," she added.

Beary explained about the voice that had been heard by the dog walker.

"That doesn't make sense," said Juliette practically. "I mean, how would

Judy Parsons have heard a warning called out from the edge of the road? She was speeding, and at this time of year, she'd have the windows closed."

"But we know someone from the brunch came down the trail and was standing near the hairpin bend, so presumably it was someone she knew. If he'd waved, he could have caught her attention. She might have heard him if she was already looking his way."

"Maybe she was talking to him on her cell," mused Juliette. "That would make more sense. If the man she was talking to saw her coming down the road and realized she was in danger, he might have hollered the warning down the phone."

"Oh, my God!" said Beary. "We've been blind. She was talking to Brandon Manning."

"But he didn't say anything about being at the roadside. He said he was at the restaurant."

"Don't you see?" said Beary. "*He* could have been the person who slipped away from the brunch. We only have his word for it that Judy Parsons kept phoning him to see how things were going. For all we know, he told her to call him as she turned onto the lake road. That would have easily given him enough time to sprint down the trail and wait at the hairpin."

"But why?" Edwina was puzzled. "And what was he warning her about?"

"Nothing. That's the evil beauty of it. Put yourself in Judy Parson's place. You're late for an important engagement, you're stressed out because you know you've been doing something illegal, and there are indications that the jig is up. You're driving much too fast and you're talking on your cellphone at the same time. That in itself is dangerous. Then, just as you're approaching the hairpin bend—just prior to the critical moment when you should slow down to take the curve—someone yells at you to look out behind you and then hollers at you to brake. What would you do? You'd glance in the rear-view mirror for a split second, then look back and see you were too close to the corner. The contradictory warning would throw you into a panic, just long enough for you to lose control of the car. You'd jam on the brakes, but it'd be too late. It's bloody diabolical."

Edwina paled.

"You think Brandon Manning tried to kill her?"

"Yes, I do. It's the only scenario that fits the evidence."

"But it might not have worked. What if she'd managed to stop in time?"

Beary looked grim.

"Then he'd have had to finish the job himself—which is what he's going to have to do now if he doesn't want the truth to come out."

Edwina stood up. Her face was ashen.

"Bertram! Remember what Anne told us. She and Brandon were going to visit Judy this afternoon. The two of them are round at the hospital now. They've probably been there since two o'clock. Adrian might be too late."

\*　　　　\*　　　　\*

Adrian turned into the parking lot and stopped by the hospital entrance. As she slid out of the patrol car, her phone rang again. It was Beary. When she heard what he had to say, she shot into the building and ran down the hallway. The first person she saw was Anne Broadbent. Anne was standing by the counter at the nursing station and putting flowers into a vase.

"Where's Brandon Manning?" Adrian demanded.

Anne pointed towards the door at the end of the corridor, but before she could speak, there was a shrill cry from inside the room. Adrian accelerated down to the end of the hall and shot through the curtained doorway.

Brandon Manning was standing by the bed. He was holding a pillow. Judy Parsons lay prone and still, but her eyes were wide open and her face was contorted with terror. Adrian lunged forward and Brandon lurched back against the window. He dropped the pillow and shoved the side table towards Adrian. It caught her off balance, and in the split second it took for her to recover, Brandon crashed through the window and sprinted across the parking lot.

He was in his car and heading out of the lot by the time Adrian reached her own vehicle. She started the siren and set off after the Jaguar, radioing to headquarters as she did so. To her relief, she was told that another officer was already on the lake road. Constable William Jackson was only a short distance away from the hairpin bend. Brandon Manning would not get far.

\*　　　　\*　　　　\*

As Constable Jackson drove alongside the lake, he put the windshield wipers on high. The rain was coming down in a torrent, pounding the glass and creating rivulets of water with every swish of the blades. He watched carefully for the approaching Jaguar, for he didn't want to end up in a fatal collision himself, and the message he had received warned him that Brandon Manning was desperate. He rounded the curve before the long, straight stretch. The hairpin bend was close now, so if Manning was coming that way, he must not be far off. Jackson pulled over to the verge and waited. From where he had parked, he could see to the top of the hill.

After a moment, he became aware of the distant wail of a siren, but before he could react, headlights flashed over the top of the hill and he saw the Jaguar racing towards him. He started his engine and put on his own siren, but the approaching vehicle did not slow down. He pulled out quickly into the road, but as he did so, the Jaguar started to do a strange, unearthly dance, veering sideways and gliding gracefully down to the bottom of the hill. Then it spun like a top towards the copse by the swimming hole. It clipped the fallen trunk of a fir tree, elevated into the air and sailed into the lake.

In the time it took Jackson to radio for help, the car had disappeared below the black water.

*      *      *

Later that evening, Beary and Edwina joined Anne for dinner in her cozy parlour. All three had decided that the privacy of a quiet meal at the inn was more palatable than dining out after the rigors of the day. The lightning storm had abated, but the rain continued in a steady downpour, transforming the ivy outside the window into a black, sodden mass and pounding the flagstones of the patio with such force that the noise of the rain drowned out the crackle of the fire.

Beary was back in his wing chair. Krypton lay at his feet, sprawled by the hearth, with his green frog tucked neatly under one paw. The flickering flames danced in the fireplace and cast a golden glow on the dog's dark fur. Anne was pouring drinks. Her face was wan, but when Beary expressed his sympathy, she smiled and reassured him.

"I'm all right," she said quietly. She handed Beary a snifter of brandy. Then she took her own glass of sherry and joined Edwina on the couch. "I'm shocked, but I'm not grieving. I wasn't in love with him, you know, merely flattered by the attention."

"You've had a lucky escape," sniffed Edwina. "Who'd have thought there was such a cold-blooded, wicked scoundrel under that appealing exterior?"

"He was pretty calculating all right," said Beary. "I had a word with Adrian before we came over and she says Judy Parsons has started to talk. It sounds like everything happened the way I suspected. Brandon yelled out as Judy Parsons was whipping towards the bend. She lost control, but she didn't fly into the lake. The car slid down the bank and lodged on the ledge. It was tilting badly, and as she tried to climb up to open the passenger door, it started to slide downwards. She managed to open the door, but Manning slammed it shut before she could get out and the impact sent the car off the ledge and down into the deep water."

"But why?" insisted Edwina. "He was rich and successful. I can't fathom what would prompt him to do it."

"Think about the things we heard at the party. His wife was the only one in the family who liked him. The rest consider him useless, and they despised him

129

and Shirley for their extravagant tastes and lifestyle. While his wife was alive, he was tolerated by the Jamieson clan, but since her death, he's been gradually demoted until all he was doing was managing the processing plant, and I imagine the salary he was getting didn't match what he needed to maintain his lifestyle. I suspect he came up with the shipping scam after his wife died, and to carry it out, he needed Judy Parson's help. She's unhappy in her marriage, so he deluded her into thinking they would marry once she divorced her husband. But then a new, much more attractive and legal source of revenue appeared. He met you, Anne. With the prospect of a wealthy wife in his future, the scam was no longer necessary, but to his dismay, Sandra Curtis got wind of what was going on, and he couldn't rely on Judy Parsons not to give way under pressure, especially since he now intended to ditch her."

"It's astounding," said Anne. "He was so cool and relaxed on the way to the hospital. When he sent me out to put the flowers in a vase, he was smiling. Why didn't I have some premonition that he meant to harm her?" Anne shook her head sadly. "I must be the world's worst judge of character," she sighed. "I've given up trying to understand men." She drained her sherry glass and stood up.

"That was a singularly unfair comment," said Beary. "Just because you're feeding me a nice meal and plying me with brandy, it doesn't mean you can slam my sex."

Anne smiled.

"I know," she said. "I don't really mean it. Brandon is certainly not the norm."

"That's right," said Beary. "Still, there is a plus side to unmasking a rotten specimen of manhood lurking in the guise of every maiden's dream."

"Oh," said Edwina tartly. "And what would that be?"

"It makes that silly idiot, Colin, look good," said Beary.

Anne looked thoughtful.

"Yes," she acknowledged. "It does, doesn't it?"

"And," Beary added, turning to his wife, "it should give you food for thought."

"Me? Why?"

"Because you might want to reassess your view that all middle-aged women would give their eye teeth for a chance to trade in their husbands for someone new and exciting."

Edwina's eyes narrowed.

"You were just pretending to be asleep, weren't you?"

"Well, what else was I supposed to do with you and Anne discussing embarrassingly intimate details that were obviously not meant for my ears?"

Edwina was saved from replying, for, at that moment, Beary's cellphone rang. His face lit up as he answered the call. It was Philippa.

"I tracked down the information you wanted," she told him. "Julian Buchanan worked with Shane Paladin during the sixties. They were in a variety show together. Paladin had just finished a gig on the coast working in a hotel in Sechelt. Julian said Paladin had been pretty close-lipped about how things had gone and had said he was thinking of giving up the stage. I could tell Julian didn't like Paladin. He said he was a weak character and bone idle. *A born lapdog* was the phrase he used. Julian assumed that Paladin had done as he'd said and quit performing because, soon after the show closed, he disappeared from view."

"Disappeared from everyone's view, actually," said Beary. "He died. Buchanan didn't know about that?"

"No. Actually, Julian figured that Paladin had procured a rich wife to support him, because there was an expensive-looking girl who used to hang around the theatre. Paladin had met her during his Sechelt gig and she'd teamed up with him again once she was back in town. He never introduced her to the other performers, but Julian heard them talking once and had the impression that she was trying to line things up so that Paladin could come and work for her father's company. He thinks she was seeing him without the knowledge of her family."

Beary's eyes widened.

"Did he ever hear the girl's name?"

"He didn't say. Is it important?"

"Yes. Could you ask him?"

"Sure. I'll see him tomorrow. I'll ask him then."

Beary chatted for a few more minutes and then ended the call.

"Well?" said Edwina, who was waiting impatiently. "What did Philippa have to say?"

Beary relayed what Philippa had told him.

"It sounds too similar to be a coincidence," he concluded. He turned to Anne and said, "You may well have been courted by the very same individual who features in your book of ghost stories."

Edwina set down her sherry glass and leaned forward eagerly. "It does seem possible, doesn't it? After all, anyone could send in an obituary notice. The newspaper doesn't demand a death certificate. All Paladin had to do was shave off his moustache and cut his hair. He'd look completely different. If people up the coast had read that he was dead, they'd never connect him with a wealthy member of the Jamieson clan who visited there seasonally."

Beary nodded. "Yes, Paladin could have been Brandon. He just had to change his name. Mind you, that would be tricky if he was trying to get in with the Jamiesons. They'd check up on him, and a false name would have prompted more enquiries."

"Oh, for heaven's sake!" cried Edwina. "We're not thinking. Whoever heard of a person being christened Shane Paladin? It was a stage name. Shane was an 'in' name in the fifties because of Alan Ladd—and given that we were told the man looked like Richard Boone, we've been utter idiots not to remember that the hero's name in 'Have Gun, Will Travel' was Paladin. Call Philippa back. See if Julian Buchanan knew what Paladin's real name was. He might not have changed his name at all."

Beary opened his cell again and punched in his daughter's number. When Philippa answered, he posed the question right away. Her answer was exactly what he had expected.

"Of course it was a stage name," said Philippa. "Sorry. I forgot to tell you that. Paladin's real name was Brandon Manning."

*       *       *

The following morning dawned sunny and bright. Beary saw his grandchildren and son-in-law off to school. Then he took MacPuff for a leisurely walk, while Edwina visited with Juliette and organized their bags for the trip home. When he returned, he opened the back of the Jeep so that MacPuff could jump in. Then he went to the house and called to Edwina to hurry up. If they hustled, they would be in time to catch the twelve-thirty ferry.

Five minutes later, after hurried farewells, Beary and Edwina set off. As they turned onto the main road, a small cavalcade of cars came towards them from the other direction. Edwina was fussing with her purse and making sure that she had remembered her keys, but she glanced up and gasped as a green pickup truck passed by. She swivelled round and stared through the rear window. To her amazement, the truck turned into the driveway of the Hampton House Inn.

"Good heavens!" she exclaimed. "Wasn't that Colin Broadbent?"

Beary nodded smugly.

"I believe so," he replied.

"What is he doing coming up here? The nerve of the man. Why can't he leave Anne alone?"

"He still loves her," said Beary. "The only reason he's stayed away is because of her lottery win. He was too proud to come back because he figured she'd think it was only because she was rich."

"But he has his other woman."

"No, he doesn't. Even before Anne had her windfall, he'd realized what an idiot he'd been. He'd already broken off with the salesgirl."

Edwina looked suspiciously at Beary. "How come you know so much about it?"

"I phoned him," said Beary, "and told him that Anne missed him, and that she needed him because she was getting mixed up with a crowd that was going to cause her a lot of grief." Beary gave a self-satisfied smirk. "I've never heard a man sound so happy," he added cheerily.

Edwina fell silent. Beary allowed himself a quick glance at the passenger seat. Edwina's studied absorption of the scenery did not deceive him for a moment.

"Just think," he purred, digging the knife a little deeper, "if Anne takes Colin back, he can move up here and operate a fishing charter out of Hampton House. What a delightful prospect. It positively gladdens the heart, doesn't it?"

"Well," said Edwina, after a moment's reflection, "you might be right. I must say I thought that Brandon was far too smooth. Even if he hadn't turned out to be a killer, he wasn't right for Anne."

"You said he was charming."

"Well, he was. But charming doesn't always make the best husbands."

"I'm glad you admitted that," said Beary.

"Neither does smugness," said Edwina caustically. "And stop rolling your eyes like that. Concentrate on the road."

"You can hardly criticize," said Beary. He smiled enigmatically. "I'm far more alert than you are," he added.

Edwina bristled indignantly.

"Why should you think that?"

"Because you completely missed an amazing sight as we passed the inn."

"What on earth are you talking about?"

"The window."

"What about it?"

"It no longer appears to have a mind of its own."

Edwina blinked. "Oh, for heaven's sake, stop talking in riddles," she snapped. "Say what you mean."

Beary gave a seraphic smile.

"The window in room twenty-one was closed," he said.

# LOST IN THE SOUTH PACIFIC

Philippa Beary was over the moon when the phone call came. She had won the leading role in *South Pacific*. The pay was good, the director was fabulous, and since Detective Constable Robert Miller had never seen her onstage, this was her opportunity to dazzle him. Nurse Nellie Forbush was the perfect role to show how she could strut her stuff. Her good friend, Milton Lovell, was in the cast too—another bonus since he'd be milking the part of Luther Billis for every ounce of comedy. "Honey Bun" was going to be a riot. She could hardly wait.

Of course, for every up there was a down, and the news that Octavia Bruni was to play Bloody Mary was something of a dampener, though Philippa felt an impish surge of glee knowing how much the gorgeous Octavia was going to hate uglying herself up for the role. Still, Philippa could deal with the usual barrage of vituperation that was part and parcel of Octavia's repertoire because everything else promised to be wonderful.

The only part yet to be cast was Emil de Bec. Philippa had heard several bass-baritones try for the part at the auditions. All of them were good, but not outstanding, so she could understand why Christian Harte was still looking, but she had enough faith in him to know he would find her a top-notch co-star. Philippa couldn't stop singing her "Cock-eyed Optimist" song. It was all too good to be true.

\*  \*  \*

By the evening of the first rehearsal, Philippa had not yet heard who her co-star was to be. However, she was sure there would be some news when she reached the hall. Milton had asked her for a ride, so she picked him up early. Although they did not have far to go, there was a football game in town and traffic was sure to be heavy.

As they inched down Canada Way, Philippa carolled songs from the show. Milton was in the mood to chat. He raised his voice in order to be heard.

"So good of you to drive me. My old banger is laid up and I'm a bit short of cash for fixing it. Maybe I can strike up a sideline in shrunken heads to earn some extra moolah."

Philippa stopped singing long enough to reply.

"I don't mind a bit," she said. She was very fond of Milton. "I'll enjoy the company."

"*I'm* enjoying the concert," said Milton, "though it would be nice if we could get a change from 'Some Enchanted Evening' once in a while. Why don't you sing your own songs?"

"The baritone has all the lovely melodies. That's the only downside of *South Pacific*."

"Well, what do you expect when it was written for Ezio Pinza and Mary Martin? You have to stop being lyric and start being peppy. Anyway," Milton added slyly, "I bet you'll be able to belt out 'I'm in Love with a Wonderful Guy' without any problem. How *are* things going with the handsome detective, by the way?"

"Okay," said Philippa guardedly. "We're not exactly at that stage yet. We're both pretty busy. We've just gone for coffee a few times, that's all."

"I thought he took you out on New Year's Eve. If all you got was coffee, I'd write him off now."

Philippa giggled.

"Of course it wasn't just coffee. It was a dinner dance at his sister and brother-in-law's tennis club. The four of us went together, and it was very formal, very lovely and very proper. We did go to the lawyers' fundraiser together as well, but that evening went nowhere because Bob ended up on duty, and since then, every time we try to make a date, one or the other of us ends up having to work."

"Oh, come on, give," coaxed Milton. "You can't convince me that there hasn't been any romantic spark. Every time we stop talking, you break back into that song. You're obviously crazy about him."

Philippa broke down. "Okay, yes, he's tremendously attractive and I could fall like a ton of bricks if I let myself, but after what I went through with Adam, I'm cautious."

"Over-cautious, if you ask me," said Milton. "Adam Craig was always a philanderer. You should have had more sense than to take him seriously. Your cop sounds like a much more reliable type. Don't be so mistrustful."

"I'm not mistrustful, just careful. If Bob's serious about me, he'll stick around. I want to get to know him."

"So what *do* you know about him? Why is he with VPD anyway? Doesn't he want to be a big shot with the Mounties?"

"No, actually. He likes the idea of staying in one place and knowing his territory. Besides, his father is dead and his mother has some health issues, so he doesn't want to be sent all over the country when he knows she needs a lot of support. He's a good son and a good uncle too. His sister has two adorable children. He brought them to Juliette's puppet show at Christmas."

"Aha!" said Milton. "A family man. Good stuff. I see a wedding in the future."

"Oh, don't be silly. And don't you dare say anything like that when he comes to the opening night or … or …"

"You'll drop me in the South Pacific? Never fear. I shall be a model of propriety. Oh, look," Milton added as Philippa pulled into the parking lot. "It's Bloody Octavia. What a good job you're playing a nurse. If she annoys you too much, you can stick a band-aid on her mouth."

As Philippa slid the Jeep into a parking spot, Octavia noticed them and gave a queenly wave.

"Isn't it amazing how she can greet you and make it look like a put-down?" said Milton. "Too bad Christian had to cast her, but, of course, she does have that glorious rich mezzo, and she can act, so she'll be incredible onstage, even if we all hate her offstage. She'll have to stick dark contacts in those glittering green eyes, though. So will the girl playing Liat. Would you believe Christian has given the part to some light-eyed newcomer from Montreal who won't even be here until next week because she's finishing up some stint in Toronto?"

"That's surprising. We have masses of talented Asian dancers in Vancouver. Why would he give the part to a Caucasian from out of town?"

"I asked Christian that. He said she's a superb actress and she's done the part before."

"Oh, and haven't we heard that a million times," Philippa said sourly, retrieving her bag from the back seat of the Jeep. "If directors had their way, there'd be one actress for every part and she could just bounce from production to production. Still, I'm not complaining. Christian chose me, and he always pulls off a first-rate show, so I'll forgive him anything."

"Did you know, by the way," said Milton, going off onto another tangent as they crossed the parking lot, "that Christian has been offered a post with the Stratford Festival. He's moving to Ontario as soon as he's through with *South Pacific*."

"Yes, I did hear," said Philippa. "Too bad. Their gain is Vancouver's loss."

"The buzz has it that his new girlfriend set it up. She's from Ontario and she knows someone on the festival board."

Philippa nodded. She never knew what Milton's sources were, but they generally proved to be right.

"Kevin Burr told me all about her," Milton continued, for once identifying his informer.

"Who's Kevin Burr?"

"The handsome stud who's playing Joe Cable. I met him at the auditions. He's a gorgeous hunky tenor, who also, believe it or not, is a hair stylist in his day job. Very high end. His lady clientele pay a fortune to have him tone up their split ends. You watch, Octavia will take one look at him and zero in like a heat-seeking missile."

"Never mind Octavia and the singing stylist. Tell me about Christian's girlfriend."

"Her name's Erica. According to Kevin, she's been living with Christian for the last three months. Kev lives in the same apartment block so he sees her all the time. Evidently she's a real cutie. A bubbly little redhead just like you. Has a lovely soprano voice too."

"Great," moaned Philippa. "Just what we need—another soprano—as if there wasn't already enough competition."

"No need to worry," said Milton. "Kev says she's going back to Ontario with Christian. Actually, she'll be leaving before him—some big family wedding in Toronto right around our production week. That's why she didn't come out for your part. Otherwise, she'd probably have got it."

"Thanks a lot, Milton. You're a real pick-me-up."

"I know," smirked Milton. "And speaking of," he added, "there is the babbling brook in question." He wagged a disapproving finger towards a handsome young man who was smoking beside the front door. "Tut-tut, Kevin," he reproved. "Bad for the voice, never mind the lungs. And we haven't even got started yet."

The man flashed a row of gleaming teeth, miraculously unsullied for a smoker. Handsome stud indeed, thought Philippa. The phrase, *beautiful, but dumb*, came to mind, though she knew she was being unfair.

His reply, when it came, was good-natured. "*You* may not have got started," he said affably, "but I've been hard at it for two hours. Christian had me come in an hour before the chorus call."

"That's what you get for being a star," said Milton.

He opened the door of the rehearsal hall and held it for Philippa. "Well, come on. Into the fray. Last year, nuns and Nazis, this year, nurses and Seabees. Off to win the war again."

The hall was already buzzing with activity as the chorus had been called a full hour before the principals. Philippa glanced around the room. She recognized several people from the auditions, but saw no one who was a likely

Emil de Bec. She hoped Christian was not having trouble filling the role. Her own performance would be diminished if she did not have a strong leading man.

She noticed Christian standing in the middle of the room. Beside him stood a petite redhead, presumably the new girlfriend, but Christian was not paying her any attention. He was talking with the musical director and the choreographer. All three looked annoyed.

"The triumvirate's collective bottoms are in a knot," observed Milton. "I sense problems."

"Just as long as the problem isn't finding me a French planter."

"So go and ask them."

"Good idea. I will."

Philippa walked over to the trio.

"You all look solemn," she commented. "Trouble?"

"Only a minor irritation." Christian's scowl belied his words. "One of the women in the chorus failed to show up."

"Maybe she got the date wrong. Did you phone her?"

Christian shook his head.

"Not yet. I will later. I've worked with her before and there were a couple of occasions when she didn't show—usually because she wasn't well. I've given her the benefit of the doubt in the past, but I did warn her that attendance is critical. If she doesn't have a really good excuse this time, she's out. Too bad Erica has to go back East for a wedding," he added, gesturing towards the pretty redhead. "Otherwise, I'd get her to fill in. Oh, sorry. Forgetting my manners. You two haven't met. Erica, this is Philippa. She's playing Nellie Forbush."

The redhead turned her bright blue eyes on Philippa and smiled radiantly.

"It's so lovely to meet you. Christian says you're enchanting onstage."

Philippa's reserve melted. The girl's friendly greeting was hard to resist.

"It's too bad I can't stick around," Erica continued. "I'd love to take part, and I'm going to miss Christian dreadfully. Still, I'm sure there are lots of singers who'd be only too willing to step in if he ends up short one ensemble player."

"Speaking of singers—" Philippa paused and turned to Christian. "Do you have someone lined up to play opposite me yet?"

"Do I ever!" Christian's voice was hearty but he failed to look Philippa in the eye. "I've rounded you up an Emil de Bec as dynamic as that matinee idol who's pulling everyone's heartstrings on Broadway. A bit young for the role, of course, but we can grey him up, and the voice is incredible."

Philippa's eyebrows shot up a couple of inches.

"Well, that's great. Is it anyone I know?"

Christian looked slightly shamefaced.

"Well, yes, actually," he said, "but I know you'll work really well together. Professionals and all that," he added.

Philippa's elation subsided.

"Oh. So who is it?" she demanded.

Christian gave a tentative smile.

"Adam Craig is coming back from Germany to do the part," he said.

Philippa heard an exuberant chortle in her left ear. Milton had come up behind her.

"Oh, my goodness, all those clinches," he gurgled. "Never mind, dear," he added. "At least you'll be able to test your resistance."

Philippa was not amused.

*      *      *

Philippa was nettled at being cast opposite her ex-boyfriend, but she knew Christian was right. Adam would be an ideal Emil de Bec, and the two of them were used to working together so there was no doubt that they would make a good team. She only hoped Bob Miller would not misinterpret the situation when he saw her being romanced on the stage by her ex.

Gradually, she rationalized herself into a better humour, and by the end of the evening, the glorious Rogers and Hammerstein songs had restored her enthusiasm for the show. She found herself still humming after the music rehearsal was over.

As she fetched her coat from the rack by the door, a man came into the hall. Philippa had never seen him before, and she wondered if he had come to the wrong place. He was medium height, but stocky, with short, almost shaven hair, and his striped business suit and expensive leather jacket were far beyond the means of most actors and singers. However, he was peering around the room as if he expected to see someone.

"Looking for anyone in particular?" asked Philippa. "Can I help?"

"My wife." The man gave her an appealing smile. He wasn't conventionally good-looking but he had a lot of charm. "She's in the chorus, but I can't see her anywhere."

"I'll track her down for you," offered Philippa. "What's her name?"

"Cynthia Borden."

Philippa did not recognize the name.

"I don't know her, but there are a few new people in the show. Let me check with our director."

Philippa left the man by the door and walked over to Christian, who was sitting with Erica on the far side of the vast room. She was surprised to hear him humming "Somewhere Over the Rainbow" as he jotted notes in his script.

Erica laughed at Philippa's bemused expression.

"Don't let it get to you. Christian always sings the hit songs from his previous productions. A month after *South Pacific* closes, 'Some Enchanted Evening' will be his favourite."

Philippa grinned. She was beginning to regret the fact that Erica was leaving town. She sensed a good-humoured soulmate in the girl. Christian was still writing notes, utterly oblivious to the discussion around him. Philippa tapped him on the shoulder and he looked up. He sounded irritated when she asked him about Cynthia Borden.

"She's the singer who didn't show up," he said.

"That's odd. Her husband is here to give her a ride. You'd better speak to him. What if something's happened to her?"

"You're such a worrywart, Philippa," grumbled Christian. "I expect there's a perfectly ordinary explanation. She's probably home with a headache and didn't call to tell him she wasn't coming—just like she didn't bother to call me."

Philippa followed Christian across the hall and listened as he talked with Cynthia's husband. The man's face fell when he heard what the director had to say. His eyes registered alarm.

"But I know she isn't at our house," he said. "I got home at seven and I was there all evening."

"How does she normally get here?" Philippa asked. "Does someone give her a ride?"

The man shook his head.

"No. She walks. We're only a few blocks away. I don't worry about her walking when it's light, but going home in the dark is a different story, especially as part of the way borders the woods. I always come to pick her up."

"Why don't you phone her?" suggested Christian. "She must have a cellphone."

"I did call. I only got her voicemail." The man began to look visibly distressed. "I've been really worried about her lately," he went on. "Her parents died in a car crash last summer and she's been depressed ever since. I thought doing the show would cheer her up, but she hasn't been as enthusiastic as usual, and she seemed particularly low this morning. God, where would she have gone? What is she doing?"

"Sounds to me like she changed her mind about doing the chorus," said Christian. "Your best bet would be to go home and wait for her to return."

Philippa was surprised at Christian's cavalier attitude for he was usually sensitive to other people's feelings. It was that ability to see what was going on inside people's souls that made him such a fine director. It was uncharacteristic for him to dismiss anyone so carelessly, especially someone who was so visibly distressed. Privately, she considered that the chorister's husband had good reason to worry.

She turned sympathetically to the harried-looking man and suggested that he leave his name and number so they could contact him if they heard any news. Ignoring Christian's impatient expression, she calmly added that it would be wise to check with the hospitals and call the police if Cynthia did not appear soon. The man nodded, his brow furrowed with tension. He took out his wallet, extracted a card, which he handed to Philippa, and abruptly left. Philippa glanced at the card; the man's name was Joseph Borden.

"He's really anxious, and I don't blame him," she said.

Christian rolled his eyes.

"I remember him from when I directed *The Wizard of Oz*. He used to pick Cynthia up all the time. Pleasant enough, but insanely over-protective."

"It's hardly over-protective to worry about someone who left for a rehearsal and didn't turn up," Philippa said sharply. "Don't be so heartless."

"I'm not heartless; I'm just using common sense. I told you, she's pulled this kind of stunt before, and that was when she was playing a principal role. That's why I only put her in the chorus this time. If the wretched creature was depressed and didn't want to come, then she'll have headed off somewhere to sulk in solitary. Gone to the mall to spend his money, or gone to Bali Hai for all I know. My problem isn't to find her; it's to replace her. Go home, Nurse Nellie, and get some sleep. We start staging next weekend."

\*           \*           \*

By the weekend, Philippa had other things on her mind, not the least of which was the prospect of her first meeting with Adam in eight months. Octavia did nothing to alleviate her tension.

"So," said the mezzo silkily, "I hear you're in no danger of falling back into your ex's arms when he arrives. The buzz is you're in love with a wonderful guy."

Philippa wilted inwardly. It had taken Octavia all of three rehearsals to weasel out details of her private life. She tried feigning deafness.

"Do tell," Octavia went on relentlessly. "Who's the new boyfriend?"

"If you're referring to DC Bob Miller, he isn't my boyfriend. We're just—"

"Good friends? God, not that old line." Octavia paused and her eyes grew shrewd. "I think I know him. Tall, dark, very attractive? Been with VPD about six years?"

Philippa nodded tersely.

"Then it's a good job you're not taking him seriously," crooned Octavia. "He had a very intense relationship with one of my high-school friends. On and off again for five years. I'm quite sure he isn't over her, so it could be on again any time."

Having delivered a palpable hit, Octavia floated to the other side of the room and coiled herself around Kevin Burr.

"Don't spit nails, darling," said Milton. "It's bad for your teeth. And don't glower. You'll get wrinkles. Is she right? Does the wonderful guy have another girl on the go?"

"No," said Philippa shortly. "The on-and-off relationship is finally and irrevocably off and has been for more than six months."

"So the ex is definitely an ex?"

"Yes. He told me all about her. She sounds like a total head-case, so it doesn't surprise me at all that she's friends with Octavia."

"True. One has to be mad to associate with Octavia," agreed Milton. "Either that, or blinded by lust like the poor lieutenant over there. She'll have him so worn out by opening night that his 'Younger than Springtime' is likely to be hoary as winter."

"Speaking of those who are young and spring-like," commented Philippa, "what's Erica doing here? I thought she was leaving on the weekend."

Milton looked across at the vivacious redhead who was lighting up the hall as she tapped her way through the routine that the choreographer was teaching the nurses.

"Ah," he said sagely, "I have the story on that."

"Naturally," said Philippa. Milton always had the story on everything.

"The wedding was cancelled," Milton said gleefully, his eyebrows soaring towards his receding hairline. "All very scandalous—'Sex and the City' and then some. The bride went to Vegas for a stagette with her girlfriends, and she ended up sleeping with some hunky football player who was there with his teammates. Predictably, one of her perfidious girlfriends blabbed to her prospective groom, and he, equally predictably, told his ladylove to take a hike, preferably on I5. Christian, of course, is happy because Erica is now going to stick around and fill in the ensemble role, so he has his girlfriend and his replacement in one fell swoop. And," Milton added with a wicked glint in his eye, "she's going to understudy your part. I mean, you can't blame him. She's such a little tintype of you."

Philippa refused to rise to the bait. Instead, she said, "So there's been no word about Cynthia Borden?"

"Haven't heard a thing. That's something I don't have the buzz on. Hopefully, her husband tracked her down, but she definitely isn't doing the show."

Milton bounced away to refill his coffee cup. Philippa tossed her empty cup into the garbage bin and glanced impatiently at her watch. She wondered how long the choreographer would take to put the dancers through their paces. She saw that Christian was still locked in discussion with the musical director, so blocking wasn't going to start any time soon. Sighing, she set down her script and turned to watch the nurses wrapping up their routine. Erica was certainly an accomplished dancer as well as a good singer and actress. A triple threat, indeed. Good job she was going back to Ontario, mused Philippa, immediately feeling guilty for her uncharitable thoughts.

The number ended in a blaze of dazzling smiles and flamboyant poses, and with one circular sweep of his arm, the choreographer dismissed the nurses and beckoned the dark-haired dancer who was playing Liat. Without missing a beat, the rehearsal pianist swung into "Happy Talk" and Liat gracefully set her palms together and laid her cheek against her slender hands. Philippa was struck by the instant change of atmosphere in the hall. Erica had been all sunshine and razzle-dazzle, but Liat was exquisite. As she mimed the movements to the song, the other performers in the hall gradually turned from their conversations and watched. The one notable exception was Octavia, who was still provocatively hovering around Kevin Burr. However, to Philippa's surprise, Kevin seemed to have lost interest in Octavia's charms. He was staring over her shoulder and his eyes were riveted on Liat. His expression was tender and adoring. He's in love with her, Philippa thought suddenly. Octavia doesn't stand a chance.

Philippa was so struck by this revelation that she did not notice a figure creeping up behind her. She jumped as she felt two arms slide around her waist and draw her into a close embrace. A soft, seductive baritone began to sing in her ear.

"'One dream in my heart, one love to be living for ...'"

Philippa resisted her impulse to lean back and enjoy the serenade. Instead, she wriggled free and pushed the hands away.

"Stop it, Adam. Cut it out!"

"Hey, get in character. We're supposed to be madly in love."

"Onstage only."

Adam looked hurt.

"I've moved out of Gretchen's apartment," he said sorrowfully. "That's all over. You might at least act pleased to have me here."

Philippa relented.

"I am pleased you're here," she admitted. "I can't think of anyone I know who'd be better in your part. You'll have all the little old ladies drooling every time you open your mouth."

"Thanks a lot," said Adam. "What about the young ladies?"

"Those too. But not me," Philippa added hastily as Adam's eyes lit up. She had no intention of encouraging him.

"Oh, well, I'll just have to wrest that luscious brunette away from Joe Cable." Adam ogled Octavia, who was still attempting to vamp Kevin Burr.

"Do," said Philippa wickedly. "Octavia will give you a run for your money." And use up most of it too, she thought complacently. Octavia had expensive tastes.

She glanced back towards the director's table. Liat's dance was coming to a close and Christian was signalling to the choreographer that he was ready to begin the blocking rehearsal. Philippa picked up her script and went to find out where he intended to start, but as she reached the table, she saw that Christian was looking past her. She turned to see what had caught his attention. A uniformed RCMP constable had entered the hall. He had stopped to speak to Lucy Wood, the costume mistress, who was measuring a chorister nearby. After a brief exchange, Lucy waved her tape measure towards Christian, and with a nod of thanks, the constable strode across the hall. Philippa felt a growing dread as the policeman approached. She hoped the reason for his presence was not what she feared.

However, when the constable began to speak, her suspicions were confirmed. Eight days had elapsed since Joseph Borden had first gone to the police to report his wife's disappearance and there had been no sign of her since. Cynthia Borden had now been officially declared a missing person.

*      *      *

After the policeman left, a hum of speculation rippled through the hall. Christian quickly quashed the chatter, but although the rehearsal continued smoothly, the tension that had arrived with the constable permeated the company for the rest of the evening.

When the break was called, the murmuring started again. Kevin Burr brought his coffee over and sat next to Philippa. She was surprised that he had singled her out since she had never received more than a token greeting from him before. She assumed that Milton's gossip mill was to blame. Most likely, Kevin had been told that she had a knack for solving mysteries, and, like everyone else in the hall, he wanted to talk about the missing chorister.

"It's a shame," he said. "She was a real nice girl."

Philippa's interest was piqued. She had not realized that the good-looking tenor knew the missing girl.

"You've worked with Cynthia Borden?"

"Yeah. We were in *Wizard of Oz* together. I played the Tin Man to her Dorothy. I liked Cynthia. She never said much. She was kind of quiet and shy, but she had a lovely voice and she was a terrific little actress. That's when she came to life." He smiled reminiscently. "It was like a shadow that became substance for a little while, and then faded back into a modest little nobody—almost as if she didn't have an identity unless she was performing."

Philippa eyed Kevin quizzically, wondering if she had underestimated him. She'd sized him up as a handsome, but vapid singing machine—the epitome of the tenor jokes that sopranos laughed over in the dressing rooms—but there could be depths to him that she had not perceived. Still, there was something not quite sincere about his larger-than-life declamation. Actors, thought Philippa, were heartless creatures. They saw every situation as an opportunity to explore their own emotions. However, if Kevin had known Cynthia Borden, he might know something useful. Curious to get his impressions, she said, "I don't recall her from the auditions. What does she look like?"

"Tiny little thing. Brown hair, hazel eyes. Like a little mouse. She was at the tryouts on Monday night. Came alive to sing 'Over the Rainbow'—a smart choice since it's Christian's song-of-the-moment—and then faded into the woodwork again."

"That's why I don't remember her," said Philippa. "I sang on Sunday, and Christian said I didn't have to come back for the recalls." Philippa looked reflective. "Christian said Cynthia sometimes missed rehearsal due to illness. Do you think there's a chance that her disappearance is related to her health problems?"

"The only health problems she had were allergies," said Kevin. "Nuts and wasp stings. She had to carry an EpiPen at all times, but otherwise she was as healthy as a horse. Christian's exaggerating."

"Perhaps, but her husband did say she was depressed. Her parents had recently died in a car crash."

"If she was depressed, it's because she felt guilty." Kevin's smooth, all-American-boy good looks seemed strangely at odds with the shrewd analysis he was offering. "She was always too busy performing or travelling with her husband to get over to see them. She told me once that she felt bad about that. It was the only time I heard more than a couple of words from her, so it must have been getting to her."

"Guilt is a pretty powerful emotion," said Philippa. "Maybe she just walked away from everything."

"No way." Kevin was adamant. "If she was depressed, she'd have used the show to revive her spirits. And there's no way she'd walk out on her husband. He doted on her. He's rolling in money too. They had everything ... a magnificent house, a fast car, designer clothes. He took her on great trips ... London, New York, Paris. You name it; she'd been there."

"What on earth does he do?"

"He's a stockbroker. He's a fair bit older than her. He saw her in *Brigadoon* six years ago when she was only nineteen and just starting out. She played Jane, that little cameo part in the last act. He fell for her on the spot. It was a whirlwind courtship. A dozen red roses arrived for her at the next performance and every subsequent night until the show closed. She was dazzled, which isn't surprising when you consider how much money he has, but she was really in love too. There's no way that she's gone voluntarily. She must have been attacked. Poor kid'll be dead in a ditch somewhere."

"They haven't found her body."

"If she was abducted by a sexual predator, he could have taken her anywhere. Her body might never be found."

Philippa shuddered. "I hope you're wrong."

"Or maybe she was killed for her jewellery." Kevin frowned like a schoolboy trying to come up with the answer to a difficult question. "Cynthia's engagement ring had a diamond the size of an egg, and she had a pendant and earring set too—Tiffany pieces, each with silver and gold leaf, and another big diamond. She always wore them. That made her pretty vulnerable wandering along the street."

"That raises another possibility," said Philippa. "If Borden was so wealthy, maybe Cynthia was kidnapped. Someone might be holding her for ransom. I wonder if there have been any demands for money. I think I'll call my brother and find out."

"What does your brother have to do with it?" asked Kevin.

"He's an RCMP detective."

Kevin's coffee-cup arm jerked, almost sending the remains of his drink into his lap.

"Really?"

"Really. A very good one too. He'll keep me posted on what's going on."

Kevin muttered something unintelligible, rose to his feet and drifted away. Philippa sighed. Sometimes, having a policeman in the family made one feel like a pariah. She wondered what the chip on Kevin's shoulder was—guilty conscience, or pique over too many traffic tickets. Irritated, she finished her coffee, tossed her cup in the bin and picked up her score. It was time to get back to work anyway.

*       *       *

True to her word, Philippa called Richard the following day. However, he had no news of the missing girl. Her bank account had not been used, her charge cards showed no activity, and there had been no demands for ransom. Borden had hired a private detective and was constantly badgering the police with leads and queries, but to no avail. Every police force in the Lower Mainland had her photograph on file and the private eye had been following every possible lead, but Cynthia Borden appeared to have vanished without a trace.

Gradually, Philippa's preoccupation with the missing chorister diminished as the demands of her role occupied her attention more and more. The weeks flew by rapidly, and as production week approached, cast and crew alike were abuzz with the excitement of the imminent opening night. The dress rehearsal was scheduled for the May long weekend, and every member of the company was happy to sacrifice the holiday Monday in order to have the run-through during the afternoon, thus allowing two evenings off prior to the opening.

When Philippa and Milton arrived at the theatre, they came through the stage door and found Octavia holding forth in the lobby. Her audience consisted of Adam Craig and Jane Fry, the stately matron who played the lead nurse.

"I don't know why 'Live From (bloody) Lincoln Centre' had to run the Broadway production on PBS right before our opening," spat Octavia. "All we need is a bunch of self-elected critics who think they actually know something coming backstage and telling us we were *almost* as good as New York."

The glass door swung open again and Erica came into the foyer, closely followed by Christian. The director was in a world of his own. He waved vaguely to the assembled performers; then, humming his favourite tune, he loped up the stairs that led to the stage. Erica remained to chat.

"Are we talking about the Broadway revival?" she asked. "I saw it when I was in New York last spring. It was terrific—way better than the TV performance. The Nellie I saw was a much stronger singer. I liked the fill-in Luther better too—I picked him out doing chorus and bit parts when I watched it on TV. He was delightful."

"Oh, God!" snarled Octavia. "See what I mean."

"Calm down, Octavia," said Milton. "I'm sure you'll be every bit as bloody as the Mary on Broadway. In a good sense, of course," Milton continued smoothly, turning his head towards Philippa so that Octavia couldn't see him wink.

Adam coiled his arm around Octavia's shoulders. "You'll be better," he said soothingly. "And I'm not worried about comparisons either. I'll take on Paolo Szot any time."

Octavia decompressed and batted her eyelashes at Adam.

"I'll take you *both* on any time," she purred. She slithered out of his hold, patted him on the cheek, and glided away in the direction of the dressing rooms. As if attached by an invisible string, Adam drifted after her. Milton grinned, rolled his eyes, and, playing an imaginary violin, sashayed down the hall on Adam's heels.

Philippa watched, amused, and gratified that she did not feel so much as a twinge of jealousy. Octavia was welcome to Adam. They might even be a good match. Both good-looking, both self-centred. Philippa was glad she had moved on. She abandoned her private thoughts and turned back to the others. Jane and Erica were gossiping about offstage love affairs. For a moment, Philippa assumed they were talking about Adam and Octavia, but as she continued to listen, she realized that they had noticed how Kevin Burr had fallen for his lovely costar. She wondered how many other people were aware of the budding romance between Liat and the tenor. Philippa glanced up at the clock; then, with a start, she saw that they had all lost track of time. The rehearsal was to start in twenty minutes. She jogged Erica's arm and pointed at her watch. Erica gasped, grabbed Jane's wrist, and the three singers scampered down the corridor.

When they entered the dressing room, Octavia had already spread her belongings along the counter and was transforming her aristocratic features into a dramatic Polynesian mask. The mezzo's green eyes had morphed to black with the aid of coloured lenses, although her own malicious glint shone through. At the far end of the counter, Liat was bent double, peering at the floor.

"No, she isn't doing warm-up exercises," drawled Octavia. "She's lost a contact lens."

"No, I haven't." Liat straightened up and held up her hand triumphantly.

Erica flopped down in the chair beside her.

"You should carry a spare pair," she said. "I always do."

She opened her case and, humming to herself, began to lay out her makeup on the counter.

"For crying out loud," snapped Octavia. "We're doing *South Pacific*, not *The Wizard of Oz*. Why does everyone around here keep humming that tune? You were singing it earlier, too," she snarled, turning to Liat.

"That's because I keep hearing it," the girl said apologetically.

"Sorry," said Erica. "Force of habit. It's Christian's—"

"—favourite song. Yes, we know, but it isn't mine, so why don't you switch to one of your own numbers, or better still, just shut up. And why don't you do something with your hair?" Octavia added snidely.

"I have," said Erica. "What's wrong with it?"

"This is the forties. Bangs weren't in fashion. You should have one of those swept-back and rolled-up dos. So should you," she added, turning towards Philippa. "Anyone would think you're playing Annie. It's so unprofessional putting vanity before authenticity."

"Oh, stow it, Octavia," said Philippa. "You're not the director."

"That's true," Octavia responded coolly, "but if Christian goes off to Stratford and starts ignoring period details, he won't last very long. And I," she added pertly, "have Martha Petrel coming to see my performance on opening night, so I want everything to be perfect."

Erica's jaw dropped.

"Petrel? The agent? She handles biggies. How did you manage that?"

"Wouldn't *you* like to know?"

Ignoring the glares of the other occupants of the room, Octavia put the finishing touches to her makeup and stood up. Then, lightly trilling "Happy Talk", she sailed out of the dressing room.

"She's probably sleeping with Martha Petrel's husband," said Jane Fry acerbically.

"Why don't you plant that rumour in time for opening night?" suggested Erica. "That would take the sting out of her tail."

"Nothing," declared Philippa, "takes the sting out of Octavia's tail. Our only hope is that Petrel will land her a job on the other side of the country. In the meantime, we have to put up with her through a four-week run."

The door flew open and the producer popped her head through.

"Programs, ladies," she announced, and plopped a pile of booklets on the counter. Philippa grabbed one for herself and passed the rest along to the others. She flipped through quickly, checking that her own information was correct and glancing at the photographs of the other performers. Then, as she came to the last page, her exuberant mood evaporated.

A colour photograph of an unfamiliar face gazed back at her from the inside-rear cover. She read the name under the picture. Cynthia Borden. A public appeal for information had been placed in the back of the program. Philippa studied the soulful eyes. They peered out from a long, narrow face, framed in dark hair that fell like wings from a centre parting. A modern-day Jane Eyre without the resilient spirit, thought Philippa. Cynthia looked fragile and a little withdrawn. No wonder Joseph Borden felt so protective towards his wife. The girl had the look of a born victim.

Philippa felt guilty. She had been so focussed on all the exciting things happening in her own life that she had forgotten about Cynthia and the frantic husband who must be a nervous wreck after six weeks of anxious speculation. Chastising herself for her selfishness, she resolved to phone her brother again to see if there had been any progress. However, the call would have to wait until she got home. This was hardly the time to detour into the role of sleuth; she had to get into the character of a U.S. army nurse. For the next three hours, the mystery of the missing chorister would have to wait. Philippa put down the program and started slapping on her makeup. Determinedly thrusting Cynthia Borden from her thoughts, she mentally transported herself to the South Pacific.

The rehearsal went smoothly and was over by five o'clock. Philippa was happy to get home. She was looking forward to a quiet dinner and an early night since she had promised to go to a movie with Bob Miller the following evening. Before she started in the kitchen, she called Richard, hoping to get the latest update on Cynthia Borden. Predictably, she only reached her brother's voicemail, so she left a message and began her dinner preparations. As she was grating cheese for her linguini, the phone rang. Thinking it was Richard, she hurried to answer, but the caller was Bob Miller. He was phoning to say he had to work the following night. The movie would have to be postponed. Philippa felt let down. Almost every time they had tried to set up a date, one or the other of them had been required to cancel. However, she hid her disappointment.

"That's OK," she said. "I'm pretty tired. I'll be better off getting an early night."

"I'll be at your first night on Wednesday, though," said Miller. "I'm bringing my mother and sister and the two rug-rats. We're all looking forward to it."

"Isn't your brother-in-law coming?"

"No. He's up in Nelson. He and Jody are moving up there in August. He's working on the house."

"That's too bad. Still, it'll be lovely to have you there," Philippa said sincerely. "None of my family will be at the opening. Mum and Dad are touring around the U.S. in their motorhome, and the others are all busy with their own activities. You'll be my only cheering section. Look," she continued, switching to the topic that was on her mind, "everyone at the theatre is wondering about Cynthia Borden. I know it's an RCMP case, but I can't get hold of Richard. Do you have any idea what's going on? Has there been any progress at all?"

There was a silence at the other end. At last, Miller spoke.

"Actually, there has been a development, but you shouldn't blab it all over the theatre, at least not until after you've opened. It'll just depress everyone."

Philippa felt a chill run down her spine.

"Oh, God! What's happened? Don't tell me she's dead."

"It doesn't look good," said Miller. "A dog-walker went into the Burnside RCMP office three days ago. She'd been walking on a trail near the Bordens' house and she had to dig in the bushes to recover a ball that her spaniel refused to retrieve. She came across an abandoned handbag so she brought it in to the station."

"Cynthia's?"

"It would appear so. The contents included her cellphone and a wallet with her credit cards and ID."

"So you think she was attacked on her way to rehearsal."

"Unfortunately, it's likely," said Miller. "The missing-person inquiry is shaping up to become a murder investigation. I'm sorry to bring bad news, but you wanted to know."

"How did Borden take the news?"

"That I can't tell you. It's not a VPD case. We just get the misper info and the updates."

"Maybe I'll go round to see him tomorrow," said Philippa. "He must be frantic. He was so upset that day she disappeared. If nothing else, I could at least relay the cast's sympathies."

"Don't you do anything of the sort," said Miller. "You stay out of it."

"Why?" said Philippa indignantly.

"Because it's an unsolved police case and you aren't part of the investigation."

"Don't be stuffy," said Philippa. "I'm not going there to investigate. I was just thinking of making a social call."

Miller's voice acquired an edge.

"For a smart girl, that's a pretty stupid idea," he said coolly. "You stay away from Borden until the RCMP come up with a definitive conclusion. Don't you know by now that whenever a woman is missing or murdered, the spouse is always in the front line as a suspect?"

"Are you serious? The poor man was devastated."

"Philippa ..."

Philippa sighed. She could tell an official caution was forthcoming.

"All right, all right. I hear you."

"Good. So enjoy your nights off, forget about solving mysteries, and concentrate on your show."

"Okay," said Philippa, "but would you keep your ear to the ground and call me if you do hear anything new."

There was a short silence at the other end. Then Miller spoke.

"All right, this is the deal. I'll get an update and fill you in, as long as you promise to stay out of it and don't try playing detective. If any information comes your way, you don't act on it. You pass it on to your brother. OK?"

Philippa crossed her fingers behind her back.

"All right," she agreed. "I promise."

"Fine," said Miller. "Now forget about the case, get some rest, and I'll see you on Wednesday."

Before Philippa could thank him, he rang off. Philippa let out another sigh. The downside of dating policemen, she thought ruefully, was that they tended to suffer from severe cases of terminal bossiness.

*      *      *

The following day was stormy. Philippa slept in, had a late breakfast, vocalized and exercised, and by noon had done everything on her to-do list.

She was still feeling rebellious at the lecture she had received the previous evening, and, with a long, idle afternoon stretching before her, she decided to go ahead with her original plan. She opened her desk and extracted a box of cards with paintings of theatrical harlequins. Quickly writing a note on behalf of the *South Pacific* cast and crew, she slipped the card into an envelope and wrote Joseph Borden's name on the outside. A sympathy call could hardly be classified as detective work, she rationalized, and Borden probably wouldn't be home anyway, so she couldn't be accused of interfering. Then she scanned the cast list that had been issued at the first rehearsal and found Cynthia Borden's address.

The rain was pounding down as Philippa drove along Canada Way. It was hard to believe that it was nearly the end of May. She put the windshield wipers on high and turned up the heater. The day was raw and cold, and the last thing she needed was to catch a chill right before her opening.

Turning off before the rehearsal-hall exit, she entered the exclusive neighbourhood where the Bordens' home was located. When she arrived at the house, which stood on a lot the size of a small park, she saw a silver-grey BMW in the driveway. Pulling in behind it, she got out and ran up the garden path. Foolishly, she did not take her umbrella as she did not have far to go, but the rain was coming down so hard that her coat was soaked by the time she reached the porch. Borden was home and opened the door so quickly that he must have seen her drive in. He looked leaner, and much older than Philippa recalled from their first meeting. She observed that his left eye had developed a twitch. Weeks of anxiety had done their work. Borden seemed surprised to see her, though not displeased. Philippa began to tell him the reason for her call, but he put up a hand to silence her, said they could talk over a drink, and invited her inside.

Kevin Burr had been right about the man's wealth. The house was a spectacular conglomeration of white rectangles, soaring skylights and furniture that looked as if it had been purchased from a Jordan's showroom. In spite of Borden's nervous state, Philippa sensed that he took pleasure in escorting her through his dwelling, and there was something very poignant about his eagerness to make her see how Cynthia had lived. He offered Philippa coffee, and when she accepted, led her into a kitchen that could have belonged on a celebrity-chef set. Here he produced a fancy concoction on a top-of-the-line latte machine. When the drinks were ready, he conducted her to a heated atrium at the rear of the house where exotic plants bloomed inside and the rain could be seen lashing the glass exterior. The choice of room was welcome as the blast of heat took the chill out of Philippa's bones. Borden set the lattes on the rattan table and gestured to Philippa to sit down. She eased her way past a giant pot with an overgrown floribunda and settled herself in a wicker chair. Borden sat down in the other chair. Behind him hung a pale yellow bougainvillea, lushly trailing down as if trying to escape from its basket. The pallid sheen of the blooms matched the sallow cast of Borden's skin, another sign that the stress of the past weeks had worn him down. He was watching Philippa eagerly, and she suddenly realized that he was hoping for news of his wife.

"I'm afraid you've misinterpreted my visit," she apologized. "I haven't heard anything new. I just wanted to come on behalf of the cast and tell you how sorry we are about Cynthia."

Borden's eye started to twitch, and he picked up his coffee mug, gripping it tightly, as if the pressure of his hand could steady the rebellious eye. He sat silently for a moment; then he started to talk about Cynthia.

Philippa listened patiently for she could see that Borden was desperate to share his feelings. It was as if he had to talk about his wife in order to feel she was still with him, but as he droned on, Philippa started to feel that he was taking possession of her as well. She tried to tune out the incessant flow and stared through the glass panes, her eyes drawn by a weathered-looking gazebo at the end of the lawn. The rough wood had turned grey in the torrential downpour and the quaint structure contrasted bizarrely with the pristine modern angles of the house. She wished that she were sitting there in peaceful solitude instead of listening to the anguished outpourings of the man seated opposite her.

All of a sudden, Borden paused. He had noticed where she was looking.

"That was there when we bought the house," he said. "It was a relic from the mansion that used to stand on the property. Cynthia loved it, so we left it intact. She went there to study her scripts. It was her private retreat."

He hesitated again, as if he had become conscious of the way he had been rambling. "I'm sorry," he said. "I must be boring you terribly. You've been very kind, coming round and listening like this."

Philippa immediately felt guilty for wanting to get away. She leaned forward and attempted to offer some encouraging words, though inwardly she was conscious of the inadequacy of the trite phrases.

Borden shook his head sadly.

"You don't have to pretend to believe she'll be found," he said. "I'm not as naïve as I sound, and I realize something bad has happened to her—but talking about her keeps her alive for me." He pointed to a stand in the corner that was piled with books and magazines. "Would you like to see her scrapbook?" he asked. "It dates from the show she was in when we met." Without waiting for Philippa's reply, he brought the album over to the table and set it between them. Philippa watched and listened as he turned the pages and talked about his wife's successes. Cynthia had been in a lot of productions, and the photographs were visible proof that she was a versatile performer who could tackle a variety of roles.

"What's that one?" Philippa asked, pointing to a colour eight-by-ten that filled an entire page. She was usually good at guessing show titles, but the combination of an Arabian princess, an Edwardian gentleman, a Mountie and a scantily dressed vamp was beyond her.

"That was a revue—Broadway excerpts. She was in the segment from *Damn Yankees*. Gwen Vernon had nothing on my Cynthia."

Borden flipped the page. Philippa instantly identified the next collage.

"*The Wizard of Oz!*" she exclaimed. "Doesn't she look adorable as Dorothy?"

"She was enchanting in the part," said Borden. "It was her first lead role and the director bullied her a lot, but he drew a fantastic performance out of her. He's the same fellow you're working with. I recognized him when I came to the hall."

Philippa stabbed her finger towards a photo of the Tin Man.

"That's Kevin Burr," she said, "though I wouldn't know it unless he'd told me he played the part. He's in our show too."

Borden frowned.

"He is?" He fell quiet for a moment and looked thoughtful. "I wonder if that's why she was reluctant to go."

Philippa was perplexed.

"I don't understand. Kevin speaks very highly of Cynthia. I got the impression that he liked her a lot."

Borden's eyes darkened.

"He did. Too damn much." Without warning, his face reddened and his voice shook with anger. The eruption was sudden and disturbing. "Kevin Burr was a menace," he snapped. "He wouldn't leave her alone. He was even after her to come to his salon to get her hair done, not that she ever took him up on the offer. It was a good job I was there to pick her up every night or he would have hounded her constantly."

Borden slapped the scrapbook shut and fell silent, but his face was flushed and his eyes glittered dangerously. Uneasily, Philippa saw that there was another side to Joseph Borden. Guiltily recalling Miller's warning, she seized the opportunity to draw the visit to a close. She stood up, but as she moved from the table, she brushed her hand against the rose bush. Feeling the prick of the thorns, she pulled her hand away, but when she glanced down, she saw that she was bleeding.

Borden's anger evaporated instantly. He leapt up and became courteously attentive.

"You must put something on that," he said solemnly. "There's a medical kit in the en suite in Cynthia's room." His colour had returned to normal and his manner was solicitous, but Philippa was anxious to leave. Borden's mercurial temperament was setting off alarm bells in her mind. She gathered up her coat.

"I'm fine. It can wait."

Borden stepped forward, took her coat, and firmly contradicted her.

"No, it can't. You don't want that puncture to get infected." He ushered Philippa out of the atrium and through to the front hall. "Go on up," he insisted. "It's the first door on the right at the top of the stairs." Philippa glanced back nervously as she climbed the stairs, apprehensive in case he intended to follow her. However, to her intense relief, he remained below.

She entered the bedroom and found herself in a boudoir fit for a princess. The furniture was white inlaid with gold, the duvet and valances were delicate shades of pink and mauve, and the latticed window was framed in frothy white lace. Glancing through the window, she saw that the room overlooked a heated swimming pool which was steaming in the steady downpour. She turned from the window and went into the washroom. It was huge, with white fixtures and pale yellow walls topped by a frieze of blue cornflowers. At the far end was a long makeup counter where she tracked down the medical kit. Above the counter was a wide mirror framed in light bulbs, and the adjacent wall held a variety of colour eight-by-ten photographs, framed duplicates or enlargements of the pictures she had seen in the album. She was glad of an opportunity to look at the pictures without the distraction of Borden's commentaries. One in particular caught her attention and she studied it for several moments.

As she returned the Polysporin and Band-Aids to the medical kit, she noticed a jewel box at the end of the counter. The lid was slightly raised, propped open by a section of a chain that was protruding over the edge of the box. Curiously, she raised the lid. Then she froze. On top of a pile of expensive-looking baubles was a pendant exactly like the one Kevin had described, and next to it were two matching earrings and a sparkling diamond ring, fused with a plain band that was unquestionably a wedding ring.

The sound of footsteps caused Philippa to whirl round, and quickly, she shut the box and stepped out of the bathroom. Borden was standing in the bedroom doorway. Stunned and confused by the discovery she had made, Philippa steeled herself to walk towards him. Smiling politely, she thanked him and passed by. He followed her down in silence and helped her with her coat. Then he opened the front door and ushered her through. His friendly smile was back in place, making Philippa almost believe that the glimpse of fury she had witnessed earlier had only been her imagination.

But his final words on parting chilled her blood.

"You see," he said. "Everything is just the way she left it. You can still feel her presence here. It's as if she never really went away."

*       *       *

Rather than risk the wrath of Bob Miller, Philippa called her brother and told him what she had seen during her visit to Joseph Borden. Richard, not surprisingly, was extremely annoyed with her. Philippa endured the lecture and promised never to do anything so foolhardy and reckless again. However, she had the comfort of knowing that the RCMP had been informed, and she knew they would follow through. Feeling she had done all she could, she set off, picked up Milton, and focussed her attention on the evening ahead.

When Philippa and Milton arrived at the theatre, they entered the stage door and found Christian talking with the stage manager. He greeted Philippa with a smile.

"You're Miss Popularity," he said breezily. "Four flower deliveries waiting for you in your dressing room."

"Wow!" said Milton. "They can't all be from the handsome detective. Who are your other admirers?"

"My parents usually send flowers from the family," said Philippa. "No idea who the other two are from."

She followed Milton down the corridor. He veered off into the men's dressing room, and Philippa went to the room she shared with the other female leads. As she entered, the scent of flowers almost overwhelmed her. The room resembled a florist's shop. Ten glorious floral arrangements lined the counter, along with a variety of single blooms and an assortment of cards.

"That's your four," said Erica, nodding towards a cluster of ornamental pots. "The carnations are from Adam. He gave Octavia flowers too. The single yellow rose is from Christian," she added. "We've all got one of those. And that fabulous Purdy's tray of chocs and nuts is from Kevin to all of us. Help yourself. The orange creams are delicious."

Philippa smiled.

"The dahlias will be from my mum and dad," she said, helping herself to a chocolate, "and the red roses will be from Bob," she added smugly. "I wonder who sent that lovely array of spring flowers. It's quite exquisite."

She dug down into the bouquet and pulled out the card.

"Oh, that's odd." Philippa frowned. "They're from Bob. Then who on earth sent me a dozen red roses?"

"You must have a secret admirer," said Erica. "Don't keep us in suspense. Read the card."

Philippa opened the envelope that had come with the flowers. Then, as she read the card, her eyes few wide.

"What is it?" Erica asked.

"They're from Joseph Borden," Philippa said uneasily. "They're to thank me for visiting him and showing him kindness. Those are his words."

Erica stared at Philippa.

"You went to see him?"

"Yes. I felt badly because we've all been so busy that we'd pretty well forgotten about Cynthia. I just wanted to convey the sympathy of the cast." Philippa paled as she remembered Kevin's description of the flowers that Borden had sent to Cynthia when he had first met her. "But roses," she said bleakly. "The last thing I need is for him to transfer his interest to me."

"No," said Erica soberly. "You certainly don't need that. Christian seems to think the man is a bit strange."

Erica fell silent and continued to apply her makeup. Philippa moved the flowers aside and sat down. As she did so, Octavia entered the room.

"What's the matter with you two?" she said. "Anyone would think those flowers were for a funeral, judging by the looks on your faces. Mind you," she added to Philippa, with a spiteful glint in her eye, "you'll feel even more funereal when you hear what I have to say. Guess who I saw last night?"

Philippa took a deep breath and opened her makeup case.

"No idea. Not interested," she said.

"Oh, you will be," cooed Octavia. "I was dining late at Earls and saw your cute detective on the far side of the room. And," she added gleefully, "he wasn't alone. He had a woman with him."

"So what. He was on duty. At some point, he has to take a break and eat. It was probably one of his colleagues. VPD has several female detectives."

"The woman wasn't a colleague," said Octavia. Philippa's heart sank. She could tell from the mezzo's twisted smile that she was getting ready to deliver a verbal coup de grâce.

Octavia picked her cellphone off the counter, opened it, stretched languidly like a cobra about to bite, and thrust it under Philippa's nose.

"She was my high-school friend," she said happily. "DC Miller's ex that obviously isn't. See. I even snapped them on my cell just in case you didn't believe me. So if he told you he was working, he was telling you a lie."

Philippa kept her face impassive, but inside she could feel her heart breaking.

"Can't wait to hear you sing 'I'm Gonna Wash That Man Right Outa My Hair' tonight," Octavia continued mercilessly. "Should be the hit of the show."

*          *          *

Philippa was not quite sure how she got through the evening, for when the curtain finally went down, she remembered nothing about the performance. She knew it must have gone well because she was vaguely aware of Adam hugging her and rhapsodizing about her amazing energy, and saying something about the fact that he'd never seen her so on top of a role. Every compliment he gave her was echoed by the people who came backstage. *South Pacific* was a hit.

To Philippa's intense relief, when Bob Miller found her, he seemed almost awed and shy, so she was able to focus her attention on his niece and nephew who were bubbling over with excitement and thrilled to chat with the star of the show. Then, before it became too obvious that she had no desire to talk with the detective, Adam appeared at her elbow and whisked her away to meet Martha Petrel, who, to Octavia's fury, had asked to be introduced to Philippa.

Petrel had been impressed by Philippa's performance, and she told her so in no uncertain terms. Promising great things to come, she placed her card in Philippa's hand and told her to call her. She continued to chat, discussing roles and possibilities, and automatically, Philippa parroted the appropriate responses. Adam kept his arm proprietarily about Philippa's shoulders throughout the exchange, and from the corner of her eye, Philippa was aware of Bob Miller watching them, his face expressionless. After a while, Miller and his sister quietly left.

By the time the agent had gone, the area had cleared. Philippa and Adam were alone on the stage.

"Want to go for a drink?" Adam offered.

"What's happened to Octavia?" Philippa said tartly, misery adding an edge to her tongue.

"Gone off in a huff, just like your detective." Adam gave a wry grin. "Sorry. Did I muck that up?"

"Not really," said Philippa gloomily. "It wasn't going anywhere."

"Then what about that drink?"

"No. Not tonight. I'm not in the mood. Maybe on the weekend."

Adam nodded and turned to go. Exhausted and deflated, Philippa followed him downstairs. The long, narrow corridor to the dressing rooms seemed as bleak and drab as her spirits. The adrenalin rush that had come with the show had evaporated and the knowledge of her success was like a sharp, stabbing pain in her side instead of the euphoria that usually followed a triumphant performance. Ahead, Adam disappeared into his dressing room. Wearily,

Philippa headed for her own room, but before she had moved more than a few steps, the men's door opened again and Kevin Burr stepped out.

"Philippa," he called after her, "could I have a quick word?"

Philippa turned back. Kevin came to join her and drew her to the side of the corridor. He looked agitated.

"What's up?" Philippa asked.

"Erica tells me that you went to see Joseph Borden yesterday. She says he sent you flowers tonight."

"That's right."

"Look, you're not thinking of seeing him again ... like, well ... you wouldn't consider going out with him?"

"Kevin, what on earth is the matter? I went round to the house to tell him how sorry we are about Cynthia. That's all."

"Yes, but you see, if he's sent you flowers, he may be going to ask you out. That's the way he operates. I mean, you were probably very sweet and sympathetic, and you're very pretty. And he can be very persuasive. I just wanted to make sure you weren't letting yourself get involved."

"Kevin, you're going around in circles and tying yourself up in knots. What exactly are you trying to say?"

Kevin flushed. Looking uncomfortable, he said, "If he asks you out, don't go."

Philippa was intrigued. She had no intention of going out with Joseph Borden, but she wanted to know why Kevin thought it was a bad idea. Cleary, the singer knew far more than he had admitted when he'd talked about Cynthia before.

"Why not?" she demanded.

Kevin sighed. "He's not the nice guy he appears on the surface," he said. "I didn't like to say anything before, but the reality is, Cynthia didn't have a very good time with him. He's totally narcissistic and he controlled her life so utterly that she was completely stifled. He separated her from her family. That's why she didn't visit her parents. It was because he wouldn't let her."

"Oh, good lord," said Philippa. "And then they died in an accident. Poor girl. No wonder she was depressed."

Kevin rattled on.

"Yes. It was devastating for her. It was the last straw after six years of mental cruelty. She completely lost her sense of self living with Borden. I told you she was a good actress. Well, acting was the only way she could come to life. That's why she was so incredibly moving singing 'Over the Rainbow' when she did *Oz*. She *wanted* to go there. Around Borden, she was a walking zombie."

Philippa's head was spinning. Kevin's change of attitude was utterly bewildering. She wondered if he would be goaded into more disclosures if she defended Borden.

"Maybe she just didn't know how to handle him," she said. "I thought he seemed kind and sincere."

Kevin's eyes bulged.

"Philippa, look … forget it. Stay away from him. He's dangerous. He used to hit her, but never where anyone could see the bruises. I know he's charming on the surface, but don't be taken in. I don't want to see you sucked into the same mess that Cynthia had to endure."

Philippa decided to go on the offensive.

"OK, Kevin, let's get this straight. You might as well know that I began to figure that out for myself, but I'd sure like to know why you didn't tell the police that Borden was violent."

"What was the point?" Kevin fidgeted uncomfortably. "Until that handbag turned up, I just assumed Cynthia had left him."

"No, you didn't. You were quite definite that she'd been abducted and murdered, and you said nothing but good things about Borden. Why the about-face? And how did you know all this stuff about Borden anyway? You told me Cynthia barely said two words to anyone unless she was onstage."

"She unloaded on me once when I was doing her hair."

"Baloney. Borden said she never bothered with hair stylists."

Kevin's eyes were showing increasing strain. He was either going to clam up or blow up. Philippa hoped it was the latter.

"I did do her hair," he muttered sulkily. "Just the one time. Look, what does it matter how I heard? I just wanted to warn you about Borden. I didn't expect an inquisition."

"Hasn't it occurred to you that if Borden was violent, he might be responsible for Cynthia's disappearance?" said Philippa. "Let me tell you what I saw at his house: Cynthia's ring, and the pendant and earrings that you said she always wore. There's a very good chance that he killed her and she's still there, buried in the garden somewhere."

Kevin's breathing became rapid and a quaver in his voice betrayed his panic.

"Now, wait a minute. I could have been mistaken about the jewellery. I didn't know for sure that she always wore those pieces … I mean … You're not going to pass all this along to that brother of yours, are you?"

"Of course I am. What did you expect?"

"Well, I'll deny everything if you do." Kevin's lips tightened mulishly. "Anyway, it's all hearsay. Cynthia didn't actually tell me herself. It was Christian that winkled it out of her. You know what he's like. Eyes like X-rays. Picks up everything that's under the surface. He's the one who told me, and he said it was absolutely confidential. Now, if you've finished grilling me, I'm going home. I've got a long drive out to Maple Ridge and I'm tired."

Looking annoyed, Kevin stalked past Philippa and headed down the hall. Philippa was startled, so it took a moment before his last statement registered, but she came to in time to call out before he reached the end of the corridor.

"Kevin, wait. Maple Ridge? I thought you lived in the same apartment block as Christian in East Vancouver."

"I did, but I moved out several mo—" Kevin stopped in mid-sentence and glared at Philippa. "It's none of your business," he said frostily and walked away.

As he disappeared around the corner, Philippa pondered on his reaction to the news that Cynthia Borden's jewellery remained at the house. Kevin knew far more than he was letting on, but on one matter, he was right. The fact that the treasured pieces were there did not conclusively prove that their owner had been murdered. There was another interpretation that made more sense. No matter how valuable her jewellery was, an abused wife would never want to keep it if it reminded her of a bondage that had crushed and broken her. Philippa thoughtfully continued down the hall until she reached her dressing-room door. As she opened it, she heard the sound of the shower running. A lyrical voice floated above the hum of the water.

*Somewhere over the rainbow, way up high …*

Philippa's glance fell on Erica's makeup case, open on the counter. The singer's spare contact-lens container lay in the top tray. Philippa picked it up and opened it. The lens, soaking in solution, was a startling, bright blue.

Reflectively, Philippa began to process a series of memories: Christian, the caring, perceptive artist who always knew instinctively the strengths and weaknesses of his performers; his unnatural indifference to the wellbeing of Cynthia Borden; the inconsistencies in everything that Kevin Burr had told her; the outright lie he had told Milton about seeing Erica at Christian's apartment; Kevin, the hair stylist, coming in an hour early on the day of the first rehearsal. Philippa could see only one possible answer that explained Cynthia's disappearance.

She looked at the Purdy's tray, still on the counter. The chocolates had been decimated, but the nuts were untouched, except for a few she herself had eaten before the performance. She noticed Erica's handbag on the floor by her chair. The shower continued to run and Erica was still singing her song.

*If happy little bluebirds fly above the rainbow, why, oh why can't I?*

Philippa went over and opened the purse. The bag held what she expected to see. An EpiPen nestled amid the other paraphernalia.

She pulled out her cellphone and punched in her brother's number, and for once, she was in luck. He answered right away. His reply to her question confirmed her suspicions. Cynthia's handbag had held everything that a woman's handbag would normally contain, but the contents had not included an EpiPen.

As she put away her phone, Philippa became aware that the room had fallen silent. The sound of running water had ceased and Erica was no longer singing. Philippa looked up.

Erica stood in the doorway of the bathroom. Her tiny frame was wrapped in a towel and her red hair, black from the shower, was slicked back against her scalp, revealing a long, thin face, which looked frail and vulnerable.

"I ... I thought everyone had gone," she whispered.

"Hello, Cynthia," said Philippa. "Welcome back."

*          *          *

On the drive home, Milton was determined to find out why Philippa had kept him waiting while she was locked in a lengthy discussion with Kevin and Christian. Knowing that Milton would be far more likely to cause trouble by chattering to everyone about the fact that there was a big secret, Philippa swore him to silence and filled him in. For all Milton's love of gossip, she knew he could be a clam when someone's personal safety was at stake.

"You're telling me that Cynthia has been in the show all along?" Milton's natural tenor went up two octaves. "Why? What was all the subterfuge for?"

"She wanted to disappear. That was the only way she could safely get away from Joseph Borden. She knew he would pull out all the stops trying to get her back, and he did too. He harried the police constantly and he hired private detectives to track her down. Cynthia admitted to me that she's been terrified the entire time. Her performance as Erica has been the performance of her life because she really believes that Borden would kill her if he found her. She's convinced that the only way she'll be safe is if he thinks she is dead. All she wants is to escape and start over. And Christian and Kevin are helping her do it."

"Why those two?"

"Christian fell in love with her when he directed her in *Wizard of Oz*. He admired her artistry, and her waif-like appeal really got to him. Borden himself told me how Christian pushed her hard to get the performance he did, but I think he also pushed her until she opened up to him. And then the inevitable happened. She fell for him too. Let's face it, she's one of those women who

163

likes to be led, and Christian is authoritative, just like Borden, except that Christian has a heart of gold and he cares about the other person's needs, not his own. Once Christian understood what was at stake, he devised a plan to help Cynthia escape—and in order to establish the character of Erica, he drew Kevin into his confidence. They were old friends, having been neighbours for a couple of years, and he knew Kevin liked Cynthia and felt sorry for her."

"I suppose it was Kevin who gave her the makeover?" said Milton.

"Yes. Borden was out when Cynthia left to go to the rehearsal, so he didn't know that she went in an hour earlier than usual. On the way, she detoured onto the trail and dumped her handbag in a bush. Then she met Kevin at the hall, and he whisked her into the washroom and dyed and cut her hair. He'd also brought the change of clothes and the blue contacts—everything she needed for her new identity. He bundled her own clothing into a garbage bag and put it in the trunk of his car. Later that night, when he got home, he dumped it into the garbage chute at his apartment, knowing it would be incinerated in the morning. Then he and Christian put on an act so that the people involved in the production became unwitting accomplices in their scheme. Christian pretended to be indifferent about Cynthia Borden. He labelled her as difficult and unpredictable, and Kevin tried to convince everyone that she was the victim of a serial killer. He struck me as rather overdoing it when he talked with me, and I put it down to histrionics, but, of course, he really was putting on a performance. He was scared stiff when he thought I was going to push the police to arrest Borden for murder. That could have blown the whole thing wide open."

Milton looked indignant.

"I've just had a thought," he said. "Kevin was using me when he told me all that stuff about Erica living with Christian for the past three months. That was a bunch of hogwash to make us believe the new girlfriend really existed."

Philippa smiled.

"Yes. He made that up, but you have to admit it was a smart move. Telling you guaranteed that the information would go through the entire cast and be taken as gospel. And once it was a known fact that Erica had been around for three months, no one would dream of connecting her with Cynthia Borden."

"I am offended," sniffed Milton. "What's more, this will cast doubt on my authenticity as a *Who's Who* of theatrical gossip."

"Oh, well. It was in a good cause. Anyway, you aren't the only one who was used. Christian knew I was related to a detective, so he told Kevin to work on me, even though he didn't tell him why. Kev was pretty startled when he found out, but he dutifully did his best to convince me that Cynthia was dead—not a very good best, as he really wasn't smart enough to carry it off, but he gave it his best shot. And the other way Christian used me was pretty tacky. I gave him an earful over that."

"What did he do that warranted an earful?"

"Created Erica. No wonder I related to her so completely. Christian used my looks and personality to give Cynthia a model for a character."

Milton laughed out loud.

"So he did. I said she was a little tintype of you, didn't I? Still," he added, "weren't they taking an awful chance? Why hide her here, where Borden expected her to be? Why not safely send her off to Ontario to wait for Christian there?"

"I think it was brilliant," said Philippa. "You've read those detective stories where thieves hide diamond necklaces in chandeliers—in full view of everyone, yet invisible because of the surroundings. Well, that's what Christian did with Cynthia. Once Borden had come to the hall and seen she was not there, he would have set his minions searching everywhere but at the theatre. Same with the police. This was the one place she was really safe."

"Lost in the South Pacific," mused Milton, "just like Luther Billis. I had no idea I was hiding Cynthia in my rubber dinghy."

"No one could know, except for Christian and Kevin. That's why they were able to 'lose' her in the show."

"So what are you going to tell your brother?" asked Milton. "Isn't that going to be tricky?"

"I'll have to tell him the truth, or at least part of it, but as long as Richard knows Cynthia's safe and alive, the police won't pursue Borden. They won't care if the case file is left open indefinitely."

"What about Bob Miller? Shouldn't you fill him in?"

"No, I don't think so," said Philippa. She fell silent, remembering that Milton had not heard the news that Octavia had so spitefully delivered earlier in the evening.

"Well, everything is certainly coming up roses for you, darling," Milton said happily. "A devoted swain, and now a top-line agent wanting to promote you. Things couldn't be better."

Not wanting to talk about the young VPD detective, Philippa took refuge in song. Milton listened in silence for a few blocks, but then, puzzled, he blurted out a question.

"Hey, what's with the new repertoire?" he demanded. "How come we're getting 'This Nearly was Mine' tonight? Where did 'Some Enchanted Evening' go?"

Philippa stopped in mid-phrase as she realized what she had been singing.

Wryly she replied, "I guess it got lost in the South Pacific too."

# THE TRAGEDY AT THE OAKS

Edwina Beary looked up from the open *Next Exit* in her lap and glowered at the procession of twisted trees gliding past the window of the motorhome.

"So this is the Deep South," she grumbled. "I'd envisioned magnolias, and oaks dripping with Spanish moss, not endless stretches of elevated highways surrounded by straggly pines and billboards with alligator logos. So much water everywhere."

"We're in bayou country," said Beary. "*Gone with the Wind* wasn't set in Louisiana."

"There were snake warnings at the welcome centre, too." Edwina's tone implied that her husband had personally stocked the lake with reptiles.

"Water moccasins," said Beary, "but the only things jumping in that pond were mullet. I'm quite sure you won't see anything larger than a turtle."

"That may be, but I have no intention of going near the water." As a road sign flashed by, Edwina became alert. She glanced down at *Next Exit*, then peered ahead and said sharply, "Turn right up there." She stabbed her finger at the windshield. "Just before the bridge."

Beary blinked.

"That can't be right. We have to cross the Mississippi if we're going to New Orleans."

"We don't have to cross it here," said Edwina impatiently. "The ladies at that travel centre—the one that boasted it was on the largest river marsh in the world—"

"Atchafalaya?"

"Yes, that one. The guides told me how to get to New Orleans via the Great River Road ... so stop arguing and go off here!" Edwina's arm flailed in the direction of the turnoff sign and the pitch of her voice leapt an octave as the land ahead disappeared into the void and the road rose into the complex series of girders that formed the huge humpbacked bridge over the Mississippi.

Beary knew better than to argue. He did as he was told. As he steered their motorhome onto Highway 1 and viewed the long stretch of singularly uninspiring scenery ahead, he raised his eyebrows and said, "And why, perchance, did the ladies at the travel centre think we'd want to take the slow back route to New Orleans?"

"Because you can't visit the Deep South without touring a plantation."

Edwina closed *Next Exit*, deposited it on the floor, and replaced it with a glossy brochure. Gloomily, Beary noted the antebellum home gracing the cover.

"I should have guessed there'd be sightseeing involved," he griped. "I suppose this entails a stately mansion tour?"

"Of course."

"Then all I can say is they'd better have an eyelash-batting Southern belle on the premises to make it worthwhile."

"I'm quite sure there will be nothing of the kind. The modern women of Louisiana know how to keep their menfolk in line without resorting to flattery," said Edwina tartly.

"Probably—and what a pity. There was something to be said for women who knew how to stroke men's egos and make them feel strong and heroic. A gentle art sadly gone with the proverbial wind."

"Tosh," snapped Edwina.

"Shouldn't that be fiddle-de-dee?" quipped Beary.

"No, it shouldn't. You're far better off with a woman who speaks her mind. Then you know exactly where you stand."

Beary wisely fell silent and concentrated on the road.

After half an hour of driving by small towns and fields of sugar cane, which alternated with an anomalous mix of trimly kept wooden houses and ramshackle shacks, they found themselves travelling alongside the levee, where the bright green grass was dotted gaily with yellow flowers. The pines of the bayous had now disappeared and oak trees appeared along the roadside. Periodically the road passed under conveyer belts and pipes that connected the river to the land on the other side of the highway.

"I didn't expect to see chemical plants amid the sugar cane." Edwina sighed at the signs of the modern world.

"Never mind; there's your Spanish moss," said Beary, pointing to a small grove of oak trees that were so heavily coated with the grey trailing fronds that the branches were barely visible. "See, MacPuff. Trees," he added, patting the husky who had padded to the front of the motorhome and was peering anxiously out the window. "How much further?" Beary demanded. "MacPuff needs a bathroom break—especially if he's going to be stuck in *Arvy* while we plod around a plantation—and I'm starving. You'll have to make me a sandwich if I'm going to survive a tour. I refuse to do any sightseeing until I've been fed."

"There's a restaurant." Edwina waved the brochure. "According to this, we can 'partake of mint juleps' on the verandah."

Beary's countenance brightened.

"That sounds more like it. This tour promises to have merit, even without Southern belles."

The road followed the bend of the river, and another huge stand of oaks, trailing with moss, glided into view. Beary smiled seraphically, the prospect of bourbon, however sullied by syrup and mint leaves, elevating his mood.

"What is this plantation called?" he asked.

"The Oaks," said Edwina.

Beary rolled his eyes.

"Couldn't they have been a little more original that that?"

"They were being original," Edwina informed him. "These particular oaks are three hundred years old."

*   *   *

The double row of oaks had been planted during the early eighteenth century, long before the present antebellum home had been built. The trees, lined up as rigidly as a battalion of soldiers, formed a long avenue leading to the big house, where the white pillars of the Greek revival building were just visible through the overhanging branches. The trees were huge, and their gnarled branches, dappled with moss and intricate folds of bark, connected to form a shady canopy over the red brick path. The effect was that of a story-book illustration from a fairytale, as if Cinderella's castle or Swan Lake should lie at the end of the magical row of trees; however, the solitary oaks that covered the rest of the grounds were more suited to a Gothic mystery, for their twisted branches, struggling up to the light or curving to the ground, appeared angry and tormented, as if the long arms of the trees would animate at any moment and ensnare the unwary traveller.

Having allowed MacPuff to christen an oak or two, Beary returned him to the motorhome, opened the vents, topped up his water bowl, and re-entered the grounds to find Edwina. She was still on the path, seemingly entranced by the arboreal symmetry of the avenue. Beary jogged his wife's arm and steered her firmly in the direction of the restaurant.

"Come on. You can admire the trees later. Lunch first."

Reluctantly, Edwina dragged her eyes from the majestic oaks and followed her husband to the low wooden building that contained the restaurant and gift shop. A fleur-de-lis on the sign by the hedge reminded visitors of Louisiana's French heritage. Beary and Edwina bypassed the umbrella tables on the porch and entered the building. To the right of the hall was an archway leading to the gift shop. Beary guided his wife past the store and into a semi-octagonal room with white walls, green wainscoting and a cluster of round tables, each surrounded by six wooden chairs. A *Gone with the Wind* poster dominated the far wall. On the adjacent wall, a round mirror reflected the brightly coloured plastic tablecloths and made the room seem larger than it was. As Beary and Edwina stood wondering where to sit, a plump, middle-aged woman wearing blue slacks, a striped blouse, and a no-nonsense manner bustled forward and herded them into a smaller atrium where there were tables set for two. She seated them on the inside wall, plopped two menus on the table and retreated back to the main room. Beary stared dolefully at the utilitarian cutlery wrapped in pink paper napkins.

"Not exactly Scarlett O'Hara, is she?" he grumbled. "She could at least have taken our drinks order."

However, he had no sooner finished speaking than a waitress popped through the door, notebook in hand. She took their order, scurried away and quickly returned with the anticipated mint juleps.

Forty-five minutes later, Beary's mood had lightened. The accoutrements might be merely functional, but the meal had been delicious. Edwina tutted disapprovingly as he polished off the gumbo-covered rice that had accompanied his braised crawfish.

"You'll have terrible indigestion," she admonished him. She flagged down the waitress to get the bill.

Beary ignored his wife's frown and mopped up the sauce with a piece of bread. "If I end up with indigestion," he said, "it will be as a result of your visit to the gift shop, not because of my lunch." He wiped his mouth with the pink paper napkin, scrunched it into a ball and tossed it defiantly onto his empty plate.

"I'm glad you reminded me." Edwina stood up. "I'll pop in there now while you settle the bill."

Edwina breezed out of the atrium. Beary contemplated ordering himself another mint julep, knowing full well that he had at least half an hour to spare, but then, on second thoughts, he decided that he would be better off following his wife around the store and discouraging her purchases. To that end, he paid the bill and went through to the shop. Just as well, he thought gloomily. Edwina had already acquired a basket laden with bags of pecans, boxes of pralines, two Scarlett and Melanie cutout books for the granddaughters, a paperback volume on the River Road mansions and a box of stationery embellished with borders of oak leaves. She was now staring curiously at a candlestick in the shape of a pigtail.

"That's rather interesting," she said.

"We don't need any more candles," Beary said firmly. "Come on. Let's get to the tour."

"In a minute. I'm going to buy one of those dolls for Chelsea."

Beary inspected the end wall where several rows of boxed Southern belles were lined up with the regimental precision of the oaks in the avenue outside.

"Those aren't dolls to play with," Beary pointed out. "She'll just ruin it if you get her one."

"No, she won't."

Edwina pulled down a box from the shelf. The doll inside was an exquisite creation, with sweetly pouting lips, bright blue eyes, and golden ringlets trailing down from a tiny garland of white flowers and pink ribbons. The doll's gown was a frothy confection of pink and white, with tiny flecks of green, which somehow heightened rather than detracted from the fragile illusion of pale Southern womanhood. Edwina read the name on the label.

"Marianne," she said. "How appropriate."

"What about the other one?" Beary was interested in spite of himself. He picked out a box from the lower shelf. "This one's a Marguerite," he said, eyeing the print on the top flap.

"No." Edwina looked critically at the doll's smoky eyes and the jet-black hair adorned with red camellias that matched the flowers sewn in the décolletage of the velvet gown. "Too sophisticated. The crimson dress is beautiful, but Chelsea would like the other one better."

Taking the Marianne doll, she swept to the front of the store and paid for her purchases. Then, deciding that she would put her packages in the motorhome before going on the tour, she left Beary to his own devices and headed back to the parking lot.

While he waited for Edwina to return, Beary ambled across the grounds and read the information plaque at the start of the avenue. It listed every slave who had served on the plantation, along with his or her appraised value. A thirty-seven-year-old Creole Negro with carpentry skills was valued at thirteen hundred dollars, whereas a sixty-two-year-old, one-armed African Negro was only worth fifty dollars. Beary felt an uneasy mix of awe and discomposure. Reading the names seemed to bring the people to life, and he wondered whether the owners of The Oaks had been kindly masters. He was about to move on to the big house, when he glanced through the trees and glimpsed a stretch of water. He went closer and saw that, on the far side of a shallow pond, there was a small graveyard surrounded by low, black metal railings. Noticing a wooden bridge, he crossed and approached the cemetery. A bench had been placed near the gate, and within the fence, behind a line of tombs and headstones, were three red camellia bushes. Beary was studying the gravestones when Edwina eventually tracked him down.

"There you are," she said. "Have you come upon anything interesting?"

"A miniature city of the dead," said Beary. He gestured towards the marble sarcophagi. "See how the whole cemetery has above-ground tombs. They had to inter their dead that way because of the high water table. A heavy rainfall would float the caskets to the surface if the bodies were buried in the ground."

Edwina shuddered.

"How horrible. My goodness," she added, nodding towards an ornate cross at the centre of the cemetery. "I wonder if that's Chelsea's doll. See the inscription."

"Marianne Hawthorne," read Beary. "Beloved wife and mother. 1798 – 1885. Well, if it is, she led a long life. An eventful one too, I expect. Right through the Civil War."

Edwina had moved on. She pointed at a tiny slab of marble. "Look at that. It's a dog's grave. Napoleon. Sadly taken. January 8, 1815." Edwina's face fell as she read on. "Oh," she murmured. "He was only two years old. That must have upset the household."

"I imagine the occupants had other things on their minds," commented Beary. "The death of a dog might have paled into insignificance."

"Beside what?"

"Beside the chaos on the other side of the river. Louisiana was fighting the Battle of New Orleans."

Edwina was not as familiar with North American history as her husband.

"I didn't know there was a Battle of New Orleans," she said.

"There most certainly was," said Beary. "A decisive victory for the U.S. at the end of the War of 1812, at which, by the way, the Duke of Wellington's brother-in-law got his final comeuppance. Ironically," he added, "American and British representatives had already signed the peace treaty in Ghent that ended the war, but no one in Louisiana was aware of the fact, so the battle raged on."

Edwina was fascinated.

"I always associate the War of 1812 with the invasion of Canada," she said, "but, of course, the Americans were fighting the British in the South too, weren't they?"

Beary nodded.

"The Battle of New Orleans made Andrew Jackson a national hero. He held off the British invasion—along with a great deal of extra help from his countrymen. The meticulously trained British troops with their swords, bayonets and Congreve rockets were trounced by a handful of American soldiers, augmented by the militia, Choctaw Indians, Baratarian pirates, volunteers, free men of colour, New Orleans civilians, and Kentucky and Tennessee sharpshooters with rifles, tomahawks and hunting knives. It's a very exciting episode in American history."

Edwina turned back towards the graveyard. "I wonder if the dog was a casualty of the war."

Beary was eyeing the tomb beyond the dog's grave.

"Well, if he was," he said, "the little chap had company. Someone called George Lockhart died on the same day. 'Nephew and valued kinsman,'" Beary intoned, reading the words engraved into the granite. "Now *he* might have died in the battle. He was only thirty-four."

"Look," said Edwina. "There's a monument amid the camellia bushes. I wonder whose grave it marks."

Beary was never one to let a boundary stand in his way. He stepped over the fence and plodded across the grass.

"You shouldn't go in there," protested Edwina. "They have it fenced off."

Beary ignored his wife and pushed his way through the camellia bushes.

"Well, well, well," he said, staring at the inscription. "It's a good job you bought the Marianne doll for Chelsea."

"What has that to do with anything?" demanded Edwina.

"Because I suspect that I've just found the grave of the black-eyed doll in the red dress. Marguerite Lockhart—another beloved wife and mother, except she isn't the beloved wife of George Lockhart, she's the beloved wife of Nathaniel Lockhart, whoever he was."

"So why should that make her an unsuitable subject for a doll for Chelsea?" Edwina asked inquisitively.

"Because," said Beary, "unlike Marianne, she didn't live to a ripe old age. She died when she was only thirty-three. And what's more," he added, avid curiosity emanating from every pore, "she died on January 8, 1815 ... the same day as George and the poor little dog."

*     *     *

When Beary and Edwina emerged from the canopy of oaks and reached the big house, they saw that the white pillars of the Grecian portico enclosed a terrace on the ground floor and a balcony on the upper floor, both of which appeared to encircle the mansion. The intricate filigree of the balcony juxtaposed with the setback of the exterior walls created the illusion of a dollhouse open and ready for play. Each door and window was topped by a transom window and framed in green shutters, which broke the predominantly white surface. Three dormer windows in the roof indicated the presence of an attic floor. Above these rose twin chimneys, encased by the same metal lacework as the balcony railing.

Several people occupied the terrace. Some were drinking mint juleps, which had been served from a bar by the front door. A huge man, sporting a

Tilley hat, khaki shorts and a T-shirt proclaiming himself a Virginian, leaned against the counter, his beatific smile advertising the fact that he had taken full advantage of plantation hospitality. The sober mien of the tiny brunette beside him imparted more than mere abstinence, but her husband seemed blissfully oblivious. At the end of the terrace, a grey-haired matron in an "I love NY" cap was sneaking interior shots through the windows when she thought no one was looking. Her companion stood in front of her, using his rotund, beer-bellied profile to shield her actions from the tour guide who was welcoming newcomers by the entrance.

The guide was dressed in a burgundy hoop skirt and a white ruffled blouse, an ensemble that contrasted dramatically with her modern hairstyle and crisp speaking voice. Edwina elicited the information that the next tour would start in five minutes, so she steered Beary clear of the bar, nudged him into the line-up, then proceeded to ignore him as she struck up a conversation with a bespectacled don from Massachusetts. Beary was vaguely conscious of alcoholic fumes wafting over his shoulder. The Tilley-hatted giant was standing behind him. Hearing Edwina's clear tones informing the professor that she and Beary hailed from Vancouver, the Virginian tapped Beary on the shoulder and initiated a discussion about the Olympic hockey finals.

Once inside the house, their guide introduced herself as Sara. The Virginian was still talking hockey, so she wilted him with a steely smile, then led the group into the dining room. This was a high-ceilinged chamber with a long mahogany table laid with blue and white dishes, wine bottles, and a luminously painted compote filled with wax fruit. A white wooden lyre was suspended over the table. Below it hung a red swag with gold tassels that reminded Beary of the proscenium on his daughter's marionette stage. Sara confirmed his guess that this was a fan. She explained how a slave boy would stand in the corner, pulling a string that would wave the fan over a bowl of ice, keeping the room as cool as if it had modern air conditioning.

Sara dutifully pointed out the *faux-bois* fireplace and allowed everyone time to admire the gilt-framed mirror over the mantel and the torchère with its gleaming brass candelabra that stood beside the door; then she led the way into the hall and stopped by a glass display case that held a side-by-side, double-barrelled flintlock pistol with a lethal-looking bayonet on the end. This, she informed her listeners, came originally from France and had been used by a merchant from New Orleans during the War of 1812.

Next, she conducted her charges upstairs and took them through the bedrooms. These were furnished with dressing tables, highboys, well-stuffed chairs and lofty four-poster beds. The last bedroom was clearly a woman's room. The swags, cushions and counterpane were all fashioned from pink velvet, and a glittering chandelier hung from an intricately carved oval at the centre of the stamped ceiling. A rosewood secrétaire stood by the window, and a brocade chaise longue had been placed by an outer door that opened onto the balcony. At the foot of the chaise was a low tabouret with matching upholstery. A lady who enjoyed her comforts, thought Beary, noting the contents of the dainty pedestal table beside the chaise. The polished satinwood surface held a decanter and a novel entitled *Paul et Virginie*, which appeared to be the same vintage as the house. Beary glanced briefly at the book; then he examined the painting on the wall opposite the bed. It was a portrait of a handsome middle-aged woman whose rounded features still displayed the sweetness and innocence of youth. Something about the fair hair and the blue eyes struck Beary as familiar. He nudged Edwina.

"Look," he murmured. "I bet that's Marianne in her latter years."

Sara stepped through the French doors and invited her flock to follow. Obediently, everyone trooped onto the balcony. The view of the grounds was extensive. Beary and Edwina could see walkers on the avenue below, and the restaurant and the family cemetery off to their left. They walked around to the other side of the balcony. From here, they could see a series of box hedges almost in the formation of a maze, and beyond this, two low, oblong buildings. These, Sara explained, were the slave quarters. She directed their attention to a tidily kept cottage nearby, which she explained was the boys' house, where any youth in the household would have to sleep once he entered teenage, since living in the house with the female relatives would be improper once he had reached an age to be interested in the opposite sex. Noting the proximity to the slave quarters, Edwina gave a sniff of disapproval, but before she could give vent to her thoughts, the tour group was ushered inside and directed back down the stairs.

The last room on the tour was the parlour. It was a dignified reception area with powder blue velour drapes and scroll-armed walnut chairs upholstered in the same fabric. Five of the chairs surrounded a pedestal table at the centre of the room. On the table stood a silver sweetmeat basket and a gilded, royal blue porcelain vase painted with colourful flowers. Another chair was placed to the right of the door, and a settee with matching plush upholstery stood against the adjacent wall. Next to the settee was a side table with intricate marquetry. It held a lamp, a snuffbox and an embroidery frame. Above the settee was a large, gilt-framed mirror with a second, tiny circular mirror embedded into the lower, right-hand corner. The wall opposite the mirror was bisected by French doors leading onto the terrace, and the connecting wall was filled by a grand piano with a lyre-backed music stool and a *faux-bois* fireplace even grander than the one in the dining room. Edwina's eye was drawn to the fireplace mantel. At its centre stood a pigtail-shaped candlestick.

"Look," she hissed. "That's like the one we saw in the gift shop."

Sara overheard and elaborated.

"That," she said, "is a courting candle." She picked up the candle, took hold of a small peg that protruded from the lower end of the candleholder and turned it. The candle rose higher and higher until almost the entire length was exposed. "If a suitor was favoured by the family," she explained, "the candle would be set high to give him lots of time with his beloved, but if he were not considered suitable ..." Sara fell silent and reversed the procedure so that only an inch of the candle remained in view. "Voila!" she said when the procedure was complete. "Only a very short visit."

Her audience chuckled appreciatively. The guide returned the candle to the mantel, then turned and pointed to the tiny oval at the corner of the large mirror.

"Now that," she continued, "is another courting device. It's a convex mirror. A chaperone, from her position on the chair by the door, could glance across and see everything that was happening within the room."

"Ingenious," breathed Edwina. "I should have had one of those when our brood was young."

"Never mind the spy mirror," said Beary. "Have a look at the painting over the fireplace."

Edwina followed his glance and gave a gratifying squeal of delight.

"There's your dolls," said Beary, "and if I'm not very much mistaken," he added, pointing towards a pug-faced lapdog at the centre of the picture, "that's probably Napoleon. The venerable grey-haired gentleman will be Nathaniel Lockhart, husband of Marguerite and father of the fair Marianne who has a stranglehold on the poor dog. Am I right?" he finished, seeing Sara looking his way.

"You've obviously visited the gift shop and the family graveyard," she replied. "I usually send people there after the tour. Yes, that's Marguerite Lockhart and her daughter, Marianne. They were both very beautiful women. The doll gowns are replicas of the dresses in the family portrait."

"But Marguerite died young," said Beary, "along with the dog and a relative named George."

"George Lockhart." Sara elaborated: "He was Nathaniel Lockhart's nephew, and a suitor for Marianne's hand." Her eyes took on a mischievous twinkle. "And that brings us to the conclusion of our tour," she said. "The Tragedy at the Oaks—a real-life mystery to tantalize our guests."

"You mean it happened right here?" said Edwina.

Sara nodded.

"Well, not exactly here," she amended. "The original Creole House was torn down and the new building was erected in 1838. However, the last owner of The Oaks was intrigued by the early family history, and she had this room restored to replicate the parlour where Marguerite and George died."

"What happened?" demanded Beary. "Was it the war?"

"Indirectly," said Sara. "They were shot by an American deserter. Or so the story goes. There was some question as to whether the soldier was a deserter or not, but fortunately for Marianne, the army major who investigated the shootings concluded that the man had run away when the British broke through on the west side of the river, after which he came to steal food from the plantation and murdered George and Marguerite when they discovered him."

"Why fortunately for Marianne?" asked the bespectacled don from Massachusetts.

"Because," said Sara, "that was the reason she gave for shooting the American soldier."

Her audience gasped.

"Listen," Sara continued, "and I'll recount the story as it was told to the major. But before I do that, I should relate the history of the family itself, for the seeds of what happened at The Oaks on that fateful night in 1815 were planted many years before."

A hush fell over the room as Sara began her tale.

*       *       *

Marguerite Lockhart, née Marguerite Valéry, was born in 1782, the daughter of a New Orleans warehouse owner whose wealth was largely the result of profiteering made possible by the Baratarian pirates of Jean Lafitte. When Marguerite was sixteen, she fell wildly in love with George Lockhart, but her father did not approve the match, for George's father was a United Empire Loyalist living in Canada. George was from a family that had been divided by the Revolution. His father had sympathized with the British during the War of Independence, but his uncle, Nathanial Lockhart, had fought hard for the American cause.

Nathanial was a lawyer who had come to New Orleans in 1789 after a financial scandal had compelled him to leave Boston. He had married a well-to-do Creole lady and, two years later, had inherited her father's plantation on the Mississippi. His wife died of malaria in 1796, and his nephew, who liked his uncle's politics better than his father's, left Canada and came to live with him the following year. George Lockhart met Marguerite within months of his arrival in Louisiana, for his Uncle Nathanial already had his eye on the beautiful young daughter of the warehouse owner.

Whereas the nephew was young, raffish and impoverished, the uncle was middle-aged and prosperous, and Marguerite did not need much persuasion from her father in choosing the older man for her husband. So she married Nathaniel Lockhart, and George left New Orleans, disillusioned and cursing her for her fickleness and mercenary nature.

Marguerite's marriage to Nathaniel was harmonious, if not a passionate love match. They had four children. The oldest was their daughter, Marianne. Of the three other children, two died of yellow fever, but their son, Louis, was a hale, sporting youth, who was the pride of his doting parents. Marianne and Louis were spirited children, quick to get into scrapes, though Louis was the more adventurous of the two. Raised to be a Southern gentleman, Louis was conditioned to believe that the man's role was to protect his womenfolk, so he cheerfully took the blame when trouble arose.

When Marianne was fourteen and her brother was twelve, they acquired a new neighbour, for George Lockhart reappeared in Louisiana. He had made his fortune, no one knew quite how, and had bought the plantation next to The Oaks. Nathaniel was delighted to have his nephew back, Louis was enthralled by this dashing young neighbour, and Marianne promptly fell in love. Marguerite was the only one who appeared to have reservations about the new arrival.

When Marianne turned sixteen, George became an official suitor, with the full approval of his uncle. Marianne blossomed as George came courting. He sat with her in the parlour, talking sweet nothings, while Marguerite sat in the corner dutifully fulfilling her obligations as chaperone. And if an occasional edge came into George's voice or the odd dart was tossed Marguerite's way, she kept her eyes on her embroidery frame and refused to be provoked. Marianne was so much in love she was blind to the atmosphere between the other two people in the room.

Come December of 1815, tensions ran high in Louisiana, for although the British assault on Mobile had been repelled, it was now rumoured that the English were going to attack New Orleans. Young Louis was at school in Atlanta, and with the uncertainty caused by the imminent invasion, Nathaniel Lockhart judged it safer to leave the boy there rather than bring him home at Christmas. Nathanial joined the militia and left his foreman in charge of the plantation. He was confident that his nephew, George, would keep a watch on his family as well, for George was not in a position to sign up and fight. Word had got about that his father was building ships for the British at Kingston, and he was suspected of lacking loyalty to the cause. Nathaniel knew otherwise, and believed the vicious gossip had been started by Henri Duval, a New Orleans merchant who coveted Marianne for himself, so he vigorously supported his nephew and left instructions that George was to be welcomed to The Oaks whenever he chose to visit.

Two days after Nathaniel left The Oaks, the British were sighted off Lake Borgne. Four days later, Andrew Jackson declared martial law. By December twenty-third, in spite of Jackson's orders to obstruct and guard the bayous, the British had landed at Bayou Bienvenu. Now, with the Crescent City threatened and every fit male commandeered into duty, Nathanial sent for the men on his plantation to join up and fight.

The bloody Battle of New Orleans continued on into the New Year. The final decisive engagement occurred on the eighth of January. However, in spite of the glorious American victory, one section of the battle went badly for Jackson's troops. On the west bank of the river, a contingent of Louisiana militia and a detachment of Kentuckians, outnumbered and out-armed, ended up running for their lives.

On the day that the unfortunate detachment of Americans scattered into the bayous in their attempt to escape the British troops, the big house at the plantation was all but deserted. Only Marguerite and Marianne remained, guarded by Antoine, the loyal Negro foreman, and attended by the slave, Celestine, who had been nurse and maid to both mother and daughter. That afternoon, George Lockhart came to check on their well-being and stayed into the evening to visit with Marianne. It was a cold night, and nerves were on edge, for no news had come of the fighting that was happening below the city.

Celestine expressed her disapproval in no uncertain terms.

"A gentleman shouldn't be coming a-courtin' when the place is all but empty and our menfolk are away riskin' their necks to save us from them murderin' redcoats," she grumbled. "It ain't fittin'."

Marguerite paid no attention. She ordered Antoine to light a fire and told Celestine that she would sit with the couple and act as chaperone. Not to be ignored, Celestine took the courting candle from the mantel and insisted that, war or no war, things had to be done properly. Marianne pertly reminded her that George was a favoured suitor, so Celestine reluctantly set the candle high. However, she warned the couple that the visit was over when the candle had burned down. Then muttering under her breath, she retreated to Marianne's room, where she determined to wait until her charge came up to bed.

Soon after the trio sat down in the parlour, Marianne told George about a poem she had written. Marguerite glanced up from the corner where she sat with her sewing and suggested that her daughter might wish to read her literary effort to her visitor. George pressed the issue, saying that he longed to hear the verse, and with alacrity, Marianne stood up and left the room. She ran upstairs to her bedroom, where Celestine watched her retrieve the poem from her escritoire. Shortly after Marianne left the bedroom—though Celestine was hard pressed to say how long it had been—the Negro maid heard Napoleon bark. She went to the door and listened, but everything was silent. She returned to the bedroom, but a moment later, she heard a series of gunshots, and at that point, the dog began barking hysterically. Then the noise abruptly ceased. Frightened, she ran out of the room and started towards the attic stairs to rouse Antoine. However, Antoine had heard the shots and was already on his way down. The two slaves ran to the parlour. There they beheld a terrible sight. George and Marguerite lay sprawled by the hearth, and another body lay just inside the French doors. It was a man dressed in the grey uniform of the Louisiana militia. Marianne knelt in the centre of the room, clutching the body of Napoleon and crying hysterically.

Over and over, she sobbed, "He shot them. He shot them!"

As Celestine stood, shocked at the scene that met her eyes, she heard steps on the terrace and Nathaniel Lockhart burst into the room. He rushed to his daughter's side and clutched her in his arms. Turning her eyes from the dreadful sight of her mother and her suitor, he called Antoine to take the dog and eased the corpse of Napoleon from the girl's arms. Then he helped his daughter to her feet and led her from the room.

Celestine followed and asked her master why he had returned. He replied that he'd been afraid for his family's safety after he'd observed the trouble on the west bank. When he'd seen the British advancing, he'd leapt on his horse and rode along the levee until he could commandeer a boat to take him across. Reaching the plantation, he assumed all was well, for everything was quiet. He saw the lights shining in the parlour window, but as he started across the lawn, he heard gunshots. He raced onto the terrace and saw that the French doors were wide open. He was met with the same terrible sight that had greeted Celestine and Antoine when they had come in from the hall.

Waving aside further questions, he took his daughter up to her room and remained there for half an hour. When he came back down, he told Celestine to attend to her mistress, and he sent Antoine to notify the military of the incident.

When Celestine went up to her mistress, she found Marianne still weeping, but her hysteria had subsided. Celestine helped her undress and tucked her into bed, and gradually the girl calmed down. Sadly, she told her maid what had happened.

Marianne's story was heart-wrenching. After she left the bedroom, she had gone back down the stairs. As she reached the hallway, she heard Napoleon barking. Almost immediately, there was a gunshot. The dog continued to bark, and terrified, Marianne crept toward the parlour. As she neared the door, there was another shot. Too petrified to enter, she stayed back from the open doorway and stared towards the convex mirror. The reflection froze her blood. It revealed her mother and George Lockhart lying lifeless by the hearth, and a man in uniform standing over them, a pistol in his hands. Napoleon was barking and jumping at the man, and as she watched, the intruder lashed out at the dog, stabbing at it with the bayonet that protruded from the end of his pistol.

Marianne knew that her father kept a loaded musket in his study. Consumed with fear, she ran and retrieved the weapon. Then she tiptoed back towards the parlour. Everything was quiet, but when she looked across to the mirror, she saw that the soldier was still there, standing inside the French doors, staring at the bloody results of his deeds. Napoleon lay immobile near the lifeless body of his mistress. After that, Marianne remembered feeling a surge of heat through her body, an insane, uncontrollable rage. She stepped into the room, raised the musket and shot the man dead.

Marianne collapsed back into sobs as she recounted the final confrontation with the soldier. Celestine soothed her mistress and assured her that everything would be all right, but she was fearful for the girl, because the state of Louisiana was under martial law, and she knew that the army would demand a full explanation. Sure enough, when Antoine returned, he was accompanied by Major William Hawthorne, a tall and imperious officer whose autocratic manner did not bode well for the household. Since he had heard the rumours of George Lockhart's British sympathies, Major Hawthorne was not immediately satisfied that Billy Pollock, for that was the name of the dead soldier, had been a deserter with a vicious streak who had killed two Louisiana residents, not to mention a dog—especially as Billy's brothers-in-arms had insisted that their comrade would never harm an animal.

Therefore, the major, who had the instincts of a Sherlock Holmes long before that character was ever conceived by Conan Doyle, employed his sharply-honed observation skills to record the details of the scene of the crime. He noted a crushed red camellia, matching the flowers on Marguerite's gown, lying at the end of the terrace. He observed that the candle on the mantel was burnt almost to the edge of the pigtail holder. He checked the convex mirror and saw that Marianne was speaking the truth when she insisted that she had been able to see a sweeping view of the room from the doorway. He was somewhat perplexed that Marguerite's embroidery frame was laid neatly on the table beside her chair, given that the entrance of the militiaman must have caused her to jump up quickly and move to George Lockhart's side. He was also troubled that the dog ceased to bark for a short period before renewing his howls, and he was bothered by the absence of bite marks on Billy Pollock's hands and ankles. He also noted some discrepancies in the timing of the shots. Antoine described a single shot followed by two shots in fast succession, whereas Celestine reversed her story and insisted that the first two shots had happened closely together and that the third had happened afterwards. Last of all, Major Hawthorne was utterly baffled by the fact that there was a residue of wax in the fire grate, and no one in the household had any idea why it was there.

However, even a cursory knowledge of ballistics was sufficient to establish that Billy had been shot with Nathaniel Lockhart's musket, whereas Marguerite and George had been killed with Billy's double-barrelled flintlock pistol, so under pressure from Nathaniel's friends, who reminded the major that Lockhart's war record was exemplary, both during the War of Independence and in the current engagement against the British, Hawthorne accepted the account and closed the case.

*   *   *

Sara ended her account and looked around the room. Her audience was spellbound. "So," she challenged her listeners, "was the major right to close the case? Any sleuths in the crowd who would like to dispute the verdict?"

The hockey-lover from Virginia was the first to venture an opinion.

"Why the hell would a deserter enter a house and cold-bloodedly murder two civilians?"

"He probably wanted food," said a lady in the back row.

"He didn't have to kill for it," drawled the Virginian. "I could see him holding a gun on them and telling them to order the servants to bring him a meal, but there wasn't any advantage to blowing them away. Something else must have been going on."

Beary opened his mouth, but before he could speak, the lady who loved New York piped up, "Well, obviously there was still a flame burning between George and Marguerite."

Edwina pursed her lips disapprovingly.

"I agree. They certainly seized the opportunity to get rid of Marianne when she mentioned the poem she'd written."

"Right on," said New York. "They'd be off their chairs and in each other's arms the minute she was out of the room. That would explain the embroidery frame being set neatly on the table."

Edwina waved a hand toward the French doors.

"And the camellia on the terrace," she said. "They would have gone outside, knowing that they could be seen in the mirror if they remained in the room."

New York was an avid reader of romance novels. She rolled her eyes with glee.

"The flower will have been crushed in their hot embrace. It must have broken off as they sprang apart. I bet they saw the deserter when they were on the terrace, and to keep them from giving him away, he forced them back into the room at gunpoint."

Edwina sniffed.

"Maybe, but it seems highly coincidental that her husband should pop in just at the moment that another militiaman killed them both."

"Well," contributed the don from Massachusetts, "that rather raises the question: Did Nathaniel Lockhart and the dead militiaman wear the same uniform?"

"Not necessarily." At last Beary managed to get a word in. "The militia was a pretty ragtag bunch. Weapons and uniforms were often whatever they had on the homestead."

"Actually," said Sara, "sources indicate they did both have grey uniforms, similar, if not identical."

"Well, then," said the don, taking off his spectacles and blinking his owlish eyes, "I'd say the solution was pretty evident."

"Surely you're not suggesting the murderer was Nathaniel Lockhart?" exclaimed Edwina.

"Why not? Just picture the scene. Nathaniel Lockhart rushes home, worried sick about his family, and is greeted by the sight of his wife and his nephew locked in each other's arms. He's carrying a musket. It's quite conceivable that he'd shoot them in a jealous rage."

"But Marianne would have recognized her own father."

The don pointed to the convex mirror.

"Not from the rear and reflected in that tiny mirror," he said firmly. "She could easily have been mistaken."

"But how do you explain the presence of the other soldier?"

"The poor idiot probably just heard the shots and wandered in." The hockey fan from Virginia was beginning to look restless. "He was a witness, so he had to be eliminated."

"Ahem," interjected Beary. "Aren't we all forgetting something? Marguerite and George were shot with the double-barrelled pistol, not with Nathaniel Lockhart's musket. Was that," he added, turning to Sara, "the weapon we saw in the hall?"

Sara nodded.

"Yes. It was kept by Major Hawthorne and passed down through various family members, ultimately ending up on display here, courtesy of the most recent owners."

"Quite a fancy weapon for a militiaman with a name like Billy Pollock," observed Beary.

"It had belonged to a French planter who was killed in the battle, so the theory was that Billy had taken it after its owner was killed," Sara explained.

"Aha!" cried the don, stabbing the air with his finger. "So who was to say it wasn't Nathaniel Lockhart who took the gun during the battle? Maybe the deserter didn't even have a gun. Lockhart could have used both barrels on his wife and nephew, then silenced the dog with the bayonet, and when Billy Pollock came bumbling through the French doors, he could have dispatched him with his musket."

Beary continued to play devil's advocate.

"I thought Nathanial Lockhart fought in the main battle on the east side of the river," he interjected. "Billy Pollock was on the west bank. Which regiment did the French planter serve in?"

"The same one as Billy," said Sara.

"All right," persisted the don. "Nathanial could have come into the room to confront Marguerite, and Pollock could have entered after him. Nathanial could have shot Pollock, and then taken the pistol and turned it on his wife and nephew. What a great way to cover up a murder. Blame it on a deserter."

"But if that was the case, why would Marianne say she killed the soldier?" puzzled Edwina.

"To protect her father, of course," said the don. "Nathaniel Lockhart was already on touchy ground, having a brother who was working for the British. If he was guilty, it was plain cold-blooded murder—but Marianne's story, on the other hand, was guaranteed to elicit the sympathy of the major. And look at her," added the don, pointing to the picture on the wall where the fair Marianne smiled sweetly down at them, her dog clutched to her chest. "How could he possibly haul those beautiful blue eyes in on a charge of murder?"

Sara laughed.

"He couldn't," she admitted. "The major was utterly bewitched by Marianne's charm. The following year, much to the chagrin of Henri Duval, Major Hawthorne married Marianne and settled in New Orleans."

"Good heavens!" said Edwina. "What did her father think of that?"

"I suspect he was past caring. He never really recovered from the tragedy of his wife's murder. People said he died of grief."

"Or guilt," said the don. "I'd say there's no question that he and Marianne concocted that story to save his neck."

"There is another possibility," said Beary.

All eyes in the room swung in his direction.

"That Marianne did kill the soldier, just as she said."

The don seemed puzzled for a moment, but then his face cleared.

"Ah, I see what you're getting at. The time lag while she went to get the musket from the study. It's possible. Nathaniel Lockhart might not have stuck around after killing his wife and nephew. He could have set off again. If Pollock had heard the shots and seen someone running from the house, he might have gone in to investigate. Unfortunate fellow, because Marianne came back and assumed he was the killer. She would have been utterly distraught, seeing what had happened to the people she loved. And then Lockhart, hearing a third shot, would have rushed back to see what had happened. It makes sense," he concluded grudgingly.

"Not if Antoine was right and the sequence of the shots was a single shot followed by two shots in quick succession."

"But Celestine contradicted Antoine. She said there were two shots, and then a single shot."

"Not in the beginning. She changed her story later. That could have been a ploy to support Marianne and her father. What's more," added Beary, with a seraphic smile, "you all appear to have missed the one detail that provides the key to the whole case."

The don's scowl could have withered an entire flower show.

"What detail?" he growled.

"Everyone seems to have forgotten about the candle," said Beary.

∗       ∗       ∗

The room fell silent. Then the don spoke again.

"What about the candle?"

Beary elucidated. "It was burnt down to the top of the holder," he said, "in spite of the fact that Celestine had set the candle as high as it could go. Yet every version of the tale says that Marianne left to get her poem soon after the visit began."

"Now this is interesting," said the hockey-lover from Virginia who was getting very irritated by the know-all attitude of the don from Massachusetts. "What are you implying?"

"That the wax in the fire grate must have come from somewhere. Put yourself in George and Marguerite's place. Marguerite's husband is away. The plantation is virtually deserted. They have just acknowledged that they still have the hots for each other, just as they did all those years ago, and all that's preventing them from finally consummating their love is the presence of Marianne. They can't bear the thought of waiting a couple of hours for the candle to burn down, so to speed up their rendezvous and get rid of Marianne early, they hustle in from the terrace and George cuts the candle in half. Then he throws the lower half into the fire, relights the upper half and returns it to the holder. And at that moment, the deserter comes into the room. And there's the picture that Marianne sees—her mother and her suitor at the fireplace with the soldier holding a gun on them."

"All you've just demonstrated is that everything could have happened exactly as Marianne said it did," the don said sourly.

"But as our friend from Virginia pointed out, and as we've all agreed, the story of the deserter killing civilians doesn't really hold water," said Beary. "We've just spent ten minutes trying to find a solution that establishes a motive for the killings."

The don started to look impatient. He eyed Beary as if he were a recalcitrant pupil who was wasting class time.

"Well, in that case, the scenario you just came up with doesn't add a scrap of helpful information. The business of the candle is utterly irrelevant."

"Not," said Beary, "if Marianne came back a minute earlier and saw her mother laughing intimately with George Lockhart as he cut the candle and returned it to the mantel."

The room fell quiet as Beary continued.

"I'm sure Marianne did feel the surge of rage that she described to the major. A double betrayal by her mother and her lover, who were also betraying the father that she adored—and then the golden opportunity for vengeance steps into the room in the form of a deserting soldier. What simpler than to get her father's musket and return to shoot the invader? Her mother and George Lockhart would have praised her for her courage. They would have been unaware of her intentions as she picked up the soldier's gun. She would have shot George Lockhart first," mused Beary. "Otherwise he might have overpowered her when he saw her aim at Marguerite, but her mother would have been so shocked when George fell that her natural instinct was to kneel and clutch him in her arms. Napoleon's death must have been an accident. Marianne flailed at him in a panic, forgetting the lethal bayonet at the end of the weapon in her hand. I expect her tears over the dog were perfectly genuine, not that they hindered her from crying out, 'He killed them!' Her self-protective instincts were pretty strong. And as our well-informed guide has told us, Marianne had a habit of letting others take the blame, witness the lickings her brother had endured in their youth. I wonder if she ever told her father what really happened."

Beary paused. No one spoke. He tilted his head and peered at their guide. She, in turn, raised her eyebrows and turned to the don.

"Well?" she said.

"Well," he repeated obdurately, "I fail to see that there's any hard evidence either way. The tragedy at The Oaks won't ever be conclusively resolved. What did happen to Marianne and the major anyway? Were they happy together?"

Sara told them the end of the story.

"After Nathaniel Lockhart's death, Marianne's brother, Louis, took over the plantation. Later, when Louis was killed in a hunting accident, The Oaks passed to Marianne. By that time, William Hawthorne had run into financial difficulties, so his wife's inheritance was a godsend, but Marianne refused to live in the house. The memories were too traumatic. She insisted that they tear down the mansion and build anew, but during her lifetime, neither a convex mirror nor a courting candle was ever permitted at The Oaks." Sara paused and threw Beary an approving smile. "Also," she continued, "many reliable sources have told how Major Hawthorne was always an exemplary husband, being most careful never to give his wife cause for jealousy—and he had a particular household rule that drove everyone to distraction."

"Oh," said the don. "And what was that?"

"He was fanatic about having all the weapons in the house kept locked in a cupboard in his study"—Sara's eyes twinkled—"and he was the only person on the plantation who had the key."

She winked at Beary and ended her tale with a simple sentence that was loaded with significance.

"Marianne," she said, "was never allowed in the room."

$*$            $*$            $*$

"Well," chortled Beary, as he and Edwina strolled back towards the parking lot, "I emulated General Jackson rather well back there."

"How so?" said Edwina, whose mind was on other things.

"I vanquished the don," said Beary smugly.

"I thought Jackson vanquished the British," said Edwina.

"Well, yes, but he wiped out the Spanish as well—much later, of course. You know, Don ... don."

"Oh, I see," said Edwina, finally getting the pun. "That was a joke."

"It was until you flattened it," retorted Beary.

Edwina ignored him and changed the subject.

"You know," she said slowly, "I've rather gone off my Marianne doll. I don't think I'll give it to Chelsea after all."

"Good," said Beary. "Take it back and get a refund."

"No. I won't do that." Edwina looked thoughtful.

"Then what are you going to do with it?" Beary asked.

"Well," said his wife, "I think I'll keep it."

"What on earth for?"

"To give to you," said Edwina sweetly, "as a reminder that fluttering eyelashes can be as deadly as a steel trap."

Looking pleased with herself, Edwina sailed through the exit gate and started towards the motorhome. A comment regarding steel traps leapt into Beary's mind, but wisely he suppressed it. He fell back his usual three paces and muttered under his breath, "Frankly, my dear, I don't give a damn."

# THE DEFENCE RESTS

Sylvia Barnwell gazed out over the sparkling blue waters of Malaspina Strait. The day was so clear that she felt she could pick out every individual evergreen on the islands that dotted the diamond-crusted sea.

"What a fabulous spot," she sighed. "Thanks so much for inviting us."

Cathy Weatherby smiled at her friend.

"Don't mention it," she said. "We love having houseguests—especially ones like you and Norton, because you have children to entertain our own urchins. Brian and Jilly are always hanging out with Janie from next door, but they're thrilled to have your three to play with. Look at them all. They're having so much fun."

Sylvia dragged her eyes away from the sweeping ocean view and cast them on the wide stretch of lawn between the Weatherbys' new home and the edge of the ravine that ran in front of their property. Chelsea's blonde curls could be seen bobbing up and down between the brown ponytail of Jilly Weatherby and the russet mop of Janie Landry as they played dollies' tea party in front of the gazebo. On the grass, Norton, Thomas and Geoffrey were valiantly engaged in a lively round of croquet with Janie's sister, Suzie, young Brian Weatherby, and Cathy's neighbour, Bonnie, who was the mother of Suzie and Janie. Adults and children alike were having a wonderful time.

"Cathy just likes showing off our new property," laughed Jim Weatherby. "We've never owned anything this spectacular before. Stay!" he added sharply to the collie at his feet that was eyeing the rolling croquet balls and inching towards the grass.

"We've been lucky," admitted Cathy. "Jim selling his business just before the downturn worked out perfectly for us. He's always wanted to retire from accounting and run a fishing charter, and after the bubble burst, properties here were going for a song."

"You did well getting this place for the price you paid," observed Brad

Landry, who was lounging in the deckchair on Cathy's right. "It was originally listed at one and a half million."

"It's a very unusual building," commented Sylvia, twisting round and peering towards the three-storey rectangle of plate glass shimmering in the afternoon sun. Above the glittering windows, she could see striped umbrellas and cultivated fronds of greenery peeking over the wall of the roof garden. "It looks peculiar from the road—especially as there are no windows facing the street and just that one vertical strip of glass on the side—but the interior is lovely."

Cathy laughed.

"You don't have to be tactful. We know it looks odd. Locals call it The Cereal Box House. We weren't too keen when we first saw it, but once we went inside, we made up our minds instantly. It's turned out to be an excellent purchase. The view's even better now than when we bought it, as the people on the other side of the ravine cut several trees down in the spring, and we love the solar heating; it's an eco-house, cheap to run and marvellous to live in."

"Great location as well," said Jim. "We're a five-minute walk from the docks and a ten-minute walk to the swimming hole on the lake. And it's only a five-minute drive around Trout Lake Road and we're at the pub."

"Or a half-hour walk," said Cathy firmly. "That way we both get to drink, and then we walk off the calories."

A jubilant shout erupted from the lawn. Thomas was waving his mallet and laughing at Brian Weatherby.

"I hit your ball. Now I get a meanie shot!"

"It's actually called a croquet," Norton corrected him.

Thomas was indifferent to terminology. Eyes gleaming, he put his foot on his ball, which was nestled against his opponent's ball, whacked it with his mallet and sent the second ball flying off to the other end of the garden.

"Stay away from the terrace," Cathy called loudly as Brian took off after his ball. She turned back to Sylvia. "There was so much rain last month that part of the bank gave way. A whole mass of earth below the terrace slid to the bottom of the ravine and part of the foundation has crumbled. I'm worried that the deck is destabilized."

"It's too bad," said Brad. "It was a perfect spot to build a terrace. Best view of the entire garden. I helped your predecessor construct it. We did it in the spring of 2009, so I still have some of the materials stored in my garage. I'll give you a hand with the repairs when you're ready to work on it," he added to Jim Weatherby.

Cathy smiled at Sylvia.

"See. We have great neighbours too."

Another yell from the grass made them look up. Suzie Landry was grinning and lining her yellow ball up against Thomas's green one. A hit with the mallet, and it was Thomas's turn to see his ball bounce across the green.

Norton shrugged helplessly in the direction of the spectators.

"They seem more interested in whacking each other's balls than getting through the hoops," he muttered.

"Stop yapping, Dad," said Thomas. "Your turn."

Norton apologized and turned his attention to the black ball. He adjusted his glasses, which were sliding down his nose, and peered at the course. Then he hitched up his baggy shorts, lined up his mallet with the target, placed his feet carefully, then tapped the ball neatly and propelled it forward. It rolled gently across the grass and stopped just in front of the centre hoop.

Sylvia gave a contemptuous sniff.

"You could have hit that through," she pointed out. "Don't be so cautious. It's so annoying," she added, turning to Cathy. "Norton never does anything without checking and double-checking every angle at least six times."

"I expect it comes from being a defence lawyer," Cathy said tolerantly.

"He's a good one, too," Jim Weatherby chipped in. He rather liked Norton, for all his idiosyncrasies. "From what I've heard, your husband doesn't lose too many cases."

Sylvia snorted.

"He bombards the court with so much trivial detail that everyone gives in from sheer tedium. Norton is excellent at research, but he's pathetic in the courtroom. If he could improve his speaking skills, he could be tops in his field. That's why I got him involved in theatre. I thought some drama experience would help him develop a bit more presence."

"And has it?"

"Not really. He's learned to talk loudly and stand up straight, so now he barks at the judge like a regimental sergeant major."

"I heard that," said Norton indignantly. "And I do no such thing."

Circumventing a quarrel, Cathy changed the subject. "I believe the people who owned our house previously were both lawyers. They were, weren't they?" She looked to Brad Landry for confirmation.

"They were indeed," said Brad. "Colin and Geraldine Gray. Very jolly couple. We were sorry to see them go—though, of course," he added hastily, "we didn't realize what a great family would take their place. And you have children too, which is even better. Colin and Gerry didn't have a family. They were a fun-loving career couple. They were the life and soul of the pub nights up here ... well, of the pub, period. They were great boozers, but a real barrel of laughs."

"Why did they sell?" asked Sylvia.

"Overextended, I suspect," said Brad. "They live in West Vancouver, so this was simply a summer place and holiday home—when they weren't travelling abroad. They really used to chuck the money around. Coincidentally, they were involved in amateur dramatics too—maybe that's a lawyer thing—and that kept them in town quite a bit, so they didn't get up here as much as they wanted to."

His wife looked up from her ball. Bonnie Landry was a slender woman with prematurely grey hair that framed her face in wildly disordered curls, but the overall effect was pleasingly attractive, mainly because of her gently smiling countenance.

"The Grays came up a lot when they first bought the place," she corrected her husband. "It was only in recent years that they spent less time here."

"Like I said, they were having money trouble," declared Brad. "They certainly weren't spending the way they used to."

"Maybe," said Bonnie. She cracked her ball and it ricocheted off Geoffrey's blue ball. "But they were doing more theatre by then, so that could have been the reason."

Geoffrey's face fell.

"Are you going to meanie-shot me?" he asked timorously.

Bonnie saw his downcast expression and smiled.

"No," she reassured him. She took her second shot and patted him on the head.

"What group did the Grays perform with?" Norton asked curiously. "Was it Deep Cove? I was in their production of *Reluctant Debutante*."

"No. West Van Players, I think." Bonnie laughed. "I have a funny story about the Grays," she added. "You remember, don't you?" she said to Brad. "That was so embarrassing."

Brad grinned.

"Bonnie was walking Laddie one evening." He turned to his wife. "It was dark outside, wasn't it? I guess it must have been winter."

"It was spring break, actually," said Bonnie, "so it must have been the March before last. It was a freezing cold night."

"Yes," Brad continued, "so all the houses had lights on. Anyway, as Bonnie went by the eco-house, she looked up at that long window on the side and she flipped right out."

Bonnie nodded.

"It was terrible. I saw Colin and Geraldine standing on the landing—well, just their silhouettes, of course—and he was strangling her."

"Good grief!" said Sylvia. "What did you do?"

"I didn't know what to do. I was in an utter panic. And then I thought of my cellphone."

"You called the police?"

"That wouldn't have been any use," chuckled Brad. "By the time a cop car drove all the way out here, Gerry could have been dead and buried. Anyway, it's a good job Bonnie didn't call the cops. Tell them the end of the story," he added to Bonnie.

"I phoned Geraldine's number," said Bonnie. "I thought, if they were having a fight, that might stop them. Anyway, she picked up. She sounded a little puffed, but she was fine. And when I asked her if she was all right, and she realized why I was asking, she broke into laughter. The next thing I knew, she and Colin were out the front door and coming up to the road to meet me. They were having hysterics. Evidently they'd been rehearsing a scene from their next play. It was Agatha Christie's *A Murder is Announced*. You can't believe how embarrassed I was."

"She was mortified," laughed Brad.

"Actually ..." began Norton.

"Dad, it's your shot," hollered Geoffrey.

"Oh, yes. Sorry." Norton dutifully reported back to the field. Cathy turned to her husband.

"You and Jim ought to fire up the barbeques," she said. "It's almost five o'clock. I'm going to pop the potatoes in the oven."

Brad obligingly rose to his feet. He beckoned to Jim, who unfolded himself from his deckchair, and the two men followed Cathy to the patio. Bonnie held out her mallet.

"Sylvia, could you step in for me for a bit?" asked Bonnie. "I have to run next door and get the salad."

Sylvia nodded and took the mallet. Bonnie walked across the grass and disappeared behind the hedge. By the time Sylvia had taken her turn on the course, Cathy had returned. Sylvia stepped to the side of the course.

"Is Bonnie not back yet?" Cathy asked her.

"No," replied Sylvia. "Your neighbours are really nice," she added.

"They're a lovely family," agreed Cathy. She glanced towards the patio to make sure Brad was out of hearing. Then she leaned in to Sylvia and dropped her voice. "Bonnie and Brad are the kindest couple you could hope to meet, which is a miracle considering what they've been through. Five years ago, they suffered the most awful tragedy. They lost their oldest son. Bobby was such a great kid. His death absolutely shattered his mom and dad."

Sylvia's face became grave. "What happened?" she asked. "Was it an accident?"

Cathy nodded.

"A hit and run. On Trout Lake Road. Bobby was walking home from the swimming hole and he was struck from behind. Poor kid was only nine years old. One of Bonnie's friends who lives round there—well, she wasn't really a friend then; she only became one after the accident—heard the thud. She was out watering her garden. She has one of those properties where the house is set back in the woods, so her drive is a long one, and by the time she ran down to the road, there were no cars in sight. She found Bobby lying there. She had her cell with her, so she called 911 right away, but there was nothing the paramedics could do. He'd been killed instantly."

"Mom!" bellowed Thomas. "Come and take your shot."

Sylvia obliged. Norton stepped forward with a twinkle in his eye and tapped his ball against hers.

"Meanie shot!" crowed Thomas.

"It's called a croquet," insisted Norton, and shot Sylvia's ball over to the gazebo.

Sylvia pursed her lips.

"That wasn't funny," she snapped.

"Part of the game," smirked Norton. "What were you two muttering about over there?" he added. Sylvia told him.

"God, that's terrible," said Norton. "Who's the woman who found the boy? Have we met her? You ought to find out her name so we don't put our foot in it if she comes round when we're here."

Cathy was listening and she interjected.

"You're not likely to meet her," she reassured them. "From what I hear of local gossip, she's on an extended trip around the world."

"Good heavens," said Norton. "What is she? A travel writer?"

"I think she inherited money," said Cathy. "I'm not really sure."

"You must be talking about Marylou Pretty."

Startled, Sylvia and Norton spun round. Bonnie Landry was standing behind them. They had not heard the neighbour return, and the expression on her face made it plain that she knew what they had been discussing.

"Marylou lives on Trout Lake Road," Bonnie went on smoothly, "but she's hardly ever there. She used to work in the IGA in Madeira Park, but she came into money and her inheritance enabled her to quit her job."

Cathy looked embarrassed, but she valiantly picked up the cue.

"Someone told me she's on her fourth overseas trip now," she said lightly.

Bonnie nodded. "That's right. This time, it's a long one, though. A couple of years ago, she decided to fulfill a lifelong dream and travel all around the world." Bonnie paused. Then, keeping her gaze steady, she continued, "And I hope she's having a marvellous time. She was very kind to us after our son's accident. She brought us flowers and never tried to avoid the subject the way people often do because they don't know what to say. We were very glad for her when she came into good fortune."

"Hey, Mom! Look!" Geoffrey hollered.

Sylvia turned in time to see her orange ball bouncing towards her. It careened off the leg of the table and rolled underneath the chaise longue.

Norton managed to keep a straight face as his wife retrieved her ball.

"Your turn, I think," he said. Tight-lipped and eyes glittering, Sylvia hacked her ball back into play. Then with an effort of will, she relaxed her clenched jaw and turned back to Bonnie.

"Cathy told us what happened," she said simply. "We're very sorry."

Bonnie compressed her lips. "We've come to terms with it now," she said, "but of course, one never gets over it. What made it even harder was the fact that the police never discovered who was responsible. But people were so good to us. Not just Marylou, but all our neighbours. The Grays spent a lot of time with us in those early years. They got to know Marylou too and became quite good friends. She was often there for dinner. They'd always have her round before she set off for another of her jaunts. I think she went to some of their theatre events too, because I remember her telling me how sorry she was that she'd be missing *A Murder is Announced* as it wasn't opening until after she'd left."

"Ah, yes," interjected Norton. "On that subject ..."

"Dad, stop talking," complained Geoffrey. "Come and play."

"Oh, all right," said Norton affably. He ambled onto the pitch and eyed the other balls. Seeing the orange ball nearby, he propelled his black ball towards it and tapped it gently.

"Meanie shot!" chorused the children.

"Croquet," said Norton, and shot his wife's ball into the flowerbed. Then, ignoring her look of fury, he hit his own ball so that it lined up neatly in front of the final two hoops.

As Sylvia set her ball back on the edge of the grass, Norton turned curiously to his hostess's neighbour.

"Has anyone heard from Marylou Pretty since she left?" he asked.

"I've had the odd postcard," said Bonnie. "The last one came from Rome. That was about six months ago."

Sylvia's eyes darkened and her brow furrowed with concentration. She swung her mallet and it cracked against the wooden ball, which hurtled across the grass and ploughed into the black ball by the end hoops. With a smile of triumph, she marched over and placed her ball against Norton's. Then she set her foot on her ball and whacked it with all her might. Norton's ball leapt forward and raced across the lawn in the direction of the stone terrace. Then, as all the children gaped in delight, it bounced against the concrete and disappeared over the edge into the ravine.

Norton sighed. He peered over the drop and assessed the situation.

"I can see it, Dad," said Thomas. "It's caught on that bush. Can I climb down and get it."

"No," said Sylvia firmly. "It's your father's ball. He has to retrieve it."

Norton hitched his shorts up over his bony knees and took hold of an overhanging branch. Then, carefully, he clambered his way down the slope. The ground was still loose from the previous rains and the descent was treacherous, but he slipped and slid his way until he reached the bush. Grabbing onto another branch, Norton stretched down to retrieve the ball. He clasped it in his left hand and inched round towards the bank. Then he froze. He slipped the ball into the pocket of his Tilley shorts and stared up towards the base of the terrace.

"What are you doing?" Sylvia cried impatiently. "For heaven's sake, come back up."

Norton ignored his wife for several seconds. Then he straightened up and carefully ascended the slope. When he pulled himself back onto the grass, he stood up and turned to Cathy Weatherby.

"I think you'd better stop this game and send the children in for dinner," he said quietly.

Cathy's face paled.

"What's there?" she asked anxiously. "What did you see?"

Norton did not answer right away. Instead, he briskly ordered the children inside to wash their hands. With uncharacteristic firmness, he overruled the indignant outburst that followed and waited silently until they had left. Then he turned to Bonnie Landry.

"Bonnie," he said, "I'm sorry to bring up a subject that's painful for you, but were the Grays up here the day your son was killed?"

Bonnie blinked, surprised.

"Yes, they were," she said, "though they went back to town that afternoon—some emergency at the office caused them to cut their stay short. They didn't hear about what happened until they returned the following month. Why?"

"Do you know if they'd been at the pub prior to driving down to the ferry?"

Bonnie gasped. "You're quite wrong if you're implying it was them who hit Bobby. Marylou saw them pass by a good ten minutes before the accident. She was quite definite about it. It couldn't have been them. I don't understand why you're asking."

Her voice faded off and her eyes suddenly filled with tears. Cathy Weatherby put an arm around her neighbour's shoulders, but her eyes remained on Norton.

"Norton, you'd better answer my question," she said. "What's down there?"

"A body," Norton replied grimly, "or rather, the skeletal remains of one. You're going to have to call the police."

\*   \*   \*

By the time the police had cordoned off the garden and finished their preliminary round of questions, it was eleven o'clock. The children were asleep, and Norton and Sylvia retreated to the guest room, exhausted and relieved to have a moment to themselves.

"How come you were such a long time with the police?" demanded Sylvia. "What were you saying to them?"

Norton finished brushing his teeth and closed up his travel kit.

"Well," he said, tightening the cord on his pajama pants and climbing into bed, "I was telling them whose body I thought it was and the reason for the murder. I must say," he added, plumping his pillow vigorously, "this bed is definitely designed to discourage visitors from staying more than a couple of days." Having softened the offending foam, he snuggled down and pulled up the eiderdown.

Sylvia stared furiously at her husband.

"Don't stop there. Tell *me* your ingenious theory."

"The clues are all there," mumbled Norton. "You figure it out."

"Well, obviously, it's related to the grilling you were giving Bonnie Landry. You seemed to be hinting that the Grays were the ones who killed her son."

"Yes, I was," muttered Norton. Sylvia gave him a prod and his face popped out from under the eiderdown. "All right," he said. "I'll explain, but it's plain as the proverbial pikestaff if you piece together all the bits and pieces Bonnie and Cathy told us over the course of the afternoon. The skeleton must be the remains of Marylou Pretty. My guess is she was blackmailing the Grays, so they popped her off. Her decision to take a world tour made it easy for them."

"So you think it was her that Bonnie saw with Colin Gray through the window of the eco-house? You think Bonnie really did witness a murder?"

"I do," said Norton. "Bonnie said the Grays were out of breath and a bit hysterical. That's exactly how they might have behaved if they were covering up a crime. The timing is right. It was just before Marylou Pretty was to leave for her trip. It all fits. The Grays were heavy drinkers, and they'd been at the pub shortly before the accident occurred. It's almost certain that they're the ones who hit young Bobby Landry. Marylou was first at the scene and she must have seen them there. She had her cellphone with her. She might even have snapped a photograph. I'm betting she lied when she said she didn't see the vehicle. All she had to do was say she didn't see a car and insist that the Grays' vehicle had passed well before Bobby came along, and she'd have them over a barrel."

"There would have been damage to their car, surely," said Sylvia.

"Actually, I gather they drove a whopping great SUV with a big bumper," said Norton, "so there probably wasn't even a dent. But I bet that's why they made that unexpected trip to town. Very convenient if any touching up did have to be done."

Norton sighed and closed his eyes. Sylvia poked him in the shoulder.

"Don't go to sleep. I haven't finished yet. Is there any evidence to show that Marylou Pretty weaselled her way into the Grays' lives and started to bleed them dry?"

Norton kept his eyes shut as he replied.

"Well, we were told she suddenly became wealthy enough to go on overseas trips, and I had the impression it was around that time that the Grays began to show signs of diminished wealth. When Marylou decided to up the ante so she could go on her world tour, it must have been the final straw—and the perfect opportunity to get rid of her. Brad said the Grays take overseas trips. The postcards Bonnie gets will have been sent by them." Norton yawned and rolled over. "The Grays are guilty. I'd bet my life on it. Anyway," he added, "I knew there was a body somewhere as soon as Bonnie told us about the incident she saw on her dog-walk."

"Oh, now you're being utterly ridiculous," snapped Sylvia. "We rehearse scenes at home when we're involved in a play. Why couldn't the Grays have been doing the same thing?"

"Because I've read the script of the play they were in," Norton murmured sleepily. "Surrey Players are doing it next year and I was checking to see if there was a part in it for me."

Sylvia did not try to conceal her vexation.

"What," she said caustically, "do your thespian ambitions have to do with your ability to play detective?"

Norton yawned again.

"Everything, actually. You see, nobody gets strangled in *A Murder is Announced.*"

Sylvia slid down under the covers.

"Oh, for heaven's sake," she groaned.

The only response was a gentle snore from the other side of the bed.

\*　　　　　\*　　　　　\*

Three weeks later, after the holidays were over and the Barnwell family had returned to town, Norton was making breakfast. As he shovelled rashers of bacon onto a paper-towel-lined plate, Sylvia drained her teacup, set it down, and turned the page on her copy of *The Vancouver Sun*. Then she gave a sharp intake of breath.

"What's up?" asked Norton.

"You were right," said his wife. She stabbed her finger at an article in the middle of the page. "The Grays have been arrested for the murder of Marylou Pretty."

"Told you so," said Norton. "Children," he called, going to the kitchen door, "breakfast is ready."

"She *was* blackmailing them. According to this reporter, they've admitted to everything. You'd think lawyers would have enough sense to keep their mouths shut," Sylvia added scathingly.

"It's probably been weighing on their consciences."

Sylvia was more cynical than her husband.

"You mean they probably know the evidence is foolproof so they'll be better off feigning a suitable degree of remorse."

Chelsea burst into the kitchen, followed by Thomas and Geoffrey. Sylvia glowered at the children, and they immediately slowed their pace and sat down sedately at the table. Norton set their plates in front of them.

"Well, whatever the reason," said Norton, "at least there will be some degree of closure for Bonnie and Brad. Personally," he added, "I hope the judge throws the book at them. I have no tolerance for people who drink and drive."

A slight smile flickered over Sylvia's face.

"You know," she said thoughtfully, as she speared her bacon and eggs, "I'm impressed."

Norton blinked. Praise from his wife was a rarity.

"Are you? Really?"

His face lit up with pleasure as Sylvia nodded.

"Yes," she said. "For someone who takes pride in his work as a defence lawyer, you created an absolutely brilliant case for the prosecution."

Norton grinned.

"That," he said, digging back into his breakfast, "must be because it was our summer vacation."

It was Sylvia's turn to blink.

"What has that to do with anything?"

"Well," said Norton amiably, "when on holiday, the defence rests."

# SORRY HER LOT

The October morning was cold, in spite of the pale winter sun, which hovered low in a white sky, glaring from behind the trees to create a bizarre collage of sharply edged silhouettes: crows on telegraph wires, a jutting chimney, the skeletal branches of a maple tree, a black dog poised in the middle of the road. The result was eerie, a Hitchcockian panorama that suited Philippa's mood. *The world is out of joint*, she thought gloomily. The Shakespearean phrase aptly described the black and white montage, for the scene resembled a photographic negative. The street was quiet, adding to the dreamlike aura, but as she approached the tract of woodland at the end of the block, the sun hit the fallen leaves, flooding the forest floor with colour as if a hand from the sky had painted an illuminated red carpet amid the black trunks. At the entrance to the trail that would take her through the wood, two large cottonwoods formed a vaulted arch, and Philippa felt as if she were entering a cathedral as she walked into the coppice. The air was colder in the wood. The ground was damp, and glittering spider webs decorated the spindly branches. At the far end of the path, a patch of mist hung over the ground, and the sun, filtered through the haze, formed a shimmering star that soared up to the highest treetop. As Philippa grew nearer, the star faded and the mist engulfed her. For a few seconds, it was hard to see; then the haze evaporated as she moved out of the trees into the parking lot of the theatre. As she stepped onto the tarmac, she startled a flock of pigeons and they fluttered into the air, the noise of their wings making her jump as it broke the silence.

Philippa glanced at her watch. She was early for her appointment and she had no desire to wait inside an empty theatre until the costume mistress arrived. There was a Starbucks around the corner. A coffee would be welcome after the chilling walk from the bus stop. The theatre was in South Vancouver and it straddled two vastly different commercial districts: an insalubrious area that Philippa liked to avoid and the up-market shopping strip where the coffee shop was located. To reach the latter, she had to cross the parking lot, and as she neared the other side, a woman came around the corner of the building. She was tall and dressed all in black. She moved towards Philippa with the air of a sleepwalker, yet in spite of her smooth gait, she looked as if she had the weight of the world on her shoulders. She passed by, unseeing, lost in her own thoughts, a woman of indeterminate age with lovely bones and eyes full of pain.

The lyrics of her first *Pinafore* solo floated into Philippa's mind. "Sorry her Lot" suited her current mood, and she wondered if this woman was also suffering from loving too well. Then, feeling cross with herself for being maudlin, she picked up her pace and hurried across to the coffee shop. A jog of caffeine would improve her spirits.

There was only one other patron in the coffee house, a young black woman, thin to the point of anorexic, with pink hair cut in short, dramatic spikes. Long earrings, like spears, hung from her ear lobes and a metal stud glinted at the side of her nose. Below her short jacket, spindly legs in boots with four-inch heels protruded from a vinyl miniskirt, and she swung one leg back and forth while she entered text messages into her cellphone.

Philippa ordered a latte. Seeing a morning paper on the counter by the window, she took her drink there and perused the headlines while she enjoyed her coffee. Nothing but gloom and doom, she noted: more peace talks going nowhere, another drug-related gang shooting, a woman murdered in a massage parlour in Rock Creek. Did they have massage parlours in cowboy country? Probably, she decided. They seemed to be everywhere in town.

The black woman's cellphone broke into a tune, which ceased as she answered the call. Her voice was loud and a little brash. She made an appointment to see her caller later that afternoon; then, ending the conversation with a throaty laugh, she stood up and clicked her way out of the coffee shop. Philippa finished her coffee and slid down from the counter stool. As she walked out, she saw a card had been left lying on the now empty table: *Lally's Lair - Haircuts, Manicures, Massage*. Philippa wondered cynically what other services were on offer. It was a good job, she thought, that Lally didn't live in Rock Creek. Then, once again, she reproached herself for her vile humour. So what if her love life was back on ice and Martha Petrel, for all her enthusiasm after *South Pacific*, had not yet come up with anything concrete. Philippa reminded herself that the lead role in *H.M.S. Pinafore* was nothing to sneeze at, and even though it was a community-theatre production, she was being paid well to do it. It was time to count her blessings and get on with the job.

*　　　*　　　*

Richard Beary read the incoming report with increasing consternation.

"We've got a serial killer on our hands," he said. "I don't care how far apart these murders were, there are too many similarities to be coincidental. Three murders over an eighteen-month period, two in solo-operator massage parlours that were offering a lot more than therapeutic services, and one in a two-person outfit that appeared outwardly a trifle more respectable, but the partner of the victim acknowledged that sometimes, for a cash payment, they would agree to a bit extra if a gentleman requested it. The phone records indicate that, prior to each murder, the victim received a call from a public phone, presumably setting an appointment for the day of the crime."

"So what are the common threads?" asked Sergeant Martin.

"All three victims were shot at close range with a sawed-off shotgun. The sound was muffled by a plastic water bottle converted into a silencer, which was left at the scene. Also, in each case, the massage bed and the sink area had been very carefully cleaned, and the victim's hands had also been scrubbed. The other similarity is that there were no towels or flannels by the sink, which suggests that the killer had received some form of sexual services and had been very careful to remove all items that could reveal his DNA."

"Any chance of them being copycat crimes?"

"No," said Richard, "because most of the details haven't been released. It has to be someone who is moving about B.C."

"Are there any other common threads between the victims, other than the fact that they were sex-trade workers?"

"Not really. Totally different types. The woman on Gabriola last summer was white, late-forties—one of those fleshy, good-natured ladies who wore floral muumuus and was quite happy to make some extra cash accommodating any gents who needed a little cheering up, as the locals put it. The Delta woman was a tiny Asian, only thirty-two, and, according to her partner, extremely businesslike. That's the only one who had a written record of an appointment for the morning she died. It was just a first name, Harry, but no doubt that would have been a false name. The partner didn't know of any regular client using that name. Then the latest girl, Chrissy Marino, was a Latino who'd moved to the Kettle Valley area with her boyfriend a year ago and set up her business out of their home. She was twenty-six and very pretty. If there hadn't been the previous crimes, we'd be looking at the boyfriend. It's hard to believe he'd take lightly the fact that she was providing sex services, but he has an alibi, the cast-iron variety."

"It's an unusual murder method for a sex killer," said Martin. "They're usually sadists who like to strangle or carve their victims up. What about the cleanliness angle? Maybe it's a holy Joe who considers he's doing a public service by wiping out practitioners of vice."

"It's possible," said Richard. "The problem we have is tracing the weapon.

There was an old shell casing at the last site, so we know he's using a sawed-off shotgun, but it's obviously not registered, and we can't trace the ammunition because heavy-shot shells are used by hand-loaders. There aren't many people following that practice these days, but the gun shops don't have to keep a record of those sales, so it's almost impossible to track the owner. However, his travel patterns, the dates of the murders, and the fact that he's a shooter who is hand-loading his ammunition provide a very definite lead. The Delta murder was in January, Gabriola was in July, and the last one in Rock Creek was October. The Delta massage parlour was close to the dikes where duck hunting is permitted, Gabriola is a big summer hangout for fishermen—"

"And Rock Creek in the fall is full of deer and elk hunters." Martin picked up the thread. "Our man could be an outdoor sportsman."

"Exactly. I think we might be looking at a hunter."

The door of Richard's office flew open and an agitated Jean Howe came into the room.

"Sir," she said breathily, "VPD just contacted us. There's been another one. The south Granville area. Another solo operator."

"There goes that theory," said Sergeant Martin. "What the hell does one hunt in the city of Vancouver?"

"Nothing legitimate," said Richard, "but my theory still holds. Maybe he's back on his home turf. Let's start checking hunting permits and find out which Vancouver residents had a draw for game in the Rock Creek area this fall. Gradually, we'll narrow it down and nail the bastard."

*       *       *

"When I was a lad, I served a term,
As a chorus singer; I was treated like a worm,
I sang my little heart out and I ate lots of crow,
And directors loved to have me in their show;
I sucked up so well as you can see,
That now I am the ruler of the Queen's navy—"

"Milton, do shut up," said Philippa.

"Why? You used to sing all the way to *South Pacific* rehearsals. Now it's my turn."

"You could at least practise the right words. Suppose you implant that version in your brain and it slips out on opening night."

"No one would care," said Milton airily. "This is going to be an *Art of Coarse Acting* production. It wouldn't matter what I sang."

204

"I sincerely hope you're wrong," said Philippa. "I have no desire to star in a turkey."

"Oh, you will, my dear," prophesied Milton cheerfully. "This will be one where your friends will come backstage and say, 'Well, darling, *you* were good.' Just be prepared to take your paycheque and run."

"I thought Riverside Light Opera had a good reputation."

"They did, under their former director."

"That's right. Keith Landry died a couple of years back, didn't he? Sad."

"You knew him?"

"Not well. I met him at the Playhouse once. He was such a dynamic man. I suppose he was the one who put Riverside on its feet."

"Yes. Keith was incredible," said Milton. "It was amazing what he could beat out of those enthusiastic amateurs. But I'm afraid his death is going to be the death of the society. His replacement is hopeless. Last year's show was so bad that all their best singers have gone elsewhere. Why do you think they've had to resort to paying people like us to come in? They used to have several good non-Equity people who could do their leads, but now they're so short of decent male singers that they're press-ganging some of the sisters, cousins and aunts into the Royal Navy and making them up as boys to fill out the sailor chorus."

"Surely a team of good Equity soloists will inspire the chorus to come up to scratch?"

"Not a chance. We principals will be a little cluster of pearls in a sea of confused swine who can't remember their moves, granting that the director actually gave them any, and who are staring at the conductor like frightened sheep, bobbing their heads in time to the music in the hope that they'll stay together—not that they'll get any help from the pit. Claude Bison used to be a good musical director, but he's been around since the ark and he's so doddery that the greatest excitement he generates these days is whether or not he'll make it through the performance without dying on the podium."

"Oh, God!" Philippa's mood dipped a couple more notches. "As if my life wasn't doldrummy enough at the moment. To think I was thrilled when they phoned out of the blue and offered me the part. I realized that they'd called me because Lorna Gay had dropped out and they knew I could whip it together in a couple of weeks, but when they told me my tenor would be Pablo Alonso, I assumed it would be a good production."

"Silly assumption. You should beware of geeks bearing gifts."

"Spare me the bad puns. I'm already depressed enough."

Milton chattered on, ignoring Philippa's dour mood.

"Oh, well, you'll find it entertaining, especially watching Pablo gritting his teeth at all that Anglo-rah-rah in *Pinafore*. He still hasn't got over the British taking back the Falklands, or rather Las Malvinas, as he calls them. He turns purple when the chorus belts out 'He is an Englishman' with all that pseudo-patriotic gusto. Still, if he acts up in the performances, we'll sick Buttercup on him."

"Who is playing Buttercup?" asked Philippa.

"Harriet March. Club secretary. Non-Equity, but a very good voice. She's a registered masseuse. Shoulders like an NFL football player and hands like elephant's feet. When she tells those sailors, 'Come to your Buttercup, buy,' they won't dare not hustle over to purchase her peppermint drops. She's very jolly, and she can do wonders for you if your muscles are all knotted up, but woe betide anyone who makes jokes about massage parlours. One wallop and they'd be out for the next fortnight. Highly respectable is our Harriet."

"Sounds like a useful lady to have around."

"Absolutely." Milton deviated onto another topic without missing a beat. "So what gives with you?" he asked. "Why is your life in the doldrums? Tell Uncle Milton. I know it has to do with your handsome detective, since he never showed his face at *South Pacific* after opening night and you haven't been talking about him at all. What's gone wrong with you two?"

Philippa told him. Milton was shocked.

"Did you confront him with it?" he asked. "For all you know, that snake, Octavia, made it all up."

"No, she didn't. She even had a photo of them on her cellphone. And no, I didn't ask him about it. What was the point?"

"Surely he wants to know why you're mad at him?"

"He doesn't think I'm mad at him. After I invented several excuses why I couldn't see him, he simply assumed that I'd got back together with Adam and stopped calling. Not that I am seeing Adam, but it was a logical guess on Bob's part because Adam was all over me while I was talking with Martha Petrel after the show."

Milton clucked disapprovingly.

"I'm appalled," he said. "For a smart girl, you can be awfully dumb at times. For all you know, you and DC Miller could be staying apart over a misunderstanding. You could at least make sure you know where you stand."

"I'm not the sort of person who indulges in lengthy discussions over relationships," Philippa snapped. "Either they work or they don't—and I don't want to talk about it, so go back to singing your silly Joseph Porter song."

"Stubborn, stubborn," said Milton. "Touchy, too. Oh well, I yield. So, changing the subject, since you're at loose ends these days, want to take in a movie on Sunday?"

"Can't. I'm going out with my parents. It's Dad's fish and game club dinner."

Milton pulled a face.

"That hardly sounds like your cup of tea—or should I say kettle of cod? Dish of duck? Mug of moose?"

Philippa laughed in spite of herself.

"That's better," said Milton. "There's the smile I like to see. You're really sure you'd prefer all those rugged outdoorsmen to an evening of my witty repartee?"

"No, I have to go. My mother seemed determined to get me there, so I broke down and promised I'd come. She said I needed a social evening to cheer me up."

"Oh, God! She's probably trying to line you up with some strong, silent elk hunter."

"Probably, but I'll survive."

Philippa pulled into the parking lot and tucked the Jeep into an end space. Then she wrapped her scarf around her face to protect her sinuses from the chill air and followed Milton into the theatre. They were greeted by a large-busted woman wearing a black T-shirt that displayed two hands imprinted on her bosom and a caption that read, *Aye, there's the rub*. Philippa correctly assumed that this was Little Buttercup.

"Handy Harriet," trilled Milton, and gave the woman an exuberant kiss. "Welcome back," he said. "She's been visiting her mother in the Kootenays," he told Philippa. He introduced Philippa to Harriet, who dragged her over to a short, watery-eyed man whom she introduced as Michael Bray, the director. Bray extended a damp hand to Philippa and smiled thinly. Then his eyes rolled away towards a young girl with a script, to whom he issued a vague directive. Leaving her looking confused, he drifted up the aisle and murmured something else to a middle-aged matron who was enjoying a coffee and a gossip with a choleric-looking man in a yachting cap. Nearby, an elderly gentleman was sleeping in an aisle seat with a score in his lap. Milton caught Philippa's eye and winked.

"See what I mean?" he said.

Philippa did not respond, for she had noticed a striking figure at the back of the auditorium. It was the woman she had seen in the parking lot when she had come for her costume fitting.

"Who is that?" she asked Milton.

Milton looked where Philippa was pointing.

"Oh," he said. "That's Jo Farnsworth. She's been around for years. She used to act, but now she sticks to production work. She's a cosmetician and she does design work too, so she oversees the makeup and she'll do the poster and program. Lovely person, but positively melancholy since dear old Keith died. She misses him terribly."

"Keith Landry? Was she married to him?"

"No, but there's a tale, and it's a tale you ought to hear."

Philippa waited patiently. Milton loved to repeat club gossip, so she was confident he would continue. Milton obliged.

"Jo has been married to Rupert Farnsworth for forty-two years," he said.

"I know that name," said Philippa. "Isn't he a children's author?"

"That's right. Do you know him?"

"No, but my dad does. They belong to the same fish and game club."

"Well, small world," said Milton. "I expect you'll get to meet him when you go to your dinner on Sunday."

"Did you say the Farnsworths have been married more than forty years? How old is she, for heaven's sake? She doesn't look much more than forty herself."

"She's sixty-three, I think."

"You'd never know it. She's gorgeous, in a dramatic sort of way. Very well preserved."

"Easy for her," said Milton. "They have lots of money and they've never had children. She's quite the pampered spouse, very much his showpiece, but she's the ultimate good wife so she deserves to be treated well."

"Nice to see a man who treats his first wife as a trophy wife, instead of trading her in for a younger model."

"No danger of that," said Milton. "Farnsworth likes his money too much to divide it up on alimony payments. Besides, he's much too comfortable to disrupt his life. Jo's the one who's made the sacrifices. She doesn't act any more as he wants her to go along on his hunting and fishing trips, even though she's stuck in a cabin while he's off having fun. They have a cottage on Gabriola where he likes to get away for writing and fishing. Jo goes along to clean, cook and make him comfortable. He'd be a fool to get rid of her and take up with some whiny blonde who wants to spend all his money and live it up in the city."

"So where's the story you referred to?" asked Philippa. "They sound like a perfectly ordinary couple with a solid marriage. How does Keith Landry come into it?"

"He's the story. Jo met him in the early eighties when he first started directing the operettas. They worked on a production of *Gypsy Baron* together. It was that instant spark that passes between two people once in a million years, and everyone could see that it was love at first sight."

"Big scandalous affair?"

"No. That's the sad part. Very much Cathy and Heathcliff, and the frustration of what was meant to be never actually happening. Jo is such a decent woman, and she knew that Rupert would be devastated if she ever betrayed him, so she and Keith just lingered on all those years as loving friends."

Maybe the fact that they never gave in to their feelings was what kept the romance so poignant, but the fact remains, Jo was utterly desolate when Keith developed cancer and she's been dreadfully depressed ever since he died. I think she regrets now that she was such a virtuous wife. Still, she sails on, like an ocean liner, steady on course and stabilizers out to cope with the waves. Poor Jo. I do feel sorry for her."

"Honestly, Milton, you should write a book. Vancouver theatre scandals—the hidden stories. How do you know all these things?"

"I listen to people. Anyway, I've done a couple of shows with Jo's brother, Abel Bowman. He's in *Pinafore* too. He's Captain Corcoran. He's a fiery sort of guy, but very fond of his sister—he's lived in Jo and Rupert's basement suite ever since his wife divorced him—and he told me the whole story."

"Well, I'm glad you passed it on to me," said Philippa gratefully. "I'll know what not to say if I run into them at the dinner."

"You're missing the point," said Milton. "I didn't say it was a tale you ought to know so that you didn't drop a clanger at the banquet. I thought you might learn something from it."

"Oh. And what might that be?"

"Follow your heart," said Milton. "Don't grow old and be full of regrets about things you didn't do. In other words, bloody well phone your cop and give him a chance to explain!"

\*      \*      \*

DC Bob Miller stared at the body lying in the corner of the dingy room, the pale green walls now splattered with red. The black girl had been tiny, which seemed to make the mangled corpse even more pathetic. Her thin legs, in ludicrously high-heeled boots, were splayed out at an odd angle. The blast of the shotgun had been high, and although her upper chest and face were a mass of blood, her velvety midriff was intact. A glittering stud shone from her navel above the low-cut miniskirt.

Miller went through the beaded curtain that separated the back room from the main part of the shop. The barber's chair was old, the leather seat cracked at the side and on the arm. A faded yellow towel was folded over the back of the chair. Curious, thought Miller. The only towels and facecloths in the back room had been neatly folded at the end of the counter, but none appeared to have been used. The towel ring by the sink was empty. Either the incriminating items had been stolen, or whoever came to see the girl had not come for her services, but merely to kill her.

Lally's Lair was on the second floor of a seedy strip mall and the two rooms comprised little more than five hundred square feet. As Miller scrutinized the room, he avoided touching the surfaces, but took everything in with his eyes. He heard footsteps on the stairs, and a moment later, a uniformed constable entered, his eyes shining eagerly.

"Sir, we have a witness, and we've got a description of the killer. A homeless man was picking up bottles in the back lane. He saw the man leave via the back door."

"Where is this witness?"

"Downstairs. I couldn't get an address because he doesn't live anywhere. Best I could extract from him was, 'Under the bridge.' You'd better come and hear what he has to say."

"What did he tell you?" Miller asked.

"I'll tell you afterwards," the PC said earnestly. "Then we'll know if he's making it up as he goes along. Let's see if you get the same description I did."

"Aiming for the detective squad?" asked Miller.

The constable grinned self-consciously.

Miller followed him down the stairs. Outside stood an ancient derelict in a worn grey overcoat, which covered a tattered sweatshirt and faded jeans. The man's hair was long, grizzled and matted. He greeted Miller with a gusty hello and a smile that exposed missing teeth and rancid breath, which, combined with the smell of unwashed flesh and the stench from the bins in the lane, was overwhelming. Miller steeled himself not to recoil and asked the man to describe the person he had seen.

"Big. Tall and bulky," was the response. "Couldn't see his face too well. He wore a hat with a brim."

"A ball cap?"

"No. Looked like oilskin. The brim went all round."

"A sou'wester?"

"No. More like a fishing hat. The sort of thing the Brits wear. He had specs. I could see those. He had a sports bag with him, and he was wearing one of those army coats."

"Khaki?"

"No. Camouflage gear. Dappled. Browns and blacks and greens."

Miller glanced at the constable, who nodded. Miller was about to dismiss the old man, when he glanced at the shopping cart in the lane.

"That yours?" he asked.

The man reluctantly acknowledged ownership.

Miller walked over to the cart and eyed the pile of scavenged goods. A faded yellow facecloth lay on top.

"Where did you find this?" he asked the tramp.

"Outside the door. Right over there." The tramp waved towards the door where the PC was still standing.

"In that case," said Miller, "you'll have to come back to claim your cart after IDENT arrive."

As the man set off, muttering under his breath, Miller turned jubilantly to the constable.

"This time, the killer's made a mistake," he crowed. "If I'm right, we have more than his description; we just might have his DNA. This is one case where VPD is going to get there ahead of the red-serge brigade. You wait and see."

*     *     *

The Burnside Fish and Game Club banquet was held at the Lakeview Rowing Club, which was an unfortunate choice in October since the row of plate-glass windows overlooking the lake gave off a biting chill that no amount of central heating could overcome. The regular female attendees could be identified by their heavy wool pantsuits or designer jeans and bulky sweaters. Edwina, snug in velvet evening pants, black silk turtleneck and beaded woollen jacket, apologized to Philippa for not forewarning her and seated her as far from the window as possible. Philippa, shivering in a short, sleeveless chiffon dress, decided the only way she was going to make it through the evening was to wear her coat, so she retrieved it from the cloakroom and sat huddled in the black winter coat with her scarf wrapped around her neck. Glamour, be damned, she thought.

Her father seemed out of sorts too, having endured a particularly onerous series of committee meetings throughout the day and, as Edwina pointed out, not having yet imbibed his usual quota of Glenlivet to alleviate the pain. He scowled at the table of trophies, which were lined up, gleaming, inscribed, and ready to be presented to the various winners after dinner.

"I can't believe old man Murphy is winning the biggest trout with a mere three-pounder," he complained. "I caught one twice that size at Owen Lake."

"So why didn't you enter it?" asked Philippa.

"Didn't have a witness," grunted Beary.

"Never mind, Bertram," Edwina said dryly. "Maybe you'll get the award for the biggest crab."

"Your mother's on a roll tonight," Beary muttered sourly to his daughter. "Fancies herself a wit. Aha!" he added. "Finally. The bar is open."

Beary lumbered to his feet, taking his roll of bar tickets, and homed in on the bartender with the precision of a falcon diving onto a field mouse. Edwina beckoned Philippa to follow her to the appetizer table, which was laid out with a potluck variety of hors d'œuvres created by the club members from their assorted catches and kills.

"I'd avoid the duck pâté," Edwina instructed her daughter. "Mr. Murphy

211

is notorious for not getting all the birdshot out. But have some of that salmon mousse. It's delicious."

Philippa tried it. It was.

"The crab dip is lovely too," Edwina continued, "but don't overdo it. There will be a full catered buffet after this. So how's *Pinafore* coming along?" she added, as they filled their plates with delicacies.

Philippa shrugged.

"Not great. The director is wishy-washy and disorganized, so the leads are basically figuring out the blocking for themselves. We'll be okay, but I can't vouch for the chorus, and goodness knows what the overall production will look like. The musical director is hopeless too. He takes my numbers at the speed of a freight train. Are you really sure you want to come?"

"Oh dear, perhaps we shouldn't have passed your name on to Jo Farnsworth. But she told me they needed a soprano in a hurry and were willing to pay, so I thought you could use the money."

"I can. It's fine. It's better than sitting idle or doing extra time at the arts council. But I'm puzzled. How come the Farnsworths belong to the Burnside Fish and Game Club?"

"Why shouldn't they?"

"They live near the Riverside Theatre. Shouldn't they belong to a Vancouver club? Dad wouldn't join a group outside his own area."

Edwina added one last shrimp canapé to her plate and led Philippa back to the table.

"Your father's a fisherman," Edwina explained. "Hunting enthusiasts are different. They go where the firing ranges are, and Burnside has good facilities. The Farnsworths will be sitting at our table tonight," she added. "They're just back from the club's annual hunt in the Rock Creek area. One of Rupert's friends who lives in Langley was on the trip, and they're bringing him with them tonight. When Jo told me he was mid-thirties and single, I said I'd bring you with us to make up the numbers—since you seem to be on the outs with that nice Constable Miller these days."

Philippa ignored the probe, and before Edwina could persevere, Beary interjected.

"And blame your mother if you don't enjoy your evening," he said, returning to the table with a glass of Scotch in one hand and a bottle of wine in the other. He plopped the glass on his placemat and proceeded to pour wine for Edwina and Philippa. "Having met the gentleman in question," he added, "I have misgivings about your compatibility, but who am I to challenge your mother's wisdom?"

"Jo said Rupert's friend is a good dancer," Edwina retorted. "Unlike present company," she added frostily. She turned back to Philippa.

"Jo's brother is coming too. I believe you've already met him."

"Captain Corcoran?"

"That's right. Abel Bowman. He doesn't hunt, but he's an enthusiastic fisherman."

A cheerful-faced woman with unruly salt-and-pepper hair and heavy-rimmed glasses came over and sat next to Beary, and a moment later, she was joined by a white-haired, affable-looking gentleman in a buttoned-up white shirt and bolo tie. Edwina introduced them as Maggie and George Parks. The couple was a study in contrasts. Maggie talked enough to allow the entire table to sit in silence if they so wished, while her husband sat quietly with a dreamy smile on his face, only coming to life if asked a direct question. As Philippa leaned back in her chair, tuning out the words and nodding appropriately at regular intervals, she noticed Jo Farnsworth coming through the door. She was accompanied by three men. Two were portly and well into middle age, and the third was a lanky giant with Clint Eastwood eyes that peered out from under a white Stetson. Philippa recognized one of the older men. He was Jo Farnsworth's brother, the singer who was playing Captain Corcoran in the operetta. Philippa smiled to see he was still wearing his yachting cap.

The other middle-aged man, who Philippa presumed was Rupert Farnsworth, was tall, like his wife, but heavily built, with a florid face that implied he was a dedicated toper. He was bald, except for a tonsure-like ring of grey hair around the base of his skull. He wore glasses, which, at a distance, reflected the light and concealed his eyes, but his mouth looked a little petulant, and Philippa was conscious of a feeling of disappointment. She liked Rupert Farnsworth's books, which she had read many times to her nieces and nephews, yet somehow, the man did not match up to her idea of how he should look. However, he took his wife's coat, hung it on the rack by the door, chivalrously handed her to her brother and went to the bar, clearly intending to order her a drink, so his behaviour could not be faulted, for all that he did not have a prepossessing appearance.

Jo Farnsworth, on the other hand, was an imposing figure. She was elegantly dressed in a long, olive green gown, which emphasized her tall, slim frame. She really was a very attractive woman, Philippa decided, and an inspiration for younger females to know that they could still look glamorous well into their sixties; but for all her smart appearance, she had the bearing of an aristocrat going to the guillotine. It was inexplicable, thought Philippa. Jo was escorted by three men, all treating her courteously and deferentially, and she was respected, and even envied, by the other women in the room. How could the loss of a dear friend weigh so heavily after two years, however much her romantic dreams had vanished with him, when she had a husband who had been devoted to her for more than forty years? Still, Philippa recalled how she herself had been bowled over by the magnetism of Keith Landry on the one occasion that they had met. It must have taken a supreme effort for Jo to stay a virtuous wife to her plain, but loyally affectionate husband, if Landry had really proved to be the soulmate she had not had the good fortune to meet before settling for marriage with a compatible, if not exciting, mate.

Philippa looked away from Jo Farnsworth and saw that she had more pressing personal issues to deal with. Clint Eastwood was peering around the room as if watching for a war party to come over the rise. Spotting Beary, his eyes swivelled to the right and landed on Philippa. Immediately, the narrowed eyes opened a millimeter and his mouth split into a predatory grin that would have filled the wide screen in the heyday of Cinemascope. Then, with the determined gait of a man about to wrangle with a feisty steer, he strode towards their table. Oh, my god, thought Philippa. I'm about to be corralled.

"Do come and join us," trilled Edwina unnecessarily. "You must be Rupert's friend."

Clint Eastwood's name, it transpired, was Hector Ridgeway. "Just call me Heck," he informed the table, before transferring his attention entirely to Philippa. By the time dinner was over, Philippa had learned most of the regulations of the Ministry of the Environment, the mating habits of assorted wild fowl and range animals, and Heck's annual schedule of events, which, co-incidentally, reflected the priority of most of the men in the club: duck and goose hunting in the winter, crab fishing in the spring, the pursuit for trout and salmon during the summer months, and the hunt for deer, moose and elk in the fall.

"Do you actually eat everything you kill?" Philippa asked. "Sorry," she added, looking at the man's size. "Silly question. Of course you do."

Heck flashed the Cinerama teeth again.

"You betcha. Healthy food too. Not pumped full of those hormones like the meat you buy in the stores."

"Don't you feel a teeny little bit of conscience, shooting those pretty doe-eyed creatures?" Philippa said wistfully.

"No, ma'am. It's called culling the species. Too bad we can't cull a few of the humans on the planet, too, when they get out of line or overpopulated."

Philippa blinked. Heck clearly was not an individual who worried about political correctness.

"You don't think that's a little extreme?" she ventured.

"Hey, nature does it. Why do you think we have earthquakes and epidemics? A war or two does the trick as well."

"Oh, dear," sighed Philippa. "I suppose we're all expendable."

Heck was not fazed by her sorrowful tone.

"Yup. We are. Coffee?" he added, picking up the pot on the table. "Maybe this'll warm you up so you can take off that big overcoat."

Philippa suddenly realized she was not chilled any more. The food, combined with body heat from a crowded banquet hall, was offsetting the icy draft from the windows. As the emcee announced that it was time to give out the awards, she slipped the coat from her shoulders.

George Parks, who had continued to leave all conversation to his wife throughout the dinner, emerged from his daze and gave Philippa a dreamy smile.

"That's a right pretty dress," he said.

Philippa smiled back at the white-haired man. Country and western manners could be right charming, she decided. Relieved to have a break from the environmental lecture, she settled back in her chair and turned her eyes toward the podium.

The awards lasted half an hour. To Philippa's delight, her father won the biggest salmon and came back to the table bearing a huge trophy. By the time the presentations were complete, Philippa barely had room for her coffee cup, for the table was covered with ornamental figurines toting rods or guns. Heck, it appeared, had cleaned up on moose, elk and geese during the course of the year, and Rupert Farnsworth had done a great deal to reduce the deer population in the interior and the fish stocks on the coast. Gentle George Parks had potted the largest duck, and his wife, Maggie, won a prize for the funniest anecdote, which was a hilarious tale written at the expense of her husband. There were children's awards for the junior members, and photography awards for those who preferred to shoot and leave their targets standing. By the time the emcee declared the formal part of the evening over, Philippa was longing to stand and stretch her legs, so she was delighted when a bespectacled gentleman sporting a cowboy hat and a beer belly came forward to start the disco music.

Heck immediately asked her to dance, and Philippa's evening transformed from tedium to delight. Heck could indeed dance, whether firmly steering her round the floor in a foxtrot or whooping it up for line dancing, and for the next two hours, she completely forgot about her problems and indulged in an orgy of toe tapping.

"I told you so," said Edwina to Beary, as they watched from their table. "She's having a wonderful time."

"Yes, dear. Well done," nodded Beary, who by now was feeling mellow. "Would you like another drink before the bar closes?" he added.

"No. I'd like to dance."

Beary accepted the inevitable and guided his wife onto the floor. Philippa beamed as her parents passed by, Beary steering Edwina with the concentrated determination of a learner driver trying to manoeuvre a semi-trailer.

"Your pappy's had a few," said Heck with a grin.

"Yup," said Philippa, who had had a few herself and was comfortably set in the country and western mood. "Mum will definitely be driving home."

"That's real nice, you being out with your parents." Heck sounded approving.

"Aw, Heck," drawled Philippa. "I like my mum and dad."

Heck appeared not to notice the twinkle in Philippa's eye.

"There are so many real cheap girls running around these days," he said earnestly. "There's not much in the way of standards any more. It's real special to meet a girl like you: real pretty, real talented and real decent. I got no time for the other types."

With a start, Philippa saw that the Clint Eastwood eyes had returned to gunfighter mode. In the fun of the dance, she had forgotten the hobby that brought the people in the room together, but Heck's hawk-like gaze reminded her. He looked like a hunter again.

When the disco shut down at eleven, the event drew to a close. Philippa had enjoyed her evening, but she hoped that Heck would not try to offer her a ride home. However, to her relief, he simply thanked her for her company, politely shook her hand, and said he would enjoy seeing her again.

"Why don't you come to the Riverside production with us?" proposed Rupert. "Then you can see Philippa onstage."

Heck's eyes lit up.

"Hey, that'll be grand."

Philippa groaned inwardly, but there was little she could say in front of the Farnsworths. However, Jo spoke up and said the words that Philippa had not dared utter.

"It won't be that great a production." Jo shook her head apologetically. "Our new director is proving very weak. But the leads are excellent, even the non-Equity ones like Buttercup."

Rupert chortled.

"I bet she is. Good old Handy Harriet. She's a masseuse," he added with a wink.

Jo stiffened. Her brother, standing beside her, didn't look amused.

"That's a tacky job for a woman," he said shortly.

"Only if the men are tacky," snapped Edwina. "There are lots of eminently respectable specialists giving therapeutic massage."

"Not the ones who are getting murdered," said Heck coolly.

"I wouldn't know," said Edwina. She turned to Philippa. "Did you see the paper? There's been another case in Vancouver. Your friend, Bob Miller, is in charge of the investigation."

Philippa sensed, rather than saw, a reaction from the people around her, but she couldn't put her finger on what it was. Jo Farnsworth stared at Philippa as if she was seeing her for the first time. Her brother was also watching guardedly. Heck had regained his vigilant air, and the smile had evaporated from Rupert Farnsworth's face.

"Is he?" Philippa said casually. "I had no idea. Come on, Dad. Time to go," she added, deliberately changing the subject.

While her parents retrieved their coats from the cloakroom, Philippa remained in the lobby and perused the display of photographs from the various club outings. She picked out Heck with his prize moose, and her father in his Hardy hat, proudly holding up his winning salmon. There was also a shot of Rupert Farnsworth, similarly attired, standing on a riverbank, a row of trout spread along the grass at his feet.

A call from her mother made her turn. Her parents were following the Farnsworths towards the exit. Heck galloped forward and held the door until everyone was through. Then he sauntered alongside Philippa and escorted her to the parking lot, where he saw her off with her parents. Beary insisted that Philippa ride in the front with her mother and promptly went to sleep in the back seat.

"Did you enjoy your evening?" Edwina asked Philippa, as she pulled out of the parking lot and set off in the direction of Philippa's condo at Westminster Quay.

"Yes. Very much. I'm glad you asked me. The dancing was fantastic. I feel badly that I didn't visit much with the Farnsworths, though. Heck pretty well dominated my attention."

"The Farnsworths are not the greatest company at the moment," Edwina observed. "Jo seems dreadfully down in the mouth these days, not that I know her well. I've just met her at the club events in the past, but she always struck me as a pleasant woman and a real lady. But these days, it's hard to have much of a conversation with her. She's miles away most of the time. Something is on her mind."

"According to Milton, she's grieving for a very dear friend who died two years ago."

Edwina sniffed disapprovingly.

"She should be over it after two years. Even women who lose their husbands get on their feet after struggling through a year of widowhood."

"I heard that," mumbled Beary from the back seat.

"Go back to sleep," said Edwina.

"I can't," complained Beary. "Not with you two yapping at the tops of your voices. And if you want to know what's wrong with Jo Farnsworth, I'd say the problem is not her fretting for some lost friend; it's her relationship with Rupert. They used to be all sweetness and light together, but these days she's distinctly chilly with him. My guess is Rupert has done something to blot his copybook, and she's found out. Her brother is rather distant with Rupert at the moment too. You mark my words; there's trouble in the Farnsworth household."

Beary fell silent again, and a few minutes later, Edwina pulled up at Westminster Quay and let Philippa off. Waving goodbye, Philippa hurried through the alley to her condo entrance. Her newspaper was still in the front hall. Picking it up, she saw that the murder had made the front page. Her eyes slid from the headline to the photograph of the victim. With a start, she realized that she had seen the girl before. It was the young black woman who had been in Starbucks.

As Philippa read on, she concluded that the murder must have occurred only a few hours after she had heard the woman talking on the phone. Uneasily, she wondered if the conversation she had overheard in the coffee shop had been an appointment with death.

*   *   *

The following morning, Philippa steeled herself to phone Bob Miller. Glad of the excuse to make contact and aware that Milton would approve, she punched in the numbers of Miller's cellphone, wondering if he would reply when he saw who was calling, or let the incoming call go to voicemail. She did not have to wonder for long. Miller answered right away. However, his voice was cool.

"Philippa, what's up?"

Philippa gulped. Friendly preliminaries obviously weren't in order. She got right to the reason for her call.

"Bob, I saw that you're in charge of the murder of that masseuse in Vancouver," she began.

"She was a bit more than a masseuse," said Miller dourly.

"Yes, well I sort of guessed that. She sounded like she was prepared to offer a lot more than a massage."

"What?" Miller's voice grew sharp. "Did you have some kind of contact with this woman?"

"Yes. That's why I called. I saw her in Starbucks the day she was killed, and I heard her making an appointment for that afternoon at two o'clock. She might have been talking to her killer. I don't know if that's any help, but I thought I should pass it on."

"Yes, you were right to call in. Thank you."

Philippa sensed that he was about to end the call. She rushed in with the thoughts that had been forming in her mind since she had read the newspaper report.

"There was something else I thought I should mention, though this is pure supposition," she said.

"OK. Let's have it."

"I was at a fish and game club dinner last night—with my parents," she added, throwing in the last bit deliberately. "Dad belongs for the fishing, but there are a lot of hunters in the club too. They talked about the places they hunt and the times of year they go, and when I read the article, it occurred to me that the murders tally closely with the hunting and fishing schedules of outdoor sportsmen. I'd say a quarter of the members of the club were in the Kettle Valley earlier this month, and a lot of them hunt in Delta on the dikes during the early part of the year. Also, in the summer, tons of them are fishing off the Gulf Islands. It just seemed a bit of a coincidence, given that all the murders were committed with a shotgun." She petered out, Miller having let her have her say without interruption.

There was a silence at the other end. Then Miller chuckled.

"You haven't changed a bit," he said. "Good sleuthing."

"You think my idea is worth following up on?"

"Actually, we already thought of it, and so did your brother. We've got VPD, the RCMP and the Delta Force working to find this guy. The problem is, although we have some significant evidence to nail him once we find him, there's nothing on record that can lead us to identify him at this point. We don't live in the type of police state where we can pull someone in at random just because he had an entry for an elk in MU 8-14, but we're working on it. Let me know if you come up with anything specific."

"I will. The sports set isn't my usual crowd, but the makeup lady for my current show is married to a hunter, so she and her husband might have some ideas. I'll keep my ear to the ground."

"What's the show?" asked Miller.

Philippa breathed a sigh of relief. At last, a personal question.

"H.M.S. Pinafore, but I can't recommend it. It's an amateur group that has gone sadly downhill in recent years. The leads are good, but the production is pretty sloppy."

"So who are the leads?" Miller asked casually.

Not Adam, Philippa wanted to say, but since she could hardly do that, she rattled off every person who had a role, large or small.

"Quite the cast," Miller concluded dryly. "Well, good luck with it. Let me know if you have any more bright ideas."

Philippa sighed as Miller ended the call. At least they'd made contact, but he certainly hadn't indicated any interest in getting together. He was probably back with the ex, just as Octavia said. She thrust the detective from her mind and headed for the solace of the coffee pot.

*       *       *

Opening night came quickly. Philippa had never learned a role so hurriedly before, but she felt reasonably confident. She was in good voice, and Pablo was a courteous singing partner who was prepared to help her through any rocky patches, so she was sure she would get by. However, she had not bothered with her usual rounds of phone calls to friends and family telling them about the show. This was one she would rather passed without notice. Other than her parents, no one she knew was coming.

She left for the theatre early. She wanted to get into costume well ahead of time so that she could sit quietly and review her score before she went on. Milton, conscientiously, was ready early too, and when he hopped into her Jeep, she saw that his eyes were sparkling and he was sporting a guess-what-I-know smile.

"OK," she said. "Go ahead. Tell me."

"I was right," he crowed.

"Right about what?"

Milton answered with another question.

"Did your handsome detective ever tell you what his dotty girlfriend did for a living?"

"No. I know she wasn't a cop. He didn't say much about her, except that she had weird ideas and they quarrelled a lot."

"And I bet Octavia didn't tell you she was a social worker."

"No, she didn't. What has that to do with anything?"

"The case Miller was called in about when he broke your date was a homicide. A woman killed her husband, and her two pre-teen children witnessed the murder. Your cop's ex was the social worker assigned to the children and she had to be present during the interviews. Afterwards, she and Miller had matters to discuss and did so over a late bite at Earls. After which, he had a drink with one of his mates and went home."

"Oh, good grief!" said Philippa. "I feel like a total worm."

"So you should," said Milton.

"How do you know all this?"

"I called him up last night and asked him."

Philippa almost drove off the road.

"You didn't!"

"Yes, I did. I copied his number off your cellphone at rehearsal on Tuesday while you were 'Sorrying her Lot' onstage. And you don't have to get cross.

Miller was glad I called. He thought you were offhand with him because you'd got the hots for Adam again. He actually thought it was pretty funny that your feathers were so badly ruffled."

"Milton, you idiot. I'll never live this down."

"Probably not. But you can bet he's going to call you again. Besides, it'll give him something to rib you about when you're old and grey. Anyway, I was partly doing it for myself, not to mention your professional credibility. I couldn't stand the way you were singing your solos. We're doing G and S, not grand opera. You've been carrying on like you're performing the second act of *Tosca*."

"I haven't!"

"You have. And our wimpy director is so clueless he isn't going to put you straight. Someone had to sort you out. Now stop bristling and concentrate before we have an accident. Remember, think operetta. Light and bubbly. No more imitations of Victor Borge doing the death of Isolde. Aha!" he added. "There it is. I knew I could make you smile."

"Oh, Milton," sighed Philippa. "You're such an idiot. And I owe you such a lot."

With a light heart, Philippa steered the Jeep along Marine Way, humming as she went.

"Well, what do you know?" chuckled Milton. "We're back to 'Some Enchanted Evening' again. Try not to muck things up this time."

*     *     *

Beary and Edwina arrived for the opening night in good time. Beary always enjoyed attending Riverside productions because the theatre contained a cozy lounge on the upper floor, lined with photographs from former productions, and well equipped with leather armchairs and an impressive stock of booze. For this reason, he always insisted on seats in the balcony, since it provided the fastest access to the bar during intermission.

As he held the door for Edwina, he saw a familiar person taking tickets. Rupert Farnsworth had been commandeered into volunteering for front-of-house. Jo, he informed them, was doing makeup backstage.

Rupert grinned as he tore Beary's tickets.

"You're upstairs and I know why," he directed him cheerfully. "Stick around afterwards, too," he added. "There's a reception."

Beary and Edwina went up to the lounge. There was only a handful of people there. Two men and a woman sat on the couch at the far end, another couple circled the walls, admiring the pictures, and Heck was present, standing at the counter, chatting with the bartender. Edwina sat down to read her program and Beary joined Heck at the bar.

"Well, hello there," Heck greeted him. "Here to see your delightful daughter?"

"We are. What about you?"

"Same reason. I hear she sings like a little lark."

"She does, indeed. What can I get you?"

"Another beer. Thank you, kindly."

Beary ordered a sherry for Edwina, Scotch for himself and beer for Heck. As they took the drinks over to the sofa where Edwina sat, Jo Farnsworth came up the stairs. She was biting her lips and wringing her hands. Beary and Edwina eyed each other uneasily. This did not auger well for what was going on backstage. However, when Jo noticed Heck and the Bearys, she greeted them civilly and offered to put their coats in the office that adjoined the lounge. As she glided away with the overcoats, Edwina looked after her solemnly.

"What on earth is upsetting her so badly? I hope to goodness it's not the show."

"She sure is edgy," agreed Heck. "Never used to be. But this last year, poor old Rupe has had quite a time with her. Every time he opens his mouth, she shoots him down like he was a clay pigeon. Must be one of those middle-aged-woman things."

"I'm sure it's nothing of the sort," said Edwina frostily. "She's probably tired of kowtowing to his every whim after four dreary decades of indulging him. That would be enough to put any woman into a depression."

"Well, dear," said Beary, taking another swig of his Scotch, "*you'll* never have that problem."

Heck wisely chose to keep quiet.

Fifteen minutes later, the chimes rang. The performance was about to start. Since the balcony was only half-full, Beary and Edwina moved over and sat with Jo, Heck and Rupert, who had now been relieved of ticket duty. As Philippa had predicted, the leads sang well, but the production was ragged and the beat from the pit plodded like a carthorse, dragging the singers along with the same lack of enthusiasm. The lighting was erratic, at one point throwing the stage into blackout in the middle of Philippa's first solo, and the set changes were far from smooth.

Eventually, *Pinafore* lumbered to a close, and the performers took their bows to a smattering of applause, for the main floor was only slightly more populated than the balcony. Beary and Edwina, having done their duty, adjourned to the bar to await the arrival of the singers and the start of the reception. Jo slipped away to help with the refreshments. Rupert and Heck remained to chat.

The cast members filtered out a few at a time, and before long, Philippa appeared and came to join her parents. To her surprise, the reception turned out to be an agreeable party, and far better organized than the show. Ladies from the chorus had provided an elaborate buffet of finger food, and the club members, who had been unsure of themselves onstage, proved to have exuberant offstage personalities and displayed sparkling humour in their post-mortems of everything that was wrong with the performance. At last, people started to leave and Edwina gave Beary the cue that it was time to depart. Beary, who was talking fishing with Rupert and Heck, ignored her.

Jo Farnsworth looked exhausted. She caught Edwina's eye, and by some mutually agreed signal, disappeared inside the office to fetch the coats. The men continued their discussion, and Philippa started to feel impatient. She was getting tired and longed to see her parents off so that she could leave. Fortunately, Jo was quick. She returned a moment later, wearing her own coat and holding a pile of winter coats in her arms. Philippa went to help her, pulling out her mother's fur and her father's wool overcoat. Jo handed Heck his quilted jacket and called her brother and husband to take their coats, which were almost identical black leather. As the men took their coats, Philippa noticed that a slip of paper had fluttered to the ground, presumably from one of the pockets.

She bent to pick it up and was about to ask whose it was when the name, Lally, leapt out at her from the page. She turned away and looked more closely at the paper. It contained a list of five Christian names. There was something familiar about them.

Then the significance of the list registered and Philippa felt a chill gliding down her spine. She could hardly believe what she was reading on the paper. The first four names on the list were the women who had been killed by the massage-parlour murderer.

The fifth name was Harriet March.

*      *      *

Miller was astounded when Philippa phoned to tell him what she had discovered.

"I can't believe this just landed in your lap," he said. "It's incredible."

"Well, I didn't make it up," Philippa said testily.

"No, of course not. So which one of these men is the owner of this list?"

"I have no idea which coat it fell from," Philippa told Miller, "but it has to be either Rupert Farnsworth or Hector Ridgeway. They're both hunters, and they were both in the right locations at the right times. You'll have to take it from there."

"Oh, we will," said Miller. "You can count on that."

He hung up and turned to DC Phil Ho.

"We've got two suspects," he said, "both from the fish and game club that Philippa's father belongs to."

"How did Philippa come up with the names? Did her dad tip her off?"

"No. One of the men is married to the woman who's doing makeup for Philippa's current show. The other came to see the production. Both men were at the theatre last night and a piece of paper fell from one of their pockets. It was a list of the names of the victims of this shooter we're trying to track down. What's really scary is that there's a fifth name on the list—another masseuse. She's also in the show, so it'll be easy to warn her and keep an eye on her, but first of all, we'll bring in the two men and get DNA samples."

"So who are these suspects?"

"Rupert Farnsworth, who's a well-respected children's writer, so it's going to be a big scandal if he turns out to be the perpetrator. Philippa thinks it's possible. Evidently, Rupert and Jo Farnsworth used to have a very serene marriage, but something has gone wrong in the last couple of years. The wife seems to have become disillusioned about her husband, which might simply mean that she's found out he's been a naughty boy, but Philippa says the woman is so distraught that it could be something much deeper."

"Like suspecting him of being a killer?"

"Exactly. And the other man, who's a fellow outdoors type who hunts and fishes with Farnsworth, has some morality issues that just might make him feel he has the right to take people out if they aren't what he considers pillars of society. But either way, we should know in a couple of days."

\*          \*          \*

By Saturday, Philippa was feeling apprehensive. There had been no word of any progress from Bob Miller—not that he was obliged to tell her anything—but she could not help wondering how his investigation would affect the people in the show. Milton sang his version of Sir Joseph Porter all the way to the theatre and she did not try to stop him. She was reluctant to discuss her concerns, even with as close a friend as Milton. Other than Bob Miller, she had not told anyone about the list. If Rupert Farnsworth proved to be the killer, there were going to be repercussions at the theatre, and she had no desire to be held responsible for the public humiliation of the popular makeup lady.

However, when they arrived at the theatre, the sight of a gloomy Captain Corcoran smoking in the parking lot intimated that the wheels of justice were already in motion. As she got out of her car, Abel came to meet her and beckoned Milton to join them. In a low voice, he warned them that Jo would not be at the theatre that night. Rupert was under arrest. Abel seemed to think Philippa knew what was going on, which surprised her. Miller would never have revealed her name. Still, Abel was aware of her association with the detective so, most likely, he assumed she was in the know.

Milton, however, was astounded.

"Rupert! The massage parlour killer? You're joking," he protested, when he'd heard what Abel had to say. "I can see him being slimy enough to suss out masseuses who are willing to rub his naughty bits, but popping them off with a shotgun? No bloody way!"

"They have an ironclad case," said Abel firmly. "DNA evidence and ballistics. They found the shotgun in the garage where Rupert has his workshop. They found his Hardy hat, too, and apparently, the man who was seen leaving the massage parlour in Vancouver was wearing that sort of hat."

"What in heaven's name is a Hardy hat?" asked Milton.

"Hardy's is a major fishing-supply business in England," said Philippa. "My dad bought himself one of their hats when we were in London a few years ago. They're very different from the ball caps that you see on most hunters and fishermen out here." She turned back to Abel. "How is Jo doing?" she asked.

"She's devastated." Abel didn't pull any punches. He threw his cigarette stub onto the tarmac and ground it viciously with his heel. "All those years of loyally staying with him because she was convinced that he was a faithful husband who adored her," he said venomously. "She thought he'd be shattered if he knew she cared for someone else. What a joke that was. And then to discover that he's a cheat, and not only a cheat who had a solitary lapse, but one who calculatedly went out and paid for what he wanted with a whole variety of women whenever he had the opportunity. I hope they lock him up and throw away the key."

Glowering, Abel took out another cigarette. As he lit it, Philippa saw that his hands were shaking.

"I still don't believe it," Milton muttered as they moved away and went inside the theatre. "Even if Rupert had been regularly spending his pocket money on sex-trade workers, it doesn't make him a killer."

"The police have pretty substantial evidence," Philippa pointed out. "I must say Abel sounds extremely bitter on his sister's behalf," she added. "All he seemed to care about was the infidelity. He didn't even mention the murders. He sure doesn't like his brother-in-law."

"I don't particularly like Rupert either," said Milton, "but he's not the only person who had the opportunity to kill those girls. From what you told me about outdoor sportsmen, half the blessed gun club could have been in the area at the same time. They might have taken turns visiting the same masseuse. Even Abel would have been on the spot, though he's not a hunter. He just tags along to keep Jo company."

Philippa stopped in her tracks and stared at Milton.

"Do you know that for sure?"

"Yes. He told me once that he often goes along. He's a keen fisherman, so he heads for the lake while the others are hunting. And he's always had a pretty ferocious temper. You've seen him throw a paddy or two at rehearsals, so you know what I mean. I'd say he's more likely to pot someone than his brother-in-law is. I've know all of them for years, and as far as I can see, the Bowmans are much more fiery types than the Farnsworths."

"So it could have been his coat," Philippa murmured.

"What are you blabbering about?" asked Milton.

"Nothing. I'll tell you later." Philippa dug her cellphone out of her purse. "I have to make a phone call. You go ahead. I'll see you downstairs later."

\*       \*       \*

The following day, DC Miller called round to the Farnsworth residence. Jo answered the door, and when she heard that he wanted to speak with her brother, she called down to the basement suite. She invited Miller into the living room but made no offer of refreshments. She stood by the window, waiting quietly for her brother to join them.

While he waited, Miller felt uncomfortably conscious of the tension in the tall, pale woman. Her face was haggard and there was an unhealthy flush on her cheekbones. It was as if she had aged twenty years since the day her husband had been arrested.

Miller heard the sound of a door opening. Then Abel Bowman entered from the hallway. He looked surprised to see Miller.

"I need to ask you some questions, sir," Miller began. "Perhaps you could wait in the other room," he added to Jo.

Jo's eyes narrowed and she stayed rooted to the spot.

"Why do you need to talk to my brother?"

"Just some routine questions, Mrs. Farnsworth. They don't involve you, not at this point."

"Of course I'm involved," said Jo. "It's my husband who's under arrest. I'd like to know what's going on."

"Mrs. Farnsworth, I know you're under a strain and this is all very difficult for you. However, you're going to have to be patient and let us do our job." Miller kept his voice calm, but his tone was firm. "Right now, I need to talk with your brother."

Jo's voice rose hysterically. "Why do you need to talk to Abel? He doesn't know anything."

Miller felt a wave of frustration. Jo Farnsworth did not seem to appreciate the fact that he was attempting to make things easier for her. He gave up trying to make her leave and turned to Abel Bowman.

"I've been told you went along on all your brother-in-law's hunting and fishing trips this year," he said.

"Yes. That's correct."

"And you live here in the basement suite of your sister's home?"

Abel nodded.

"And you stay with them in their cottage on Gabriola Island during the summer?"

"Yes, I do."

"What's the purpose of these questions?" Jo interjected. "I don't understand what's going on."

Miller ignored the outburst and continued talking to Abel.

"Could I get an account of your whereabouts on the afternoon of October the tenth of this year?"

"Why are you doing this?" Jo cried. "Abel has nothing to do with it."

"Mrs. Farnsworth, please don't interfere. If you can't control yourself, I'm going to have to take your brother in to the station for questioning. So I must ask you to keep quiet."

Jo's face registered utter panic. Her eyes went wild and the control she had maintained for so long collapsed. Hysterically, she screamed at Miller as if she had not heard a word he said.

"Why are you here? You have your case. DNA is positive proof. The facecloth on the doorstep of that whore's place is all the evidence you need. Leave Abel alone."

Miller stopped as if he'd been pole-axed. He stared, bewildered, at Jo Farnsworth, and as her eyes met his, her face crumpled and she dissolved into sobs.

"Mrs. Farnsworth," Miller said slowly, "how did you know that the facecloth we found was on the doorstep of Lally's massage parlour?"

*      *      *

Later that evening, after Rupert Farnsworth had been released and his wife was in custody, Miller wearily reviewed his report. Pretty depressing, he thought, to end like that after all those years of marriage. Jo Farnsworth had been destabilized by a mixture of grief, rage, disillusionment and humiliation, but he still found it hard to comprehend how she could have justified her killing spree, let alone set her husband up with such premeditated venom. Miller was repelled by the calculated way she had systematically set out to eliminate every one of the masseuses that Rupert had visited. Was it just so that she could frame her husband for the murders? Or did her hatred extend to the women as well? Whatever the convoluted reasoning behind her actions, the woman was clearly unbalanced.

Miller flinched inwardly, remembering how Jo Farnsworth had admitted her crimes and boasted about what she'd done. She was a trained cosmetician who knew all the tricks for disguising women as men—she had coolly informed them that all makeup schools included a unit on that subject—and she had put her training to deadly use when carrying out her plan. Each time she was ready to strike, she had made up her face, donned Rupert's hunting gear, put on his spare glasses, and used his sports bag to conceal his sawed-off shotgun. She had booked appointments, always picking times when her husband wouldn't have an alibi, and had shot the women one by one. After each murder, she had cleaned the surfaces, washed her victim's hands, and stolen a towel and facecloth to make it appear that a male client was removing traces of his DNA. Then she had calmly waited, sometimes for months, until her husband's hunting and fishing schedule provided her with the opportunity to deal with the next name on her list.

The last part of the report was even more chilling for it described how Jo had set out to implicate her husband for the final murder. She had led her husband to believe she was willing to provide the services he'd sought elsewhere. One massage, and she had the incriminating facecloth to plant on the doorstep of Lally's Lair. Miller felt deeply disturbed by the whole squalid affair. He also felt angry at the way Philippa had been used. He'd thought at the time it was an incredible coincidence that she'd been the one to discover the killer's list of victims, but now he realized she had been targeted because of her association with him. It had been a despicable way to bring Farnsworth's name to the attention of the police.

Rupert Farnsworth had been shaken by his wife's revelations too, especially when he realized that it was his confession to her more than a year ago that had triggered the terrible series of events. It had been during their summer stay on Gabriola Island. Soon after his visit to the massage parlour there, he had come out in a rash. Terrified that he'd picked up a sexually transmitted disease, he had mustered the courage to own up, since he could not risk passing it on to his wife.

The news had sent Jo Farnsworth right over the edge. She had cried for a week, and when she stopped crying, there was nothing left except a terrifying cold anger. She had grilled him and harassed him until she heard every single detail. After a few weeks, she seemed to calm down, although the coldness continued. Rupert could not break through her reserve. However, he had no idea what a terrible vengeance she was planning. And how could he, thought

Miller, for who would ever imagine that an outwardly gracious lady could conceive of, let alone embark on, such a lethal journey of retribution?

Even Philippa, who had a remarkably detached, analytical mind, had never suspected Jo Farnsworth. Philippa had been horrified when she heard the outcome of the final visit to the Farnsworths' home. Miller had called her, realizing he should break the news gently before she had to face another performance, but he felt guilty remembering the sorrow in her voice as she listened to what he had to say. He had known Philippa long enough to realize she was something of a stoic—she wouldn't let anyone see or hear her cry—but he was willing to bet that the tears had flowed once he had rung off. The whole business was a sad, sorry mess. Feeling tired and dispirited, Miller closed the file and stood up. It was time to go home.

*      *      *

By the closing night of the show, Jo Farnsworth's arrest was the lead story on the front page of *The Vancouver Sun*. Philippa was still giving Milton rides to the theatre, so she knew she would have a lot of questions to answer once she picked him up. Predictably, the inquisition started the moment he got into the car.

"I can't tell you much more than was in the paper," Philippa insisted. "Bob called and told me the outcome, but he was pretty cagey about the details. He just said it was all pretty sordid and I didn't want to know."

"Oh, that's sweet," cooed Milton. "He was being chivalrous. Anyway, what about this list you picked up? Why was Harriet's name on it? I'll never believe *she* was having hanky panky with Rupert."

"No, of course not. Little Buttercup is a model of respectability. She had nothing to do with it. Jo added her name, knowing I'd be sure to alert the police if I thought Harriet was in danger."

Milton whistled.

"Fancy Jo being capable of murder. Those poor women … how could she have been so pitiless? I'm still having trouble processing it. She's the last person I would associate with violence. She always seemed so serene."

"Her serenity was based on the belief that she had a good marriage. When that illusion was shattered, I think she went mad with rage. It wasn't as if she could walk out on Rupert and go to the man she'd loved all along, because he was dead. Can you imagine how bitter she must have felt?"

"I guess she was pretty unstable under that calm surface," observed Milton. "Stable people can compartmentalize, so even if one facet of their life is malfunctioning, they can cope and keep going, but unstable ones sink under the pressure. Just think, when I compared her to a cruiser gliding across the ocean, I wasn't far off. I just didn't realize she was the *Titanic*. The water surged over the top and flooded all the compartments. Poor sad Jo."

"'Sorry her lot who loves too well,'" said Philippa quietly.

"What?"

"My solo. That's the line that came into my head the first time I saw Jo Farnsworth. I just didn't know how true it was."

Philippa fell silent for the rest of the drive, and her sombre mood continued once she reached the theatre. Backstage, everyone was speculating about Jo Farnsworth's arrest, but Philippa deliberately avoided entering into the discussions. She had no wish to publicize her part in bringing the popular club member to justice, so she secluded herself in her dressing room and applied her makeup in silence. From the corridor outside the room, she could still hear the buzz of gossip, but the voices were hushed and the atmosphere was subdued. The whole cast had been shocked and saddened by the newspaper headlines. However, as curtain time approached, the mood in the theatre gradually began to change. Vocalists warmed up and the energy started to rise. The ripple of anticipation at the beginners' call grew to excitement as the sailors' chorus reached the stage and heard the hum of voices on the far side of the curtain. Tonight was predicted to be a full house because the friends and family of the cast and crew always liked to attend the closing-night party. Of necessity, Philippa quelled all thoughts of the Farnsworths and concentrated her mind on her role.

Once on stage, the discipline of performance took over, and the show seemed to flash by quickly. The bows came and went, and then the curtain came down for the last time. Principals and chorus alike hurried downstairs to get ready for the party. However, Philippa took her time removing her makeup and changing for the gathering. She was glad the show was over, even though there was nothing looming on the horizon, but she was reluctant to mingle, knowing that people would still be talking about the tragedy of Jo Farnsworth. However, Milton had promised to stand guard and defend her from awkward questions, so she steeled herself, slipped into a black cocktail dress and made her way to the upstairs lounge.

When she arrived at the top of the stairs, she picked out Milton right away. He was standing by the bar and his smile was bright enough to illuminate an amphitheatre. Beside him stood Bob Miller.

"Well," said Philippa, as she joined them at the bar, "this is a surprise. I didn't expect to see you here."

Bob grinned.

"I thought I might as well come out and cheer you on, seeing as you've been so helpful."

"So? Dare I ask what you thought?"

"Well, *you* were good. You too, Milton," Miller added, sensing a reaction at his elbow.

"It's okay," said Philippa. "You don't have to lie. We know it sucked."

"I wouldn't say that, but it certainly wasn't the glittering performance you gave when I came to *South Pacific*. That had real bite."

"Possibly because of the mood I was in," said Philippa caustically.

Miller chuckled. "Well, from what Milton here tells me, that performance had so much intensity that you've been singled out by an influential agent. Sounds like I did you a favour."

"Right," snapped Philippa. "Like the time you arrested me and saved me from a bad date. Maybe we'd get along a lot better if you stopped doing me favours."

"Careful, DC Miller," cautioned Milton. "She's getting cross. Now, behave, children," he added. Milton wagged a finger at Philippa and sailed away to chat with Buttercup on the far side of the room.

"Sorry," said Miller. "I shouldn't tease you. What can I get you to drink?"

"A glass of white wine would be nice. Was the show really awful?" she added, as Miller ordered her drink.

"No. The production was pretty amateurish, but the leads were good. I enjoyed the singing. And your friend Milton is hilarious. He's quite a ham." Miller's face became serious. "He's a good friend, too."

"Yes, I know."

"I'm glad he called. It was good to clear the air, especially as I'm going to be away for a while."

Philippa looked startled.

"What? Where are you going?"

"Well, for starters, as soon as this case is wrapped up, I've got leave for a few weeks. My mother has decided to move up to Nelson with Jody and Hal. She wants to be near the grandchildren, but she's still very frail and I'm going to give her a hand. I'll be staying there through Christmas. Then ..." Miller's voice tailed off and he looked a little uncomfortable. "Well," he continued after a pause, "I'm going to be quite busy with work for a couple of months. I won't have time to call, but I'd really like to get together when things settle down."

Philippa gave him a straight look.

"Please tell me you haven't volunteered for an undercover assignment."

"Sure. I haven't volunteered for an undercover assignment."

"I don't believe you. Oh, do be careful. Why can't you stick to normal detective work?"

Miller looked irritated.

"Why don't you stop jumping to conclusions?"

"I don't jump to conclusions."

"Yes, you do. You jumped to one about me earlier this year, very unfairly too."

Philippa sighed.

"Yes, I did. All right, I won't ask questions or say anything to anyone. Just, whatever you're doing, get back safely."

"Hey, I believe you're worried about me."

"Well, of course I am. I worry about Richard too. You're in a dangerous job. So take care of yourself."

"I will. You take care too. No getting into trouble in my absence. Is that a pact?"

Out of the corner of her eye, Philippa saw Milton watching from the other side of the room. Even from a distance, she could see that his owlish eyes were wide and twinkling.

"Agreed?" persevered Miller. "How about a toast? To better things in the future."

Philippa flashed Milton a smile, and then raised her glass to Miller.

"Yes," she said sweetly. "I'll drink to that."

Milton, watching from the far end of the lounge, raised his own glass to Philippa and made the victory sign with his other hand. However, Philippa had turned away. She and DC Miller were totally absorbed in a private conversation.

Milton did not mind. He smiled and went back to chatting with his friends, but periodically, he glanced across to the laughing couple standing by the bar. For every show that closed, he thought happily, another opening was sure to follow.

# THE MYSTERY OF THE CHRISTMAS TRAIN

Richard Beary had one inviolable rule. Never allow a girl to meet one's family on a first date. Nothing spelled death to a potential romance like a premature introduction to a surfeit of boisterous and opinionated Bearys, led by a matriarch whose cozy chats as she assessed the newcomer resembled an interview with the Grand Inquisitor. Whenever Richard felt it was appropriate to introduce a girlfriend into the family circle, he took care to break her in gently. No more than one or two Bearys at a time.

Therefore, there was one outing that Richard always attended alone. Every December, the Beary clan convened en masse for a festive visit to Stanley Park and a ride on the Christmas train, revelled in by senior and junior Bearys alike. The event was always followed by a late supper at his parents' home. Richard enjoyed this annual jaunt, for it provided him with an opportunity to socialize with his nephews and nieces, who seemed to have grown like weeds every time he saw them. But the train expedition was a solo outing. Dates were out of the question.

However, one year, temptation appeared in the form of a new neighbour who had moved into his apartment block. Larissa Swinton would have made the stoutest man weaken. Her soft blonde hair, delectably alluring lips and pouter-pigeon bosom brought Scarlett Johansson to mind, and her baby-blue eyes held an ocean of promises. However, her luscious curves were well protected, for the young divorcée, in addition to her mouth-watering attributes, also possessed a ten-year-old son called Billy whose vice-like grip on his mother was as immovable and effective as a medieval chastity belt. It was obvious that the route to the winsome Larissa's heart was through her son, for she made it quite plain that she would be delighted to go on a date as long as it was a child-friendly activity and Billy could come too.

Sorely tempted, Richard reminded himself of his rule.

And broke it.

*       *       *

Evangeline Wellburn scowled into the mirror as she watched her daughter arrange her steel-grey hair into a neat chignon. Evangeline could have easily afforded regular trips to a hair salon—Mr. Wellburn, before he died, had amassed a fortune from the mining industry, all of which had passed to his wife—but then, what were spinster daughters for if not to wait upon their mothers in the interest of household economy?

Evangeline's mood, never benevolent, inevitably deteriorated as Christmas approached. There were so many more relatives around to irritate her, and their presence served to remind her of their failings. Evangeline felt particularly cantankerous at the prospect of the evening ahead. She had no faith that the younger generation of Wellburns would have improved since the last time she saw them.

"If I discover that Ross has been gambling again," she announced vehemently, "I'll disinherit him."

Faith Wellburn ignored the outburst and stuck another pin into the bun. However, Evangeline's sister, Prudence, who was fiddling ineffectually with a scarf, which simply refused to hang into the smart folds that the saleswoman had demonstrated in the shop, looked up, horrified.

"Oh, no, dear! You can't do that. He's your grandson, after all."

"He's a lazy, deceitful good-for-nothing, and it would do him good to have to go out and earn a living. And I mean what I say. I've done with bailing him out, and none of you are to do anything to help him either, or you'll be written out of my will too."

Evangeline glowered at her daughter and her sister, as if daring them to contradict her. Faith's gaze remained impassive.

"There," she said calmly, patting her mother on the head. "All done. What jewellery would you like to wear tonight?"

Evangeline snorted.

"My rose pendant, of course. You know I always wear it for our annual dinner at the Sylvia."

"Yes, dear, but remember, we're all going to Stanley Park beforehand to take little Georgie for his first ride on the Christmas train. Do you really think it's a good idea to wear something that valuable trekking around the park?"

"Don't argue. Get it out."

Faith shrugged and fetched the royal blue case from the drawer of Evangeline's dresser. She opened it and took out the pendant, which glittered and sparkled in the light as it dangled from its fragile gold chain. She caught it in her hand and examined it more closely; then she frowned.

"It looks like one of the claws is loose," she said. "Perhaps this should go in to be repaired."

"Nonsense. Bend it back into place. It'll be fine."

"A stone could come loose," Faith cautioned her mother, as she slipped the chain around the crepey folds of Evangeline's neck.

"It's insured," snapped Evangeline. "Stop fussing. If it needs repairing, you can see to it after Christmas."

"Yes, I will. You don't want to lose any of those diamonds."

Evangeline looked around irritably. "Where's Dorothy?" she demanded.

"She's downstairs ordering the taxi." Prudence gabbled the information, rushing to offer reassurance that Dorothy was usefully engaged. Evangeline could ruin a social event very quickly if she were allowed to sink below her customary level of ill humour. "It should be here any moment."

"It better be," said Evangeline. She put out her arm so that Faith could assist her in hauling her obese form up from the dressing-table stool. Prudence hurried forward with Evangeline's brown mink coat and helped Faith maneuver her mother into it. Faith wrapped a heavy shawl over the shoulders of the coat and plopped a matching fur cloche onto her mother's head. The result looked like a malevolent Mummy Bear. Goldilocks, thought Prudence whimsically, would never have dared sit on *her* chair.

Evangeline waddled towards the door, but before leaving the bedroom, she turned back and glared at her daughter.

"And if I see you tip the cab driver," she grunted, "I'll treble what you gave him and take it off your housekeeping money."

*     *     *

Richard perceived the gravity of his error within minutes of picking up Larissa and her son. The conversation, what little there was of it, was punctuated with frequent demands from Billy, all of which took precedence over anything Richard had to say. Richard's attempt to divert Billy by loaning him his Blackberry was politely and firmly vetoed.

"Billy doesn't play computer games. Very bad for the psyche."

The pattern continued throughout the journey.

"How about a visit to the petting zoo before we go on the train?"

"Oh, no. Billy has allergies."

"Popcorn for the ride?"

"We don't do junk food."

"Chestnuts, then? They're always good."

"I don't think so. They're so high in fat content."

"Well, we can at least get a hotdog. I didn't have time for dinner."

235

"Billy can't have wieners. He gets a reaction from the nitrates. I'd rather you avoided them, too, and set him a good example. He gets very upset if people are eating something that he can't have."

"What sort of reaction does he get from hot dogs?"

"He's ADHD. Food additives have a terribly negative effect on his behaviour."

Richard sank deeper in gloom. From what he had seen during the drive, Billy's behaviour was already bordering on delinquency. How much worse could it get? Glumly he brooded on the evening ahead. There were some things that even a pouter-pigeon bosom could not adequately compensate for, and he suspected that Billy the Kid was one of them.

*       *       *

It was the perfect evening for a ride on the Christmas train. The snow that had fallen two days previously had been cleared from the paths, yet still lay on the grass and trees, turning the park into a Christmas card scene. The sky was cloudless, with a bright moon and sparkling stars, and the air was crisp and cold. The chestnut and hot-chocolate vendors were doing a roaring trade. The smoky aromas from the concession stands hung temptingly on the air as Bertram Beary strolled behind his wife, who was busily snapping pictures of the reindeer, toy soldiers and gingerbread houses that adorned the network of paths leading up to the Stanley Park Junction.

"When life gives you a lemon," Beary intoned philosophically, "make lemonade."

"What?" Edwina lowered her camera and stared at her husband.

"Typhoon Freda," responded Beary. "1964. High winds wiped out a mass of trees, just like the windstorm that raged through the park five years ago. The clearing that was created by Freda was used to build the miniature train circuit, and it's been one of Vancouver's biggest attractions ever since. But it's certainly grown since then," he added, peering across a sea of Santas toward the avenue of glistening lights.

Edwina was barely listening. She had found a solitary Nativity scene tucked behind Santa's toyshop and was pointing her camera its way. She took one last shot and joined her husband on the main path.

"We'd better head down and find the others." Edwina glanced at her watch. "They're probably already in line."

"I thought you pre-booked on the Internet."

"I did, but there will still be a lot of people in our time slot. We want to make sure we're all on the same ride. This is supposed to be a family outing," she reminded him pointedly, then set off briskly in the direction of the ticket office.

"Well, well, well," said Beary, as they neared the station. "We're not the only family out in full force to ride the Christmas train. That's Evangeline Wellburn and her brood."

"I don't know them," said Edwina.

"Mining money from way back. The father croaked once he'd made his fortune and bought his family a luxury mansion on South West Marine. No doubt a merciful release. He wouldn't have enjoyed a golden retirement in that household—one crotchety wife and three downtrodden spinsters. Neither of Evangeline's sisters ever married, though I believe one had a fiancé who was lost in World War II. Anyway, they both moved into the Wellburn mansion. The daughter remained single too, poor thing. Imagine a lifetime of bondage to that."

Beary nodded towards the huge, fur-swathed matron with the predatory eyes. Three other women bobbed around her like tugs escorting a log boom. Two of them looked frail and elderly. The third was a stolid, middle-aged woman, dressed in a sensible wool coat. Unlike her older companions, she had an air of calm resignation, as if indifferent to whatever barbs were emanating from the mink mountain.

"Who are the others?" asked Edwina, pointing to the cluster of people at the rear who had paused to admire the glittering maple tree that towered above the tents and drew all eyes upward. Its trunk and branches were entwined with glowing rings of red and white, and nearby, the Canadian flag, cleverly fashioned from lights, hung between the treetops.

"The middle-aged couple is Evangeline's son and his wife. It's through them that I know about the family. Caleb Wellburn is on Vancouver City Council."

"*His* wife certainly doesn't look downtrodden." Edwina eyed the bleached blonde whose trim figure was encased in Armani jeans and a white mink bomber jacket.

"No. Evangeline's daughter in law likes the good life, and Caleb seems to be able to provide it."

"Who are the younger ones?"

"The weary-looking woman carrying the little boy is Caleb's oldest daughter. I think her name is Trudy. She's divorced, so I'm told. The bored young thing in designer leather is her younger sister, Mary, and the smarmy-faced individual who looks like he stepped out of a movie about Wall Street is her brother, Ross. Expensive tastes, high-end drugs and an indolent nature, according to those in the know. The son has been a particular thorn in his father's side. He's a gambler. Regular little card sharp too. Been caught cheating more than once and the family has had to bail him out to the tune of thousands of dollars. He contributes a great deal towards his father's high blood pressure."

"Sounds like people we want to avoid," said Edwina firmly.

"Can't," said Beary, nodding towards the line. "Not unless you want to avoid your own daughters. The Wellburns just got in line right behind our mob. They must be booked for the five-thirty rides too. Still, you don't have to worry. Caleb will not be able to remember where he knows me from—we only met a couple of times at GVRD meetings—so he'll be embarrassed and pretend he hasn't seen me, and Evangeline will be so incensed when we elbow in front of them that she'll utter a few pithy comments about line-jumpers and then give us the cold shoulder. Now, let's go and get a bag of chestnuts before we join the others."

Beary proved correct. When they wriggled in beside Philippa and Juliette, who, along with Sylvia, were keeping the children in line, Caleb Wellburn gazed off into space and his mother emitted one shrill protest, then fell into an indignant silence which lasted all of two minutes before she started in again on her unfortunate sisters and daughter. The Bearys contentedly munched their chestnuts, listened to the chatter of their grandchildren mingling with the tinny sound of the carols jingling from the speakers, and tuned out the litany of complaints from the rear. While they waited for the minute hand on the station-turret clock to inch down to the half-hour, Beary stamped his feet to keep warm. He noticed that clouds of mist rose from his mouth every time he uttered a word.

He was contemplating buying some cups of hot chocolate to warm their hands and insides, when a small figure hurtled into his knees and gave him a big hug.

"Hi, Grampus!" It was Chelsea. "Daddy took me to the petting zoo," she shrieked. "I patted a goat!"

Norton slid into line beside Sylvia. He waved the remains of a hotdog at Chelsea.

"Don't you want this?" he asked.

"No," said his daughter. "I just want my popcorn."

Norton shrugged, handed her the bag of popcorn and finished off the hotdog.

Chelsea skipped forward to join her brothers and cousins, all of whom were sharing an assortment of chips, popcorn and chestnuts while they watched Philippa texting on her cellphone.

"Why is Auntie Philippa smiling at her phone?" asked Chelsea.

Jennifer grinned. "She just got a 'Merry Christmas' message from Constable Miller," she said.

"Where's Uncle Richard?" demanded Thomas. "If he doesn't hurry up, he'll miss the ride."

"Maybe he got called in to work," suggested Philippa, putting away her phone.

"No," said Edwina. "I spoke to him an hour ago. He was on his way to pick up a friend."

"He's bringing someone with him?" Sylvia raised an elegant eyebrow. "That's a first."

"I know," smirked Edwina. "It must be someone special."

"There he is!" cried Juliette. "Over by the hotdog stand."

Edwina swung round. Richard was purchasing a hotdog and glancing about surreptitiously. Seeing his parents, he loped over to join them, chomping rapidly on his hotdog as he did so.

"I thought you were bringing a friend," said Edwina.

"She's coming," sighed Richard. "Her son had to go to the bathroom."

Edwina's eyebrows arched eloquently. "Her son?"

"She has a little boy. She's divorced."

"Oh." Edwina managed to infuse a paragraph of meaning into the word. "Don't gobble your food like that," she added sharply. "You'll have terrible indigestion."

"Is that her?" cried Philippa, pointing towards a voluptuous blonde who was walking around the boardwalk that surrounded the artificial lake. Periodically, the woman turned to urge on a youth who was squawking at the ducks and pretending to machine gun the display of nutcracker soldiers and carollers on the stage at the centre of the water.

Richard nodded and gulped down the rest of his hotdog. He tossed the napkin into a nearby bin, stepped forward and waved.

Larissa waved back, said something to her son, and then came forward to join Richard. Billy held back truculently, but as Richard began to introduce Larissa to the Bearys, Billy's glance grew calculating. In a flash, he was at his mother's side, but his eyes were on the row of junior Bearys.

Thomas thrust his bag of popcorn forward.

"Want some?" he asked.

Billy grinned and held out his hand.

"I'll have some chips, too," he said.

Larissa opened her mouth to protest, but at that moment, the attendant lifted the rope to admit the five-thirty bookings into the inner line and the crowd swept forward. Scooping a handful from each bag, Billy melted into the cluster of children and disappeared through the gate. Richard shrugged apologetically at his date. Larissa did not look amused.

\*　　　　\*　　　　\*

When the Bearys reached the platform, there was no one else ahead of them. Fortuitously, the couples at the front had all squeezed onto the previous train. Watched by the glowing, life-sized polar bear on the far side of the track, Edwina efficiently lined up her family into twos, allowing one trio in the form of Philippa, Laura and Chelsea, since the two younger girls were small enough to wedge into one bench alongside their slender aunt.

A whistle heralded the approach of the train, and the little black engine, merrily sporting a Canadian flag on either side of its cowcatcher, came trundling down the track.

"Good stuff," said Beary. "We're on 374." He turned to his grandchildren and pointed to the approaching engine. "That's a replica of the engine that pulled Canada's first transcontinental passenger train into Vancouver in the 1800s," he informed them.

"Cool," said Geoffrey, who shared his grandfather's enthusiasm for local history.

The train rattled in, slowing to a halt in front of the polar bear, and discharged its occupants, who swiftly dispersed and disappeared through the exit gate. The conductor lifted the chain, and the Bearys surged forward and clambered into their seats. The older members of the family moved towards the rear, sitting with their mates and taking advantage of the opportunity to send the children forward to sit with their young unmarried aunt and uncle. Philippa hauled Chelsea and Laura in beside her and directed Jennifer and Geoffrey to the seat directly in front. Then Richard and Larissa took the next seat forward and settled Thomas and Billy in front of them. The two ten-year-old boys appeared to have struck up a popcorn-fuelled alliance. They were also playing games on Thomas's Blackberry. Richard sighed. Larissa's lush Scarlett Johansson lips had compressed into a razor-thin line.

The Bearys had taken up seven of the twelve seats in the small carriages. It was only once everyone was settled that Edwina noticed that her family had filled the mid-section of the train and left seats at either end, which was not the most considerate thing to do since there was another large family group behind them. However, the Wellburns did not seem to mind being split up. Caleb and his wife climbed into a seat at the rear behind Juliette and Steven, and they signalled to their oldest daughter to bring her little boy to sit in the seat behind them, which was the last seat on the train. The other Wellburns headed for the remaining three seats at the very front. As two of them languidly slid onto the bench in front of Thomas and Billy, Richard looked up and frowned. The young man with the bored-looking redhead in designer leather seemed familiar. Richard had been too preoccupied with Larissa and her son to observe the other people in the line-up, but now his attention was caught.

Evangeline Wellburn moved into his line of vision, surrounded by her trio of satellites, who fussed about her as they wedged her into the seat in front of the young man and woman who had caught Richard's eye. Immediately, Richard realized why he had recognized the young man. He was Ross Wellburn, Evangeline's grandson, and the redhead was his sister. They had both come to the attention of the RCMP before, and Richard had twice had run-ins with the arrogant matriarch of the Wellburn family when the junior members had been misbehaving.

Evangeline was so huge that she spread over the entire bench. Richard wondered where the other three women would sit, since no one could fit beside Evangeline and there was only one bench seat left at the very front of the train. He watched, fascinated, as Evangeline's entourage tried to make her comfortable. He decided that the stout woman in the black wool toque must be Evangeline's daughter. She bustled about competently, impervious to the complaints emanating from the mound of fur. She pulled the sleeves of the brown mink coat down over the gloves and wrapped the shawl higher so it snugly encased her mother's neck. The other two women appeared well over eighty, so Richard assumed they were the matriarch's sisters. One seemed a little more assertive than the other. She was dressed in a camelhair coat and a matching beige cloche hat, and she held onto Evangeline's purse until she was ready to take it. The other sister wore a long plaid coat and a red mohair beret, and she fussed rather ineffectually, tucking up Evangeline's collar and straightening her shawl, until a brusque command from the daughter made her fall back. Evangeline's daughter, Richard noted, had picked up a thing or two about command from being browbeaten by her mother. There was a definite pecking order in the quartet.

A whistle from the conductor caused everyone to sit up. Evangeline's daughter slipped into the front seat, followed by the sister in camel hair. The plaid sister scurried away. Richard swivelled round to follow her progress and saw that she had joined Trudy Wellburn and her little boy at the very back of the train. Everyone was on board, and with a loud toot from the engine and a tiny jerk, the train rolled forward into the tunnel of brightly lit arches that began the ride.

Richard had been around the circuit many times before, but he always got a kick out of the lighted displays and the happy cries of the children as they spotted Santas, elves, reindeer, carollers and gingerbread men; not to mention the Arctic wolves whose pens were incorporated into the enclosure. The train rounded a corner to reveal a mass of glittering lights, and Chelsea's shriek of delight could be heard by everyone on board, even over the lively rendition of

"Winter Wonderland" that was accompanying the ride. The little engine towed the coaches past a stand of gleaming candy canes, then rounded a corner and passed a row of illuminated toy soldiers.

"Winter Wonderland" morphed into "Up on the Rooftops"—the latter's bouncing rhythm steadily keeping pace with the clickety-clack of the train wheels—and beyond the snow-laden bushes, Richard could just make out the black silhouette of a second engine gliding parallel to its CP 374 counterpart. Another train was heading for the crossing. Then, as the track curved, it was lost from view.

Richard glanced to the left and saw Scrooge's gravestone looming out of the darkness. Then the train lurched round another corner, the music switched to a First Nations chant, and a big screen, lit with huge, drifting snowflakes, came into sight on the right. In front of the screen, an actor in a bear costume danced and waved to the people on the train.

A loud roar, followed by a series of *ack ack acks*, erupted from the seat in front. Billy had his pretend machine gun out again, and to Richard's surprise, Thomas was joining in his seatmate's antics, hooting boisterously and strafing the dancing bear. However, he stopped abruptly when his uncle gave him a sharp prod in the back.

"Smarten up, turkeys," rapped Richard.

Billy turned and gaped at him.

"Cut it out," Richard reiterated in his sternest policeman's voice. Billy glared back at him, but he fell silent.

"What did you expect?" said Larissa primly. "They're full of junk food. It was bound to manifest, and it's hardly fair of you to get cross with them. I thought the way you spoke to them was really quite excessive."

*Just be glad my mother wasn't the one sitting behind them.* The thought crossed Richard's mind, but wisely, he did not say anything aloud. Larissa turned her head away pointedly and stared out the left side of the coach.

The train accelerated towards the tunnel. Larissa continued to keep her back towards Richard. The icy chill emanating from her shoulders was colder than the frosty night air. I will be so glad, thought Richard, when this ride is over.

The train thundered into the tunnel. Out of the blackness loomed luminous white murals on the tunnel wall. As they flashed by, Richard saw that they depicted the various provinces.

All of a sudden, as the carriage whipped by Saskatchewan, an ear-splitting shriek rent the air. It was followed by a series of screams, which continued on as the train burst out of the tunnel.

And Richard got his wish. The engine driver put on the brakes and the train ground to a halt. The ride was over.

\*           \*           \*

Evangeline Wellburn was hysterical. She sat, scarlet-faced, still wedged in her seat, screaming accusations to the white-faced train conductor.

"My pendant! It's gone! He ripped it off my neck! Somebody get me off this wretched train."

The engine had stopped on the trestle bridge that crossed the artificial lake, and only the first five seats of the carriage had emerged from the tunnel. On either side of the track, a wide stretch of water separated the train from the shore. A statue of a moose rose out of the water on the right, and it stood, stolid and silent, as if impervious to the frenzied woman's cry. The clamour of anxious voices could be heard inside the tunnel. Richard signalled to the engine driver to remain seated; then he climbed out and carefully inched forward so that he could look the raging woman in the eye.

"Mrs. Wellburn, calm down please. I'm an officer with the RCMP. I'd like you to tell me what the problem is."

Evangeline blinked, then glared suspiciously at Richard.

"How did you get here so quickly? Where's your uniform?"

Richard whipped out his identification and held it in front of the woman's face.

"I'm Detective Inspector Richard Beary," he said. "I'm here with my family, but I can help you sort out whatever problem has arisen. Now tell me exactly what has happened."

"My diamond pendant has been stolen, and my grandson, who is sitting right behind me, will be the person who took it. I demand that you search him at once."

Richard glanced towards Ross Wellburn, who was looking remarkably complacent for someone who was being accused of theft.

"Are you quite sure the pendant is missing?"

Evangeline tossed off her shawl and ripped open her coat. She looked apoplectic.

"Of course, I'm sure. Look. It's gone."

Faith Wellburn interjected. "She's right, Inspector," she said. "She was wearing it and it's definitely not there."

"Is this a valuable item?" asked Richard. "What would it be worth?"

"It's valued at ten thousand dollars," said Evangeline.

Richard managed to refrain from whistling. This was more serious than he had realized.

"Why do you say your grandson stole the pendant?" Richard asked Evangeline. "When did it go missing?"

"In the tunnel. He reached out and tore it from my neck. The chain is fragile. It would have broken very easily with that much force."

"You felt the pendant being pulled away?"

"Yes. Didn't I just say so?"

"Mrs. Wellburn, you're wearing a shawl and a heavy fur coat. Presumably, your pendant was inside both. It would have been rather difficult to get at."

"He slid his hand down inside my collar, you fool. He grabbed the pendant; then he yanked it off my neck. What's so difficult about that?"

"So you actually felt someone's hands on your neck?"

"Yes."

"Where exactly did the thief touch you?"

Evangeline looked irritated, but Richard's authoritative air quelled her instinct to retort, and she answered him, "Here. On the right side of my neck. I felt his hand slide down, and then I felt a hard tug against my neck."

"Then you weren't necessarily grabbed from behind?"

Evangeline gave him a scathing look.

"Well, my daughter and my sister aren't going to yank my jewellery off my neck, so it had to have been Ross. He's the one who needs money. Search him."

Richard looked sombrely at Ross Wellburn.

"I think I will have to," he said, "unless someone can produce the missing piece. In fact," he added, including Evangeline's daughter, sister and granddaughter in his glance, "unless it appears forthwith, I will have to bring all four of you down to the station to be searched. However, right now I want you all to stay exactly where you are."

Richard turned and spoke to the engine driver.

"I want you to proceed to the station. I'm going to instruct everyone to remain seated with their hands inside their compartments. The ride will have to be closed off until I have questioned the people on board. While I'm doing that, I'd like you to arrange for the park staff to get a flashlight and search the tunnel."

The driver nodded. He waited while Richard worked his way to the entrance of the tunnel and gave the passengers an edited version of the reason for the delay. Then, once Richard had returned to his seat, the train trundled forward and continued around the circuit. The Christmas music still jangled from the speakers, but the murmur of voices on the train had taken on a subdued tone and the twinkling lights served as a reminder of the diamonds that had vanished inside the tunnel. The lights also matched the dangerous glitter in Richard's companion's eye.

The train finally reached the station, and the driver climbed down and went to inform his colleagues of the situation. With a murmured apology to Larissa, Richard hopped out onto the platform and moved forward to the Wellburns. As he reiterated his instructions to them, he heard footsteps and looked up to see the plaid sister hurrying towards the front of the train. Behind her was Caleb Wellburn.

"What has happened? Are you all right, dear?" The plaid sister rushed to Evangeline's side.

"I'm going to have to ask you to keep back," Richard said firmly.

"But that's my mother you're talking to," sputtered Caleb. "What's going on?"

"Mrs. Wellburn has lost a piece of valuable jewellery."

Caleb paled.

"Not her rose pendant? Christ! It's worth a fortune."

"So I gather."

"When was it taken?" quavered the plaid sister.

"In the tunnel. Someone clutched at Mrs. Wellburn's neck. Have you any idea who—"

Richard got no further, for Caleb turned on his son in a fury.

"Ross, you little bugger!" he bellowed. "This isn't a joke. Give it back right now."

Ross Wellburn steadily met his father's gaze.

"I didn't take it," he said.

"It's not fair to pick on poor Ross," trilled the plaid sister. "He gets blamed for everything."

"With good reason," snapped Caleb. "Keep out of it, Prudence."

"Now," Richard told Caleb, "the tunnel is being searched, and we're all going to remain where we are until the parks staff report back to me. Unless the pendant is recovered, I'm going to bring your family down to the station—even those who were at the back of the train. Everyone might have some information to contribute. And the people sitting in the seats behind and in front of Mrs. Wellburn will have to be searched. You can all wait here while I call for a squad car. You'll have to shut the ride down until we're out of here," he added to the conductor, who assented gloomily. The line had more than doubled in the last half-hour and there would be a lot of disaffected customers to placate.

Richard pulled out his phone and put a call through to the station. Then he went to speak to the members of his own family, all of whom had been watching the proceedings with avid interest.

"I've got to stay for a bit. Sorry about this. There's no point in waiting around. You might as well head back and start dinner. I'll be along as soon as I can." Lowering his voice, he drew Larissa aside. From the corner of his eye, he noticed that Billy's eyes were gleaming with excitement. Larissa's, on the other hand, held as much warmth as a pair of ice cubes.

"You can get a ride with Philippa," Richard said apologetically. "I might be a while. I'll join you as soon as I can."

Larissa met his glance coolly.

"I think I'll call a taxi and head home," she said.

"Nonsense." Edwina stepped forward and intervened. "Bertram and I will drive you. If you're determined to go home, we can drop you on the way. That way we'll be able to have a nice cozy chat." She turned to her grandson. "Thomas, you come with us to keep Billy company. By the way," she added, fixing both boys with a steely eye, "I hope that wasn't you making that awful noise when we were on the train. I could hear it all the way at the back, even over the music."

Thomas and Billy smiled angelically and shook their heads.

"Hmm," said Edwina. "Well, come along. Let's get moving."

Grinning, the two boys fell in behind Edwina. Larissa glared at Richard as if expecting him to intervene, but Beary planted himself between them and offered Larissa his arm.

"Off we go," he boomed. "A stiff drink will put you back on form. And if we hear machine-gun fire coming from the back seat, we'll make those two little mugs get out and run behind the car."

Richard watched them go, finding, to his surprise, that he didn't care one way or the other what the outcome of his mother's talk with Larissa would be. With a spring in his step, he turned back to the Wellburns. A couple of hours sorting out the mystery of the Christmas train promised to be far less onerous than spending the rest of the evening with a pouter-pigeon bosom that was topped by an even more protuberant pout.

*　　　　　*　　　　　*

However, Richard's feeling of relief evaporated very rapidly, for an hour later, he had to admit to being utterly baffled. The search had produced nothing. The train and tunnel had been examined carefully a second and third time, the surrounding area had been scoured, and a thorough investigation had been carried out to ensure that no other person could have been hiding in the tunnel. The valuable pendant had simply vanished. It was nowhere to be found.

After interrogating the members of the family, Richard understood why Evangeline was so sure that her grandson was the culprit, for he had a history of drug abuse and gambling debts, and no matter how many times he had been bailed out and promised to reform, he had always slipped back into his old habits. The only person that appeared to have any sympathy for him was his Great-Aunt Prudence.

Prudence was an interesting old bird, Richard thought, for all her dithering ways. She chattered to him cheerfully, veering off topic to inform him of little Georgie's amazing ability to print his name at the age of two, or of her sister's brief career as a secretary before family demands compelled her to give up her job. With a childlike giggle, she even told him of her own rebellion when she became engaged to a young man who was the son of a touring magician, much to the chagrin of her family, although her courage to defy her mother was ultimately never tested for, sadly, her fiancé died during the war. But there was no doubt that Prudence was the softhearted member of the Wellburn clan. She expressed indignation over the accusations against Ross, and she felt that he had been so put down over the years by his father and his grandmother that it was no wonder he'd gone off the rails. Wearily, Richard dismissed her and leaned back in his chair. He'd learned nothing that was of use, and for all Prudence Wellburn's protestations, he instinctively felt that Evangeline's guess was correct. Ross did not have the pendant, yet there was something about his smug expression that convinced Richard that the young man was guilty.

*Damn*, thought Richard. *How the hell did he do it?*

He came out of the interview room and glanced down the corridor. Ross was standing at the end of the hall, talking with his sister. Prudence Wellburn was walking towards them and, when she reached her nephew, she gave him a big hug.

Richard scrutinized the elderly woman thoughtfully. If Ross was guilty, then his doting aunt was the most likely person to be his confidante. Recollecting the scene at the train station and all the preliminary activity before the ride began, Richard began to formulate an idea. Suddenly he was sure he knew how the pendant had disappeared.

He called out, "Miss Wellburn, another word, if you don't mind."

Prudence looked up, startled. She held a hand to her chest and raised her eyebrows, the gesture clearly asking, *me?* Richard nodded, and the old lady slowly returned down the corridor. Richard ushered her back into the interview room and shut the door.

Five minutes later, they emerged again. Prudence led the way, and they proceeded back to the reception area, where Evangeline was waiting with Faith and Dorothy. Prudence joined them and sat down next to Evangeline. She put an arm round her shoulder in an affectionate gesture.

"Try not to fret, dear," she said. "I'm sure it will show up."

Evangeline sniffed.

"Don't be ridiculous. It's stolen, not lost."

"Are you quite sure it was around your neck during the train ride?" asked Prudence. "You didn't take it off at any time?"

Evangeline's countenance took on an ominous shade of red.

"Of course I didn't. I told you, I felt the hand on my neck when it was stolen."

"Dear, you have been rather forgetful lately," Prudence continued. Faith and Dorothy looked at each other amazed. Prudence rarely argued with her sister, and she couldn't have failed to notice the warning signs of an imminent eruption. Evangeline was rumbling like a volcano, yet Prudence persevered. "Why, only the other day, you said you had lost your spectacles," she said, "and two minutes later, they turned up in your coat pocket."

"What are you talking about?" snapped Evangeline. "Are you getting senile? I did no such thing." She thrust her hands into her coat pocket in a dramatically indignant gesture. "As if I'm likely to put a ten-thousand dollar pendant into my coat—"

She stopped abruptly, and her roseate hue paled to ashen white.

Slowly, she pulled her hand out of her pocket. Then, eyes bulging, she held up the diamond pendant.

*     *     *

When Richard arrived at his parents' house, dinner was over, and Juliette and Philippa were in the kitchen helping their mother clean up. Beary was also in the kitchen, preparing a Spanish coffee to reward Edwina for her hard labour. Sylvia and Norton were lolling on the living-room chesterfield, gradually lowering the contents of a bottle of wine, while Chelsea and Laura, closely watched by MacPuff, were examining the presents under their grandparents' tree and thwarting Minx the Manx in her attempts to purloin her wrapped catnip mouse. Thomas, Geoffrey and Jennifer had disappeared into the den to watch the latest Harry Potter movie. Larissa and Billy were nowhere in sight. Larissa, Edwina apologetically informed her son, had insisted on being taken home, in spite of all her efforts to be friendly and hospitable.

Beary let his wife have the say that she was obviously determined to have. He poured his son a Scotch and replenished his own glass, while Edwina produced the plate of leftovers that she had set aside for Richard. Then, firmly ordering her inquisitive family to go to the living room and hold their questions until Richard had eaten, Edwina sat her son down at the kitchen table and let him devour his dinner in peace.

As Richard swallowed his last mouthful, Beary reappeared, Scotch bottle in hand. He refilled the glasses again and followed Richard into the living room to join the rest of the family.

"Well, go on," urged Philippa. "Tell us. What was the outcome of the mystery of the Christmas train? Did your search produce the culprit?"

"No," said Richard, settling himself comfortably in an armchair. "None of the four had it on them, and it wasn't anywhere on the train or in the tunnel. The search didn't produce a thing."

"So you didn't get it back?"

Richard grinned.

"Well, we did and we didn't."

"What's that supposed to mean?" demanded Sylvia. "Do you know who stole the blessed pendant or don't you?"

"Oh, yes. We know who stole it. It was Ross Wellburn, just as his grandmother said. She was quite right about the fact that he slid his hand down her neck. He reached around to the side, rather than from behind, since that made it less certain that he was the culprit. But it was him."

"I don't get it," said Norton. "If you didn't find it on him, where did he hide it?"

"He didn't hide it," laughed Richard, "because he didn't take it. Oh, all right," he added, seeing his relatives starting to look distinctly unmerry in spite of the festive season. "I'll put you out of your misery."

Richard paused to enjoy some more of his Scotch. Then, setting down his glass, he explained. "Ross Wellburn has caused his family nothing but trouble, but he has one sympathetic relative who adores him and will do anything to help him out of the messes he gets into. I suppose it makes her feel important. Poor old Prudence Wellburn never married and never had a child of her own, so she dotes on her nephew's son. Whenever he's in trouble, he runs to her, and she has intervened with his grandmother on numerous occasions, pleading with her to bail him out. But this time, she knew Evangeline wouldn't help, so she conceived of a plan to get Ross off the hook. You see, the pendant wasn't stolen when Ross slid his hand down his grandmother's neck and yanked at her collar. He just did that to make it appear that the robbery had occurred in the tunnel. Prudence had undone the chain when she was rearranging Evangeline's scarf before the ride. She slipped the pendant up into the sleeve of her coat. Then she went and sat in the very last carriage of the train, neatly taking herself out of the list of suspects. It was quite a feat of adroitness," he added, "but the old girl has some surprising talents, one of which is sleight of hand. In her youth, she was engaged to a magician's son and she learned all kinds of tricks from him ... some of which, unfortunately, she also taught her nephew, not suspecting he would use the skill in a variety of socially unacceptable ways."

Philippa's eyes bulged.

"That sweet-looking little old lady stole a ten-thousand dollar pendant because Ross Wellburn needed money! I find that hard to believe. And why did you say that you 'did and didn't' get the pendant back? There's something more you haven't told us."

Richard nodded.

"Yes, there is. You see, we didn't get the pendant back. We merely recovered the fake duplicate that had been created some months ago."

"Aha," said Beary. "Now this is starting to make more sense."

"Exactly," said Richard. "Ross stole the pendant from his grandmother's room last March. He had a copy made through one of his disreputable contacts, and then he substituted the fake in the jewellery box. But he didn't realize that there was a loose claw on the new necklace. Faith Wellburn noticed it and announced that she was going to take it in to be fixed after Christmas. The subject came up when they all arrived at the park, so Ross was thrown into a panic because he knew the theft would be discovered if a jeweller had a close look at the replica. Evangeline Wellburn was already threatening to cut him out of her will if he didn't smarten up, and that would have been the last straw."

"So that's why Prudence Wellburn agreed to help him," said Norton. "She would never have stolen the real jewellery for him, but she was willing to act out a charade in order to cover up his crime. Logical." Norton refilled his wife's wine glass and topped up his own. "But if all you've done is recover the fake pendant," he said gravely, "Ross Wellburn is still up the creek without a paddle."

"Yes," said Richard, "and it serves him right."

"Did you arrest him for the theft of the original pendant?" asked Edwina.

"No. How could I? It hasn't been reported. I simply advised him to go to his grandmother and confess."

"Do you think he will?" Sylvia asked sceptically.

"Not right away. He'll be going twenty-four/seven to retrace and reclaim the pendant before the fake goes in for repairs, but if that fails, he'll have no choice but to own up. There's a chance that his grandmother might become reconciled with him in time if she sees that he's prepared to pay for his rotten behaviour, but he's going to have to walk the walk and demonstrate that he really has changed his ways."

"But in the meantime," chuckled Beary, "he's definitely on Santa's naughty list." He drained his glass and turned to go back to the kitchen. Edwina took the glass from his hand.

"Yes, and someone else will be on Santa's naughty list if that bottle of Glenlivet gets any lower. I'll put on a pot of coffee."

"Where's your Christmas spirit?" grumbled Beary.

"Not in the Scotch bottle," said his wife.

Edwina started for the door, but then she paused and turned back to speak to her son. Richard noticed that her brow was furrowed anxiously, an unusual phenomenon in his mother.

"I hope you're not too upset that your friend didn't come back to join us," she said to Richard. "I tried so hard to be friendly, but she was quite determined to go home. I wanted to make her feel welcome, but I have a feeling she thought I was prying. I was just trying to cheer her up and get her to talk about herself, but I'm terribly afraid I might have made things worse." Edwina paused, as if assessing her son's reaction. Not seeing any signs of annoyance on Richard's face, she continued more confidently. "Still," she ventured, "I honestly believe it might have been for the best. I really don't think, dear, that she was your type. For all her good looks, I think you might have found her just a tiny bit irritating in the long run."

*In the short run too*, thought Richard. He smiled contentedly and settled back in his armchair. There was something very comfortable about his parents, in spite of all their foibles. And sometimes, there was even an advantage to having the Grand Inquisitor for one's mother.

But all the same, next year, he would remember to follow his inviolable rule.

# Also by Elizabeth Elwood

## MYSTERY STORIES

*To Catch an Actress and Other Mystery Stories*
*A Black Tie Affair and Other Mystery Stories*
*The Beacon and Other Mystery Stories*

## PLAYS

*Casting for Murder*
*Renovations*
*Shadow of Murder*

WATCH FOR THE NEXT BOOK OF BEARY MYSTERIES

# The Path of Evil and Other Mystery Stories

The kidnapping of a teenage movie idol brings Philippa and DC Bob Miller together when it appears that a visiting member of the Beary family might be involved; Richard is put on high alert by a threatened assassination during a vice-president's visit; and Sylvia and Norton face a dilemma when a rape case that dates back to London of the Swinging Sixties puts them on opposing sides in the courtroom. While the younger family members tackle a variety of challenges, Beary and Edwina take a day trip in the *Optimist* and find themselves embroiled in the curious incident of the boat dog in the night. Enjoy these and other intriguing stories in the next book of Beary mysteries.

Website: www.elihuentertainment.com

# AUTHOR'S NOTE

The stories in this volume are set in the Greater Vancouver area and on the Sunshine Coast of British Columbia, with one exception where my characters visit a plantation in Louisiana. Therefore, many of the settings described may be familiar to residents of those areas. However, the assorted political groups, theatrical associations and characters in the various stories exist only in the imagination of the author and bear no relation to organizations or people in real life. Also, some of the settings, including the city of Burnside where Beary resides on Council, are composites of several different locations and do not really exist. Gastown does exist as a popular tourist venue in Vancouver; however, I have added an imaginary block to encompass the area that includes the Old Chandler and the arcade on the far side of the street.

Several acknowledgements are in order:

First, my appreciation to Patty Jackson of the Sunshine Coast who provided me with the intriguing piece of local folklore that inspired the story, "The Window in Room 21".

"Tragedy at the Oaks" resulted from a wonderful trip to Louisiana, travelling in *Arvy*, who really does exist. The setting for the story was inspired by a drive down River Road where we saw several plantations and enjoyed a fascinating tour of Oak Alley. The story, initially suggested by the tiny cemetery with the dog's grave, later evolved after I read Robert V. Remini's book, *The Battle of New Orleans,* while we were visiting the city of that name. The task of linking the historic details of the battle, so well outlined in Remini's book, with the mystery that had formed in my mind during the plantation tour proved to be a fascinating challenge, and one which I hope the reader enjoys as much as I did.

The other stories have many sources of inspiration: Vancouver's historic Gastown; VPD's fine dog squad; the exciting 2010 Winter Olympics; the fabulous Lincoln Centre revival of Roger and Hammerstein's *South Pacific*; and last, but not least, a delightful visit to Stanley Park where we rode the Christmas train.

Thanks, once again, to my husband, Hugh Elwood, who assisted with research and kept me straight on details relating to outdoor recreational activities. Thank you also to Lorraine Meltzer for her invaluable assistance with editing my manuscript.

A final note is necessary regarding the dedication in this book. The Vagabond Players, the oldest continuously operating community theatre in B.C., has provided me with constant support over the years. The society has now premiered all three of my plays and launched each one of my books. Therefore, it seems entirely appropriate to thank the members of this great company by dedicating this book to them.